"You _____ **east,"**
Belle _____

Adam caught her wrist, stopped her from leaving. "And what bothers you most about that? The fact that you would like to reform me? Or is it the fact that you don't want to reform me at all and that you rather like me this way?"

He caught up to her, pivoting so that he was in front of her. She took a step backward, then to the side, butting up against the wall. Then he caged her between his arms, staring down at her. Her blue eyes were glittering, her breasts rising and falling rapidly with each breath.

"This is the only thing worth exploring. Not what could be, but what you have. The fire that burns between you and another person. For all you know in the days since you've been here the entire world has fallen away. And if we were all that was left… Would you not regret missing out on the chance to see how hot we could burn?"

*Three innocents encounter forbidden temptation
in this enticing new fairy-tale trilogy
by* New York Times *bestselling author Maisey Yates…*

Once Upon a Seduction…

Belle, Briar and Charlotte have lived sheltered lives,
far from temptation—but three billionaires are
determined to claim them!

Belle has traded herself for her father's freedom—
but the dark-hearted Prince keeping her prisoner
threatens to unleash an unknown sensuality…

Meanwhile Briar awakens to find herself abducted
by Prince Felipe—who blackmails her
into becoming his royal bride…

And Charlotte is reunited with the billionaire who
once climbed a tower to steal her innocence—and
Rafe is about to discover the secret consequences!

Find out if these young women can tame their
powerful men—*and* have their happily-ever-after!

The Prince's Captive Virgin
June 2017

The Prince's Stolen Virgin
August 2017

Rafe and Charlotte's story
October 2017

THE PRINCE'S CAPTIVE VIRGIN

BY
MAISEY YATES

All rights reserved including the right of reproduction in whole
or in part in any form. This edition is published by arrangement with
Harlequin Books S.A.

This is a work of fiction. Names, characters, places, locations and
incidents are purely fictional and bear no relationship to any real
life individuals, living or dead, or to any actual places, business
establishments, locations, events or incidents. Any resemblance is
entirely coincidental.

This book is sold subject to the condition that it shall not, by way of
trade or otherwise, be lent, resold, hired out or otherwise circulated
without the prior consent of the publisher in any form of binding or
cover other than that in which it is published and without a similar
condition including this condition being imposed on the subsequent
purchaser.

® and TM are trademarks owned and used by the trademark owner
and/or its licensee. Trademarks marked with ® are registered with the
United Kingdom Patent Office and/or the Office for Harmonisation in
the Internal Market and in other countries.

First Published in Great Britain 2017
By Mills & Boon, an imprint of HarperCollins*Publishers*
1 London Bridge Street, London, SE1 9GF

© 2017 Maisey Yates

ISBN: 978-0-263-92524-1

Our policy is to use papers that are natural, renewable and recyclable
products and made from wood grown in sustainable forests. The logging
and manufacturing processes conform to the legal environmental
regulations of the country of origin.

Printed and bound in Spain
by CPI, Barcelona

Maisey Yates is a *New York Times* bestselling author of more than thirty romance novels. She has a coffee habit she has no interest in kicking, and a slight Pinterest addiction. She lives with her husband and children in the Pacific Northwest. When Maisey isn't writing she can be found singing in the grocery store, shopping for shoes online and probably not doing dishes. Check out her website: maiseyyates.com.

Books by Maisey Yates

Mills & Boon Modern Romance

Carides's Forgotten Wife
Bound to the Warrior King
His Diamond of Convenience
To Defy a Sheikh
One Night to Risk It All

The Billionaire's Legacy

The Last Di Sione Claims His Prize

Heirs Before Vows

The Spaniard's Pregnant Bride
The Prince's Pregnant Mistress
The Italian's Pregnant Virgin

One Night With Consequences

The Greek's Nine-Month Redemption
Married for Amari's Heir

Princes of Petras

A Christmas Vow of Seduction
The Queen's New Year Secret

Visit the Author Profile page
at millsandboon.co.uk for more titles.

To my dad.
Remember when you took me to see
Beauty and the Beast when I was seven?
I think all of this is your fault. And I love you.

CHAPTER ONE

Once upon a time...

BELLE LOOKED UP at the imposing castle and tightened her coat more firmly around her petite frame. It was surprisingly chilly tonight on the small island country nestled in the Aegean Sea between Greece and Turkey.

Of course, when she had first heard of Olympios she had been put in mind of the Mediterranean. Bright white homes and searing blue skies and seas. And perhaps, in the daytime, that was what it was. But here at night, with the velvet darkness settled low around her and that damp air blowing in from the ocean, it felt like something completely unexpected.

The fortress in front of her, on the other hand, was almost far too expected. It was medieval, and nothing but the lights flickering in the window gave any indication that it might be part of the modern era. Of course, she could expect nothing less from a man who had gone to such great lengths to seek revenge on a photographer.

A man who had captured her father in the act of taking pictures and imprisoned him to get revenge for something as innocuous as photographs that were set to be published without his permission.

Belle supposed that she should be afraid. After all, Prince Adam Katsaros had proven to be unreasonable. He had proven to be inhumane. But she was bolstered by the same rage that had infused her veins from the moment she had first heard of her father's fate, even now.

It seemed that she was insulated from fear, which was strange considering she'd spent a lot of her life feeling afraid of almost everything. Of losing her father and the haven she'd found with him after her mother had abandoned her when she was four years old. Of the potential inside herself to become a tempestuous, selfish creature driven by passions of the flesh, as her mother had been and probably still was.

All that fear was gone now. Had been from the moment she had first boarded her plane in LA, all the way through her layover in Greece, and through the flight that carried her here to Olympios.

She could only hope that her bravado lasted.

Tony was going to be so mad when he found out she'd done this. Her boyfriend of nearly eight months had always wanted to be more involved in her life. But she resisted. Just like she'd been resisting serious physical intimacy. That was part of all her fear stuff.

She'd never had a boyfriend before, and she was accustomed to her space and her independence. Surrendering any of it just didn't sit well with her.

Which was an ironic thought, considering what she was prepared to do here today.

She was surprised to find that the palace was more or less unguarded. There was no one about as she walked up the steps that led to a rough-hewn double door. She was tempted—not for the first time since her arrival on the island—to check and see if her phone calendar had been set back into the last century. Or, perhaps, a few centuries ago.

She lifted her hand, unsure as to whether or not one knocked on doors like this. In the end, she decided to grasp hold of the iron ring and pull it open. It creaked and groaned with the effort, as though no one had dared enter the large, imposing building in quite some time. However, she knew that they had. Because only a few days ago her father had been brought here. And—if rumor was to be believed—he was being imprisoned on the property.

She took a cautious step inside, surprised by the warmth that greeted her. It was dark, except for some wall sconces that were lit across the room. The great stone antechamber possessed nothing like the sort of comforts she would have expected from a palace. Not that she was in the habit of being admitted into palaces.

No, the little seaside home she and her father lived in in Southern California was as far from a palace as it was possible to get. It wasn't even Rodeo Drive.

But this wasn't exactly what she had expected from royalty. In spite of her lack of experience, she did have expectations. She might never have been admitted into the lavish homes and parties that celebrities threw in Beverly Hills, but her father's business was photographing those events. So she had a visual familiarity with them, even if it wasn't based in experience.

"Hello?" she called out into the dim chamber, vaguely aware that that might not have been the best idea the moment the word left her mouth and ricocheted off the stone walls. But, that adrenaline that had wrapped itself around her like an impenetrable suit of armor remained.

She had a mission, and she was not going to be frightened out of carrying it out.

Once the prince understood, he would be more than happy to return her father to her custody. She was certain. Once he understood about her father's health.

"Hello?" she called again. Still nothing.

She heard a soft sound, footsteps on the flagstone floor, and she turned toward a corridor that was at the far left of the room, just in time to see a tall, slender man walking toward her. "Are you lost, *kyria*?"

His tone was soft and kind, faintly accented and nothing like the harsh, brutal surroundings that she found herself in. Nothing at all like she had imagined finding here in this medieval keep.

"No," she said, "I'm not lost. My name is Belle Chamberlain and I looking for my father. Mark Chamberlain. He's being held here by the Prince…and I…I don't think he understands."

The servant—at least, that's what she assumed he was—took a step closer to her, his expression becoming clearer as he moved nearer. He looked…concerned. "Yes. I know about that. It is, perhaps, best if you go, Kyria Chamberlain."

"No. You don't understand. My father is ill, and he was supposed to start treatment back home in the States. He can't be here. He can't be…imprisoned, just because he took some photographs that the Prince doesn't like."

"There is a lot here that protects the Prince's privacy," the man said, as though she hadn't spoken. As though he were simply reciting from a well-memorized book. "And whatever the Prince says is…well, it is law."

"I'm not leaving without my father. I'm not leaving until I speak to the Prince. Also, your security is shockingly lax." She looked around. "Nobody stopped me from entering. I imagine it was far too easy for my father to gain access to him. If he wants to keep his life private, then he should work harder at it." The celebrities her father photographed went to great lengths to avoid his telephoto lens. She was not impressed with the setup the Prince had here.

Perhaps it was a little bit callous of her to look at things that way. But, she had been raised the daughter of a paparazzo, and that was just the way things were. Celebrities capitalized on their images, and relied on the fact that they were public commodities. Her father was simply a part of that economy.

"Believe me," the man said. "You don't want to speak to the Prince."

She drew up to her full height, which, admittedly at five-three was not terribly impressive. "Believe me," she countered. "I most certainly do want to speak to the Prince. I want to tell him that his tyrannical tactics, seizing an American citizen, all in the name of his precious vanity, are not the least bit impressive to me. In fact, if he has issues with his presumably weak chin, subtly rounded jawline and hollow chest, perhaps he could take some of the money he has saved by not renovating this palace and invest in a good plastic surgeon, rather than imprisoning a man for taking a few photographs."

"Weak chin?" Another voice sounded in the darkness. Much different from the voice of the servant. It was deep; it resonated there in the stone room, resonated inside Belle. And then, for the first time, she knew fear. An intense, trembling kind that skated down her spine and reverberated in her stomach. "That is a new accusation, I have to say. However, suggestions that I go visit a plastic surgeon are not. I find that I have lost patience with going under the knife, though."

"Prince Adam," the servant said, his tone clearly intended to placate.

"You may leave us, Fos."

"But, Your Majesty—"

"Don't bow and scrape," the Prince said, his tone hard as the stone walls all around them. "It is embarrassing. For you."

"Yes," the man said, "of course."

And then, the one person who she felt might be her ally shuffled back off into the darkness. And she was left with a disembodied voice that was still shrouded in the inky blackness.

"So," he said, "you have come to see about your father."

"Yes," she said, her tone unsteady. She took a deep breath, tried to get a grip on herself. She was not easily intimidated. She never had been. She had spent her childhood going to private schools that she was far too poor to have gained admittance to, if not for a trust fund previously established by her long-deceased grandfather.

Everyone there knew she was there on charity, and she had been forced to grow a spine early. Everyone was always teasing her. For being poor. For always having her head in the clouds—well, she had her nose firmly planted in a book. But, those stories, those fictional worlds, were her armor. They allowed her to insulate herself. Allowed her to ignore the taunting happening around her.

She had survived a childhood surrounded by the mocking glances and cruel words of the children of Hollywood royalty. Surely she could face down the Prince of a country that was the size of a postage stamp.

She heard a heavy footfall, an indication that he had moved deeper into the room, but she still couldn't see him. "I arrested your father," he said.

"I know that," she said, doing her best to keep her tone steady. "And I think it was a mistake."

He chuckled, but there was no humor in the sound. It lay flat in the room, making it feel as though the temperature had dropped. "You're either very brave or very stupid. Coming to my country, my home, and insulting me."

"I'm not sure that I'm either. I'm just a girl who's concerned about her father. Surely you can understand that."

"Perhaps," he returned. "Though, I find it difficult to remember. I have not worried about my father in quite some time. The cemetery keeps him in good comfort."

She wasn't sure what she was supposed to say to that. If she was supposed to say that she was sorry that his father was dead. In the end, she imagined that he probably didn't want her sympathy.

"That's what I'm afraid will happen to my father," she said. "He's sick. He needs treatment. That was why he got the pictures of you in the first place. He needed money to cover the cost of the treatment that the insurance wouldn't. This is his job. He's a photographer. He's—"

"I have absolutely no interest in paparazzi scum. That kind of thing is forbidden in my country."

"No freedom of the press, then," she said, crossing her arms and planting her feet more firmly against the stone floor.

"No freedom to hunt people down as though they are animals simply because you wish to collect photographs."

She huffed. "I doubt you were hunted down. I was able to gain admittance to the palace easily enough. My father is an experienced photographer, and I bet it was even easier for him."

"He was also caught. Unfortunately, he had also already sent the photographs off to his boss in the United States. And, as his boss is unwilling to negotiate with me—"

"I know. The photographs are planned to go out in an exclusive later this week. I spoke to the *Daily Star*."

"But they are so invested in the fact my interim leader's tenure has now come up, they want the monopoly on these photographs for when I make my decision about my rule."

"If I *had* been able to negotiate with them," Belle continued, "I wouldn't have come myself. But, I imagined that they didn't explain to you about my father's illness."

"Am I supposed to care? He does not care about *my* afflictions."

Rage poured through her. "Are your afflictions going to kill you? Because his will. If he doesn't get back to the US and get himself into treatment, he is going to die. And I won't let that happen. I can't. You want him sitting here wasting away in a jail cell? For what? Your pride? He can be of no use to you."

She heard him as he began to pace, his footsteps echoing off the walls. She could just make out a dark shape, movement. He was large, but that was all she could gather.

"Perhaps you have a point. Perhaps he is of no use to me. Beyond the fact that I feel the need to make him an example."

"An example to who?"

"Anyone who might dare to do similar. Is it not enough, what was done to my family already? The press feel the need to come back and add insult to injury near the third anniversary of the accident? I will not allow it."

"So, you'll let a dying man rot away in your palace then. Haven't you ever heard that two wrongs don't make a right?"

"You mistake me," he said, his tone suddenly fierce. "I am not trying to make anything right. What has been done to me can never be made right. I want a pound of flesh."

She heard his footsteps, and, she realized, he had turned away from her. That he was beginning to walk away. "No!"

"I am finished with you," he said. "My servant will show you out."

"Take me." The words left her trembling lips before she had a chance to think them through. "Instead of my father. Let me take his place."

"Why would you want to do that?" She heard his footsteps drawing nearer to her again. She blinked hard, cursing her inability to see through the thick darkness.

"*Want* is a strong word. But, I'm not currently in need of medical treatment. If I stay here in your palace for however long the sentence might be…I'll be fine." There was the matter of her scholarship, of the fact that she was supposed to be getting her master's in literature. But, for her father's life, she would easily sacrifice a piece of paper.

"And what good will that do?"

"Just tell everybody that I'm the one who took the pictures. That I am the one who caused all this trouble. Use me as your example." He said nothing. It was so still and silent in the room that she thought he might have left. "Please."

"If we do this, I am not simply letting you off with such a bland public story. No."

"I thought you wanted to make an example of him."

"I did," he said, his tone hard. "However…I think there are more creative uses for you."

A shiver ran through her. Fear. "I don't think you want me for…for that."

"You mistake me. If I wanted a whore, I could have one summoned easily enough. You…you're beautiful. Uncommonly so. And I find myself in an interesting position."

"What?"

"Your father didn't decide to get my photograph on a whim. In the last three years, an interim ruler has been governing in my stead. But that…that period has ended. His term has ended. And I have a choice to make. Whether or not I abdicate for good, or take control of what is mine."

The air rushed from her lungs, a strange metallic taste on her tongue. "And…and you've decided?"

"I will not hide away forever," he said. "I will reclaim my throne. And in that I will make my example. I and my country will not remain broken. And I will not be kept under siege by the press."

"Well I…I don't know anything about ruling a country. I can't help you with that."

"Silly girl. I don't need your brain. I need what I myself no longer possess. I need your beauty."

She could scarcely understand the words he was saying.

"So, you have a deal," he said.

He'd given her no time to react to his previous statement. The swift proclamation stunned her. She nearly stumbled, nearly fell down to her knees.

"I…I do?" She still wasn't sure what she'd agreed

to. Helping him somehow with this reclamation of his kingdom. But she had no clue what that actually meant.

"Of course. I will have Fos go and tell your father that he's free to go."

"I…" She didn't know what to say. She certainly didn't feel anything like triumph. Instead, she was terrified, a bitter cold spreading through her midsection. She was a prisoner now. She had agreed to take her father's place in this madman's castle. "Can I…can I see him before he goes?"

"No," he said, "that would only cause unnecessary tears. And I find myself low on patience this evening."

"I don't…what do you want me to do?"

"You have heard it said, I imagine, that behind every successful man is a woman? You will be that woman. Something to help soften my…image."

He turned away again, his footsteps indicating that he was walking away, and panic gripped her. "Wait!"

He stopped. "A servant will come and show you to your room."

She imagined by "room" he meant "dungeon." Another shiver wound through her, fear spiking her blood, making her feel like she had been drugged. "At least let me see you." She refused to think of him as a monster looming around in the darkness. That would only give him more power. He was just a man. As she had been ranting earlier, he was probably a man with a weak chin.

A man who was afraid to show himself because he was cowardly. Because he was the kind of tyrant who wouldn't allow anyone to say anything about him that wasn't expressly approved by him. She had nothing to fear from this man. And when she saw his face, she would know that for sure.

"If you insist." Footsteps moved toward her, and his shape became clearer as he drew closer. Then one foot moved into the pool of light at the center of the room. Followed by the rest of him.

She had been right in her assessment of him as large. He was almost monstrous in stature, broad and impossibly tall. But if his height weren't enough to make her shiver in fear, his face would have accomplished it.

She had been wrong. He did not have a weak chin. Neither did he have a rounded jaw. No, there was something utterly perfect about his bone structure, which made the damage done to his features seem like a blasphemy shouted in a church.

His skin was golden brown, and it was ruined. Deep grooves taken from his face, a deep slash cutting through one eye. Deep enough that she wondered if he had vision on the side. He might have smiled, but it was difficult to say. The scar tissue at his mouth, so heavy on the one side, kept his lips from tipping up fully.

In that moment, she was certain that she had not been taken captive by a man. No, she had been taken captive by a beast.

CHAPTER TWO

PRINCE ADAM KATSAROS was no longer a handsome man. The accident that had stolen his wife from him had also stolen his face. But, he found it of little concern. He was not a good man anymore, either. And that made it seem slightly more poetic, his outsides matching what remained within.

Though, taking a woman captive was a bit much, even for him. Still, he was not inclined to change his mind now. When she had put the offer on the table, he had accepted it gladly. Mostly because he knew that he could use her. That he would be able to use her much more sufficiently than her father.

If what she said was true, if the old man was in fact dying, he had no interest in keeping him here to do just that. Yes, he wanted to make him an example. Yes, he wanted to reinforce his power, his hard line that he drew against all forms of entertainment media and the low, crawling worms who harassed and tormented their subjects simply for being famous, for being royal.

But, he had no interest in causing anyone's death. Additionally, he had a feeling that this woman could be infinitely more useful. His seclusion was coming to an end, and while he would happily stay in the darkness forever, it could not be so.

The agreement he had signed with the viceroy had very definitive terms. And if Adam didn't step in, an election would take place in the fall. So would go his bloodline, which had ruled Olympios for hundreds of years.

And, lost in his grief and pain though he'd been, he was not so lost that he would abandon all that his family line had built over the centuries.

But he needed another headline. One that extended beyond his scars, and a beautiful woman coming into public view by his side would add another dimension, another story, to the mix.

It was exactly what he needed, though he had not known it.

He would simply need the proper venue in which to use her.

He curled his hand into a fist and looked down at his marred skin. Sometimes, he was tempted to ask himself if he was overreacting. But then he was reminded. It was easy to be reminded. The reminders were all over his body.

At that moment, his phone rang, and he cursed. Because it was his friend—if that was the appropriate word—Prince Felipe Carrión de la Viña Cortez.

He punched the answer button on the phone and lifted it to his ear. "What do you want, Felipe?"

"And hello to you too," came his friend's lazy response. "I have Rafe on the line, as well, just so you know."

"A conference call?" Adam asked. "What sort of trouble are you in?"

His hot-blooded friend had a reputation for causing

international incidents, and it wouldn't surprise Adam if he was involved in yet another scandal.

Truly, he, Felipe and Rafe could not be more different. Were it not for their friendships formed at a particularly strict boarding school, he doubted they would have two words to say to each other now.

But, Felipe and Rafe had kept him from receding completely into darkness over the past few years. And for that, he owed them. Or, at least, for that he didn't growl at them every time one of them made contact.

"No trouble," Felipe said. "However, I am planning a party. You see, it is the fiftieth anniversary of my father's rule. And, likely the last he will see. Of course, I should like to invite you both."

For the first time since getting on the line, Rafe spoke. "And are you allowing service animals at your event?"

Felipe laughed. "Perhaps, Rafe, it is time you found yourself a lovely partner to help lead you around."

"As appealing as that is, I have yet to find a woman keen on playing the part of guide dog."

Five years earlier Rafe had been blinded in an accident, and though Adam didn't know the details, he suspected that a woman had been involved somehow. But, Rafe wasn't the type to share the details of his life. Unlike Felipe and himself, Rafe was not royalty. He had not been born with money. Instead, he had become the protégé of an Italian businessman at a very young age.

That man had paid for Rafe's schooling, and had gotten him a position at his company. Until Rafe's accident. But, it was that accident that had propelled Rafe to the next level of his success. Now he was unquestionably one of the wealthiest and most powerful men in Europe—royal blood or not.

But, whatever had happened, his friend had been completely changed by it. Adam understood.

Growing up, he and Felipe had been hellions. Utterly unconcerned with the state of their education, where Rafe had taken everything seriously. He had been there on borrowed money, and he had been incredibly conscious of that.

Adam and Felipe had spent most of their time pursuing women; Rafe had studied.

Now here they were. All a bit battle worn, except perhaps Felipe. Though, Adam always wondered about his seemingly carefree friend. In his experience, few people were actually carefree, and those that seemed the most dedicated to such facades often had the most structural damage beneath the surface.

"Now," Felipe said, "I'm sure that isn't true. Once a woman gets a look at the size of your…bank account, certainly she's more than willing to fulfill whatever duties you might require."

"Your confidence in me is astounding," Rafe said.

"Well," he continued, "you certainly possess more charm than our friend Adam."

Adam gritted his teeth. "Regretfully, I doubt I will be able to attend your ball."

"That," Felipe said, "is expected. But unacceptable. The fact of the matter is I'm going to be ascending the throne of my country soon. My father might have walled us off, made us insular, but I don't intend to keep it that way. I want to align myself with you, Adam, with your country, and with you, Rafe, and the industry that you could bring to Santa Milagro.

"I know you have been in exile for the past few years, Adam, but with your viceroy's tenure coming to an end, and the recent sale of those photographs of yours to the tabloids, I think it's time you took matters into your own hands. Your visage—such as it is—is going to filter out into the public soon enough. You might as well make an appearance along with it, Adam. Prove that you are not a coward."

"I'm not," he said, quickly losing patience with Felipe. "However, exposing myself in the public arena holds no appeal."

"Certainly understandable. I'm sure if Rafe could hide away, he would do so, as well."

Rafe laughed, but the sound held no humor. "I'm not disfigured. Only blind."

"Mostly blind," Felipe countered. "And anyway, what better way to take back the control. I know you despise the paparazzi for what they did to you. For what they did to your family. Are you going to let them have control of the story? Publish photographs of the Beast of Olympios and whatever headlines they wish to accompany it? No, come now, Adam. The man I knew in school would not allow such a thing."

"And the man you used to know had a soul. Not to mention a face."

"If not for yourself, do it for Ianthe."

Had his friend been standing in front of him, Adam would have hit him for bringing his wife's name into this. But, at the same time, he couldn't deny he had a point. A point he had come to for himself already, but Felipe didn't know that.

"Take your control back," Felipe said. "Make this

unveiling of your own making. Make Olympios yours again."

This was it, he realized. His moment. The power play.

The precise way and place to use his beautiful captive.

"When is this party?"

"In just over a month," Felipe said. "We can only hope my father holds on until then."

Adam could tell that Felipe didn't particularly hope any such thing. He knew that the two men had a complicated relationship, though he didn't know the details. The three of them talked details as little as possible.

"I'll be there," Rafe said. "I have no reason not to go."

"And you'll bring a date?"

"Absolutely not."

"I will," Adam said, his voice soft.

"You?" Felipe asked, not bothering to disguise the surprise in his voice at all.

"Yes. I have a recent acquisition that I look very much forward to showing off."

"Adam," Felipe said, "what have you done?"

"Just the kind of thing that suits a beast."

Belle was surprised when she was shown not to a dungeon but to an elegantly appointed bedroom with a four-poster bed covered by brocade curtains and festooned with pillows.

"I thought I was a prisoner?" She turned to ask the servant.

She'd been made to surrender her phone, but otherwise, everyone was being…nice to her. Well, everyone except the Prince himself. She doubted nice was a thing he did.

"There are enough rooms in the palace to keep even a prisoner comfortable," the man said drily.

"You don't approve of him," she said. "Do you?"

He lifted a shoulder. "He does not require my approval. Neither does he take any heed of my disapproval."

"Is he…is he crazy?" The disfigured man who had sought such destructive revenge on her father, and who had accepted her in trade could hardly be sane. Still, she felt like she needed to figure out exactly what she was dealing with.

He seemed to have a plan. A way he wanted to…use her to come back into the spotlight. She could only hope that plan meant there was a finite end to her sentence.

"He is not unaffected by the accident that caused those scars," the man said carefully. "That is about all I can tell you."

"Okay," she said, wrapping her arms around herself, shivering, because suddenly she felt cold. She turned to face the window, the small, narrow notch giving her a slight view of city lights reflecting on the sea. "Has my father gone already?" She turned again, to find her companion gone.

For some reason, the withdrawal of the servant made her feel isolated. Utterly alone. A chill swept over her, bone deep and intense. She had agreed to stay here, with a potential madman, for an unknown amount of time. There was no one here to protect her. Her father was likely long gone, and really, there was nothing he could do for her. He had to go and seek out his treatment; he couldn't stay behind.

She wondered if the Prince had even told him that she had traded places with him.

That thought made her stomach tighten. The thought

that it was entirely possible no one would know she was here. She hadn't told Tony where she was going, because she'd known he would try to stop her.

No, no one would have any idea she was locked up in a medieval castle. What if nobody ever looked for her?

No. She wouldn't think of it like that. The way he had talked…he'd made it sound like he very much intended to be seen in public with her. Which meant her being here wouldn't be a secret. But…

What would her father think? What would he do?

What would Tony do if he knew she was being held at some strange man's castle? She tried to imagine Tony taking on Adam. Her boyfriend's more…refined frame would be no match for Adam's monstrous form.

Adam was…

She thought back to that moment when he'd stepped into the light. That hard, scarred face. His incredibly muscular body. She shivered.

Thinking of him made her heart pound, made her skin tingle. It was a strange sort of fear. One that coursed through her veins like fire.

One that felt almost not like fear at all.

She heard heavy footfalls, and realized she had left the door open, had left herself exposed. She moved quickly toward the entrance, intent on closing it tightly, on giving herself some security. But, she didn't move quick enough.

There he was.

He was…she wasn't sure she had ever seen a man so large. Six foot six, at least, broad and muscular. His face was even more shocking in the bright light of her bedchamber.

His dark eyes were watchful, and yet again, a window into how beautiful he might have been before he had been altered like this.

"Do I frighten you?" he asked.

"Isn't that your intention?"

"Not specifically."

He didn't elaborate, though. Didn't give her any idea of what he might be doing specifically. "So, do I go before a judge and jury? Or are you basically it?"

"This is my land. And I am the law of it."

"In other words, you can do whatever you want."

He nodded slowly. "Yes. In other words."

She drew herself up to her full height, ignoring the shiver that wound through her. "What exactly do you intend to do with me?" It took a lot of courage to ask that question, especially considering she didn't know if she wanted the answer.

"I intend to make you pay," he said, the promise on those dark words licking down her spine. "But first, I should like you to join me for dinner."

"No," she said, the denial moving quickly from her lips, before she had a chance to think better of it. "I don't want to have dinner with you."

"Why not?"

"Because you're my jailer. Because I find you uncivilized."

"And hideous," he said, flashing her a slight smile, a brief glimpse of straight, white teeth, "I imagine."

There was no good way to answer that. He was... *hideous* wasn't the right word. Damaged. Terrifying. Compelling. But certainly not hideous.

"Show me anybody who wants to have dinner with the person keeping them captive," she said, rather than responding to his previous statement.

"That's the thing about being a captive," he said, his tone dry. "Choice is typically quite limited."

"What are you going to do if I refuse to go with you?" She planted her hands on her hips and took a step forward. She had to do this. She had to test him. Maybe he was a madman. Maybe he was going to go full Henry VIII on her. Off with her head, and all of that. Maybe he would do something even worse. But, until she tested the boundary, she wouldn't know what manner of man she was dealing with.

"I will pick you up, put you over my shoulder and carry you down to dinner whether you want to go or not."

"I don't want to."

Without missing a beat, he closed the distance between them, curved his arms around her waist and pulled her up off the ground, laying her over his shoulder. She was stunned. By his strength. By the ease at which he held her. By the heat of his body.

He was just…so very hot. And it burned her all over, even in places where they didn't touch. He moved, and she wobbled, grabbing hold of his shoulder to keep from falling. Then he turned and carried her from the room.

CHAPTER THREE

SHE WAS LIKE fire in his arms. That was all he could think as he strode out of her chamber, her lithe body wiggling over his shoulder as he carried her down the hall.

He braced one hand on her lower back, gripping her calf with the other. It had been three years since he'd had his hands on a woman. And suddenly, he was conscious of every one of those years. He had been far too lost in the bleakness of it all to think of it in those terms until this moment.

He had not thought of being with a woman. Hadn't thought of touching one. He had only been conscious of his bed being empty as far as it being empty of his wife. Not being empty in a way that meant it might need to be filled by someone else.

But now she was hot beneath his fingertips, smooth, and very much alive. So different from the last time he had touched a woman and found her cold, icy and lifeless.

He gritted his teeth, clipping his jaw down tight as he continued to cart his protesting captive down the stairs and toward the dining room.

"How dare you?" she shrieked, pounding one fist against his back.

"How dare I feed you?" He laughed. "I truly am a monster."

"You could have sent me a crust of bread up to my room," she continued to protest.

"Yes, but alternatively you can sit and eat with me, and you can have lamb."

"Maybe I don't want to eat a baby animal!"

"Are you a vegetarian?"

"No," she said, sounding small, and slightly defeated in her response. "But still."

"If you have serious issues eating small, fuzzy things, you can always indulge in the vegetables and the couscous. Plus, there will be cake."

"I could have eaten that in my room," she said, wiggling, that movement of her body against his sending a jolt of sensation through him. He ignored it.

"No, *agape*, you could not have, because it is not on offer."

He stepped into the dining room, and set her down neatly in the chair next to his own. She looked up at him, her eyes wide. She truly was beautiful. Her dark hair was captured in a low ponytail, her blue eyes glittering in the dim light, distrustful, but nonetheless lovely. She had full lips, the kind he could vaguely remember enjoying back in the days when he had indulged in such pleasures.

Then, there was her body, which was pleasingly round in all the right places, as he had observed while carrying her from her room.

"What do you want from me?"

"I would like for you to eat. With the dramatics kept to a minimum."

She frowned, her expression stormy. "You did not

allow me to trade places with my father so that you could feed me."

"No," he said, "perhaps not. I allowed you to trade with your father because you asked me to allow it. And as I mentioned before, I thought, that just maybe you might be of more use to me than a dying man."

She recoiled. So completely that it was nearly comical. "What sort of use?"

There was a time when a woman would have leaned in at such a suggestion, touched his hand, touched his arm, perhaps made things even more intimate by placing her hand on his thigh. But, those days had long since passed.

He let his eyes wander back to those beautiful rosy lips. And just for a moment, he imagined crushing his ruined mouth right up against them. Yes, she would most certainly take offense at that.

"Oh, anything I can think of. Propping up a wobbly desk, perhaps?"

Her eyes narrowed. "Be serious for a moment."

"Don't be silly. I'm always serious." At least, he had been for the past few years. Until these past few moments.

But, other than his friends, who he communicated with primarily over the phone, he only ever talked to his stripped-down staff. To Fos, the man who had been his father's right hand for as long as Adam could remember. And to Athena, his cook. Otherwise, the staff tended to rotate, and they kept out of his way.

Belle was one of the first new people he had spent any time with in longer than he could remember.

"Seriously deranged." She sniffed.

A few moments later, Athena appeared, along with

kitchen staff carrying trays. "Tonight," she said, casting
a swift glance over to Belle, "we have lamb with mint
and yogurt, couscous and assorted vegetables. For dessert there is baklava."

"Thank you," he said.

Athena lingered.

Adam sighed heavily. "Have you something to say,
Athena?"

"I don't approve," she said, her tone stiff.

"And I don't care," he returned. "Leave us."

Athena cast him a sad glance, and then turned the
same look onto Belle. Then she shook her head and
walked out of the room.

"Neither of your servants approve of you," Belle said,
looking the food over critically.

"And my captive doesn't seem to fear me," he said.
"I must be doing something wrong."

"I came all the way from California to face you down
and get my father out of your dungeon. If I was going to
freak out, I would have done it already." She tilted her
chin upward, her expression mutinous. And a little bit
too committed to defiance.

"We shall see. Eat."

He took his own command, digging into the food with
relish. He picked up one of the lamb shanks, gnawing it
close to the bone. He became aware a moment later of
Belle's watchful gaze on him.

"What?" he asked.

"I assumed that… I assumed that royalty would have
some sort of exemplary table manners. But, unless your
customs are different here…"

He set the meat down onto his plate. "Are you determined to insult me at every turn? I served you dinner. I

installed you in a very nice room. All things considered, I find you ungrateful."

"I'm sorry—am I not expressing adequate gratitude for my imprisonment?"

"You are a prisoner of your own design. You could have left your father here."

"Right. I could have left my father here to die."

He lifted a shoulder. "Plenty of people would have. A great many people possess more self-interest than that."

"My father raised me," she said, conviction in her tone. "He's all I have. And it might be easy for you to dismiss him as nothing more than a paparazzo, but he's everything to me. And you didn't even let me say good-bye to him."

"I'm hardly going to keep you captive for the rest of your life," he said. "Don't be dramatic."

"He's sick," she insisted. "He might die while I'm away."

Adam felt an uncomfortable stab of conscience. He was not in the market for his conscience to make any kind of resurgence. Not now. "I truly hope that isn't the case. However, he was well enough to sneak into my palace and collect photographs of me only a few weeks ago. Then he sold those photos and would do nothing to reclaim them. Tell me," he said, "since you are so well versed in matters of popular culture, do you know exactly how I got my scars?"

She looked down, shaking her head.

"All it took was a relentless photographer harassing my driver on a night with poor driving conditions," he said, his tone hard. "And in the end, damage was done that could not be undone."

He didn't see the point in bringing up Ianthe. If she didn't know, he wasn't going to discuss it. Not something so intensely personal. Not pain that belonged to him, and him alone, so unquestionably.

"I…" She looked away from him, and she had the decency to look ashamed. "I didn't know. I didn't. But, my father didn't endanger you."

"No," he said, his tone dripping with condescension. "He only broke into my home and invaded my privacy."

"He's harmless," she said. "I mean, I know that a lot of people don't understand the paparazzi thing. And I guess it can be a little bit…intense."

"They are nothing but leeches. Bottom-feeders who leech off the fame of those who have either talent or power."

"Fine. But my father isn't a leech. When my mother decided she didn't want me he took care of me. He's always taken care of me. And yes, he did it by taking pictures of celebrities. That's what fed me, all of my life. But nobody else was going to feed me," she said, her voice vibrating with conviction.

"There are plenty of other lines of work to be in."

"Says the Prince who was born with his job. Other people have to work. And not only that, they have to work hard to get work in the first place."

"Are you lecturing me on how hard life can be?" He sat back in his chair. "Excuse me while I get a pen and paper so that I can take notes."

"I'm sorry about your accident. My father didn't do that to you."

"But he was intending to use my personal tragedy for his gain." He laughed. "In fact, he has succeeded."

"Yes," she said, sputtering. "But it isn't that simple.

He isn't doing it to hurt you. He needs help. He needed to be able to afford his treatments."

"Your justifications are hardly going to impress me. There is absolutely nothing I hate more than the press. Particularly the kind of fake press your father is a part of. But, it is of no matter to me. There is nothing I can do to prevent the publication of those photographs. Believe me—I have tried. But, I have figured out a way to take control of the situation."

"What's that?" she asked, clearly skeptical.

"I have not appeared in public since my accident. That's why those photographs are so valuable, you know. Because everybody's curious. How badly am I disfigured?"

She blinked. "You haven't been in public...at all."

"No. I think I mentioned when we first met—"

"When you took me captive."

"If you prefer. I think I mentioned that I have someone ruling in my stead. However, the time frame on our agreement is running out, and if I do not regain control of the country, a general election will result. And so it will be the end of the monarchy as we know it." He looked at the little woman sitting across from him and twisting her hands in her lap. "I would have thought you would have done a bit of cursory research on me before you tore off to my kingdom and offered to become my prisoner."

"There wasn't time. Whatever you think about my father, I hope that you can understand that I love him."

"Love doesn't matter except to the people it is between," he said, thinking of his wife. The press certainly hadn't cared that he'd loved her. They were always tormenting her, always working to dig up a scandal. "It is precious to no one else," he finished, the words bitter.

"Tell me. Tell me your plans. Since I clearly factor into them."

"I intend to keep you here with me, and then I intend to present you to the world as my mistress."

Belle felt as though she had been slapped. "Your...what?"

"My mistress. As I said, I have not been seen in the public eye since the accident. But, now those photographs are going to be published, and it is forcing me out of my seclusion. I suppose it had to happen eventually. I dislike greatly having my hand forced, but the timing coincides with an event that is politically expedient for me to attend."

He began to eat again, just as he had done earlier. There was something feral in the way that he handled his food. In his posture. He wasn't at all the way she imagined a prince might be. Though, when he talked about how long he had been away from the public eye, it all made a bit more sense. He had been here, she assumed. Nearly alone in this castle, answering to no one but himself. Clearly, performing for no one at all.

His manner was rough, his manners nonexistent.

Of course, she could expect little else from someone who had taken her prisoner over some photographs. Well, as a trade for a prisoner who was imprisoned for photographs.

And he had said he needed her for her beauty. So she supposed she shouldn't be shocked that this was where it was leading.

But a mistress. Such an old-fashioned word, and certainly not one that had ever been applied to her.

She wasn't sure anyone would believe it. She didn't know how to act the part of a vixen. Or even someone mildly flirtatious.

She'd met Tony at school, and if not for him coming into the university library every day around the time she was studying, asking her what she was reading, the two of them would never have started dating. She'd been oblivious, and only his persistence had brought about the first date.

Oh. Tony. He would be…

"I can't do that."

"You don't have a choice. You agreed to be my prisoner, and so, here you are."

"But…but…I can't have the whole world thinking I'm with you!"

He lifted his hand, drawing his fingertips across her cheekbone, leaving a trail of strange fire in his wake. "Yes," he said, his tone dry. "I can see how that would be a grave humiliation for you."

He'd misunderstood, but she saw no point in correcting him. The why didn't matter. Not to him.

She looked down. "I don't suppose you would have a hard time finding somebody else who wanted to go with you."

"Yes," he said, "I'm very wealthy, and very powerful. But, a great many men are. And very few of them have my ill humor or destroyed features."

"So," she said, "you just want me to be your date?" Spoken plainly like that, it scared her slightly less.

"Oh, it is a bit more than that. I shall present you to the world as my lover, and with that there will be certain expectations. You will be required to keep up the farce or… I will continue to pursue action against your father."

She felt helpless. And she felt…well she felt like a prisoner. "I have a boyfriend." As if bringing Tony into the mix would discourage him.

"Not anymore."

Her heart twisted. "You can't just do that. I mean, you can't force me to break up with him."

"You don't need to do anything half so dramatic as that. But you will not be allowed to speak with him. In fact, I think I like this scenario even better. I hope he comes forward and complains to the media about the woman who jilted him for this." He gestured to himself.

"Why do you want this?" she asked. "Just to hurt me? Because of my father?"

"No," he said, hard and firm. "I need to return to the spotlight as I left." He laughed then, dark and merciless. "Which is difficult enough. And I will be damned if I allowed myself to be an object of pity. Of scorn. When I walk into that ballroom, in front of the world, it will be as though I never left. Yes, I am scarred now, but I will have a woman on my arm, and there will be no doubt that as easily as I stepped into your bed, I will step back into the throne room."

"And when…and when the party is over?"

He lifted a shoulder. "You will be free, of course. And we will concoct a story about our drifting apart. I could hardly settle down so quickly, after all. Someday, yes. But after a suitable succession of women such as yourself."

The arrogance, the confidence inherent in that statement should have enraged her. Instead she felt…hot.

"I need my phone back," she insisted, thinking again of Tony. Forcing her thoughts back to him.

"No."

"But, I have agreed to your terms."

"And yet, you are not a guest. You are my captive. I cannot have you making contact with the outside world that I don't approve of. You are the daughter of the lowest form of life that I can think of on this planet, and I have no guarantee that you are not also a photographer, or that you wouldn't also act as one if the opportunity presented itself. In fact, it would be rather a clever ploy, don't you think?"

She supposed it would be, but she honestly hadn't thought of it. "Well, I'm not. I'm getting my master's in literature."

"What do you do with a degree like that?"

"Teach mainly. But, my point is I don't move in that world. I don't condemn my father, but I'm not following in his footsteps either."

He spread his arms wide. "And yet, here you are. You followed in his footsteps close enough."

"I'm not hungry," she said, looking at her barely touched food.

"I still am."

"I want to go to my room."

He waved a hand. "You will go when I'm finished. I suggest you eat, because there will be nothing served to you after."

"I'm done."

"It is not in my best interest to have you show up at our big debut looking half-starved. I should like your curves to be able to fill out a ball gown."

Heat flooded her cheeks. "I don't care what you want my curves to do. They aren't yours. I'll put on a show for you, but you don't get access to my body."

The air between them suddenly seemed to freeze; then

it heated again. He stood from his chair, moving over to where she was sitting. He leaned in and he reached out slowly, drawing his fingertip across her cheek. She was mesmerized, held captive by his face. By every groove and imperfection in his skin, by the twist at the corner of his mouth and that slash that ran over his right eye. With him this close, she could see that it didn't impact his vision. No, he saw. She had a feeling he saw so deeply into her that he could see just how fast her blood was rushing. How hard her heart was pounding.

"I will have access to whatever I like," he said, his tone soft. "And you would do well to remember that."

"I already told you—"

"You have a boyfriend. Yes. But, I have taken you prisoner in my castle, Belle. Ask yourself, do I seem like the sort of man who is concerned about whether or not someone has a boyfriend?"

"Given that…" She swallowed hard, trying to fight the fluttering in her stomach. "Given the fact that you have taken two people prisoner in the space of forty-eight hours, I imagine you don't care about things like boyfriends, no."

"You are correct." He settled back into his chair, and a wave of relief washed over her. But, she also felt a lingering chill from his withdrawal. "You see, it is an interesting thing, having everything taken from you. When you shrink your world down to a palace, to the grounds, it gives you a lot of time to reflect."

"Yes," she said, "clearly, you had your own *Eat, Pray, Love* moment and emerged extremely enlightened."

"Not entirely. Instead, I had a lot of time to think about what matters. And what doesn't."

"What matters to a man like you?"

"Survival. That's all that matters. That's the beginning and end of it. There are no rewards given for the manner in which you live, Belle. It would do you well to remember that."

"You have the audacity to comment on what my father does for a living while you say morality doesn't matter?"

"Because it hindered my survival. And, as previously stated, that is the only thing that matters to me. When you have nothing else, the elemental need to breathe is all that keeps you going. Yes, survival is the beginning and end of everything. When everything else falls away, the only thing that remains is that indrawn breath, and the seconds that stretch between it and the next. Sometimes, it is simply all you have to live for." He took another bite of his dinner. "The living. Not the manner in which you live, not anything you possess. We are all creatures driven by that need."

She shook her head. "Not me. I like books. And I like the ocean. The sun on the sand, and how warm it feels against my skin." She saw something flicker in his dark eyes, and for some reason she felt her cheeks heat. "Those things are deeper than survival. And they matter. Because they're what make survival matter."

He laughed, but the sound carried no humor. "You would be surprised. There was a point in my existence when I looked around, and there was nothing. Nothing but an empty palace, dark, void of life. When every part of my body hurt, when I could barely get out of bed. And I would ask myself why I was still breathing. The answer was not books or the sun on the sand."

"What was the answer, then?" she asked, in spite of herself.

"Because I'm simply too stubborn to allow death to

win. Sometimes, that's all the reason you have. So it is the reason that suffices." He stood then. "I am finished. Come. I will show you back to your room."

"I don't need you to."

"Yes," he said, his voice uncompromising, "you do. Because, I need to establish a few...ground rules."

She bristled. She wasn't accustomed to being told what to do. That simply wasn't the way her father had raised her. No, her father had seemed perpetually out of his element with a small child. But, he had loved her, and Belle had given him as little trouble as possible because she could see how hard he tried. Because from what she could remember of her life with her mother, she was much better off with her father.

He kept her on a very long leash. He had never imposed much in the way of strictures. She fixed her own dinner, chose her own clothes, decided when she would go out at night and when she would stay in.

Having this man suggest that she would be following anything like rules burrowed underneath her skin and prodded her.

Not that she'd ever done much with that freedom. But it was the principle.

Somehow, she managed to bite her lip and keep from saying something. But, the minute she did that fear crept back over her. A reminder that she didn't know who he was, not really. And didn't know what he was capable of.

It was so hard to take it all in; it kept hitting her in fits and starts, in little snatches. Probably because if it all landed on her at once, like a ton of extremely archaic bricks, she would lose her mind completely.

"If ever you are hungry, just let Athena know. She will feed you."

"I can't just…get my own food?"

"I never do," he said.

"Well," she said, "that is not particularly surprising."

She followed him down the long corridor, back to the stairs. "There is an exit that way," he said, gesturing to the left. "It will take you out to the gardens. You're welcome to explore anyplace you want on the grounds. Also, the ballroom, the libraries, all of that is open to you. But my quarters are not."

"Okay," she said, feeling a strange sense of relief. Really, she did not want to go to his quarters. Just the thought made her stomach clench up tight.

"My chambers encompass the east quadrant of the palace."

"An entire quadrant?"

He arched a brow, pausing midstride. "I take up a lot of space." Then he turned away from her and continued walking. That simple statement was truer than he probably realized. He most definitely took up a lot of space. And all the air in whatever room he was in.

"Can I at least…?" She took a breath. "You won't give me my phone. I need something. I need some way to get in touch with people."

"That is impossible. Not at the moment. I have my own agenda, and my concern is that you have your own, as well. I cannot have them conflicting."

He didn't sound the least bit regretful. "So you just intend to keep me cut off from the world?"

"It isn't so bad."

It was dawning on her, creeping up over her like a chill, that she was committed to staying here with a man who had not been outside palace walls in several years. A man who clearly didn't understand why anybody would have an issue being so isolated. It wasn't even an issue of him lacking sympathy or humanity.

He had no understanding. For why she might want more. For why she might need more.

A person could shrivel up into a husk and die here, and the master of the manor would never even have had the slightest inclination she was in danger of doing so.

"I don't…" It suddenly dawned on her when they approached her bedroom door that she had nothing with her. No clothes. "I don't have anything to wear." She had been wearing the same jeans and jacket since she had embarked on her journey yesterday.

"I can have something procured for you. You will get it tomorrow. Tonight, however, there is nothing I can do for you."

"But…I…I have nothing to sleep in."

He looked at her, his coal-black eyes burning through her skin, leaving her feeling hot, restless. "Then sleep in nothing. It is what I do."

For some reason, those words forced an image of him with acres of golden skin exposed. She wondered where his scars extended to. If all of him was so rough and tragically torn, or if parts of him were still whole.

And once more that strange sensation overwhelmed her. Made her scalp prickle, made her heart beat faster.

She gasped and jerked away from him.

He regarded her closely for a moment, and she sensed a strange current arcing between them; for some reason she was incredibly conscious and aware of the amount of restraint and strength it was taking for him to hold himself there, still and steady. She had no idea just what he was restraining himself from doing, or why she was so confident in her assessment of him.

She wasn't sure she wanted to know the answer to either thing.

"I will leave you," he said, his tone hard.

Then he turned away to go, and she found herself strangely wanting to stop him. To prolong the moment.

So she took another step away from him, holding her hands down at her sides and keeping herself resolutely still.

He walked away from the room, and back down the corridor. She let out a breath she hadn't known she'd been holding. And then she sprang into action. She forced the door shut, and locked it, hoping that it would hold. Then thinking it was probably silly because if anybody had the key to the door, it was her captor.

Her heart began to thunder hard, and she placed her hand against her breast, trying to catch her breath. She was shaking, shaking and trying not to cry. But then she wondered why she was bothering.

She let out a gasping sob, one tear trailing down her cheek. She turned and threw herself on the bed. She was alone. Really alone. Her father didn't know where she was, Tony didn't know where she was.

She had no way to reach them. She had no way to get help if she needed it. She simply had to trust the man holding her here.

Her wounded, strangely beautiful captor, who seemed to bring ice with him whenever he entered a room.

She closed her eyes, waiting for sleep to claim her. And as her thoughts began to swirl around in a confusing circle, she kept picturing his dark eyes. Dark eyes, set in a ravaged face, that were windows to an even more ravaged soul.

Thoughts of him made her restless. Made it impossible for her to breathe.

I will present you to the world as my mistress.

Memories of those words, of that voice, set off a quiver low in her belly. And her final thought before drifting to sleep was that if this was fear…if it was anger, it was unlike anything she had ever felt before in her life.

With those words still resonating inside her, she was forced to recognize, as sleep claimed her utterly, that she felt neither fear nor anger toward him.

But she refused to name the things she did feel. Which were far more monstrous than he could ever be.

CHAPTER FOUR

THE CASTLE FELT DIFFERENT. Adam had to wonder if it was
because of the woman who was currently residing in it.
He did not like to give her presence that much weight.
There were often women and residents here in the castle, various staff members who he did his best not to
interact with. Plus Athena, who had been with him for
more than a decade.

Belle's presence should make no difference at all. And
yet, it was as though he could feel her in the air. He gritted his teeth. Perhaps Felipe was right. Perhaps he was
starting to get a little bit too close to insanity thanks to
his years of isolation.

To be so much a part of a place that he could sense
the presence of a new person…yes, that was perhaps a
bit close to crazy.

Though, crazier perhaps, was that flash of heat that
had flared up when he had placed his hand on her last
night. He should not have done so. It had touched something inside him, awakened something. Something that
was far better left asleep.

For the first time in recent memory, he felt restless.
Usually, he was content to conduct his business within
the confines of the palace walls, or, if he was feeling

like a change of scenery, on the grounds. Often, a burst of energy could be dealt with in his gym.

This was different. He didn't like it.

He prowled the halls of the palace, his staff members making themselves scarce the moment he approached. He was clearly radiating his foul mood.

If there was business to take care of as far as the country was concerned, Fos would have approached him already. But, he had not seen his adviser today at all, so that meant he lacked for specific direction.

Given the circumstances, he disliked that greatly.

A maid scuttled by, and Adam stopped her with a warning look. "Have coffee sent to the library," he ordered.

"Forgive me, Your Highness, coffee is already there," she returned, bowing slightly.

"Why?"

"For…the lady. Was that not… Athena told me to serve her when she asked, and where she asked."

Of course she had. Obviously, his housekeeper had seen fit to override his handling of his own captive. "You did nothing wrong," he said. "You may go."

He continued on his way to the library. And there he found her. She was sitting in an armchair, her legs tucked beneath her, wearing the same clothes she'd had on yesterday. Yes, that was right; she'd told him she had nothing else to wear. He would have to ensure that something was procured for her.

Her attention was so focused on the book that was sitting in her lap that she didn't look up when he came in.

"Enjoying the story?"

She jumped, looking up, her blue eyes wide. "I was," she said, her tone dripping with disdain. Her pale cheeks had a rosy flush to them, and he wondered if she was embarrassed about something. Or, if she was angry. Likely, it was anger.

"What is it?"

"Nothing you would be interested in," she said, closing it, keeping her finger tucked between the pages, holding her spot. She reached over to the table that was placed next to the armchair and picked up a mug that he assumed contained coffee.

Next to that mug was another, and beside that was an insulated carafe. He moved nearer, picked it up and helped himself to a cup.

"I was told I would find you here, along with the coffee," he said.

"And so you did." She gave him a sideways glance, her lips pressed against the edge of her mug, poised as though she was about to take another drink. "You said that I could go in any room I wanted, as long as I didn't invade your quarters."

"I did say that."

"Then why are you…prowling around looking vaguely disapproving? You're the one that wanted me here."

"Yes, *agape*, and you're the one who offered the trade. So a little bit less outrage from you would perhaps benefit us both. I gave you what you wanted."

"Well, preferable would have been to free both my father and myself."

He laughed and set his mug back down on the table. "But, that would benefit me in no way. You cannot expect me to do something simply because it is the right thing, can you?"

Adam had lost touch with what was right and what was wrong long ago. He would hardly allow this little

waif to come in and lecture him when she had no idea
what sort of man he was. No idea of the realities of the
life he had lived. And the weight of his responsibility
that was beginning to crush him now.

The simple truth was, he did have to get back out into
the public eye. The more he pondered what Felipe had
said, the more he realized his friend was delivering him
the salvation that Adam had been looking for.

He had been mired in the darkness for too long.

But, for the sake of his country—because he certainly didn't give a damn for his own sake—he needed
to change course. He had to take control, and he had
known it was coming but…

Since the discovery that photographs of him had been
taken it had been like he was walking out of a thick fog.
The reality of the fact that the outside world still existed
hitting him harder than it had in the past three years.
The arrival of Belle and the phone call from Felipe had
only cemented those things.

It had driven home what he'd known already: That it
was time. That there was no question about whether or
not he would take his rightful place.

"Well, I always hope that people will do the right
thing," she said, her tone stiff.

"Come now, this facade doesn't suit either of us.
Surely, you must assume that people will do what benefits them. Your father makes a living off that principle,
does he not?"

She shifted, the color in her cheeks darkening. Yes,
it was definitely anger. "I suppose."

"We talked about this already. Survival. That is why
we're all here. To make it to the end. To prolong the distance between that moment of our birth and the moment

we take our last breath, as best we possibly can. And if in between those moments we can find ways to thrive, then I suppose we will."

"I suppose," she said again, the words muttered darkly.

"But you must understand that it is not my own self-interest that pushes me here. But the interest of my country. Viceroy Kyriakos is a good man. But he is not a Katsaros. It is not his legacy."

"Obviously."

"It is time for me to make a stronger show for my country. For a while, I thought that a ruler such as myself would seem like a weakness to my people. That no one would want to see me so diminished. So, I was content to rule from behind the scenes. I did what I could to ensure that my people would not be a laughingstock, with a ruler who is disfigured as I am."

She winced at his words, but she didn't correct him. There was no dancing around the truth. He was disfigured. There had been a time when he and Ianthe had been media darlings in Europe, when they had been the most beautiful royal couple, the most photographed. But now he found himself without his princess, and without any appeal whatsoever.

It wasn't about vanity. It was about control. About the unknown. About giving this tragedy over to the world. He was reluctant to do so. For a great many reasons. But, his reluctance could carry on no more.

"And, as an added bonus, you will get to experience what it means to be on the other end of the photographer's lens."

She winced. "What do you mean?"

"Well, surely you have deduced that we will make the

news—that was why you protested so last night, told me about your boyfriend."

"Well," she said, "yes."

"You have no idea the sort of headline we will create," he said. "Before the accident I mostly made waves here in Europe. But, the wider world will be interested in my return from the darkness, I have no doubt. As the deadline for my return approaches. Just as they will be morbidly interested in what horror the accident has brought upon me. I'm certain that there will be a salacious tabloid headline to that effect any day now. But, to emerge shortly thereafter, with a beauty such as yourself on my arm...well, that will be a story."

Again, he held off mentioning his wife. She didn't need to know.

"Of course, there can be no question about you making contact with your boyfriend. I can have nobody on the outside able to call the validity of this relationship into question."

"My father certainly won't believe it," she said. "And, even though he's likely in the hospital at this moment, he probably still has access to a phone."

"Really?" Tension gathered in his stomach, and he couldn't quite work out why. "You think your father won't believe that you came to speak to me, that I enticed you to stay. That I offered you beautiful clothing, jewelry...pleasure. That you were swayed by such things?"

She looked away. "Of course he won't believe that."

"Because I'm ugly? I assure you, Belle, a man in my position does not need to be beautiful. And a man with my skills doesn't need physical perfection to bring a woman to completion."

This time, when her cheeks turned red, he had a feeling it was from something else. The same thing affecting him. Molten heat that was coursing through his veins. For the second time in the space of twenty-four hours desire stirred inside him. What he was saying to her… he believed it to be true. Of course he could bring a woman pleasure in the dark. He didn't need his face restored in order to find all the places on her body that would make her cry out, that would make her wet with her need for him.

Again, the issue here wasn't vanity, but the desire to do so. It had been absent for long enough that he had thought it was another casualty of the accident. Another side effect of his loss.

Now he wondered. Now, with his body roaring back to life, he more than wondered.

In fact, he didn't wonder a damn thing. He was starving. That was what he was.

"I don't intend to find out," she said, her tone clipped.

"That's right. Because you have a boyfriend. How is he? *Pretty?*" She made a small, outraged squeak at that. "But does he know how to make you scream?"

She stood up quickly, holding her book up against her chest. "You're awful."

"I'm the monster who took you prisoner. If you expected me to be anything different, you were only going to be disappointed."

She gave him a look of pure umbrage, then made a movement like she was going to storm out of the room. He reached out, taking hold of her book, his fingertips brushing against hers, sending trails of lightning up his arm and down through the center of his body.

"You lost my place!" she shouted, her tone indignant.

"I'm sure you'll find it again." He turned the book over in his hands. "What is this?"

"Anna Karenina."

"Doesn't she get hit by a train?"

"Yes. At this moment it's something of a fantasy of mine. As it's preferable to my current situation."

He reached out, sifting his fingers through her hair. He expected her to pull away, to jump back. She surprised him by freezing instead. Her mouth dropped open, her eyes turning glassy. "I don't think that's true," he said.

"What? That I'm having a fantasy?"

"Oh, I believe that you're having a fantasy. I just don't think it has anything to do with being hit by a train."

He slid his hand to her cheek, drawing his thumb across her silken skin, brushing the edge of her lips. That seemed to mobilize her. She jolted, then pivoted to the side, stepping away from him. "I'm only here because I wanted to save my father. For that, I'll do anything. For right now, our only agreement is that I make an appearance with you at whatever event you feel I need a gown for. If you want something else, you're going to have to come out and say it. If you require my body, then I can lie down and take it, but you had better rest assured that it will be under sufferance. But don't play this game where you act as though you might be able to seduce me. That would be impossible."

"I've never had to force a woman into my bed yet," he said.

"I suppose that's hard for you to know, considering you're royalty and all. How can anyone refuse you?" She drew in a sharp breath and took a step away from him, and he thought for a moment that she was finished. But then she continued. "Also, I'm curious if you've propositioned a woman since…you know. You might find it more difficult now."

Her eyes glistened as she said the words, the color high in her cheeks, almost as though she felt guilty for landing such an unerring blow.

He was hardly going to let such an insult stand. He reached out, grabbing hold of her arm and dragging her back toward his body. She lost her balance, falling against his chest, her palms pressing against his muscles. She looked up at him, eyes wide.

He gripped her chin with his thumb and forefinger, holding her steady, and his mouth crashed down on hers.

CHAPTER FIVE

IT WAS A PUNISHMENT. There was no doubt about that. There was nothing ambiguous in the way his lips met hers, nothing gentle, nothing tentative. It had nothing to do with giving, nothing to do with pleasure. He tasted like rage. Maybe even hatred.

Belle was too stunned to do anything. Too shocked to fight back. So she stood, immobilized, trapped in his strong arms, pinned beneath the hard wall of his body.

He shifted, angling his head, forcing her lips open, his tongue sliding against hers. She gasped, and the action allowed him deeper access.

She waited. Waited for something like horror to overtake her. Waited for a surge of adrenaline, the kind that was supposed to come when you were in situations that were deadly. That gave you the strength to lift cars, and all other manner of things. Surely, some of that should come to her rescue now. Give her the strength to fend off one hard-bodied prince.

But it didn't. Instead, something else stole over her. A betraying heat, a kind of strange, languid feeling that started in her stomach and spread outward toward her limbs. It made her want to melt against him, and without being aware that she'd made the conscious thought to do so, she found herself doing just that. Curving her body around his, going pliant against the mountain that was Prince Adam Katsaros.

It was that strange feeling from before. That she had been calling fear. That prickling heat that spread over her skin. It came together here. In a brilliant flash. When his lips met hers, it became so very horribly clear.

His mouth might be too damaged to smile, but it had in no way affected his ability to kiss.

She had never imagined a kiss could feel like this. So raw, and rough and devastating. It wasn't good. It wasn't sweet; there was no connection in it. She had kissed only one other man, Tony, and the thing that she liked about kissing him was that it made her feel close to someone.

This was not that. This was hard, and it was angry, and it had breached her defenses and touched her in places she didn't know a simple meeting of mouths could reach.

And it made her heart beat so hard she thought it might tumble out of her chest. Made it impossible for her to think, impossible for her to breathe. Her knees went weak, and she curled her fingers around his shirt, keeping herself from melting into the ground as best she could.

He reached up, forking his fingers through her hair, curling his hand into a fist and growling as he tugged hard, changing the angle of their kiss yet again to something so impossibly deep it made her head swim. He growled again, and something in that sound pierced through the fog that had surrounded her.

What was she doing? Allowing this…this monster to kiss her like this? He had taken her father prisoner, and then he had taken her prisoner, as well. She had a man waiting for her back home who cared about her, who would be horrified to see her in this position and would never subject her to such a thing.

And here she was, betraying him, betraying herself. Allowing herself to be swept away on some crazy tide of physical need.

She pushed him, at his chest, his shoulders, but he was immovable. So she bit his lip.

He roared, pulling backward, his dark eyes fierce. "You will regret that," he said.

"My only regret is that I was in a position where it was possible to put my mouth on you in any capacity."

"And yet," he said, that ruined face of his contorting into a sneer, "you trembled in my arms."

She hated him even more for that, because it was true. Because she had felt…well, she didn't even know what it was. Some dark, sexual need she had not even been aware she possessed the capacity to experience.

"That's what prey does in front of a predator," she spat. "It trembles. Because it knows it's going to get eaten."

He laughed, and the dark sound reverberated in her. Made her shiver. "Yes, indeed. A few more moments and I would have devoured you whole."

"You disgust me," she said, wishing very much that speaking the words would make them true. "No wonder you're alone! No wonder you've been hiding away from your country. Your face is the least of your problems. It's not the thing that makes you a beast."

She whirled around, running down the corridor as quickly as possible. She was blinded by anger. Blinded by fear. But the worst thing was, it wasn't him she was afraid of. She ran, not looking back, taking twists and turns in the labyrinthine set of halls that carried her to unfamiliar places she hadn't yet seen before.

Finally, she stopped, satisfied that he wasn't coming after her. She put her hand on her chest, trying to catch her breath. She looked around, stunned by the darkness around her. By the strange sense of abandonment here in this portion of the palace.

She took a cautious step forward, looking up at the paintings that lined the walk, seemingly laden with dust.

It was like she had wandered into a different building. No evidence of staff here at all, no evidence that anyone had set foot here in years. She moved over to a door and pressed it open slowly, looking inside and finding furniture that had been upended. A table lay on its side, a couch fallen over onto its face.

She closed the door again and continued on down the hall.

Then she saw another door, with a sliver of light coming from beneath it. Her breath caught in her throat, her limbs still shaking from the kiss, from the run, from… everything.

She looked back behind her, then back at the door. She tested the handle and found that it gave. She looked over her shoulder again, then quickly stepped inside.

The source of light was two wall sconces above the fireplace, casting a dim glow in the room. The curtains were drawn tightly shut, also covered in a slight film of dust that suggested they hadn't been opened in a long time.

There were bookshelves that were half-empty, a chair with a broken leg turned over onto its side. One of the walls had a dark stain at the center, something that resembled an explosion of liquid, as though a glass had been thrown against it, the liquid spraying out.

She took another step forward, and saw a glittering trail of crushed glass that supported that theory. She wondered how long it had been there. Because, nothing about it looked recent, and yet, no one had cleaned it up.

She made her way farther into the room, her heart thundering so hard that she could feel the pulse echoing in her temples. She took another step, something crunching beneath her foot. She looked down and saw a vase, or, the remains of one. And there were roses, shriveled up and blackened, spread out among the broken shards.

She bent down, picking up one of the dried buds, brushing her fingertip over the shriveled and darkened edges.

She turned around, and saw a framed photograph facedown on the table the vase had likely fallen off. She reached out, touching the gilt edge gingerly, tilting it upward.

The image in the frame made her heart stop.

There was a woman, pale, blonde and beautiful with a wide smile on her face. There was a man standing behind her, looking equally joyous. His large hand was resting on her stomach.

Her rounded stomach.

She looked at the man, stunned by his beauty. By his sheer masculine perfection. But that wasn't what held her focus. It was his eyes. Those dark, piercing eyes that were all too familiar.

Adam. Before the accident.

She scanned the picture for clues. His left hand was on the woman's stomach, a wedding band on his finger. His wife. His wife, who had been carrying his child.

She knew two things for sure. There was no wife, and there was no child.

She gasped, pressing her hand up against her mouth, dropping the frame. It made a loud cracking sound as it hit the surface of the table, and she scrambled to reclaim it, to make sure she hadn't done any damage.

"What are you doing here?"

The low, steady voice, piercing the silence of the room made her turn, the picture still clutched tightly in her hand.

Adam was standing in the doorway, his face dark with rage.

"I didn't…this is…these are your quarters, aren't they?" These quarters that looked uninhabited, that bore the evidence of fits of uncontrolled anger. This was where he lived. And it wasn't only her that wasn't allowed here. She had a feeling not a single member of his staff had set foot here since…since his accident.

"Yes," he said, his tone as dark as their surroundings. "I warned you not to come here."

"I didn't mean to," she said.

"Right, you simply found yourself in a part of the palace that was clearly separate and thought you would explore. Don't you think," he said, moving toward her, reminding her of a large predator, "that perhaps a place kept dark, with doors kept closed, should obviously be private?"

"I didn't mean—"

"The picture," he said, the words seemingly pulled from him, "give it to me. If you have damaged it in any way…"

She turned it so that it was facing her, and looked down yet again at the smiling faces. It wasn't the scars that made him look so different than he did in this photo. It was the bleakness. Something was missing from him now, extinguished. Gone completely.

"It's okay," she said, her hands shaking as she extended them, handing the picture to him. "It's fine."

"Set it down on the table where you found it," he said, not making a move toward it or her.

She complied, then moved away from it quickly, afraid somehow that by being near it she might do something to damage it. This thing that was clearly so precious to him. She felt awful, twisted up, shattered like the glass beneath her feet.

"I didn't...I didn't know," she said, her tone muted.

"And are you satisfied? Are you satisfied with seeing my loss? This," he said, drawing his hand across his cheek, "this is just a warning. A demonstration of what you will find if you look inside me. Honestly, it is a kindness. If I still looked like I did in that photograph, if I were unchanged...it would almost be worse. Better that I be destroyed both inside and out, yes?"

"You were married," she said, not quite sure why it came out that way. It sounded flat and stupid in the silence of the room once it was spoken.

"Yes," he returned. "You really should have looked me up before you came here. You might have learned some things."

"I know," she said, her breath freezing in her lungs. "But I...I just didn't..."

"That is why I don't allow paparazzi in my country. That is why I have no tolerance for it," he said, something in his voice fraying, unraveling as he spoke. "Do you think I would allow that scum to set foot in this place? After what they did to me?" His voice rose, along with his rage. "After they stole my wife from me?" He reached down, picking up a glass from the sideboard to his right. "After they stole my son?" He hurled the glass at the wall, and it shattered, leaving yet another pile of broken glass on the floor that she knew no one would do anything to clean.

She understood then. What she was seeing. It was the map of his grief. The evidence of moments when it had all become too much and he'd had to wreck his surroundings. Because his destroyed face wasn't enough. Because his destroyed soul wasn't enough.

"Adam…" It was the first time she had spoken his name out loud.

"Get out," he said. "Never come back here. This is not for you."

"I'm sorry…"

"Do you think I want your apology? Do you think I want your pity? Unless you can bring people back from the dead, you can save your breath. There is no resurrecting what is killed. There is no fixing this. There is no fixing any of it." He grabbed another glass, hurling it at the opposite wall. It exploded just like the first, the sound making her jump.

He took a step toward her, curling his fingers around her arm, holding her tight, so hard that it hurt. "Go," he said, "before I do something we both regret."

He released his hold on her, and she stumbled back, brushing her fingertips over her arm where he had just held her. She lingered for a moment, and she felt…she felt torn. He was scary, so of course part of her wanted to run.

But he was also injured, and not in the way that she had initially thought. It was so much worse. So much deeper. And a part of her felt broken in response.

Without thinking, she extended her arm, reaching toward him. He jerked back, like a wounded animal. "Go," he said again, his tone fractured.

And this time, she complied.

Adam considered taking dinner in his quarters. He rarely did that, because he did not allow anyone—even his housekeeper—to come into the section of the palace he had once shared with Ianthe.

But, then he realized that he was dangerously close to allowing Belle to dictate what he did in his own palace. The rest of the world had been closed off to him for long enough that he was hardly going to allow anything in his castle to be closed off to him, as well.

He figured she would probably avoid taking dinner with him anyway. So, when he walked into the dining room and saw her sitting in the same spot she had occupied last night, he was surprised.

After the kiss in the library, and the scene in what had been his wife's parlor, he had expected her to take refuge in her room. But, here she was.

"I hope there's cake tonight," she said by way of greeting.

"If you put in a request Athena will make sure there is cake," he returned, taking his seat next to her.

She looked down at her empty plate, and she kept her focus there until the dinner of chicken and vegetables was served. They ate in silence for a while, nothing other than the sound of silverware scraping over the plates sounding in the room. Then she sighed heavily.

"You wish to say something?" he asked, not bothering to ponder the fact that he could read her so easily.

"Yes," she said, "and I know that you probably don't

want me to say anything, but I can't keep things to myself. It's hard for me."

"Really? Other people find it so easy. It's most certainly not a matter of self-discipline and practicing restraint. By all means, do go and say whatever is on your mind."

"I'm not going to take a lecture from you about restraint, Adam," she said.

There was something about the way she said his name—about the fact that she said his name at all—that struck him like a blow to the stomach. How long had it been since someone had said his name to him when they were so near each other?

It was all so "sire," and "Your Highness," "Your Majesty" this and that. No one called him Adam except for his friends, and then it was only over the phone.

"I have a title," he said, as a reminder to himself most of all.

"Yes, I know. I could use it if you want."

"No," he said, deciding then that he would rather hear her say his name. "You are to play the part of my lover, and so you should seem somewhat familiar with me."

"Anyway. Adam. I am sorry. It makes more sense now. Why you put my father in prison for what he did. Why you don't allow paparazzi on the island. Why you don't have any patience or tolerance for it. You…you lost your wife in the accident."

"I didn't lose her," he said, his throat feeling scraped raw. "She died. Losing someone implies that you can find them again. Ianthe isn't missing. I'm not going to lift up a couch cushion one day and find her there."

Belle shook her head, a tear sliding down her cheek. She reached up and wiped it away, and he marveled at it. At the fact that this woman shed a tear for his pain.

"I do know that," she said, biting her lip and nodding. "It's a terrible thing to say. That your wife is dead. I can't imagine what it must be like to actually feel the loss. And she was…"

"She was eight months pregnant," he finished for her. "And, yes, our son died too."

She looked down, delicate fingers clenching into fists. "I wish you would have told me."

"Why?" He leaned back in his chair. "Because it makes me less of a monster? It makes you less my prisoner? Neither of those things is true."

"It makes me understand you. At least, a little bit."

"Do tell me all the things you understand," he said, keeping his tone deliberately dry.

For some reason, his stomach tightened. Thinking about her trying to understand. Thinking that she might just.

"The man that I saw in that picture…he wasn't a monster."

"No," Adam said. "He was one of the most celebrated royals in all of Europe. Renowned for his looks as much as for his temperament. He is a stranger to me."

He could barely remember being that man, and more to the point, he often didn't like remembering it. But, there were nights when he wandered down the halls, wandered down his memories, and ended up drunk in that room. It never ended well. It always ended with things broken. Just like his life.

"He's part of you," she said, her tone muted.

Adam shook his head. "He's not. He's dead, along with everyone else."

"Well," she said, softly. "I think that's terribly sad. Seeing as you're still breathing and everything." She looked up at him, the steel in her blue eyes belying that softness in her voice.

"Have you ever lost anyone?"

"I might lose my father. I lost my mother emotionally when I was a child. That emotional loss? Well, that one hurts worse, in some ways. If my father dies, it isn't because he chose to leave me. My mother...she didn't want me. That's a particular kind of pain."

"You don't know," he said, keeping his voice hard. "Until you have held someone in your arms while they die, someone you love, and felt them growing colder? You don't know."

He felt that cold spreading inside his chest now. That ice.

She cleared her throat. "I don't. You're right."

She reached across the expanse of table, placing delicate fingertips over the back of his hand. Her skin felt so hot against his. Especially in conflict with the memory of all that cold.

She began to draw away, and he pressed his other hand over the top of hers, holding her against him. For some reason, he was reluctant to break the contact. No, he knew why. He felt his body stir, heat flooding his veins where before there had been only ice.

She made him warm. She made him feel. And he wanted to cling to that. Wanted to cling to her.

Her eyes widened, and her tongue darted out and slicked over her lower lip, leaving it glistening, tempting. He could not forget the way it had felt to have her lips pressed against his. To delve deep inside her mouth and taste her, consume her.

There was something powerful in it. Something magical. Something he had not experienced in a long time.

Touching another person, needing another person. At least physically. Yes, physically, he was ready for that.

He had spent a long time in this house, essentially alone, doing nothing to satisfy the growing hunger inside him. For touch. For a woman. Ignoring it so completely that he had been able to convince himself it no longer existed.

"I could try to understand," she said, the words broken. "I could try."

He lifted his hand from hers, reached out and cupped her chin, holding her face steady as he continued to look at her. She was lovely, like a rose, beautiful as her name suggested. There was something simple to her, something wholesome. She was not overly made up, though that could perhaps be because of what had or had not been provided for her by his staff.

Her lips were red, her cheeks dusted with color. Like petals strewn across new-fallen snow. Something striking and rich against the stark white. He wanted to gather all that to himself, take it, taste it, make it his.

There was a time when he had been a man who had collected beautiful things. Who had *enjoyed* beautiful things. But he had forgotten that man, and he had forgotten that simple pleasure. He was remembering it now. But this need for her was different, it wasn't simply about collecting, but about possessing.

It struck him then that he didn't particularly want to take her out in public with him, drag them both into the light. Rather, he was much more interested in bringing her down into the darkness with him. Indulging in this yawning passion that had opened up inside him, seemingly endless, fathomless. So impenetrable that not even he could quite work out what it was, or what it would take to satisfy.

If he had just a few hours alone with her in the darkness, perhaps he could find it. Perhaps they could sate it. Together.

He leaned in, and she made a sound that might have been a protest, cut off by the firm press of his lips against hers. If it had been a protest, it wasn't evidenced in her response to the kiss. No, she didn't push back. Instead, she softened against him, a sigh escaping as she seemed to melt beneath his touch.

He didn't touch her anywhere but at that spot on her chin, where he held her firm as he continued the kiss, sliding his tongue along the seam of her lips until she capitulated, until she opened to him, begging him to take it deeper with that simple movement.

When he pulled away to catch his breath, she was trembling, the color in her cheeks even more vivid against the stark white of her skin. "I really do have a boyfriend," she said, her voice husky. "And I'm your prisoner."

"I can see how that would be a problem," he said slowly, "for you. I don't understand why I'm supposed to be perturbed by either."

"I suppose you wouldn't."

She did not sound outraged, however. She sounded drugged.

"I could make your stay here more enjoyable for the both of us."

She shook her head slowly, drawing back from him, removing her hand. "We should just eat dinner."

A lock of dark hair fell forward into her face, and she did nothing to sweep it away. He examined her, the

gentle curve of her delicate neck, the stubborn set of her
jaw, that subtle slope on her upturned nose. He watched
her and said nothing all through dinner. She was his captive, it was true, but in some ways she was beginning to
hold him captive, as well.

It wasn't good for a man to be celibate for so long. In
his grief, he had allowed himself to forget his physical
needs. He would not do so again.

"What do you like?" he asked.

She blinked rapidly. "What?"

"You are not my prisoner," he said, not quite sure
when he had decided to take this tactic. Perhaps when
he had first felt her skin beneath his hands, how soft
she was. Perhaps it had been then. "You will help me
step out for the first time, and in order for us to accom-
plish all that we need to, all that I need to, I need for the
two of us to be somewhat united. If we are to present
ourselves as lovers to the world…it must be believable.
The chemistry…*that*, I believe, will be the least of our
problems. However, more than occasionally you look as
though you want to finish the job my accident started."

She shifted uncomfortably. "I can't imagine that you
would think I would have…easy feelings toward you.
And just because I feel sorry for you—"

"You do not enjoy my kiss because you pity me," he
said, his tone hard, firm. He had felt her melt beneath
his touch, had felt her respond to him. That was more
than pity.

At least, if he could be trusted to remember what desire felt like.

She went stiff. "There's no point talking about it."

"Because you're ashamed." He examined her more
closely. "Is it because of my face?"

"No," she said, almost comically fast, "I'm not ashamed because of your face. I…I *should* be angry at you. And, I have a good boyfriend. He's very nice. I like him. You asked me what I like. I like Tony."

"I see," he said. "Your cheeks do not turn pink when you talk about him. They get pink when you look at me. When I kiss you."

"My face turns red when I get mad," she said, that stubborn jut to her chin even more pronounced than usual. "That's all."

"I could easily prove it's more than anger, Belle, though I imagine there is an element of that. If mostly anger at yourself. You want me." A lick of heat skated over his veins as he said it. As he allowed himself that confidence. There had been a time when he had been certain of a woman's desire for him. When he'd never had reason to doubt. He had never even put himself in that position one way or the other since the loss of Ianthe.

Doing so now…recognizing her need…it made him feel things he had thought long since dead.

"Impossible," she said, the word a hushed whisper. "Because I like Tony. And I like books. I don't like fearsome, angry men who seclude themselves in their palaces."

"No," he said, his tone sardonic. "You don't like me. You just pity me. Though, I have a feeling you would like to demonstrate that pity for me in a very physical manner."

She jerked back as though she had been slapped, and something in him regretted that. Regretted that step backward when he had been attempting to build an inroad. But she was making it difficult. Was making it impossible. She wanted him, and he didn't see why she was so intent on denying it. Certainly, she had a boyfriend, but he was back in California; he was not here. And, if Tony were a compelling lover at all, she wouldn't be so drawn to Adam.

When he had been with his wife it had been a simple thing for him to eschew the pleasures of other women. He had loved his wife and no one else, so no one else had tempted him. Belle, however, was tempted by him, no matter what she said about lovers and captivity.

"You really are kind of a beast," she said, standing up. He caught her wrist, stopped her from leaving.

"And what bothers you most about that? The fact that you would like to reform me, that you would like for your time here to mean something and you are beginning to see that it won't? Or is it the fact that you don't want to reform me at all, and that you rather like me this way? Or at least, your body likes me this way."

"Bodies make stupid decisions all the time. My father wanted my mother, and she was a terrible, unloving person who didn't even want her own daughter. So, forgive me if I find this argument rather uncompelling. It doesn't make you a good person, just because I enjoy kissing you. And it doesn't make this something worth exploring."

She broke free of him and began to walk away, striding down the hall, back toward her room. He pushed away from the table, letting his chair fall to the floor, not caring enough to right it as he followed after Belle.

He caught up to her, pivoting so that he was in front of her. She took a step backward, then to the side, butting up against the wall. Then he caged her in between his arms, staring down at her. Her blue eyes were glittering, her breasts rising and falling rapidly with each breath.

"This is the only thing worth exploring. Not what could be, but what you have. The fire that burns between you and another person. For all you know, in the days since you've been here the entire world has fallen away. And if we were all that was left…would you not regret missing out on the chance to see how hot we could burn?"

She shook her head. "But the world hasn't fallen away," she said, her trembling lips pale now, a complete contrast to the rich color they had been only moments ago. "It's still there. And whatever happens in here will have consequences out there. I will help you, Adam, but I'm not going to give you my body. I'm not going to destroy that life that I have out there to play games with you in here. You're a stranger to me, and you're going to remain a stranger to me. I can pretend. I can give you whatever you need when it comes to making a statement for your country. But beyond that? I can't."

Then she turned and walked away, and this time, he let her go.

CHAPTER SIX

BELLE BARELY SLEPT. Her room was beautifully appointed, the bed plush and lovely, but after what had happened with Adam—again—she had been unable to relax. Not because she was afraid of him. If he wanted to force himself on her, he could have done it already. He would have done it already. It wasn't force that scared her.

It was the potential for seduction.

She shivered as she got out of bed. For the first time, she made her way over to the ornate wardrobe. When Fos had come in with her clothing yesterday she had simply asked for a comfortable outfit to wear, and then, last night when she had come back to the room after dinner she had dug blindly for a pair of pajamas.

She hadn't really examined the contents. She needed clothes, obviously, but she had a feeling the purchase of those clothes was all part and parcel to the mistress ruse.

All the better for rumors to abound about the sudden purchase of a woman's wardrobe by the Prince of Olympios's personal shopper.

The large piece of furniture was heaving with clothing. From lacy underthings to beautiful ball gowns. She could hardly believe it. Every item was more beautiful, more extravagant than the last. The fabrics were exquisite, so much so that she could scarcely bring herself to touch them. But then, once she did, she had a difficult time not touching them, because they felt so wonderful.

She and her father had lived a comfortable, simple existence in Southern California. Most of her life was spent in cutoff shorts and flip-flops, though, she took it up a notch by wearing jeans to class at school.

But mostly, she was accustomed to the more casual vibe of the West Coast of the United States. Certainly, she wasn't accustomed to things like this.

She dug around for a while until she found a gray T-shirt that was made of material so soft it made the casual garment feel like a luxury. Then she found a pair of ankle-length black pants and a simple pair of black slip-on shoes.

She pulled her hair back into a ponytail and examined her reflection in the mirror. "Very Audrey Hepburn," she said to herself.

She wasn't sure why she cared what she looked like at all. In fact, she was mostly pretending she didn't care, which was why she had chosen the most unassuming pieces that had been provided for her. Because she didn't want to look like she was putting on a show for Adam. She didn't want to encourage herself to put on a show for Adam.

He was…well, he was barely civilized. He clearly didn't remember what it was like to be around people. Evidenced by his table manners. And his manners in general. He was tragic, his life story painful for her to even think about, even when she was angry with him.

No one should have to go through what he had gone through. To lose a wife and a child, an entire future in one night…it was more than any one person could be expected to bear. And, it was clear that Adam had not born it particularly well. He had been altered by it. Utterly and completely. So much so that he felt the man he had been was dead.

Her heart twisted, and she placed her hand to her breast, rubbing it slightly as she walked out the door of her bedroom. She didn't know what she was doing. Where she was going. To get food, she supposed. It was tempting in some ways to stay holed up in her room. To hide from him. But, then she really would feel like a prisoner. She needed to keep from going crazy.

And as difficult as it was to deal with him sometimes, she needed to continue to interact with him. So that she could play her part as lover to his satisfaction when they had to go to that party of his. So that he could begin to see her as a person and not simply a means to an end.

Or a means to his physical satisfaction.

That thought made her shiver. And she drew her arms tightly around herself as she continued to wander down toward the dining room.

She moved through the labyrinthine halls, and came around the corner, pausing in her tracks when she saw Adam standing there, large, imposing and more than a little bit terrifying. But not in the way he had been the first time she'd seen him. This was different. Deeper. Something that whispered in her ear that he was dangerous in a way she had never experienced before.

"There you are," he said, a dark light in his eye that made her feel…something. A kind of strange, shimmering heat that started in her midsection and radiated outward.

"Were you looking for me?"

"I was about to be."

She shifted her weight from one foot to the other. "I was just going to get coffee."

"It will have to wait."

"Come on now. Coffee waits for nothing."

"It will wait for me. I am Prince Adam Katsaros."

She couldn't help it. That made her smile. It even made her laugh a little bit. He frowned.

"Are you laughing at me?" he asked.

"A little bit. I suppose it's been a long time since somebody has laughed at you. So, it's probably good for you."

"That is open for debate. However, I have something to show you, so I'm not going to stand here and engage in one with you." He extended his arm. "Come with me."

She eyed him. "Suddenly you have manners?"

"Perhaps I'm beginning to remember them. As you remind me of other things long forgotten, as well."

"What is that?" she asked, stretching her arm out slowly and curling her fingers around his forearm gingerly.

"My desire."

She nearly drew back as though she had been burned, but he pressed his hand over hers and stopped her. His dark eyes burned into hers, and she really did feel like she was being scalded. From the inside out.

"I'm not sure what to say to that," she said.

"Well," he responded, "then I consider it a good topic of conversation. Because I think this is the first time I have successfully shocked you into silence. Did you suppose that I was entertaining women here in my isolation?"

"I know some girls like to think they're the first,

Adam, but I never really considered that I might be the first of your captives."

"You are. Until your father breached the security of my palace, no one has tried to draw me out of my seclusion. My story is far too tragic for such a thing. And, until your father, when the media realized they weren't going to get a story out of me, they left me alone. Actually, I imagine it's because the press caused my accident that they do leave me alone. It wasn't enough they had done it once before to royalty, but then they did it again. Things need to change."

"I know." She admitted that she had a little bit of a purposeful blind spot when it came to the kind of work her father did. Mostly because it had put food on the table all her life. And also because in her opinion her father was a good man. He did what he could in the economy they lived in. But…when things went this far, when they put people in danger, cost people their lives, he was right. It had to change.

"You know," she said, still clinging to his arm as he led her down a hall she hadn't been in before, "my father wasn't always a paparazzo. He used to travel around and take pictures of world events. Go behind enemy lines, all of that. But, then he ended up taking care of me, and he couldn't travel the way that he used to. Plus, it's hard to make a living that way. People don't like to see how ugly the world is—they would rather get a look at the beautiful people. And yes, to a degree get a look at the ugly side of the beautiful people so that all the normal ones don't feel like they're quite so bad off."

"Well, I will certainly have that effect on the masses. A little bit of tragedy porn to go with dinner."

"You make me see the other side of it," she said. "Not

just the fact that sometimes the photographers go to dangerous lengths to get the picture, but…the fact you didn't do anything to have your privacy invaded like this. Apart from the accident, nobody has a right to you. They don't own you just because they know your name."

"Well, thank you for that stamp of approval," he said. "Without it I'm not sure how I would have held to my conviction that I was entitled to my privacy."

She stopped moving and stamped her foot. "I'm trying to tell you that you changed my mind. Maybe you could be a little bit nice about it."

"Maybe," he countered, "you could stop expecting me to be nice."

She huffed. "I should."

They stopped at a pair of double doors at the end of the hall, and she looked at him questioningly. "I have something to show you," he said simply. Then he pressed his palms flat against the doors, pushing them open.

The room was dark, curtains that stretched from floor to ceiling covering all the windows. He turned, pressing a button, and she heard the faint rustle of fabric, followed by a shaft of light piercing the darkness. All the curtains began to part, revealing bookcases. Everywhere. Extending from the high arched ceiling down to the marble floors, ladders stationed every few feet, to allow access to the upper shelves.

"What is this?"

"The library."

"But, you said that I was in the library yesterday." She turned in a circle, feeling awed by her surroundings.

"You were in one of the libraries. This is the main library, the one that houses my entire family history. The history of the country. Additionally, every great work of literature to come out of Olympios. Also, classics from the rest of the world. There are some modern works of fiction over here…popular works and more obscure works. If it's been written, it may very well be in here somewhere."

"I don't…why are you showing me this?"

She turned to look at him, at that scarred, rough face that was starting to become familiar to her. He was no longer shocking, and she didn't view the ridges on his skin as imperfections. Rather, they were simply a part of him. And those eyes, dark and fathomless, containing a wealth of pain…they made her feel.

"You said you liked books," he said, his voice flat.

"So I did," she said, taking a tentative step forward, walking to the nearest shelf. She let her fingertips drift over the spines, marveling at the collection in front of her. "Of course," she turned back to him, trying to steel herself against the feelings that were rioting through her, "I also said that I liked my boyfriend," she pointed out, "but, he didn't materialize. Neither did a way for me to contact him."

"Sadly," he said, "that is still not possible. However, I would like to point out that you look far more enraptured when you talk about books than you do when you talk about him. And, frankly, you look more excited when you kiss me than you do when you speak about this other man."

"It's not all about excitement," she said, her tone dry. She sounded prudish to even her own ears. *How annoying.* "Sometimes it's just about feeling taken care of. Feeling like someone is there for you. They're stable. He cares about me. I feel like we have a future together. When I'm done with school." She ignored the fact that she didn't feel the kind of churning sexual excitement that she felt when she was around Adam. Ignored the realization that hit her just then that suggested if she felt even half what she felt for Tony as she had felt for Adam over the past couple of days, there was no way she would still be a virgin. Resisting Adam—who had taken her captive, who was hard and scarred and nothing like anything she should be attracted to—was much harder than anything ever had been before. But somehow, she had managed to resist Tony for eight months of dating.

Adam wasn't wrong. She did find books more exciting than she found Tony. And that was somewhat problematic, she realized.

"Passion is a key part of love," Adam said. "And if not of love, then at least of life. My life…what you walked into, that is what life looks like without passion. It is dark, and it is isolating. You have not lost anyone the way that I have. You could have passion. Why don't you?"

"I didn't say we didn't have passion. I just said passion wasn't everything. My mother…she…she's famous. Well, she's the daughter of a very famous actress. And she essentially paid to have me swept under the rug. My father could make a spectacle of her, I suppose, but it would compromise certain things that were put in place for me. And, not only that, it would drag me out into the press, and he doesn't want that for me." She laughed. "I suppose that highlights the fact that he does see what he does as an invasion of privacy, since he wouldn't want it for his own daughter. But my point is she's the kind of person who follows passions. Drinks deep of life, and does all that stuff that's fun and New Age sounding. But, she didn't do anything with her responsibilities. She didn't want to take care of her own child. I would rather have stability. I would rather have security than anything so capricious as passion."

"I suppose you have felt loss," he said, something changing in his expression. "I underestimated that." He shook his head. "Emotional passion…I have no desire to experience such a thing again. Hope destroyed is something best never resurrected. But physical passion…" He took a step toward her, that light in his eye turning predatory. "Getting caught up in that, getting burned by that…that is something that I miss. And I wonder, have you ever experienced it? What does your boyfriend make you feel, Belle? Is he a pretty-boy surfer? Or maybe just a model with soft hands. A hollow chest and that kind of hungry look about him with sunken-in cheekbones. That's very Californian, isn't it? Probably nice to look at, but does he know how to touch you?"

His voice grew rougher, lower as he drew closer. "I am not a pretty man—that point can't be argued. But I would know how to touch you. I can give you so much more than just a library. I can make you forget your name while you call out mine. Can he do that? Three years. Three years and I haven't wanted another woman. How could I? My wife…she was beautiful. And more than that, I loved her. But I am tired of having an empty bed. I'm tired of walking around with all this fire inside of me and nowhere to spend it. Something tells me you're more like me than you would care to admit."

Belle couldn't breathe. She was lost in this moment, lost in him, in the tendrils of flame that wrapped around her with each word he spoke, stoking the heat inside her hotter, higher.

It wasn't him she was afraid of. No, it really wasn't. It was herself. Because for the first time in her life she wanted to reach out and take the reckless thing. The wrong thing. She had always felt so grateful for the stable environment provided by her father. Because she could remember living in her mother's house. Living in all that turmoil until she had been shunted off, sent to live in that little beach bungalow with her dad.

And there at least had been stability. He had loved her, once he had known she existed. He had taken her in gladly. Then she had met Tony at school, and he had seemed perfect in that very same way. Nice. Caring. Patient.

Adam was none of those things, and yet she felt like she was perilously close to being carried away on a tide of something that felt a lot like lust.

"Tony is very nice," she said, the words sounding as bland as Adam had implied her boyfriend was.

"I imagine he's very nice in bed, as well," Adam said.

He did not say "very nice" as though it was a compliment.

"He…he respects me."

"That's very interesting. What does it mean, I wonder? Does it mean what I suspect? That he doesn't want you? At least, not in the same way that I do. Which has somehow been conflated with respect. An excuse, perhaps, that allows women to put up with tepid bedroom experiences?" He laughed. "Respect. Synonymous with beige walls and sex once a week that takes less time than the human-interest piece on the evening news."

Her cheeks got hot. "No," she said, "that isn't what it means."

"Oh, I think it does in some circles. Why is it that respect is never equated to a man worshipping his lover's body? To being so hungry for her he can be satisfied by nothing else? In my opinion, if a man you're sleeping with respects you, he should respect you enough to make your knees weak and your throat raw from screaming his name all night."

She didn't correct him and say that he was respecting her desire to wait to be intimate. She didn't know why she held that bit of information back. Possibly because her airway was currently constricted, and it was making it difficult for her to talk. And her thoughts were a little bit jumbled, which made forming sentences difficult, as well.

She didn't want to tell him that she had no idea what he was talking about. That she had never screamed any man's name in her entire life. And that she wasn't exactly sure what could feel quite so intense that it would induce her to do that.

It hit her then, that the low, twisting sensation in her stomach, the slow, long pull that she felt starting there and moving down lower, was connected to a deep desire for him to show her.

It was embarrassing, just how innocent she was. How little she knew. She blamed her mother in that regard. Not just her absence, though, it wasn't as though her father wanted to sit down and have a conversation with her about the facts of life.

No, she wasn't sheltered. That wasn't it. It was just that she had chosen, deliberately, to ignore as much about that sort of thing as she could. Because she connected her mother's abandonment with passion. A passion for life, for men, for money and clothes and parties that had been severely curbed by the addition of a young child to her life.

So, Belle had resented it. All of it. She had clung to

her simple existence, to being happy with what she had. The breeze blowing in off the ocean, the feel of a book in her hands. Dating Tony was an experiment, for sure. She enjoyed his companionship, she liked kissing him, but she had shied away from the rest of it because she was afraid.

Afraid of something she hadn't quite been able to put a name to. But, she could put a feeling to it now. It was fire. That fire that Adam ignited low and deep inside of her. A fire she was afraid—once it was able to burn freely—would never be extinguished.

She was afraid she would forget herself. Forget who she was, and what she had once wanted. Because certainly, that was the fate of her mother. Who had forgotten about love, and about the important things, because of that restless fire.

She also realized that while she was rejecting all of it internally, while she was keeping silent to avoid drawing herself in deeper, she also wasn't running away. No, she was standing here in this library, in a shaft of light, with Adam advancing on her, his dark eyes glittering. Just standing there, doing nothing to try to put distance between them.

She wanted this. She wanted him to take control. To make it so the decision was no longer hers. She was too afraid to decide on that last step. To close the distance between them. To admit to herself that she wanted to know. That she wanted to know what might make her cry out his name, and that she wanted it to be his name specifically.

How was that fair? How was that possible? When Adam had taken her father prisoner, taken her captive, as well? When she had a nice, sweet, patient man waiting for her back in California? How could she feel any of these things for this dark and tortured soul in front of her?

She didn't know. Perhaps, it was that element of helplessness. Of the choice being taken from her. Perhaps, that was why it felt possible. Why it felt necessary.

In this castle, removed from the reality of the world, far removed from that little piece of the world she had carved out for herself. From school, from friends, from books and boyfriends. From the familiar California coastline and the easy breeze that blew through there.

She was in his domain. His country. This mountainous island nation, where the wind ripped sharply through the crags and peaks of the unbending mountains, where it whistled around the turrets of the palace and created a sense of restlessness rather than a sense of ease.

It was also far removed from reality, like something in a fairy tale.

Or, something from a fantasy that she would never have allowed herself to have anywhere else.

"I like it when you say my name," he said, his voice rough, the dark notes skimming along her skin, making her shiver. "I should like it even more if you said my name in bed."

She looked up at him, her lips feeling suddenly dry. She slipped her tongue out, traced the edge of her own mouth. And suddenly, she was very aware of the fact that he had done the same the last time he had kissed her.

She didn't think that she had been drawing his attention to her mouth intentionally, but when his gaze sharpened, when his focus moved lower, she wondered. Questioned herself a little bit more deeply than she wanted to.

Yes, she was trying to remove her own culpability in this situation. But, if she were honest…and then she couldn't think anymore.

He reached out, his fingertips brushing her chin, tilting her face upward. Then he traced along the line of her jaw, to her lower lip, following the path her tongue had just forged. Then he continued on, at the other side of her face, along her cheekbone and back again, to that delicate spot just beneath her ear, and down the side of her neck, which made her tremble.

Those strong hands on such a vulnerable part of her should have been terrifying, or at the very least somewhat repellent. But, she found herself entirely unrepelled. Instead, she wanted to melt into that firm touch, encourage him to take an even firmer hold on her.

She gloried in it. In his strength, his power, next to her delicate frame.

She couldn't explain it. She couldn't even rationalize it to herself. But, that didn't make her move away from him. Didn't entice her to break their contact.

She looked up, meeting his eyes. Those eyes that she had seen lit with happiness in a photograph, but were so dark now. She lifted her hand, her fingertips brushing the rough skin on his cheek. Then she drew back quickly, as though she had been burned.

Adam reached out, curving his fingers around her wrist, holding her tight. He raised her hand slowly again, placing it back where it had been a moment before. There was something needy there, written across his face.

She adjusted her position, so that she was facing him square, both of her hands on his face now, resting just above his jaw. Her thumbs touched the corners of his mouth, and a deep sound rumbled in his chest. Something that sat between a growl and a purr of satisfaction.

Her fingertips brushed up against the scar tissue next to his lips, but she didn't flinch. Didn't pull away. She hadn't known him before. Yes, she had seen that photograph, but it wasn't the Adam she knew. It wasn't the Adam she found so compelling. It was a piece of the puzzle that was the man who stood before her, a piece that mattered. That meant something. But, it certainly wasn't what compelled her. The idea that he had been a more beautiful man once.

He was the man who drew her in now. The man who compelled her to leave behind a lifetime of restraint. The man who made her question so many things about herself. About what she wanted.

He dropped his hands to his sides, then reached out, grabbing hold of her hips and holding her steady as she continued to touch his face, slowly, softly.

She raised her hand, sliding her thumb down that thick ridge that ran through his eyebrow, down along to the edge of his eye. "You can see all right?" she asked.

"Yes," he responded. "Lucky, I suppose. Though, I have never considered much about the accident to be lucky."

"Well, I guess *lucky* might be a stretch. But not adding more trauma by losing your sight is certainly something."

"Honestly, I would not have cared. Until recently, there was nothing to look at." Those words sent a spiral of pleasure winding through her. She tried to remember if Tony had ever told her she was beautiful, or ever implied it the way that Adam just had. If he had, it didn't stand out to her. But, she knew for a fact that

Tony had kissed her, and right now she couldn't remember it at all.

She could only remember what it was to kiss Adam, which was something else entirely. Something new. Something fully unto itself.

"In all of this darkness… I had forgotten that I could see," he said. "Looking at you—at your beauty—it reminds me. You remind me of the few pleasures that are left to be had in this world."

Sex. He meant sex. Nothing deeper, nothing more lasting than that. And even if he did, she couldn't leave her life, she couldn't leave her father, and…what? Marry the Prince of some small island country? A man she barely knew? *No.*

So it was fine, really. That he was only talking about the physical. Because it was the physical that held her in thrall at this moment, surely. It certainly wasn't anything else. Certainly wasn't anything deeper. It couldn't be. It was impossible.

She wasn't sure that it mattered. At least not now.

Because whatever this was, it was stronger than anything else. Stronger than any other force, than anything tethering her to the past, or reminding her of the future. This moment, this feeling, this need, was bigger, brighter, fiercer than anything could ever be.

"Adam…" And she didn't know what else to say. Because the feelings, the need, had grown too big and it blocked out all the words, all the things that were spinning around in her head. She wanted to tell him that he wasn't ugly. That he might be a beast, but that she wasn't certain she cared.

Words fled, but desire didn't. And so, keeping her hands on his face, she pulled upward onto her toes and leaned in, closing the distance between them and taking his lips with her own.

It took only a moment for Adam to claim control. For him to wrap those arms tightly around her and press her back against one of the bookshelves, a shelf digging into her lower back. She didn't care. She didn't care at all. Not about the discomfort, not about anything but the hot, hard press of his mouth against hers.

But this time, his hands did not stay contained to one place. This time, those large, warm hands roamed over her curves, sliding up to cup her breasts, his thumbs moving over her nipples. She gasped, arching against him, ignoring the slight pain when her shoulder blades met with the corner of a book.

No one had ever touched her like this. No man had ever touched her there.

She should be outraged, she should be…something. Virginal. Afraid. She didn't feel any of that. She felt completely caught up, swept up in this madness that had rolled in between them like a cyclone.

Then his hands moved lower, gripping hold of her hips tightly, drawing her against the hardness of his body, showing her the evidence of just how much he wanted her. She moved her hands, sliding them around behind his head, then pulling herself closer until she was wrapped around him.

His hands moved lower still, down beneath the waistband of her pants, between her thighs. She gasped as his fingertips slid over the smooth, silken fabric of the panties she was wearing. She was…well, she was terrified of the feelings that were rioting through her, but she was also completely enraptured by them. He pressed harder, and she could feel dampness gathering there, and she wondered if he could feel it too, through that thin fabric as he continued to torture the sensitive bundle of nerves.

She forgot to be horrified. Forgot to be embarrassed. There was nothing but the fierce, blinding need that he was creating with the magic of his touch, with each pass, each stroke. She arched against him, moving her hips in time with the movement of his wrist.

She was shivering, shaking, a coil drawing tight down at the base of her spine and spreading down even farther, internal muscles she hadn't been aware of before pulsing as he continued the sensual assault, continued kissing her, long and deep, his tongue sliding against hers. Continued stroking her between her legs, amping up her arousal to an impossible capacity that she hadn't known existed inside her.

Then one fingertip drifted beneath the edge of the fabric of her panties, his hot skin making contact with her slick flesh as he drew his finger slowly forward, using her own wetness to ease the friction while he tormented the source of her desire.

And she broke. Shattered utterly, completely, waves of need washing over her, followed by shivers of satisfaction that went deep and seemed to ebb and flow on and on. She couldn't take any more; she was sure of it. But she didn't have the words to say that, couldn't form a coherent thought. And so, he didn't stop. He moved forward, pressing one finger deep inside her, the invasion so intimate, so unexpected that she cried out.

"Adam!" Then he rocked his palm forward, pressing down hard on the place where she ached for him. She had been wrong before. She hadn't shattered. That had only been a crack. Now she shattered completely, reduced to nothing but glittering dust at his feet as she cried out his name over and over again, clinging to his shoulders as the intensity of her release swamped her, left her knees weak, left her body spent.

And when it was over, her throat was hoarse from calling out his name.

She understood why now.

She forced herself to meet his gaze, her cheeks turning pink as she did so, as she looked at the pure, unmitigated hunger in his dark eyes. Oh, yes, she understood. Why women lost their minds for passion, why they would spend their nights gladly with a man like him, and forget everything else.

And it was that that had her wiggling out of his embrace, fighting to get free, to get some distance.

"I need to…" She gasped, trying to take a breath. "I can't breathe."

He let go of her, taking a step back, his hands raised slightly as though to demonstrate that he was going to allow her this distance.

Her eyes filled with tears, her whole body beginning to tremble. She felt…well, in spite of the fact that she was fully clothed she felt naked. Exposed. He hadn't even seen her body, but she felt as though he had seen something even more private, something that she had kept hidden, desperately, even from herself.

"I need coffee," she choked out.

And then she ran from the room, leaving behind the first man to make her understand passion. The first man to ever make her confront what she had always feared about herself.

That given the chance, she would prove no better than her mother, no better at all.

CHAPTER SEVEN

BELLE AVOIDED HIM rather skillfully over the next few weeks. And his body rebelled against it. But, Adam himself thought it was perhaps best not to push. He had to keep his eyes focused on the prize before him. Which was the party, and his great debut to the public.

His Viceroy had announced that Adam would be making a public showing, and had intimated that it was time for Adam to resume his rule.

All was going according to plan.

Other than those photographs, hastily published the previous week.

But, they had been poor quality, and while the story had certainly created a sensation, it hadn't done as much damage as he'd thought they might. They had also paled in comparison to the real story. The fact that he had decided to step back into power.

Ultimately, the real control was still with him. He had a chance to write the next headline, and it would all come down to how he—how they—presented him on the world stage.

Considering that, he needed to keep Belle from looking like she was terrified of him. As she had looked at him in the library. He had to wonder if she was afraid of him, or if she was disgusted with herself. For losing herself in the arms of a man who might as well be a beast. Who was wholly unattractive and possibly the absolute opposite of the man she fancied herself in love with.

He was not vain. But for the first time he allowed himself a moment to mourn the loss of his looks. Now that he actually wanted to seduce a woman, it mattered.

Of course, in many ways he had seduced her; it had just left him unsatisfied. Had he been thinking clearly, he would have ripped her clothes from her body and buried himself inside her before satisfying her the first time. That way, they might have both come to a better conclusion.

He scowled, pacing the length of his room. Felipe's party was tonight, and Adam was wearing a tuxedo for the first time in years. A new one had been made and fitted for him just this week. He'd had nothing to do over the past three years but spend time working out in his gym, and he was far too large now to fit into the suit he had once worn.

As Fos finished straightening his tie, Adam looked at his reflection and thought it fitting. That he could no longer even wear the clothes he had once worn, and that the more streamlined physique he had once sported was also gone.

Three years ago he'd had the sort of aristocratic form suited to a tuxedo. And the face to go along with it. Now, even with a suit that had been custom made, he looked like a panther being dressed up as a house cat. And his scars certainly didn't help.

In some ways though, he found it fitting. Why should he step back into this life with ease? Looking as he had? He had changed. Utterly and completely.

"You might consider being a bit nicer to the girl," his adviser said, partly under his breath, as he brushed something off the shoulder of Adam's suit jacket.

"I gave her a library," Adam said.

"Yes," Fos returned. "And yet, she still avoids you as though you carry a particularly virulent strain of the plague."

"I'm a monster—haven't you heard?"

"It is not your face that makes you a monster, Your Highness."

"I don't think I asked for a commentary," Adam said.

"You didn't. But, you intend to make your debut with her tonight, and it might be best if she didn't look afraid of you."

"I have no control over that. I have done my best, at least, as well as I can do under the circumstances. The circumstances being that she is my prisoner."

Fos nodded. "I can see how that might make it difficult. Perhaps, make an effort to appear human. That might help both with Belle and with the ball."

"I didn't say I needed help with either."

"But you do."

Adam snorted. "Trust me. It isn't that she doesn't like me. It's that she likes me a little bit too much."

"Yes," Fos said, "I get that feeling. But how are you going to entice her if you don't remove the fear?"

"Some women like fear."

"Some women who are not as sweet as she is, I think."

"I don't want her to like me," Adam insisted. "I might want her in my bed, but that is a different matter."

"You're determined, then. To stay under this curse? To stay miserable? Because I think she's the one that could fix all of this."

Adam turned to his friend, forcing a grim smile. "There is no fixing this. What's done is done. All I'm after is a little bit of satisfaction, if it's on offer. And a chance to take back my reputation. A chance to assert myself as a strong leader for my country. I'm not asking for anything else."

"And if you could?"

"I have no interest." He looked back at his reflection, a reflection that he didn't often ponder. What point was there? All he could see on his face was a road map of the destruction that had been wrought in his life. He didn't like pondering it at all. "I suppose," he said, "this is as good as it gets."

"You have yet to see your date," Fos said. "Believe me. She is as good as it gets."

The old man had not been wrong, neither had he been exaggerating. When Belle appeared in a golden gown that conformed to curves he had had his hands on, glittering like a trophy, her dark hair swept to the side, cascading over her bare shoulder in ringlets, he felt as though he had been punched in the gut.

Arousal that had been with him, clinging to him, gnawing at him like a wild beast made itself known all the more as he looked at her. He wanted her. He wanted her more than he had wanted anything in the past three years. In truth, she was the first thing he had wanted in all these years. Because there had been nothing he wanted beyond drawing the next breath since his loss.

But she was a hunger. Fierce and unquenchable.

He extended his arm, and she looked at it as though he were offering her a snake. "Come," he said, his tone much harder than he had intended. "You can't look afraid of me when we walk into the ballroom. It will not do."

"I'm not afraid of you," she said, stepping toward him, the dress swishing around her legs. "There." She looped her arm through his. "See?"

He led her through the corridor, more brightly lit than usual. The double doors to the palace opened wide, and outside was a car. He had a strange sort of flashback, a return to a life that lived only in dreams now.

He stopped, a sudden lump in his throat surprising him, an ache that started there and extended all the way down through his chest, immobilizing him.

"What's wrong?" she asked, looking up at him with luminous blue eyes.

"I haven't…I haven't actually been in a car since my accident. Not that I can remember. Yes, I got a ride home from the hospital, but I was heavily sedated at the time. Otherwise, all my treatment has occurred here at the palace."

She tightened her hold on him. "Are you afraid?"

He shook his head. "No."

It was just that this felt a lot like the night he had left the palace with Ianthe. And only one of them had returned. He didn't think that would happen tonight; he was not so superstitious. It was just…it was difficult not to feel connected to that other time. To that old grief.

He felt a featherlight touch on his cheek, against his ruined skin, followed by the slow, hot press of her lips just by the corner of his mouth. "I'm not afraid of you," she said again. "And everything will be fine tonight. It will."

She moved her hand down his arm, slipping her fingers through his and drawing them down between the two of them. She was holding his hand. Such a simple gesture, and utterly unsexual, and yet, he felt it burn hot inside him.

He imagined that every touch from her would burn hot inside him now.

"It's okay," she said, her voice soft.

He didn't need comfort. But, there was something to be said for it.

It was surprising to him how easy it was to get in the car, how easy it was to go on those winding roads he had been on the night of the accident. All the way to the airport.

Her mouth dropped open slightly when he told her they were going on a private plane to Santa Milagro. "I didn't realize…"

"Well," he said, "we are on an island. You didn't think we were going to drive the whole way, did you?"

"I guess not."

An hour later the wheels on the plane touched down in Santa Milagro, a mountainous country wedged in between Portugal and the Andalusian region of Spain. Sun washed and golden in the day, it glittered tonight. The lights of the city twinkling in the hillside, mirroring the stars that glittered overhead in the velvet blue sky.

When the door to the plane opened, and a limo pulled up to the base of the stairs, Belle's eyes went wide.

"Okay," she said, "this is definitely the most extravagant arrival I've ever made a party. But then, I'm wearing the most extravagant dress I've ever worn. With the most extravagant man I've ever known."

He looked down at her, smiling slightly. "You think I'm extravagant?"

"A massively muscled prince who looks like he might

Hulk out of his suit at any moment? Yes, that is a little bit extravagant."

By the time they got into the car, the similarities between tonight and the night of the accident had begun to fade. He didn't even think about it when he got into the back of the limousine, and Belle took her seat right beside him, her hand still linked with his.

She was comforting him, he realized, which he thought was funny considering this was far more outside her comfort zone than it was out of his. Or, at least, than it would have been only a few years ago. But, he allowed it because he liked the feel of her soft skin against his. Because he enjoyed touching her. And he very much enjoyed her touching him.

"We won't be going back to Olympios tonight," he said casually.

"We won't be?"

They rounded a curve on the road, coming up to a set of wrought iron gates that opened when the car drew near. And then a palace came into view. A thousand times more ostentatious than his own, lit from bottom to top so that the whole place looked as though it were dipped in gold.

"No," he said, "we will be staying here."

"Wow. So…I forgot to ask you. How do you know Prince Felipe? Did you go to prince school together?"

"We did go to school together. But it wasn't prince school."

"Okay. I guess princes just gravitate toward each other?"

"To a degree. But, we do have another friend. And he is not a prince. In fact, Rafe is from a very poor family. He had a benefactor pay for his education. You will meet Prince Felipe and Rafe tonight. And I will introduce you to them as my lover, as well."

"You're even going to lie to your friends?"

"Is it a lie?"

Color bled into her cheeks. "We didn't...that is...we didn't exactly—"

"You did," he said simply, not minding so much that she was clearly embarrassed, because he was unsatisfied, and wasn't that so much worse.

"Perhaps," she bit out. "But we still didn't...all the way."

"That gives us something to look forward to." The car stopped, and the driver got out and opened their door. He extended his hand. "And it gives you something to think about for the evening. Happy thought to hold on to as we make our entrance, as we are about to do. We are going to be announced, and you cannot look angry at me. Rather, you need to look as though you just came from my bed."

Her cheeks were thoroughly flushed after that comment, and by the time they walked up the wide, ornately decorated walkway into the doors that led to the ballroom, he was fairly satisfied that she looked as though he had had his way with her in the car.

Sadly, that was not the case, or his body wouldn't ache as it did.

When they arrived at the top of the stairs, a hush fell over the room.

The herald straightened when they arrived and addressed the crowd. "Presenting Prince Adam Katsaros of Olympios and Belle Chamberlain of California, USA."

She went stiff beside him as they began to walk down the stairs, holding on to him as they moved deeper into the room. Clearly, she wasn't used to being stared at like this. Well, neither was he. Or rather, he was, but this was the first time he had been stared at because he was something less than beautiful.

People looked at him with mouths wide-open, their expressions full of pity, full of shock. And he felt…he felt nothing. He felt strangely in control. As he moved into the room with the most beautiful woman in attendance on his arm, with a strange sense of power rolling over his skin.

People were afraid of him. They had never been afraid of him before. There was something about that that made him feel as though he was in even more control than he had been before. Yes, before people had been his sycophants. Had done everything they could to try to get a favor from him, to get his attention. But now? Now people made way for him as he walked through the room, parting as though they were the sea and he was performing a miracle.

They continued moving through the crowd, making their way to the center of the dance floor. Couples swirled around them, also giving them a wide berth as though he might reach out and grab one of them if they came too close.

"Would you care to dance with me?" he asked.

He looked down at Belle, and he saw that there was no fear in her eyes when she looked back at him. No, she wasn't looking at him like everyone else in the room. She did look terrified. But she was looking at him with a mixture of awe and wonder, and a kind of fascination that he was certain would be his undoing.

"Yes," she said, extending her hand.

He caught it in his own, pulling her toward him. She

braced her hand against his chest, pressing her fore-head against his shoulder as he swept her up and into the rhythm of the music that filled the room.

People continued to dance around them, though some stopped and stared openly, clearly fascinated by what-ever the story might be between the disfigured Prince and the beautiful American who looked at him like a man, and not a curiosity.

And then, all that faded into the background. Years spent in solitude made it preferable in many ways to shut out all the extravagant sensory input that surrounded him. More people than he had seen in any one place in years, more light, more sound.

All of it seemed to go fuzzy around the edges as he looked down at Belle. She consumed him. His vision, his need, his body. Tonight, they would be staying in the pal-ace in Santa Milagro, and most certainly if he asked his friend to provide them with separate bedrooms he would.

Felipe wouldn't even question it. Oftentimes, men in their circumstances had to do things for appearances, and a facade of chastity was not outside the realm of those needs.

But he would not. Because tonight, he was intent of taking Belle Chamberlain to bed. He could not keep her; he knew that. It was not feasible. But, he could have her for a little while, and he would. *Boyfriends be damned. Decency be damned.*

Her hand was so small in his, so fragile, and while the suit, the surroundings, didn't seem to fit at all, this did. However he had changed over the past three years, however he had come to reform until he no longer fit the position he had been born into, he had been forged into a shape that seemed to fit her just fine.

Her gold dress glittered beneath the lights, but the gown didn't shine more brightly than she did. He thought back to what his adviser had said earlier in his room. About her being the woman who could potentially break the spell of darkness he had been under.

She was light. So, he could see how the other man might think that. But the darkness inside him was the kind that would consume light, not the kind that could be flooded out so simply. The guilt, the pain that he carried with him, would simply leech all that beauty out of her eventually. He would not subject either of them to such a thing.

He had felt one woman die in his arms already; he would not kill this one by inches over the course of years spent in his presence.

But, that did not mean he couldn't satisfy his need for her.

When the song ended, he brought them both to a standstill, lifted her hand to his lips and pressed his mouth against her knuckles. And when he looked around at the people watching them again, their expressions had changed.

Everything was working the way he had intended it to. Because now they saw a man. A man who was with a woman, who was clearly human, and not simply an object to be pitied or feared.

But, for the first time he was concerned about the headline that would be plastered across papers around the world tomorrow. About what they would say concerning Belle. Initially, he hadn't cared if she was hurt, because she had involved herself, because she had come to vouch for her father, in his mind he had imagined it some sort of poetic justice that she become an accessory to his revenge, as well.

Now he wondered.

Her mother was the child of somebody famous. She did have a boyfriend, as she continually pointed out. There would be ramifications for her. The words that would be used to describe a woman who would warm the bed of a man simply because he was powerful, disregarding his looks, would not be kind at all.

He felt a twinge of regret at that. But he could afford nothing else. Nothing deeper. All he could do was make the headline true.

He would push all that to the side for now, and focus on the way she was looking at him. Take everything he could have tonight, because after tonight, when reality hit, when the media had weighed in on the spectacle, it would be different. Things would change.

And she would leave.

He had to let her go after; there was no other choice. Because he certainly couldn't keep her.

He looked around the room again, saw Felipe standing in the back talking to a redhead who was wearing a very brief, very shiny dress. Then, in an isolated corner, he spotted his friend Rafe.

Of course, Rafe would stick to the outer edges of the room. His vision was severely compromised, and though he claimed he could sometimes see light and shadow, Adam wondered how serious it was truly. He had been lost in his own hell for so long that he had left Rafe alone in his.

Adam preferred to be alone in his hell, so part of him assumed that Rafe wanted the same.

"Come," Adam said. "I will introduce you to my friends."

He wasn't certain why he was doing this. Wasn't sure what the point was. But, he found himself crossing the broad expanse of the ballroom, making his way toward Rafe.

"Belle," he said, placing his hand on her lower back, a sign of possessiveness, even if it was one his friend could not observe. "This is Rafael Marelli, but the two friends he has call him Rafe."

Rafe angled his head and looked in Belle's direction, but it was clear that his dark eyes were unseeing. "And the two friends Adam has hardly call him at all," Rafe returned. "It's nice to meet you."

"Belle," she said, extending her hand. "Belle Chamberlain."

Again, seemingly on instinct, Rafe reacted appropriately, lifting his hand slowly until his palm came into contact with hers; then he lowered his head and kissed her knuckles, just as Adam had earlier. Adam felt a surge of rage, possessiveness, overtake him.

"There is no need for that," Rafe said, releasing his hold on her hand, as though he sensed Adam's irritation. "I'm not going to try and steal her from you, Adam. Though, I can see how you would be concerned. Since you have found a woman willing to tame the rather savage beast, she might be a good bet for me, as well."

"Adam." The voice of Prince Felipe came from behind them. Adam turned briefly, and so did Belle. Rafe stayed as he was. "You actually came." His friend assessed him slowly. They hadn't seen each other in years. Not since the scars had healed over. When he had been incapacitated, Felipe had come and seen him, but in the years since he had seemed dedicated to respecting Adam's desire for solitude.

"I said that I would," Adam said, "and I don't pretend I'm going to do something and then sidestep. I tell you how I feel up front—you know me well enough to know that."

"And who is this?" Felipe asked, his sharp eyes turning to Belle.

"Belle," she said, receiving a kiss on the hand from Felipe, as well.

"Adam doesn't like that," Rafe said, his voice dry.

"You're far too perceptive, Rafe," Felipe said. "It's one of the most annoying things about you. You should miss more than you do, God knows."

"Maybe my other senses are heightened."

"You were always like this," Felipe said, waving a hand.

"Is this all you intended it to be?" Adam asked, directing the question at Felipe.

"The party? Yes. Though, my father is unable to attend due to his ill health."

"Somehow, I imagine the citizens of your country are not overly saddened by that," Rafe said.

"Of course not," Felipe said, "but we cannot say that. I am poised to take the throne soon, of course. And I am assuming that the woman on your arm is discreet, Adam, as you are the most discreet man I know."

Belle shifted beside him. "I'm not going to repeat anything I hear tonight," she said, nodding. And Adam believed it. Even though she was the daughter of a paparazzo, he believed it.

He marveled at that for a moment. That he could find that kind of trust in her. That he had found it so effortlessly. It was simply there, and he felt as though he couldn't talk himself out of it even if he wanted to.

"Good," Felipe said. "I know Rafe prefers to be mysterious. He would hate for that aura of disinterest to be compromised in any way."

"There is no compromising what is real," Rafe said.

"I have to circulate," Felipe said.

"Does that mean you're going to try and talk a woman into your bed?" Rafe asked.

Adam was particularly amused by this because Rafe hadn't even been able to see Felipe talking to the red-headed woman earlier. But, regardless, he knew their friend.

"Of course not," Felipe said. "I don't have to try. I will succeed." He turned to go, then paused, regarding Adam closely. "It's not that bad."

Then he walked away. It took Adam a moment to realize he probably meant Adam's face.

Then he looked back at Rafe. Who of course had shown absolutely no shock at the change in Adam's appearance. Rafe had been blinded before the accident.

He remembered what Belle had said, that it was lucky Adam had not lost his sight. Rafe had lost his. Though, he had retained his looks. However, Adam had the feeling that meant next to nothing to his friend, who had emerged from whatever had happened to him changed. And not simply because of the loss of his sight, Adam was certain. There was something else to it. Something deeper.

"It's good you're here, Adam," Rafe said. "If you've changed, I wouldn't know."

His friend's words were so in line with what he had been thinking that he had to laugh. "Of course not.

Though, I have been informed that it is not my scars that make me a beast."

"That is true," Belle said, her tone muted.

And he didn't know why, but it struck him uncomfortably, that she seemed to think he was a beast still, when he had hoped that she saw him as a man.

"We will let you return to your brooding," Adam said. "Felipe would say that women like that."

"If they do," Rafe said, lifting his drink to his lips, "I wouldn't know about that either."

Adam took Belle's arm and led her back toward the dance floor, pulling her into his hold. "Are you up for another dance?"

She ignored the question, but moved easily into step with him. "Rafe is blind?" she asked.

He realized that it might not be apparent if you didn't know. Though, it was obvious to Adam, who had known him before, and who had witnessed the change in his demeanor, and mannerisms. "Yes," Adam responded. "Not from birth. Five or six years ago. Something happened and he sustained a head injury, though he is reluctant to give the details. You think I am a private man, but you will find Rafe bests me."

"And Felipe is the easygoing one?"

Adam chuckled at that. "Felipe is nothing but a carefully constructed facade. I would say, without hesitation, that he is perhaps the most private of all of us, and does the very best at hiding it. Which I think is what ensures he stays that way."

"Why did you cut yourself off from your friends? They seem like such good friends," Belle said.

"Sometimes you want to stay wounded," he returned, realizing how true it was the moment the words left his mouth. "You don't want anyone to fix you. I wanted to live in my pain forever. My wife was dead, my son… sometimes all of it hits me so hard it still takes my breath away. And in those moments I don't want anyone there. I don't want anyone to tell me it will be okay. Because how can it be? I almost wanted to feel bleak and hopeless forever because then the enormity of their loss could always be felt. Sometimes it feels good to dwell on the dark things."

She was quiet at that. "I understand." The words were simply offered, but they did something to him. Just as everything about her seemed to do.

"You agree then," he said, not quite sure why he was pushing the topic. "That I'm a beast inside as well as out?"

"Inside, at least," she said. "You must know that I think…that I am attracted to you." Her cheeks turned pink. "I think I have demonstrated over and over again that I find you somewhat irresistible."

"In spite of all of this?" he asked, indicating his face.

"Perhaps because of it. I can't separate the scars from the man I first met. Yes, I have now seen pictures of you without them, but they aren't you. Not to me."

He pondered that for a moment. "But inside…"

"I didn't say it was a bad thing." She was silent for a moment after that. "There is something about it that I find compelling. I associate passion with a lack of control, and I've always been… I've always hated it. I lived with my mother until I was four. I have small snatches of memory of what it was like to live in her house. I didn't like it. It was so chaotic. Everything was so over the top. But I was also devastated when I had to leave. Because it was the only life I knew. Because she was my mother and she gave me away. And I missed her. I cried for her every night. For the longest time. But, when I stopped crying I got angry. And it's like you said. You want to hold on to those things, to those dark feelings, so that you can make sure you're changed by them. So that you can understand why something happened, so that you can understand those terrible, dark places you were forced into." She looked up at him. "For me, that meant trying to find a way to learn from her lessons, so that I wouldn't do anything like what she did to me to anyone else."

She lifted her hand, allowing her thumb to trace that particularly heavy ridge of scar tissue by his mouth. "You're forcing me to look at passion differently," she continued. "It is that beast inside of you, that wild thing that lets you take whatever you want, that is made entirely of need and not of lies or protection…that's what calls to me. It's what I wish I could find inside of myself."

He reached up, grabbing her wrist, drawing it to his lips and pressing his mouth to the tender skin there. Neither of his friends had kissed that skin. It was much more intimate. Much more sensitive. And it was all his. She was his. "I could help you find it," he said, his voice rough, his body hardening at the thought.

"Please," she said, the word a whisper. "Please Adam. I want you."

CHAPTER EIGHT

SHE KNEW EXACTLY what she was asking for. But she was tired of pretending it wasn't what she wanted. She had been determined to make it his responsibility. And then, when he had done all those things to her that had made her shake and shiver, that had affected a small earthquake inside her body, she had run away.

Had avoided him as diligently as she possibly could. As if she could wait him out. Until the timer was up on her sentence.

But, she was done with that. Done with it completely. Tonight, she was cocooned in fantasy, at a ball in a beautiful palace with the only prince who would ever rule over her heart. Yes, in the end she would have to sort everything out with Tony, and she was probably being a bad person, giving herself to another man when she had avoided doing that with the man she'd been dating for months.

But for some reason, in Adam's arms everything seemed clear. Desire, need and that hungry thing inside her that might be a beast.

She was so tired of pushing it all down. So tired of pretending to feel nothing, of forcing herself to want nothing. She had clung to that stability she'd been given by her father, to every easy, responsible thing that had come her way, because she had been certain it would be the key to protecting herself from further injury. The key to protecting herself from hurting other people. And here she was, considering doing something that would certainly hurt at least one person.

That made her stomach seize up tight. But, it was something she would have to deal with later. If she had a phone on her, she would deal with it now, but she had been prevented from making any contact with the outside world, so she couldn't. And anyway, it was probably for the best. That she was cut off from all that safety, from that familiarity.

In many ways, being taken captive by Adam had led to a strange kind of freedom. She wasn't beholden to anyone. Didn't have to be the perfect daughter, didn't have to be an example of anything. She was cut off completely from all her responsibility, from everyone who knew her. Everyone who knew her as Belle Chamberlain, the very levelheaded, bookish girl who led with her head and never her heart. And certainly never the needs of her body.

None of those people were here to judge her. None of those people were here for her to please or impress. And without that…

She wanted him. And she would have him.

"Adam," she said, his name a plea on her lips. "When do we get to leave the party?"

He growled, drawing her up against him, his arm like a steel band around her waist. "Now," he said, that voice shot through with iron just like the rest of him.

She found him leading her off the dance floor, out of the ballroom. "Where are we going?" she asked.

"I assume that Felipe readied the room I normally stay in when I come to visit."

"Oh. Did you often stay here? With—"

"No," he said quickly. "We never stayed here together. This is not about her. This is not about recapturing some kind of memory, or stepping into the past. I can promise you that. My marriage is entirely separate from this. I swear to you."

A wave of relief washed over her. She didn't know why it mattered. It shouldn't. This wasn't about emotion; it wasn't about love. Yes, Adam had tapped into something inside of her, had captured a part of her that no one else ever had before. Awakened it. But, she didn't need to compete with his wife. Adam had loved his wife; she could see it in that expression of pure happiness on his face in the photograph in his room. He'd had a future set before him, a hope and joy that had been ripped from him. She could never presume to understand it. Would never ask that he relinquish any kind of hold on it.

She didn't want him to push his wife out of his heart. She simply wanted a space with him for now. That was all.

She knew that people were looking at them, that guests and staff members alike were regarding them with curiosity as they made their hasty exit.

Adam paused for a moment, reaching into his pocket as his phone buzzed. "A text from Felipe, who has indeed informed me that my room is prepared. And confirmed the location. Clearly, he was paying attention."

"A good friend to have," she said, her voice sounding thin even to her own ears.

She wondered if she should tell him now. About her inexperience. But, she didn't want to do anything to compromise what had grown between them. And that meant changing any perception he might have of her. It was too late. They could have a postmortem after, because she doubted she would be able to affect the role of experienced woman with any kind of skill. She would wait until after.

He was so large and sure beside her, and she gloried in that strength as he took the lead, sweeping them both through the halls effortlessly. His confidence, his certainty, filled her with her own.

There was something about his strength that made her eminently conscious of how delicate she was, and yet made her feel all the stronger for it. It was some kind of magic. That she could feel small, fragile and yet also as though she held this large, impossible, impenetrable man in the palm of her hand. That she had the power to affect him. That she had power in this situation at all.

If it was a dream, she didn't want to wake up from it. If it was fantasy, she was in no hurry to get back to reality.

Finally, they arrived at a set of ornate red doors that she knew led to the bedchamber. Her heart slammed up, seeming to hit her at the base of her throat, making it impossible to breathe.

Adam must have noticed the sudden fit of nerves. Because he reached out, smoothing her lower lip with his thumb. "You have nothing to fear from me. I want… I want this," he said, his voice growing frayed. Raw. "I was going to give you some kind of speech. Beautiful words. Something seductive, I suppose. But I am out of practice. And all I can offer you is honesty. I want to lose myself in you. I have spent years wandering through the darkness, losing myself there. And you…

you are light to me, Belle. I want to lose myself in that, if only for a little while. I know that it can't be more than a night. I know that after this I must let you go, as I have promised. But, just for a while. I want to be lost in something beautiful. And you are the most beautiful thing I have ever seen. I may have seen beauty before my accident, before my loss, but I didn't see it the way that I do now. It could never have meant as much to me then. After so many years of ugliness, so many years of solitude. So many years of darkness. You cannot know what it means to have you touch me." He cupped her cheek, his hand large, rough, his expression earnest. "I don't know how many women I've been with. I never bothered to count. For years, there was only my wife, but before that… I was a prince, I was young and handsome and powerful and I made the most of that. It doesn't matter. Because a single touch from you, your fingertips on my face as it is now erases all of that. It is so much heavier—it has so much more value. Now, as the man I am today, it is without price. I am not a man given to speeches. I'm not a man given to emotion. But I am full with both now. And I want you to know that. You are not my prisoner. I have grown to suspect that I might be yours."

Those words washed over her, threw her, warming her, making her feel a flood of that earlier certainty, that earlier strength. Yes, this was the man she wanted. This was the moment. Because it meant everything. Because it wasn't simply about being carried away on a tide of passion. It was a decision, a need, given in to with the full cost clear to her.

Because it would rattle the fabric of the life she had left behind, because it would change the situation Adam had been living in for the past three years. Because both of them would leave it marked as indelibly as Adam had been by his accident.

That was what she wanted. That was what she craved. To have this chance to affect someone's life so profoundly. To affect her own so deeply.

When she had been removed from her mother's care, she didn't think the woman had lost a moment of sleep over it. In fact, she had likely thrown a party. She had managed to make no change in the life of her own mother, and that wounded her deeper and more profoundly than she had ever realized before this moment.

But Adam would remember her. He would think of her. No matter who came after her, she would always be the first woman to touch him after he had been so changed. After he had been scarred. She would always be the first woman he had chosen.

Dear God, how she craved this. How she hungered for being chosen.

So, she stretched up on her toes and kissed him, lost herself in him, in this. Poured out everything inside her that he seemed to think was light, and committed herself to giving her all. To giving all of herself.

When they parted, they were both breathing heavily, her heart fluttering in her chest like a bird trapped in a cage. "Please," she said, not caring if she was begging. "I know that you want whatever you see in me, the light, the beauty. But I want everything inside of you." She put her hand flat on his chest, felt his heartbeat rage beneath her palm. "I don't need you to change. I don't want you to. I don't want you to stop being a beast. I want you to show me how to be one too."

"I can do that." He pushed open the doors, drawing

her into his arms and propelling them both into the room. Then he closed the door firmly behind them, leaving them shrouded in darkness, shrouded in privacy. She thought for a moment that he might leave the lights extinguished. But he did not. Instead, he flicked the switch, bathing them in light. Leaving no chance to hide from this moment. From what they felt. From what they were about to do.

It made it all the more terrifying, certainly, but it also made it feel more real. More stark. She wouldn't be able to block it out in the misty haze of darkness, and she found herself grateful for it.

Because if this was her big, loud moment, she should allow nothing to temper it. Nothing at all.

"I want…I want to see you," she said, the words coming out with a bit more of a stutter than she would have liked. But, she was a virgin, after all, and the confidence that she was clinging to was tenuous at best.

A strange expression crossed his face. "I had not thought anyone ever would again. Not as I am now."

He undid the knot that held his bow tie to his throat, then cast the strip of black fabric onto the floor. He began to undo the buttons of his shirt, exposing a glorious wedge of tanned, toned chest as he did.

She was held captive by him, by that sheer masculine beauty.

She saw shirtless men at the beach all the time, and given that it was Southern California, a lot of them had that perfect gym-sculpted look. But, most of them were waxed within an inch of their lives, leaving behind none of the glorious, masculine chest hair that graced Adam's body.

As he let his shirt fall to the ground with his tie, revealing a sculpted, toned body that spoke of his physical strength, she found herself mourning that current trend of minimizing a man's testosterone.

She loved it. She loved how feral it was. How untamed. But then, given the fact that she loved that this man was a beast, it didn't surprise her that she felt that way.

"The rest," she said, her throat growing tight.

He kept his dark eyes fixed on hers as he reached down, working the belt free, then undoing the closure on his pants, as well. He pushed the pants and underwear down in one motion, leaving him gloriously naked for her appraisal.

She had never seen a naked, aroused man in the flesh, and nothing had prepared her for the sight of Prince Adam Katsaros in all his glory.

Truly, she hadn't known men could be quite so large. Or quite so hard. And that wasn't just the most intimate part of him, but all of him. He looked as though he were fashioned from the rock, life breathed into him by some kind of mythical creature. And since she felt as though she were lost in a fairy tale, that didn't seem fanciful at all.

"What is it?" he asked, his voice surprisingly gentle given the brutally masculine sight he affected before her.

"You're just…*beautiful* seems an insipid word," she said. "And nothing about you is insipid. But you take my breath away—that much I know."

"I'm not sure I'm worthy of such compliments. However, I am happy as long as you are happy. And as long as I can entice you to reveal your beauty to me."

She reached behind her back clumsily, her fingers shaking as she felt for the zipper on her dress. She wanted to do this. For him. Wanted to be the first woman that he saw naked after all these years. But, she had a hard time, the tiny zipper catching itself on the folds of fabric and sequins. "I'm nervous," she said.

A smile curved his lips, lips she could never think of as ruined again. And his smile…she could never think of it as compromise. It was his. And she could see it now, could easily read it, regardless of whether or not anyone else would ever be able to recognize it in quite the same way she did.

"Let me," he said, that gentle tone combined with the firm touch of his hands at her hips putting her instantly at ease.

He dealt with her zipper deftly, her dress falling loose at her waist, then to the floor, a golden pool around her feet.

She was left in nothing more than a pair of whisper-thin underwear. Her dress didn't require a bra, so her breasts were bare to him.

He had already touched her there, had already put his hands on her intimately, and she found she wasn't embarrassed in the least.

Especially not when he clenched his jaw tight, the obvious restraint it was taking for him to hold himself back speaking to how deeply she affected him.

She liked that. Gloried in the fact that she tested him. It did make her wonder about Tony. No, she would not have liked him to pressure her, but that was something separate entirely. He didn't look at her like this. Didn't look at her with all this naked need, with this barely repressed desire.

Maybe if he had, she would have wanted him.

Except, she knew that wasn't true. Knew that part of

herself had always been waiting for Adam. Even before she had known who he was.

He surprised her by dropping to his knees, pressing a kiss to the tender skin beneath her belly button before grabbing hold of her panties and dragging them down her thighs. He was eye level with the most intimate part of her then, and that made her feel exposed. Naked, when before she hadn't felt that way.

"Adam—" Her words were cut off as he leaned forward, pressing his face to her inner thigh and inhaling deeply, the rough, sandpaper quality of his evening stubble on the fragile skin there sending a shiver of pleasure up her spine.

Then he turned to her, tasting her deeply right where she ached for him most. She stiffened, and arched back, and his hand clamped down hard on her lower back before sliding down to cup her rear, drawing her back forward, holding her to his mouth as he subjected her to a sensual assault that far surpassed anything she had imagined possible.

He wasn't Prince Charming. Wasn't the soft, smooth fantasy man she had always imagined she might end up with. But then, she imagined Prince Charming would never think of doing something quite like this.

The intensity of his desire was evident with each pass of his tongue, and when he brought his hands in—stroking her, teasing her—she lost her mind completely. Lost the ability to analyze anything that was happening. She simply gave herself up to sensation. To him.

To passion. She didn't feel so afraid of it now, not when it had consumed her so beautifully, not when he consumed her so beautifully.

Her orgasm washed over her like a wave, different

from that time in the library, where it had felt so fraught and fractured. This time, it was warm and comforting, rolling through her with building intensity, going on and on and leaving her gasping for air.

He rose up slowly, kissing her stomach, her rib cage just beneath her breast and then her lips. He kept one palm cupping her butt, the hold possessive, a demonstration of strength that made her knees weak. He pulled her naked body up against his, let her feel that hot, hard length that clearly proved his desire for her.

He pushed his fingers through her hair, pulling her hard into the kiss. She felt wrapped in him, consumed by him, his scent, his heat, the strength and hardness of his body, and when he walked them both to the bed she didn't feel afraid. She didn't feel nervous; she didn't feel unsure. This was Adam, and she wanted him. Whatever that might mean, whether it might hurt, or whether it might leave her heart feeling torn after…it didn't matter. At least, it didn't outweigh the overwhelming need she felt to be joined to him in this way.

Adam lowered her slowly onto the plush mattress, gripping her thigh, moving his hand down behind her knee, teasing the sensitive skin there as he lifted her leg slowly, draping it over his lower back, moving himself into position between her spread legs.

He flexed his hips forward, sliding that thick arousal through her slick folds, making her gasp, building her arousal back up, impossibly, perfectly, to the heights it was just before her last climax.

She reached up, grabbing his face, holding him steady, looking in his eyes as she rocked her hips against him, in time with his movements, making them both gasp. He moved to the side, and she tried to stop him, bereft as the cold air washed over her when he removed himself.

"What?"

"If I know Felipe…" He opened up a drawer on a nightstand next to the bed and produced a box. "Yes," he said, "I do."

They were condoms. He opened them, taking out the plastic packet and tearing it quickly before rolling the protection over his length. She watched, fascinated, because she had never seen it done before, because she was fascinated by everything about him. By the strength in his hand as he gripped his own shaft and smoothed the latex over himself.

Then he was right back where he had been only a moment ago, positioned at the entrance to her body, one hand gripping her thigh, another pressed into the mattress by her face. He lifted her gently, the blunt head of his arousal pressing more firmly against her as he did.

A slow, intense stinging sensation began to build, burn as he moved deeper inside her, joining their bodies together, filling her, stretching her. She gritted her teeth, screwed her eyes shut tight, bringing her hands back above her head and balling them into fists, her nails digging into her palms as she did her best not to show him her distress.

He flexed his hips forward an inch more, and she gasped, her eyes flying open wide. But he wasn't looking at her. His unfocused gaze was somewhere behind her, his jaw held tight, the chords in his neck standing, demonstrating how hard-won his control was.

Something about that made her heart clench tight, made the pain begin to recede. Watching him, watching how profoundly it affected him, how deeply he felt it. She focused on that, she focused on him, and, as he slid in deeper, she felt herself expand to accommodate him, felt it grow easier to take him, felt her desire to take him build.

He growled, thrusting inside her to the hilt, tightening his hold on her thigh and drawing her up hard against him. It took her breath away, overwhelmed her. For a moment, she didn't think she could possibly endure it. Didn't think she could possibly withstand it.

When he began to move, it was intense, it was rough and it was raw. She could see that this was different from everything else that had occurred before. That had all been about giving to her, giving her pleasure. In this moment, he was claiming his own. Was expending the years of frustration, loneliness, pain in her body. Was using her to find his own release. And somehow, that gave her strength.

She wanted to be this for him. Wanted to be all that he needed, because nobody else could be, and nobody else would be. Because he had asked no one else. Because he said he wanted no one else.

She clung to his shoulders, met his each and every thrust, and as she did, as she gave herself over to this, over to him, all the discomfort faded. Or maybe it didn't fade; perhaps it simply blended into the growing pleasure that bloomed in her midsection and spread outward, taking root deep inside her and made it so she couldn't think, couldn't breathe.

There was nothing but him. But the rough feel of his whiskers against her cheek, then the slick slide of his tongue against hers. The scent of his body, masculine and spicy, his hardness over her, inside her. Everything was Adam.

She had never felt like his captive, not fully. She had

never acted like a prisoner, had never given him the proper deference, as he had been the first to point out. But now…she felt fully taken captive. Utterly and completely.

He was rough; he was demanding; he was everything. She did her best to meet it, did her best to soften when he needed her to soften, to return force when he required it. When his teeth scraped along the edge of her lip, she returned the favor with a bite of her own and was rewarded with a low, feral growl.

Pleasure built inside her, blending in with the luxurious feel of the bedspread beneath her, and the hot weight of Adam above her.

She felt it when his control began to fray, and she lifted her hands, gripping his face, tracing that thick scar tissue that created a map of his pain across his skin. And when he shuddered, gave himself up to his own release, something deep and dark began to pulse inside her.

Her release hit when his did, and there was something different about this one too. It wrapped around them both, held them both in thrall; they shook together, clung to each other as the storm took them both over.

He moved his hands to her face, held on to her tightly and pressed his forehead against hers, then closed the distance between their lips and claimed her mouth in a kiss. One that mimicked everything that had just happened between them.

And then he pulled her against the side of his body, cradling her against him, his breath hot on her cheek, his large hand splayed possessively over her stomach.

She had thought they might talk. About her inexperience. About what had happened. About what came next.

She realized they couldn't talk about any of it, not

without addressing the *next*. And she didn't want to. She wanted to stay here. In the moment. With nothing behind her and nothing in front of her. In this moment, in this night, where she could be as free as she wanted.

Where she could hide with him. Glory in him.

So she didn't speak at all. Instead, she turned her face to his and kissed him, a hand pressed lightly to his shoulder.

It was all he needed. He consumed her lips on a growl, and they both let themselves get caught up in passion again.

CHAPTER NINE

HE WANTED TO keep her prisoner forever. That was the thought running through Adam's head the next morning, all the way back to the airport, on the flight that took them back to Olympios.

Belle was intoxicating. Being with her was being able to touch the light again, if for just moments at a time. His beautiful, innocent captive who had never been with a man before he'd been with her.

He had known after. In the middle of all of it there had been no thought, and he'd had no ability to process what the tension in her body, that slight resistance as he'd slid deep inside her, had meant.

He supposed it should make him feel guilty. The fact that he—the man who'd taken her prisoner, who had left her with so few choices—should be the first to have her.

But he was a man capable of taking her prisoner, so guilt wouldn't be coming to the party anytime soon. No, instead he felt replete with a kind of bone-deep satisfaction he couldn't recall feeling before.

But it would fade. Later today when he sent her back home to California on his jet, it would fade.

He had to let her go. He had no other choice.

He had done it. He had gone out in public, and what

the world would think of it remained to be seen, but he also didn't want it.

He didn't want Belle's suffering. He didn't want revenge. Not on her, not on her father. Whatever rage he felt over Ianthe's death—over his son's death—it was still real. But they couldn't be brought back, no matter who he punished. If he took the photographer who had caused the accident prisoner, locked him away for the rest of his life, Ianthe would still be dead. His future, his heart, would still be gone.

And in his quest to rectify something that could never truly be repaired, he would destroy that one beautiful, light thing that still remained in this world. Belle. He could not. And he would not.

She had been subdued during the plane ride, and was growing even more so on the car ride back to the palace. She knew; she knew that this was coming to an end. The fact that she seemed upset about it only drove home the point that it was the right thing to do.

The fact that she had begun to feel sorry for him, the fact that she felt some sort of connection with him, was probably the most despicable part of all of it. If she would think of him ever after this, if she would miss him, want him, when he could never be a man worthy of those things…then he had truly created an environment wherein he could never fully release her.

Part of him reveled in that, because he was only a man. Enjoyed the idea that somewhere, someone would think of him. Would miss him. Would want him.

But he didn't want it to be her. He wanted her to go back to her boyfriend. To enjoy that bright California sunshine and all the security and freedom she had spoken of when she talked of her home.

He didn't want her here. In the darkness with him.

She had told him she wanted to learn how to be a beast, wanted to learn how to embrace her passion. And if he had managed to help her with that, if she could only carry that back with her, if it made her happier, if it made her life better, then that was a good thing.

The alternative was something he didn't want to consider. That he had infected her with his darkness, and that over the course of the next few years it would continue to spread inside her until she matched him. If his darkness was so strong that it had blotted out her light, he didn't suppose he could ever forgive himself.

Have you ever forgiven yourself for anything? For your wife? For your son? What does this add? Nothing.

He shrugged that off, but as they approached the gates of the palace he saw something that sent a shock of adrenaline down his spine. Immediately, he was on alert, ready to fight, ready to defend the woman at his side. Because there were people surrounding the palace, people with cameras, microphones, video equipment. There were vans; there was a damned helicopter circling overhead. They had come back to a circus.

"What is this?" he asked no one in particular, because he knew that Belle didn't have the answer either.

The limousine slowed, his driver clearly hesitant to go on. Adam pushed the button that lowered the divider. "Can you drive through them?" he asked.

"I'm sure that if I continue to drive, they'll move eventually," the driver said.

"Test that," Adam returned, his voice hard.

"What's going on?"

"You should know well," Adam said, pulling his

phone out of his pocket and opening up the web browser. "It's the paparazzi."

"I didn't talk to anybody," she said, her voice shaking. "I didn't."

"I know that," he said. "You were with me the entire night, remember? And not only that, but last night we made our public debut. So this is hardly a complete shock. Though, I have to confess I didn't think this would be the result." There had to be something else. Something more. Yes, there were a great many headlines talking about his first appearance in the public eye since his accident had occurred, but that wasn't enough to cause this kind of frenzy. Not when there were already photographs. There was nothing new to be gained…unless…

He pulled up a headline for an American newspaper, and that was when he saw it. "What is your boyfriend's name?"

"Tony," she said. "Tony Layton."

"Yes, he is not happy. And that is why these people are here."

"What?"

He handed her his phone; there was no point keeping it from her. If she wanted to dial her father or her boyfriend, or the National Guard, she was welcome to do so. He'd been invaded already, and she was already set to go. So what did it matter?

Her mouth fell open, her eyes widening with shock as she looked down at the screen. "He's claiming that you've kidnapped me. That I'm brainwashed. Stockholm syndrome." She put the phone down, meeting his gaze. Then she reached out, pressing the button that divided them from the driver. "Stop the car," she commanded.

The driver did so, mostly out of shock, Adam imagined. He was about to open his mouth to contradict Belle, but the car had stopped and she was already getting out the passenger-side door.

"Hey! Do you want to listen to a third party, or do you want to hear the story from me? I am not Prince Adam Katsaros's prisoner. I am his fiancée. I have chosen to be here with him. I'm in love with him, and we are going to get married."

Belle was completely numb with shock, unable to believe the words that had just come out of her mouth. She had claimed to be Adam's fiancée. Had claimed they were getting married. When she had seen Tony's words in bold in the news article she had lost her mind completely. This was passion, she supposed. That total insanity she had feared for most of her life. Had feared would overtake her completely. And it had.

She couldn't regret it, though. As she stood there, facing down the horde of paparazzi, that was the thing that surprised her the most. That she wasn't filled with remorse or regret. That she wasn't beset by fear. She had always imagined that she would be horrified if she were ever to give in to such impulses. That she would hate all the changes in herself. That she would feel like she had failed in some way.

But, that wasn't the case. She felt…everything felt clear. Quiet. Everything felt like it was moving in slow motion. Which could indicate that she was in shock rather than having a moment of clarity, but she liked the clarity idea better.

Somehow, over the course of the past weeks, she had been made into the person she was always supposed to become. In Adam's arms, in Adam's bed she had found a part of herself that she had kept suppressed for a long time. Had found a part of herself she hadn't known she needed to find.

Now that she had…she felt more full, more whole than she ever had.

She felt brave. She realized that was the biggest difference. Yes, it had taken a great amount of bravery to come here and free her father, and that had been something of an out-of-body experience. Something beyond her typical capacity for strength.

It had felt foreign then. Strange.

This felt like part of herself. Like it was the most instinctual, easy thing in all the world to defend Adam, to defend the man she had fallen in love with.

Even that realization didn't scare her. Even if it should. It felt as calm and clear as everything else. Of course she loved him. That was why this was simple. That was why there was no other option.

She was not going to allow a torch-carrying mob to accuse him of being a monster. Was not going to allow reporters, the media, to invade the sanctuary that he had ensconced himself in for so long. Not when they were the ones who had caused all his pain.

She wouldn't allow it. She couldn't.

The roar that came from the reporters when she made her revelation was almost deafening, cutting through that sense of calm she had felt only a moment before. But, it didn't penetrate. Not deeply. She was still sure of her course.

"Do you want to listen? Or do you want to make wild guesses about what the truth might be? I can tell you everything," she said. And even though she was pretty sure they hadn't been able to hear the exact words she had spoken, they did quiet down.

"I was not kidnapped. I have not been tricked, and I have not been manipulated. Prince Adam Katsaros is not forcing my hand in any way. In fact, he was going to allow me to return home to avoid damaging my reputation. But I refused. I am refusing," she reiterated. She looked back at the car, saw Adam sitting inside, staring out at her, his expression fierce.

"How dare you go after a man who has already been through so much," she said, her voice trembling. "How dare you believe these lies?"

"Yes," one of the reporters in the back of the crowd spoke loudly. "But you can't blame the public for being suspicious. Beauty might love the beast in a fairy tale, but not in real life."

Rage spiked through her. "You will find that there are a great many women who prefer a beast," she said, her words crisp. "Prince Charming might be a good dancer, but a beast has other qualities to recommend him."

She knew that was going to land her a very salacious write-up. But she didn't care. It was true. He was the one she wanted, him and no one else.

Then Adam got out of the car, slowly. He was so large, his presence so vital, so intimidating, that she felt the reporters shrink back.

"I think what my fiancée is trying to say," he said, his deep, rich voice rolling over her skin, sending little tremors through her body, "is that we have a particular connection. If it doesn't make for a clever headline for you, I can't say that I'm particularly sorry. But it is time for me to move on, time for my country to move on, from the tragedy that was caused at the hands of this kind of overzealous media. Your responsibility is to report on world events, events that would inform or protect the public. Last I checked, who might be sharing my bed is not one of those events. You may show yourselves off the palace grounds and out of my country, or you will find yourself thrown in prison. And if you think I'm exaggerating, there is a photographer I can put you in contact with who will let you know that I never bluff." He looked across the car, his eyes meeting hers. "Come, *agape*—we should go home now."

That was easy enough that Belle knew he was not going to be quite so biddable when they were alone. But still, she found herself obeying his command. Following his lead and getting back into the car.

"Drive," he commanded, and the car began to move again.

"I couldn't let that headline stand," she said, justifying herself before he even said a word.

"Neither could I," he responded. "Though, I'm not certain your solution would have been mine."

"You can always retract it later. Engagements break up all the time."

He turned to face her, his dark eyes blazing. "Is that what you were hoping for?"

She shook her head. "No. Actually, I wasn't. When I said those words it was with the full intention of marrying you. Becoming your wife in every sense of the word. After what we shared together last night...I was never going to go back to Tony. And, I'm not sure what the hell he was thinking making an announcement like this. Yes, I did need to call him and break up with him. But, since you wouldn't give me a phone, that's hardly my fault."

Something shiny and black hit her lap. And she realized that Adam had flung his phone to her. She shot him a bland stare. "Thank you. But, this might have been helpful last night."

She picked it up, and with shaking fingers dialed Tony's number. He answered on the second ring. "If you have any more questions for me, I will be doing a press conference this evening," he said, his voice much harder and more authoritative than she was accustomed to hearing.

"Tony," she said, "it's me."

"Belle?" He sounded…not exactly relieved. "Why didn't you call me before?"

Adam was glaring at the phone, a murderous glint in his eye. She put the phone away from her ear and turned the speaker on so that Adam could listen in, since she had a feeling he would leap across the car otherwise.

"I didn't have a phone before," she said. "But I do now. I'm nobody's prisoner. Please stop telling the press that Adam is a criminal of some kind. He's not. He's kind, and he's been through so much."

"So, you're saying that you left me of your own free will, and didn't tell myself or your father where you were, and that you presumably cheated on me during that time? After claiming that you were waiting for some kind of magic connection." He made a scoffing sound. "I didn't touch you the entire eight months we dated, and now you're sharing a bed with this monster?"

"He's not a monster, Tony," she insisted. "And I'm sorry. But the only crime committed was mine. I wasn't faithful to you, but I also never intended to come back home to you. Before I ever touched Adam I realized that things needed to be over between us. And the order that

I did things in could have been changed. But the result is the same nonetheless. I'm marrying Adam."

"You're *marrying* him?" Tony's voice was incredulous, filled with disgust. "You refused to allow me to share your bed for eight months—you wasted my time making me believe that someday I could gain access to your body if I paid my dues, and then you spread your legs for him immediately, simply because he could offer you a castle? Because he could give you money? I'm sorry, seeing as you were a virgin, Belle, I had no idea you were such a whore."

Suddenly, the telephone was wrenched from her hand.

"I would watch what I said about my fiancée," Adam said. "Belle is going to be a princess, and her husband possesses no small amount of power. I will not hesitate to bring the full weight of that power down upon you if you persist in speaking of her this way."

"Hey," Tony said. "I'm an American, and I don't have to take anything from you. I have free speech."

"Yes," Adam countered, "and we'll see how well that free speech serves you once no one will do business with you. Because, as you say, the United States is a free country, and with full information people are allowed to make their own decisions. If they decide not to associate with you because of a few well-placed words on my end, well, that is freedom and action, is it not?"

"You bastard," Tony countered. "I'm not going to let you intimidate me. I'm going to keep talking. By the time I'm through with you, everybody will understand that you brainwashed her. She wouldn't even let me get to second base, and now she's banging you? I don't believe it. I'm going to expose you for what you are. Some kind of animal who traps women and then convinces them that the money that you offer is somehow worth the price of getting naked with somebody that messed up."

"Go to hell," Belle hissed, hitting the end button on the phone. She looked up at Adam, her expression fierce. "I'm sorry about that. Unfortunately threats about impacting his business prospects probably won't hurt him. He's a lit major like me. He was willing to accept a lifetime of poverty, and he's much more likely to escape it by tattling to the press."

Adam laughed. "Do you imagine he hurt my feelings? I'm not that easily wounded. However, he might make himself a problem."

"That's why we have to get married," she insisted. "It's the only way to keep everybody from beating down the palace doors."

"Make no mistake—a royal wedding creates its own kind of furor. However, it would be nice to be dealing with that sort of headline rather than an angry mob."

"He had no right," she said.

Adam leaned forward, taking hold of her chin. "He had *every* right. If a man carried you away from me, kept you from me, I would destroy him without mercy, without remorse. As I just proved when your boyfriend said those things about you."

"I think it's safe to say that Tony isn't my boyfriend anymore."

"I suppose he's not." He released his hold on her. "Still, I can't say that I blame him. Though, I am curious. Why did you make him wait? What was it about me that made you decide it was time to be with a man?"

She lifted a shoulder, gazing out the window at the palace. "I told myself all kinds of things. About passion, and about fear. And, maybe some of it's true. I told myself I didn't want to be like my mother. That I wanted to be more selective. That I wanted to make sure I was ready for a stable life, children, marriage, if I was going to get into having sex. But, the bottom line is that I didn't want him. I would have had to put aside a lot of doubt to sleep with him. I would have had to…work to bring myself to the point where I felt I could. With you, I found myself fighting the need to. It was entirely different. It took no restraint to resist him."

His gaze was like molten fire, and she felt her cheeks heating beneath his stare. "I don't care about the scars," she continued. "Or maybe…maybe that isn't even it. Maybe it's just that I find them beautiful. It's difficult to say that, because I know they represent so much suffering. But, all of that is part of you. And I…I'm happy to marry you, Adam," she said, not quite possessing the bravery to tell him that she loved him. Not just yet.

"I'm not certain I can say I'm happy to get married," he said, his voice rough. "But I am more than happy to share my bed with you."

Those words should have diminished the moment, should have made her feel reduced, badly, she supposed. But, instead, she felt them hit her with the full weight of marriage vows. Adam, who had spent the past three years alone, was happy to share his bed with her.

Maybe it wasn't a confession of love, but it was something. It was something she was going to take, hold close and view as a little bit of hope. Hope that someday, the beast might learn to love her in return.

CHAPTER TEN

BELLE'S ANNOUNCEMENT TO the press was hardly the end of the speculation. Headlines exploded across newspapers around the world. Not just tabloids—but reputable news sources—speculating on the nature of his relationship with this unknown woman from California.

Adam didn't particularly care for all the attention. But, ensconced in the palace it was easy to pretend it wasn't happening.

Or, perhaps more honestly, ensconced in Belle's arms.

It was easy to forget the rest of the world when he was in bed with her. If the entire kingdom had burned down beyond the palace walls, he would not have noticed.

Of course, Belle's transition from prisoner to fiancée had meant making some changes. He had begun to sleep in her bedroom every night. Additionally, he had provided her with a phone, a computer, everything she needed to make contact with the outside world. She had chosen to stay with him, and that meant there was no reason to keep her cut off. In fact, doing so would only prove him the monster the world seemed determined to believe that he was.

He took a sip of coffee and looked down at the newspaper sitting on the top of the stack. The one proclaiming his general monstrosity the loudest. He had to wonder if it wasn't true.

In many ways, all that he was accused of doing was true. Except for the part about him forcing himself on her. Except for the fact that she had chosen to stay with him. That she was the one who had jumped out of the car and announced an engagement the two of them had never discussed.

He had been set to free her. And, yes, they had never discussed that in detail, but he was certain she had been aware of the fact. He had said that after their debut he would concoct a story about the breakup. She had to have known.

Discomfort lodged itself in his chest.

And, even more darkly, he wondered if what they were saying was true. Stockholm syndrome. That she was only identifying with the person who had taken her captive because of some complex psychological break she had undergone at his hands.

Regardless, he was unwilling to do much about it.

This, while not in his plans, was ideal.

The media was fascinated by Belle, and the fairy tale that would be constructed out of the two of them finding love after tragedy would be a triumphant one indeed.

In fact, he had a ring in his pocket, and he was prepared to make sure that she was bound to him as publicly and permanently as possible. So, all these ruminations on his end were just that. They were never going to turn into anything more.

He was unwilling to do the right thing, if the right thing meant releasing her.

In her arms he had found something next to salvation, and he was determined to hold on to it.

When she walked through the wide doorway and into the dining room his heart constricted. She was—unquestionably—beautiful. He could see why everyone, from the media to the public, doubted why she had chosen to be with him.

A strange thing, to be in this position. He and his late wife had been considered a perfect match in every way. And now he was with a commoner and she was considered his superior. It didn't wound him, but it did make him wonder. What exactly she saw in him, and why.

There was nothing inside him that was superior to any man. Sure, he owned the palace, and he imagined that gave him some sort of advantage. But he could not imagine Belle being that manipulative. Could not imagine that sort of thing mattering to her.

She was happiest curled up in a corner with a book. And she could do that in a tiny cottage as easily as she could in a castle.

She saw something in him…and for the life of him he himself could not see it.

"Good morning," she said, somewhat subdued.

She was wearing a simple sundress that conformed to her curves in a casual way. The soft fabric skimmed her shape in a delicate fashion. The skirt fell well past her knee, swishing with each step. It shouldn't be erotic. It should be sweet if anything. And yet, he felt himself respond to it with a hunger that shocked him. Every time he saw her he felt as though he were in the midst of a long sexual drought. When, in reality, he had had her only a few hours earlier.

Perhaps it was simply the result of those years of celibacy. But, he doubted it.

"Is everything all right?"

She scrubbed her eyes. "I was up early talking to my father. He's, of course, very concerned about the situation. And, about the part he might have played in it."

"In all honesty, he played quite a large part in it. Without him, we would not be here—is that not so?"

She shot him an exasperated look that he couldn't quite figure out whether or not he deserved. "I suppose you could make that argument, Adam, but I don't want to. I don't want my father to feel as though he is somehow at fault for my engagement."

"Does there have to be a guilty party in an engagement?" He feared that with theirs there might be.

"No," she said, taking a seat a few chairs away from him. She was clearly agitated. And some of it was obviously directed at him.

He had been married to Ianthe for nearly three years, so he was familiar enough with women glaring angrily at him from across the table. Still, with Belle it surprised him. In part because he had committed a vast variety of sins against her, and she had been surprisingly docile about a great many of them but was now looking furiously in his direction only a few hours after he had given her a substantial amount of pleasure. And since then, had had no interaction with her.

One thing had not changed during his seclusion, it appeared. Women were inscrutable.

"Would you like some coffee?"

She sighed. "Do I ever not want coffee?"

"Not in my experience," he said, taking hold of the carafe and pouring her a cup, sliding it in her direction. "But, in my experience you are also not usually so prickly for no reason. Typically, I have to take you captive to earn this level of ire."

"It was just difficult, that's all. Talking to my father and trying to explain the situation."

"And the headlines?"

She looked away. "It's strange. Being the subject of so much scrutiny. I don't like it. And, this is kind of proving your point about the media, and challenging a lot of my perceptions about my upbringing. All in all it's been a little bit of a confronting couple of days."

"I don't suppose people are ever really capable of lingering over the trials of others. They possess too many of their own. Why should the public—struggling financially, working hard to make ends meet—concern themselves with the fate of the rich and famous? With their privacy. There is pain that wealth and status can't erase, but when you are struggling with more, why should you take that on board? Similarly, people in my position are not spared pain. And when it happens, it feels as real as it does for anyone else."

She nodded slowly. "I suppose so. But this is horribly…invasive. And I think that it's cruel. It makes me want to hold a press conference and detail all the things I like about you so that people have no doubt that I'm here of my own free will."

"A press conference is unnecessary," he said, his throat feeling tight all of a sudden. "But I wouldn't mind hearing your list."

She looked away from him, her cheeks turning pink. He liked that—in spite of everything they had done—she still blushed like an innocent. "I'm not sure it would be good for your ego."

"What ego? I'm a terribly scarred man who has lived the past three years in total darkness. It could do with a little bit of boosting. Especially considering the general hideousness of my visage is the topic of conversation around the world."

"Fine," she said, looking down into her coffee. "I would tell them how much I liked the fact that you seem to enjoy it when I talk back to you. That whatever we have between us, you've never made me feel I had to earn it. That for some reason, around you I'm able to be more myself than I've ever been with anyone. Ever. I've spent most of my life trying to behave, trying to be a good person. And being here with you, there was so much freedom to just…not do that." Her blue eyes met his, a strange smile on her lips. "I know that sounds weird. But, I was your prisoner, so I was hardly going to behave in a manner designed to impress you. It was like all of that just faded away. My concerns about being seen as…I don't know."

She blinked rapidly, then cleared her throat and continued. "I thought that passion was the enemy, but it isn't. I had to blame something. When your own mother doesn't want you, you have to find a reason. And then, you have to take that and…make it a lesson, I guess. I had to find a purpose behind what I had been through. The fact that my mother abandoned me, gave me away… and I bound it all up in this idea that giving in to what you wanted could only ever be selfish. But instead of fixing anything I just lost pieces of myself. And with you, I found them. So that's why I'm here. I guess it's not exactly the story the media is looking for, since it doesn't involve a lot of drama and emotional manipulation. But it's the truth."

There was a deep, intense truth in her words that resonated inside him. That he recognized. That reminded him of pieces that had been lost over the years, that he had found only with her. But, he didn't say anything about it.

"And here I thought it had something to do with my magic hands," he said instead, doing his best to smile at her. Smiling. It was a foreign facial expression now. Lost in all that time spent by himself. And yet, he often wanted to do it for her. To show her that she made him feel something.

"They certainly help," she said, a smile tugging at the edge of her own lips. "I would tell them about that too. You know that's what I meant, don't you?" She stood slowly from her chair, making her way toward him. She leaned forward, putting her hands on his thighs. "When I said that Prince Charming was underrated? I would much rather have a man like you. Suave and sophisticated… it doesn't appeal to me. Not in certain rooms, anyway."

He reached up, pressing his palm against her cheek. "You're very bold for a woman who was only recently a virgin."

"I think I always was. But I hid it. And now that I'm not hiding it anymore, I really can't bring myself to hold it back at all."

He moved his hand around to the back of her head, curling his fingers into a fist and holding her fast. "Tell me more."

Her smile turned slightly wicked. "I like the way you hold me. Like this. Like you're never going to let me go."

"A man is tempted to believe that you rather enjoyed being taken prisoner, Belle," he said.

"I suppose I did. I was freer as your prisoner than I ever was before."

His certainty faltered. It was a strange thing to say, and while he would like for it to be true, while he would

like it all to make sense, he was afraid that if it did…
it was perhaps more along the lines of what the newspapers were shrieking about than any kind of organic
emotion.

He released her then, unease stealing over him. But,
before he could let it take over completely, he reached
into his pants pocket and pulled out the small velvet box
that had been in there since he got up this morning. "I
have something for you," he said, placing it on the table.

She made no move toward it; instead, she stared at
him with a confused expression on her face. "What is
it?"

"Don't you want to open it?"

"If it's what I think it is, I think perhaps you should
open it."

He had not intended on proposing to her. They were
already engaged, so he didn't quite see the point to it.
Also, he had done this once before. It seemed strange to
do it again. With a different woman. Not because he was
still so deeply in love with his late wife. He had loved
her; he always would. But, it had been a love based on
practicality, one that had grown to be romantic over time
and with the addition of marriage vows. They'd made a
commitment, and he had been happy to make it.

No, that wasn't what gave him pause. Any sort of feeling that he was repeating the past didn't sit well with
him. Not when he could never revisit that place. Didn't
want to. He was not the same man who had put a ring on
Ianthe's finger all those years ago. And he didn't want to
begin this as he had begun that engagement in the past.

Still, she wanted this. And she asked for little enough
that it would be cruel of him to deny her. He reached out,
pressing his fingers against the top of the box.

"I have done this once before," he said slowly. "At a ball. If you were curious. I was wearing a tuxedo, not jeans as I am now. And, she was in a ball gown, not a simple dress. There were people all around, rather than the solitude. She knew it was coming. And I got down on one knee. She was the expected choice for me, and I was perfectly happy to make that choice. I felt a great deal of affection for her, and that affection grew into love. My life had been charmed up until then. As had hers. I had never been denied anything I had ever wanted, and I had never lost anything."

He tapped his finger on the top of the box, then continued. "In the years since that moment, both my parents have passed away. And then, only a year later I lost my wife, my unborn son. All of my hopes for the future. Whatever I thought it might look like, it was all changed in that instant. And so was I. I'm telling you all this because I want you to know I do not expect our marriage to be what my first marriage was. It cannot be. Because I am not the same man. But when I promise myself to you, I want you to know it is with the full weight of knowledge of what can be gained in this life, and what can be lost." He slid out of his chair, getting down on both of his knees, not one, because that seemed a silly gesture for a man of his age, a man of his cynicism. This seemed fitting for a man about to make a vow. "I want you to be my wife. To stand with me as I move forward into this new phase of my life, this new era for my country. It will not be easy. Speculation will always exist. And I am still me, and we both know there is nothing easy about that. But I will be faithful to you. And I will pledge my loyalty to you. To our children. I swear to protect you."

That promise was like granite, because he had failed

to protect a wife and child once before. But how could he promise less to Belle now? Even knowing just how human he was. How likely he was to fail.

Still, it sat like ice in his stomach, recriminations coming at him from every which way. How dare he make this promise when he had failed so badly before? How dare he put all this on a woman he had forced into his life, into his darkness?

How dare he try to capture this light, when he had nothing to give in return?

Still, in spite of all that, he opened up the box, revealing a large blue stone he had chosen because it reminded him of her eyes. He didn't tell her that. He said nothing as he wordlessly took the piece of jewelry from the box and slid it onto the third finger of her left hand. "Be my wife," he said, a command more than a question, "and I will be your husband."

"Yes," she said simply, her tone steady, never wavering. "And next time I talk to my father, this is what I'll tell him. That when you asked, I said yes. And that I never once wished I had given a different answer."

She might. Someday, inevitably, she would. But he said nothing about that either, and instead rose up onto his feet and claimed her mouth with a kiss. He deserved none of this. But it was being offered to him, and he could do nothing but grab hold of it.

Belle looked at the ring on her left hand for probably the millionth time since Adam had put it on her finger yesterday. It was…it was both surreal and perfectly real all at once. She could feel the weight of it. And not just of the gem, but all the words he had said when he had placed it on her finger.

She felt…well, she supposed she didn't feel the way a lot of women might about the proposal. She was glad that he had brought up his first proposal, his first marriage. She was glad that he was sharing those things with her, because in a great many ways he kept her separate from the deepest parts of himself. From his past.

It was unspoken, but she still wasn't allowed in his part of the palace. Sure, he spent less time there than he once had, opting to spend his nights in her room instead of in his quarters. But she wanted…she longed to share his bed. Not just hers. She didn't know why it felt essential, only that it did.

She rubbed her chest, trying to ease the ache of her heart. She knew why. She knew exactly why; she just didn't want to dwell on it. It had to do with loving him. And when she had told him all the things, all the reasons why she was with him, she had left that out yet again.

She felt like a hypocrite. Waxing rhapsodic about how brave she was with him, how free she was to be herself. When in reality she was hiding one of the biggest parts of herself. When she had first come to his palace she'd had nothing to lose by being herself with him. And, again, when she had imagined their association had a definite end date, it had been easy for her to throw herself into an affair with him, not worrying about the future. About what he might think of her. As long as he had wanted her in the moment, nothing else had mattered.

But, it was more than that now. Now, it was forever. And so, she was back to behaving the way she always had. Hiding little bits and pieces of herself, holding back anything that felt a bit too raw, a bit too close to her heart.

Suddenly, with the blinding moment of clarity—sitting there in the library that Adam had told her she could use as her own—with the sun sinking down behind the mountains, she realized that all this was about protecting herself, not anyone around her.

She wasn't afraid of passion because of what it might make her. No, she was afraid of passion because of how it might hurt when it was over. Because the rejection from her mother had wounded her so deeply, so profoundly, she had never wanted to be subjected to such a thing ever again.

And so, when it had been only passion with Adam, it had been easy to show him. But now it was more than that. Now it was love. It was all of her, and she was so profoundly afraid that he would reject it that she had gone into hiding once more.

She stood up, placing her book down on the side table by the chair, rubbing her eyes, which were growing fatigued in the dim light. Then she looked back at the ring on her hand. "Adam." She whispered his name, brushing her fingertips over the jewel.

Such a strange thing that this man had captured her so completely. Body and soul. That he made her want to risk things she had kept safe and locked tight for years.

She wanted to give him everything. But, that meant being brave. That meant risking herself. Well, all that was what had gotten her here in the first place. That uncharacteristic showing of bravery that had carried her from California to Olympios in the first place.

She took a deep breath and picked up her phone, scrolling until she found Adam's number—the phone was particularly handy here in the palace, where simply wandering around and finding somebody was about

as difficult as searching for someone in a small city—
and sent a text.

I'm in your room.

It was a risk. But it was one she was willing to take.
She wanted to join all the pieces of herself together, the
little fragments she had kept separate, kept buried in
order to best protect herself. And to do that, she was
going to have to force Adam to do the same. They could
no longer compartmentalize their existence. There could
be no lines, no walls and no wings of palaces between
them.

She took a deep breath and walked out of the library,
heading toward that forbidden, protected part of the palace.

This would go one of two ways. Either Adam would
send her back to her room. Or, he would open up those
forbidden, protected places inside of himself.

She truly hoped it was the latter. But she had no confidence in that.

All she had was hope. So right now, it would have
to be enough.

I'm in your room.

When the text had appeared on Adam's phone, he had
been in his office seeing to some administrative work.
He had not expected to hear from Belle, since she had
informed him she was reading a book, and he knew
that meant she wouldn't be ready to go to bed for hours.

But the timing of the text was less surprising than the
contents. His room. She never went to his room, and he

never invited her. She had not gone into that wing of the palace since she had discovered the photograph of him and Ianthe. That had been fine with him. In her room, there was no baggage, the ghosts of the past didn't loom quite so large overhead and the darkness didn't feel quite so impenetrable.

But for some reason, she had now crossed that invisible line, and it was clear she expected him to come and drag her back over it.

He gritted his teeth, standing from his desk and striding from his office. He moved down the hall quickly, his footsteps echoing in the empty corridors. His heart was thundering, hard, restless adrenaline pumping through his veins. Need, anger and a simple, driving force to see her standing there pushed him on. He had no idea what he was feeling because he felt everything. It made it impossible to zero in on one thing. To make sense of any of it.

He made his way down to the end of the hall, passing the sitting area he had found her in last time, and going straight for his bedchamber. One thing had become abundantly clear on his journey from his office. He needed her. He couldn't wait to have her. Even if it would be trespassing on sacred ground to do so, or, perhaps most especially because it would be. He felt sick. With longing, with anger, with a desire that had captured him and taken him over completely. Until he couldn't breathe, couldn't think.

He pressed his palms against the double doors and pushed them open.

Belle gasped, then turned to face him, her eyes wide, her expression that of a deer caught in the headlights of a car.

She was standing in front of his bed. A bed he had shared with his wife. This room that he had shared with his wife. It was still so heavy with memory, with the past. With guilt.

The fact he had allowed himself to sleep elsewhere over the past week had been something of a luxury. Normally, he forced himself to stay here. To linger in it. For his sins, it was a small price to pay.

"What are you doing here?" he asked, his voice deceptively soft.

"I...I thought it was time," she said simply. "Don't you?"

He began to pace the length of the room. "It will never be time. There is never a time for this."

"You have to let me in sometime," she said, and he knew she didn't mean just into the room. "Otherwise, I think our marriage is going to be a lonely one."

"This was our room," he said.

She nodded slowly, then swallowed hard, visibly. "I know. And I'm not...I know...I don't want to replace her. Like you said, this isn't the same. We are not the same, and I understand that. I respect it. Everything you've lost matters to me. I know you might not believe this, and I don't know if you want to hear it, or if it even helps. But in a way I care for her too, even though I didn't know her. Because you did. Because you do. Because losing her hurt you, because you loved her, and the destruction of that has made you the man you are."

She had no idea. She didn't understand. And he didn't want to help her. Because he simply couldn't... he couldn't share it. And more than that, he couldn't stand changing the way she looked at him.

"I just don't want to be locked out," she said. "I don't

want there to be vast spaces closed off to me because of the pain in them. You can share it with me. I will never tell you not to feel it."

He knew that she wasn't just talking about rooms in a castle. "Why would you do that? It doesn't make any sense. Why would you want to carry any of this?" He could feel the full weight of his grief just then, his guilt, oppressive, dark and destructive, and he didn't want her to bear any of that. He couldn't stand it if he knew she had been touched by this, tainted by it.

"The usual reasons," she said, her voice small. "I'm only asking you to do this, because I'm going to do it too. Because I'm going to open myself up to you, and I'm going to stop protecting myself. Protecting my pain. You don't have to tell me the same thing. You don't have to feel the same… I just want you. Whatever that may be. However much it may be. And I want that because I love you."

Those words seemed to reverberate in the relative silence of the room. Or maybe they weren't echoing in the room, but inside of him. Loud and endless, and painful.

And he had no response to them. So he did nothing at all, nothing but stand there looking at her as those words sank down inside him, like rain on dry, cracked earth. He had nothing to give back to her, but he let this wash over him, let it fill him, flood him.

She approached him slowly, her hand outstretched. She pressed her palm lightly against his chest, her fingertips skimming over his skin, over his nipples, down his stomach. He took a sharp breath, arousal joining in with that insatiable thing that had absorbed her offer of love for all it was worth.

He responded to her, to her words, to her touch,

with every part of himself. His heart was thundering so hard he thought it might burst through his chest, his lungs burning, as though they were too full of air, and yet he could feel himself drowning here above water. And his body…he was so hard he hurt. With his need to press himself against her, join himself to her, in the tight, wet heat of her body. Where everything else was blocked out, all the pain, all the recriminations of the past. When he was inside Belle there was nothing else. He was lost in her, consumed by her, and he needed that badly.

Right now he needed it more than air, and he did not possess the restraint to turn away from that need. She moved closer to him, her hand pressed firmly against his stomach as she leaned in and kissed him, gently at first. Even though it took all the control he possessed he allowed her to guide the kiss, allowed her to dictate how hard and soft it was, allowed her to be the one to instigate invasion.

When her tongue slid along the seam of his mouth he felt a growl resonating inside his chest. He could not be civilized with her, and she had never professed to want it. So, he saw no point in pretending he was anything other than what he was.

That was when his control snapped.

He wrapped his arm around her waist, crushing her to him. He was so very aware of the fact that she was small, delicate and breakable, and that he was testing her limits. But he needed to. He needed to test her against him, against this despair that ravaged him, against the darkness that was always pressing in. Especially here. Never more than here.

Ghosts and regret. Shame and doubt. They loomed

large, they loomed dark, oppressive. They were omni-present, but this was where they lived.

And with Belle's hands on his body, with her lips fused to his, he could feel light inside of him. Could feel a fire burning at the center of his chest, heat and need that blotted out those demons, that darkness, that cold.

It was a small miracle, happening inside him, all around him. She was a miracle.

And she loved him.

A surge of violent emotion assaulted him and he kissed her harder, walking her back—not to the bed—but to the wall. He flattened his palms against it, on ei-ther side of her, his body flush with hers, the hard length of his arousal cradled between the softness of her thighs.

He reached down, grabbed the neckline of that beau-tiful dress she was wearing and tugged hard. A sharp tearing sound filled the room as the fabric fell away, exposing her breasts. He gazed at her bare skin appre-ciatively. Hungrily.

"Had I known you were sitting in the library naked beneath your dress I could never have left you alone," he said, each word thick with desire.

"Had I known that," she said, reaching up and touch-ing his face, "I would have made sure to announce it."

He grabbed hold of her wrist, drawing her hand up above her head, pinning it to the wall. Then he reached for her other hand, repeating the same motion, holding her fast with an iron grip.

She arched against him, her breasts brushing against his chest, that soft flesh, the tightened buds of her nip-ples a sensual assault he had no desire to escape.

With his free hand he reached down, grabbing what remained of her dress and tearing it away. It left her in nothing more than a pair of silk panties that rode low on her hips.

He slipped his fingertip beneath the waistband. Teasing her. Teasing himself. "Did a member of my staff choose these for you?"

"Yes," she said, the word trembling, as her whole body trembled when he continued to slide his finger back and forth, not quite grazing her intimate flesh.

"Somebody deserves an increase in pay. I want to see more." Loosening his hold on her, he moved one hand to her hip and turned her so that she was facing away from him. Then he immediately returned his hold to her wrists, keeping her captive, but this time revealing the elegant line of her spine to his appreciative gaze.

She was bent slightly at the waist, her back arched, her rear thrust out slightly. He curved his hand around to her stomach, sliding it down slowly, then around to her hip until he was cupping her ass.

Her skin was bare, fully revealed by the thong cut of the underwear she had on.

"Exactly what I had hoped for," he said, leaning in slightly, adjusting his grip on her wrists and hip so that he was holding her fast. He arched himself forward, pressing his hardened length to the center of her supple flesh.

She gasped, then made a low, keening sound as he rocked forward harder still, increasing the pressure each time. He slid his hand forward, this time delving completely beneath the silken fabric of her panties to where she was wet with her desire for him.

He pressed the heel of his palm against that sensitized bundle of nerves at the apex of her thighs, then slowly rocked back toward the entrance of her body, sliding his finger slowly into her slick folds, teasing her with the promise of penetration.

She wiggled against him, shuddering out his name, a prayer, a curse. He would take it as both, and happily.

They stayed like that for a while, him pleasuring her with his hand, keeping her pinned against the wall and his body. She rocked her hips in time with his rhythm, arching into his arousal each time she did.

It was hell. And it was heaven. He needed to end it, needed to bury himself inside her, but also, something in him wanted to prolong it for as long as possible. To stay here like this, suspended in limbo, where neither of them was satisfied, where neither of them could ever get enough.

Where the fire burned bright and hot, and he felt like he was standing in the light after so many years in utter darkness.

"Adam," she said, the word ragged. "Adam…please."

He stilled his movements, cupping her sex, keeping the pressure firm. "Please what?"

"I need you. I need you inside me."

A jolt of desire washed through him, and he found himself completely powerless against that simple request. That simple expression of need. He had her pinned against a wall, had her caught between that uncompromising place and his body, rock hard with need for her, and yet, he was the one who had no power. He was the one who felt weak enough to drop to his knees in the face of this blinding need.

With a shaking hand he worked his belt free, undid the closure on his slacks and pushed his pants and underwear midway down his hips. Then he hooked his finger around that insubstantial strip of fabric at the back of her panties and swept it aside.

He groaned at the view before him. The rounded curve of her ass, that sweet, tantalizing view of her feminine flesh between her partly spread thighs.

He could not resist her. He didn't want to. He wanted nothing more than to be buried in her.

He positioned himself at her slick entrance, sliding in just half an inch, testing her readiness, allowing her desire to bathe the head of his arousal.

He swore, grinding his teeth so tightly together he thought for sure he might reduce them to dust.

He grabbed on to her hip again, leaning in with his other hand, pressing her wrists more firmly against the wall, he flexed his hips, drawing her rear back farther as he slid deeper inside her. She gasped, a shiver running down her spine, through her body, and he felt it echoing inside him.

She lowered her head for a moment, and then looked back at him, those blue eyes colliding with his, the electric shot from that unexpected eye contact reaching all the way down to where they were joined, causing him to surge up even more deeply inside her.

He flexed his hips and she groaned; then he withdrew, slamming back into her. He moved his hand around to the front of her body, stimulating her sex with his fingertips as he established a steady rhythm designed to drive them both insane.

She whimpered his name, over and over again, driving him closer, faster than he wanted. He wanted it to go on forever. And like this, it wasn't going to.

He freed her wrists, taking hold of both hips and

driving himself hard into her one last time before he withdrew.

"What?" she asked, her tone dazed.

"Trust me," he returned, his voice a stranger's even to his own ears.

He turned her so that she was facing him, claimed her mouth in a deep, hard kiss before taking her into his arms and carrying her to the bed. He set her on the edge of the plush mattress. "Lay back," he commanded.

She complied, her legs dangling over the edge, her head tossed back, her breasts thrust high. She was like a beautiful virgin sacrifice being given to the monster in the manor. And yet, even realizing that, believing it, he would not stop himself.

He was the monster, after all. Past the point of re-demption. But if he had a hope of coming close, it would be inside her.

He gripped her thighs, drawing her legs up over his hips, urging her to wrap them around his body. She com-plied. Then he thrust deep inside her again. She gasped, throwing one arm over her face as he thrust down into her from where he stood at the edge of the bed.

"Adam," she whimpered. "Adam, I need—"

"This," he finished, punctuating the word with a hard thrust. "You need me inside you."

She nodded, reaching up and taking hold of his fore-arm, drawing her fingertips down to his wrist before moving his hand to her lips. Then she darted her tongue out, sliding along the edge of his finger before sucking it deeply into her mouth. He jerked inside her, the sur-prising contact nearly pushing him over the edge then and there.

She met his gaze, drawing his hand even closer to her lips, taking a second finger inside and sucking hard.

He jerked his hand back, pressing his palms firmly into the mattress as he gave himself up to the riot of need roaring through him.

He was not considerate. He did not give her pleasure the full weight it deserved. But he could not think of anything else. The demons that always hovered at the edges of this room were tearing at his skin, trying to get past the defenses that had been built up between himself and Belle. With each flex of his hips, every time he drove himself home into the tight heat of her body, he was able to prolong the inevitable. Was able to hold on to that little spark of light she had planted inside his chest.

He held her hard—too hard—and he knew that he was going to leave bruises behind on her beautiful hips, evidence of how his blunt fingertips had dug into her flesh. He knew that he would leave marks all over her, not just on her skin, but inside her, as well.

He would break her. As he had broken everything.

She loves you, a mocking voice said. *What have you ever done to have a woman love you? And yet, you have earned the love of two different women. And you failed the first one so badly.*

He pushed the thought away, enraged that it had managed to penetrate this moment, that it had managed to get beneath his defenses.

He wrapped his arm around her waist, drawing it down to her lower back, lifting her off the mattress slightly as he moved them both back so that they were fully on the bed. He thrust in, long and slow, pinning them both to the soft surface, pressing her completely beneath his weight. Reveling in the feel of being flush against her soft, perfect form.

He alternated between quick, shallow pulses of his hips and long, slow glides that took him all the way to the hilt.

She flexed beneath him, meeting him thrust for thrust, her internal muscles beginning to pulse around his length.

She tossed her head from side to side, reaching out and grabbing his shoulders, her fingernails biting into his skin. He hoped that she would leave scars. He hoped that she would make him bleed. He hoped that he would never recover from this. From her. That as much as he would leave an imprint on her body, she would be one on his.

Of all the scars that he bore, he would be proud to bear hers.

It would be the one beautiful mark on his body.

The others were simply signs of failure. Of selfishness. Of the rash behavior of a young husband who knew about nothing but pleasing himself. Who had thought his wife's concerns were silly, and who had prized the comfort of his reputation and of his political alliances more than her comfort.

He had paid. They had all paid. All because of him.

He deserved to look as he did. He deserved all that and more.

What he did not deserve was for Belle to be moving beneath him so sweetly, for her to say his name as she did. For her to love him, when he was more a beast than she would ever know.

But he would take it. Because he did not possess the strength to turn it away, to deny her, to deny himself.

He slammed his hips down hard, his pelvis making contact with that place where she was most needy for him. And he felt the explosion detonate inside her. Her body pulsing around him as she found her release. She lifted her head, sinking her teeth into his shoulder as her orgasm overtook her. And it was that, that primal active possessiveness, that pushed him over the edge too.

On a growl, he gave himself up, spilling himself deep inside her beautiful body, staking his claim in a way he had absolutely no right to.

He deserved nothing, least of all this. But he did not possess the strength to do anything but give himself up to it. To her.

Being marked by her would be the only thing that gave him pleasure, solace, once she was gone.

And he realized, as the remnants of his orgasm washed over him, that he would have to let her go.

The headline didn't matter. Not in comparison with her happiness.

He could not allow her to stay here. He could not allow this woman to stay in this dark, oppressed palace with all these demons simply to gratify himself. He could not allow her to bind herself to him without knowing what he was. And more than anything, he could not allow her to love him. Not him.

Because whether or not he loved her in return didn't matter. Eventually, he would break her. As he broke all things in his life.

The only solution was to allow himself to sink deeper into his own brokenness. Only then would she be safe from him. Only then would he not be a danger to anyone.

He rolled off her, breathing hard, lying on his back

and staring up at the ceiling. A ceiling he'd stared at countless nights, replaying his feelings over and over again. Replaying that moment he had reached out to touch Ianthe to find her skin ice cold, to find her already gone before help ever arrived at the accident scene.

Compulsively, he reached out, brushed his fingertips over Belle's cheek. She was living. She was warm, and she was bright.

And unless he let her go, she would not stay that way. Because he knew exactly how this ended. With darkness. With cold.

"You have to leave."

Belle was still catching her breath, trying to orient herself after the force of the climax that had just ripped through her body, leaving her weak and breathless. And then Adam said she had to leave.

"Are we going to sleep in my room?" She had thought for a moment that they had made progress, that he had finally let her in, but, now he wanted to get out of the bedroom. She supposed there were steps to take, and she couldn't be too angry if they were small.

"No," he said, his voice hard. "Not just out of my bedroom. You need to go back to California. You should go back to Tony."

"What are you talking about?" Panic scurried through her like a team of nervous field mice. "I don't want to go. We are engaged. You just gave me a ring."

"You can keep the ring. I don't care. Sell it, if your father needs more money for his treatment."

"I…I don't understand. We made love. We—"

"It was a mistake. All of it. I was being selfish. I was allowing you to sacrifice yourself in order to save my reputation, but I do not require that, Belle. And you should not subject yourself to it."

"I chose it," she protested, "because I love you."

He turned away as though she had slapped him. "You do not love me. Read a headline or two about our relationship, Belle. You have Stockholm syndrome. You have begun to identify with your captor because I cut you off from the outside world so effectively."

"You insulting bastard. How dare you tell me what I feel and don't feel like some amateur pop psychologist? I know my own mind. And I know what I feel."

"Or, you think you do," he bit out.

Rage fired through her. "So, you're going to gaslight me? Tell me how it's actually been so that you can try and deny my feelings?"

"You don't know what you feel."

"Why not? Because I'm a woman, and I'm simply too softheaded to understand my own heart?"

"No," he said, "because you don't know the man that you chose to take to bed. I have never told you the whole story about that night my wife died. I have never let you know why it is I think I'm a monster. You think it's because of these scars?" He sat up, his muscles rippling with the motion. "I don't give a damn about my scars. About the loss of my pretty-boy face. What the hell does any of that matter? I was a monster long before that accident, and all that did was reveal who I actually am. Selfish. Hideous. At least now my face serves as a warning."

"Stop it. Unless you're actually going to back that up with facts I don't want to hear any of it. It's all drama. It's all you running away from something that feels too real for you to handle. You've been hiding for so many years that you've forgotten how to stand in the light."

"No, I know exactly how to stand in the light. In *your* light. And I would steal it, Belle—trust me. Use it all up until you were just as dark as I am."

"Maybe *you* should trust *me*. Maybe you should trust that I'm strong enough to know what I want, to know that I can handle this."

"Do you want to know what kind of husband I am?" He shook his head. "I am selfish. I prized my own reputation, my own happiness above all else. My wife was very pregnant when she died. And she didn't want to go to the gala that evening. No, she wanted to stay home and put her feet up. But I told her in no uncertain terms that it was not to be done. It was important that I be seen there, you see. That I make an appearance, that we make an appearance, because as a couple we were quite the darling in the media. I needed her to come there and look radiant. To look like the happy princess carrying the future of the nation. I wanted to present a specific moment to the media. We were beloved by some of the press, but hounded the rest. Popularity always has two sides. And there were rumors about her, about us, I wanted to dispel. And so, even though she wanted to stay home in bed, I pressed the issue."

"Adam…" She tried to take a breath but she felt oppressed by the pain that was coming off him in waves. It made it difficult to stay sitting up, much less speak. "You can't blame yourself for that. It isn't as though you could have ever known there was going to be an accident. It isn't as though you could have anticipated—"

"It doesn't matter. Of course I couldn't have. I cannot predict the future. And of course I blame the photographer who just *had* to get the photo. Who was determined to try and shove a camera in my poor wife's face, to make more snide comments about her past, about the fact that she was a woman with a certain reputation before she married me, and that I couldn't be certain the child was mine." His expression was fierce. "Of course the child was mine. I knew her. I knew who she was, and that she was faithful to me. But the media was intent on making her into some kind of caricature. Something she was not. I don't blame myself for that. But, I cannot forgive myself for insisting on trotting her out in those circumstances. For not listening to her when she said she was too tired. For not honoring her as I should have done. I loved going out. Being seen. Being part of that glittering world. Why do you think I removed myself from it so effectively after her death?"

She felt as though she had been stabbed in the chest, as though she might begin bleeding out all over the brocade bedspread. Of course, of course he had kept himself locked away. Because he blamed the fact that he liked to go out, the fact that he enjoyed his status. The fact that he had enjoyed that aspect of royal life, and that it had betrayed him. Of course he had punished himself like this. Keeping himself away from people, away from women, away from even his subjects—whom she imagined he loved. He had cut himself off from everything. Everything but this pain. And he had fashioned for himself in this corner of the castle a mausoleum, not to his wife and child, but to his failure.

A monument to his grief and his guilt. She couldn't blame him. Not really. After all, her entire life was a monument to the pain that she felt over her mother's rejection. Her fear of being rejected again. But she didn't blame herself, not really. She never had. Yes, it had made her afraid, but she had always known that the culprit was her mother. That there had been nothing a four-year-old girl could do to make her mother love her more.

But Adam was awash in regret. In what might have been. Adam didn't just have grief, hadn't only experienced loss; he had taken that loss into himself entirely. And he was determined to punish himself forever for it. He was punishing himself now.

He would punish them both, so that he could live in his grief and guilt forever. She thought back to what he had said when they had landed in Santa Milagro. About how part of him wanted to hold that pain, that darkness to his chest forever, to make it matter, to make it mean something.

But it was more than that. He was consigning himself to eternal punishment, eternal damnation. He had played the part of judge, jury and executioner. She wished so much that she could take it all away.

But she couldn't. She knew that without a doubt, sitting there across from him, naked body and soul, that she couldn't take it from him if he didn't want to release it. And living like this…with all these cracks between them, all of these walls, would be the death of her eventually. Oh, not literally. Because whatever the world said about him, whatever he thought about himself, he was not that brand of monster. But emotionally… after all these years of living with so much of herself repressed, she couldn't imagine submitting herself to such a thing again.

To live with a man who was determined to reject the love that she had dug so deep inside of herself to offer him.

But she didn't want to leave him. Part of her wanted to stay forever, regardless of the fact that it would end in her destruction, because at least, if she went down, it would be in a blaze of glory. At least, it would be experiencing the kind of passion she had only ever dreamed of before. The kind of passion she truly hadn't imagined actually existed.

She reached out and put her hand on his shoulder. "I love you," she said again. "And nothing that you can say is going to change that. Nothing that you tell me is going to change that. You think that you're going to uncover some hidden darkness inside of yourself that's going to make me rethink everything?" Her heart felt like it was being squeezed in a vice. "Adam, I have lived my whole life shoving my feelings down, shoving down my desires. I thought I was happy. I thought that the sort of easy moving through life like that was the answer. The answer to happiness, the answer to stability. But it isn't all about *easy*. It isn't all about *happy*. I would rather struggle here with you, deal with this pain, this deep, dark emotion that you feel, fight with you, scream at you, make passionate love with you, than go back home to my safety net. I don't want easy, not anymore. I want real. I want to feel real. I want to *be* real. And I did with you. I do. This is what I want. This crazy, messy thing that we have here. Don't try to protect me from it, because it's the best thing that's ever happened to me. You're the best thing that's ever happened to me."

He shook his head slowly. "I don't want you here. I thought that perhaps it was the answer. I thought that perhaps if I took you to bed here, I could start over, that I could forget. But it isn't only that I can't. I don't want to."

Those words hit their target, lanced her like a sword. She also knew that they weren't right, that they weren't real, that he was protecting himself with them. She could see it, could see it in the despairing look in those dark eyes. He didn't want this, but he was not holding her prisoner; he never had been. He was holding himself captive. And he seemed determined to never allow himself to be released.

She got off the bed, moving to the center of the room, standing there, naked and completely unashamed. "You're going to have to tell me again. If you want me to go, Adam, I'm not going to force myself on you, but you have to look at me and tell me that you want me gone. What happened to you—what happened to your wife and your son—was a tragedy, and you had no control over it. You've lied to yourself, you've taken that guilt onto yourself, and in a lot of ways I understand why. Because you're afraid of being hurt again."

"No," he said, his voice rough. "I'm not afraid of being hurt again. I'm afraid of the damage I can do when I forget who I am and what I am. When I allow myself to fully buy into all that is supposedly good and elevated about me. When I treat myself as though I truly am royal, as though I deserve some sort of greater consideration than those around me. I know how much destruction it can bring. And I will not become that again."

"You're afraid of being hurt again," she persisted, her voice trembling now. "And I don't blame you. My mother isn't dead. She simply rejected me, and I live with that same fear. So I'm standing in front of you now risking that, because I feel like when it comes to love you should do nothing less but risk your whole self, your whole heart. And, I also believe that love is honest. It doesn't just tell you what you want to hear. So, I'm going to tell you the truth. You didn't make the choice to lose her. You would never have chosen to lose your son. But you're choosing to lose me, to lose this, to lose what we could have. Adam, I can never replace her. And maybe…maybe you'll never love me the way you loved her. I don't need that. I just need the best you can give now. I just need you to try. And I need you to choose me. To choose us. Choose life instead of death. You didn't have that choice before. It was an accident. You had no control. But you do now, and you're choosing to kill us. Don't."

She was ready to beg. To get down on her knees. She would; she would do it gladly. Anything to keep him, to keep this. She had no pride where he was concerned, where this was concerned. What good would pride do her?

She had been a child when her mother had sent her away. Packed up her frilly little room that had been more a testament to her mother wanting to appear like a good parent than it had ever been about Belle's taste.

And then she had put her in a town car, bound for her father's house, and told Belle she wouldn't be coming back.

It had broken her. Shattered her world. She had screamed and screamed, determined to make her mother hear her pain, her fear. But her mother had turned away, and so Belle had wept and shouted, all alone in the car except for the poor driver, who was simply following orders. A creature of woe and utter despair.

But she wouldn't dissolve. Not now. Not with him.

And she would be damned if she let Adam do this, if she let him retreat back into the darkness without the full force of her light shining on him. She wasn't afraid to be loud. Not now. She wasn't afraid to love, wasn't afraid to rip her chest open and spill the contents before him.

Because without him, there was no heart to protect.

He was her heart. He was everything. And she was determined not to lose him. If she did, it wouldn't be for a lack of fighting. Of that she was certain.

"Perhaps you're right," he said, his voice as blank as his expression. He leaned over and flicked on a lamp, the harsh sideways light casting his scars into even sharper relief, the peaks and valleys of his ruined skin looking even more exaggerated now. As though all the darkness, the ugliness, the pain from the inside him was bleeding up through his flesh. "Perhaps I am choosing this. To let you go. But, that is my prerogative. Don't you understand? This is what I want. This is what I am. I am nothing more, and I can give you nothing more. We had fun these past weeks, or at least, something close to what a man such as myself can call fun. I have certainly enjoyed the luxury of escaping into your beautiful body, but it is not love. I've had love," he said, the words choked. "I had love and it's dead. This is not that. And if it is what you want, you should go. It is a kindness that I'm sending you away, Belle, rather than lying to you and telling you what you want to hear. I can keep you here, and I can keep your body for my use, but it is not something that would make you happy. So, if I were you I would retreat gracefully, and with the understanding that I am actually doing you a great service by sending you away."

His words cut deep into her, stabbing into her lungs, making it so she couldn't breathe. And yet, somewhere in the back of her mind, she knew it wasn't the truth. Because of what he said about doing her a kindness. Because, if he were even half as cruel as he was pretending to be now, he would not extend her that kindness. If it was all about sex, all about her body, then he would keep her. Because it would cost him nothing to live. The only reason he was lying was so she would leave.

It hurt. It wounded her down deep. To know he felt that what they shared wasn't love. That it was lesser than what he'd had before, because it was bigger, greater and brighter than anything she had ever had in her life. Than anything she had possibly imagined.

"Do you really want me to go?"

He nodded slowly. "It would be best."

"So you're going to stay here and lick your wounds. And open them over and over again, never letting yourself heal because you're comfortable with this pain and afraid of experiencing any new pain?"

He moved off the bed, so fast that she didn't have any time to react. She backed up against the wall, her movements wild. Adam's hand came up, resting lightly on her throat. "It is not so I don't get hurt again. I do not possess the ability to be wounded any further than I already have been. But if you don't leave, you are destined to be hurt by me. The door is open now, Belle, and it may not be in the future. If I were you I would run. Far and fast. Go back to Tony. Go back to the beach. Go back to your father. He is sick, after all, and perhaps it would be best if you spent what could be his remaining days with him."

His words hit hard, but then, they had been designed to. To wound, to inflict the maximum amount of damage.

And because he knew her so well, better than anyone ever had, they hit their mark unerringly.

She nodded slowly, and he lowered his hand, taking a step back, his expression blank.

"Then I'll go."

She didn't want to. And each step she took matched

the rhythm of her heartbeat, a heartbeat that wounded her with each and every pulse. That cut her deep as though the entire organ had transformed into shattered glass.

She didn't want to go. She wanted to stay. She wanted to turn herself around and fling herself at his feet and beg him to allow her to stay. Beg him to allow her to accept the crumbs of his affection.

But she didn't. Not for her pride, because truly, pride had no place in this. She didn't because she knew that if Adam was ever going to realize he could be hurt, if he was ever going to realize that what they had was real, that something in him had changed in the weeks they'd been together...she had to. She had to go in order for him to learn. If there was any chance he might grieve her loss, she had to allow him the opportunity to do so.

But it cost her. Each footstep feeling like a lead weight, each breath like a knife down her throat.

By the time she reached the edge of the corridor, she ran back to her room, not caring if any of the staff members were around to see her distress. When she reached her bedchamber she looked all around, at all the things in the room that had become part of this life that was only borrowed. None of it had ever been hers. Not the clothes, not the sumptuous bed, not the dark, scarred prince that had changed her forever.

She should pack. She should call for a ride to the airport. She should call Athena to bring her a pot of tea and tell her everything would be okay.

She did none of those things. Instead, she took a deep breath, flung herself down face-first onto the bed and wept as though her heart were breaking.

Because it was.

* * *

"She's gone. I do hope you're happy."

Adam rolled over in bed, squinting against the light that was flooding his room. He thought for certain he was hallucinating, because it seemed as though Fos was standing in the center of the room, glaring at him with disapproval.

"Who is?"

"Belle," the other man returned. "But then, I imagine that was your goal."

His adviser never came into this part of the palace. All members of staff were forbidden. It was private. It was where Adam kept his pain, and until last night he had never willingly allowed anyone to step inside of it.

For all the good it had done. So, she had left. It was what he had wanted after all. He should feel more triumphant. Instead, he felt nothing but a lead weight in his chest.

"Yes," Adam returned. "I did send her away. It was time."

"She cared for you."

"And if that doesn't show how precarious her sanity is, nothing will."

"Then I suppose mine is, as well," Fos said. "Because for some misguided reason I care about you too. And I care about whether or not you sink beneath the weight of your grief. You had a chance with her. You had a chance to fix some of what was broken. I cannot understand why you would not cling to that for all you're worth. Very few people would have come in here and dedicated themselves to understanding you the way that she did."

"A great many women would love to marry me. I don't have to be handsome. I don't have to be charming.

I am royalty, and I can make whatever woman weds me a princess. It's hardly a great feat on my part."

"But you don't need another princess. You need somebody who can see past all that is broken in you. And on a good day, I can barely do that, and I have known you since you were a boy. What you had with Belle…it was the only thing I can see that would ever cast out this darkness. And if you would just stop carrying around so much guilt, you might be able to make room in your arms for love."

Adam laughed, a low, bitter sound. "Love. What has love ever done for me? Absolutely nothing. Nothing but destroy me. And what did I ever give to the woman I loved besides a premature death?"

"Death happens," Fos said. "Life isn't fair. But you are a prince—you are not God. You didn't orchestrate the accident that night. And if you were selfish, then you are no less than human. We are all selfish from time to time. My wife died thirty years ago, and I still remember everything that I did wrong. I still regret so many things, things I would do differently now, that as a young man I did not possess the capacity to do. But that is life. We cannot hang on to those feelings forever, or how else will we live through the day? You're only a monster because you've decided to be."

He turned to go. "You're finished, I guess?" Adam asked.

Fos sighed heavily. "I might have to be."

On that ambiguous note his adviser left him sitting there in bed as a strange ache began to grow and spread in his chest.

It hurt. It hurt so much, reaching across the bed and

finding nothing there. Almost as much as reaching out and feeling his late wife's cold skin.

Suddenly, rage and pain roared through him like a beast and he reached out, grabbing hold of some trinket or other that was on his bedside table. He hurled it across the room. It did nothing to ease the feelings rioting inside him.

He threw his covers off, not caring that he was naked, and stalked down the hall, into the sitting room that often bore the brunt of his rage.

Too much furniture was already destroyed. Already turned over onto its side. He reached up, grabbed a painting of his father from the wall and flung it across the room, feeling somewhat more satisfied when the frame broke, when the canvas bowed. The old man had died and left him too. Why should he leave his painting there to mock him? Like every other thing he had lost. It was too much. It was too much to be expected to endure.

He walked by a chair and kicked it onto its side, stomping heavily on the leg, breaking it in two. So much rage inside him. So much anger. And no one to blame. Nothing to rage at. Ianthe was dead. She was dead, and she was never coming back. His son was gone before he ever had a chance to draw breath. And none of it was fair.

They had both been gone before Adam had a chance to save them. There had never been a chance. The only chance would have been if he simply hadn't gone, but he had, and for all that he was he couldn't go back and remake that decision.

They were his future, they were his heart, and they were gone.

But for some reason, as he thought those words, it was

Belle's face that swam before his mind's eye. He pressed his hand against his chest, trying to ease the ache there.

He walked across the room, not caring as he stepped on broken glass, dried flower petals and pieces of furniture. And then he reached the photograph. The one with his wife smiling so radiantly, and with him…with a face he no longer recognized, a light he no longer recognized.

His future and his heart. Three years ago that had been her. It had been her and the child she carried.

But that future, that heart, was for a different man.

Now when he thought of wanting something, when he thought of loving something…it was Belle.

Somehow, she loved the scarred, dark man he had become. She had stood there offering him those things he had thought lost to him forever, and he hadn't even realized it. She was right. She had been right as she had stood there, shouting him down as though she had nothing in the world to fear. He was a coward. A coward who used his grief as a shield, used it to protect himself from ever caring again.

Yes, he had craved those snatches of light that she had given him, but mostly, he had been content to hide in the darkness where nothing could find him. Where nothing could reach him.

And if he stayed here in the darkness, it would certainly offer its own kind of protection. There would be no surprises. Grief, old memories and pain would be a constant. He would be the master of that pain, though. And it would never have the opportunity to master him. It would never sneak up from the depths and shock him, destroy him the way that it once had.

If he stayed here like this, if he stayed alone, he knew exactly how his days would be spent. He knew exactly what he would have stretching out before him. A future full of nothing, a blank endless slate destined never to be filled.

But if he claimed Belle, if he accepted her love, if he admitted to himself that he might love her in return, if he wanted again, hoped again, needed again, then God only knew what the result might be.

Perhaps she would tire of him. Perhaps he would destroy her eventually. Perhaps death might take her, as it had been so cruel to him before. If he cared, if he wanted, if he *needed*, then the future was a bright, riotous unknown filled with hidden patches of darkness and uncertainty.

And if he stayed here—if he stayed like this—this room full of broken memories and dead flowers would be all he ever had.

He bent down, sweeping his fingertips over those dried-out rose petals. How long had they been there?

Years. They had died along with everything else. He hadn't brought any new life into this place since. He picked one up, rubbed it between his thumb and forefinger, grounded into dust. Dust. Death. That was the only thing he had here. Regret, and guilt, and memory.

And she was right. He blamed himself because at least then there was something to be angry at. Because at least then he could make a sick kind of sense of it. And more than that, it allowed him to stay here. To justify never moving forward. To justify this selfish, closed-off existence that was a monument to his wife and son in a way that served no one. Not his country, not their memory and most certainly not his heart.

Fos had spoken of magic spells last week in regard to Belle. And right now Adam felt there might be some truth in their existence. Because standing here, he felt as though he were bound in chains. Chains that were as real as any that could be seen by human eyes. Fos had told him that Belle was the one with the key. The one that possessed the ability to break the bonds. But, Adam had a feeling that wasn't entirely true.

Belle was the reason. But he was the one who would have to do it.

There would be no certainty. No certainty that she would forgive him for the horrible, untrue things he had said to her in his attempt to drive her away. No guarantee that life would continue on smoothly and he would have her until he drew his last breath. All these things required a step taken in faith, taken in bravery and taken in love. The very idea of doing it seemed impossible. Seemed utterly untenable. And yet, he found himself taking a step forward, and then another. And while he knew very little about the way his life might end up, in the moment he knew exactly what he was walking toward.

It was light. It was pain. It was pleasure. It was love. It was Belle.

He took his phone out of his pocket, still holding the dead rose petal in his hand. And he dialed Fos's personal phone. "Flowers," he said when the old man picked up. "We need flowers in the palace again."

Between long hours spent in oncology, and then long hours spent caring for her father while he felt ill with the aftereffects of his treatment, Belle felt wrung out and gritty by the time she walked out the back door of their modest home and wrapped a sweater around herself to fortify her body against the sea breeze blowing in off the waves. She walked down the stairs, kicking her shoes off as she reached the sand, making her way down to the water's edge.

If a human could be stale, Belle certainly was. She felt brittle, as though the slightest bit of pressure could break her in half. She felt tired. Broken.

And she couldn't even blame it all on her father's treatments, or the clear physical toll they were taking on him. No, this was all to do with heartbreak. It was all to do with Adam. When she had arrived back home teary-eyed and pale, her father had railed against her monstrous captor with all the strength he had in his frail body. But, Belle had only managed a weak smile, and told him that Adam truly wasn't as awful as he had been made out to be.

Of course her father had protested.

"He took you prisoner over a few photographs!"

"You don't know what he's been through. He's very private. And he's endured so much pain. Just because he was born royal doesn't mean everyone has a right to stare at him, and to dissect his pain."

"You aren't thinking clearly. Obviously he's done something to you during the time you spent with him."

She had nearly laughed at that. "Yes. He stole my heart."

Her father hadn't found that to be a satisfactory answer. What was it with men always trying to tell her what she felt? Always trying to tell her that her feelings were wrong or irrational. She was getting tired of it.

She took a deep breath of the salt air, trying her best to wash herself clean, to let in a little bit of this freshness so that she didn't feel quite so claustrophobic. It was strange what a broken heart did to you. Made everything feel heavier. Even the air.

She looked down at her left hand, at that ring she should have taken off but hadn't yet. She touched it, twisted it around idly as she continued to gaze out at the sea.

Adam. Oh, Adam.

"Belle."

The sound of her father's thin voice carrying toward her on the breeze caused her to turn. And there he was, standing there, leaning against the rail on the deck. And beside him, bathed in the sunlight, stood a taller, more imposing figure.

She looked down at the ring, half-suspicious it had called him here. Or, more likely that this was a hallucination brought about by her desperation.

"I was going to throw him out," her father said, "but I don't have the strength to handle someone his size on a good day."

"You don't have to do that," she said, feeling dizzy and breathless.

Adam walked past her father without saying a word, heading down the stairs and onto the beach. He paused, kicking off his shoes next to hers. Her father shook his head and walked back into the house, leaving her alone on the beach with Adam.

"You came," she said, her voice trembling. "You really did."

"There is nowhere else on earth for me to go," he said simply, making his way toward her. "There is a place I could stay. I can continue on living in the darkness as I have been. But…it isn't what I want. Not now." His hands were in his pockets, his gaze focused on the ocean behind her.

"What did you come here to tell me, Adam? Did you come here to let me know all the other ways I don't measure up to your wife? Did you come here to tell me that you want to take me prisoner again even though you don't have feelings for me?"

He looked at her then, his gaze fierce. "No. Of course not."

"Then I could do with a less dramatic buildup, thanks. Can't you see that I'm here breaking apart? Trying my very best to keep myself together, to keep on breathing, and then you show up. You show up like some...vision out of a dream, that I can hardly believe I'm standing in front of, and you haven't even managed to get to the point of why you're here. It should be the first thing you say. The reason you are here. That should be—"

He cut her off, pulling her into his arms and pressing his mouth to hers. His kiss was urgent, savage, and she reveled in it. Because it called out the savagery in her. Called to that dark, messy place inside her that only Adam had ever reached.

"I love you," he said. "Is that direct enough?"

"Yes," she said, feeling dizzy and breathless. "But you said—"

"Everything you thought about me is the truth. I lied. I lied to us both. I said horrible things, hurtful things, so that you would leave me because I am a coward. Because I thought it best to break my own heart in a way that I could control. When I decided to do it. Not in ten years. Or ten months—depending on how long you could possibly put up with me. Depending on how long it would take for you to finally realize that I'm not a man you love. I'm just a beast that took you captive."

She shook her head. "You're not bad. You're not a beast to…you're…you're everything to me."

"I don't deserve that," he said, his voice rough. "I had sunk so far into my own darkness and I didn't even want to be reached. But you reached out to me when I gave you no reason to, and you started to love me when nothing in me was lovable. I don't understand it, Belle. Because I couldn't understand it, I feared it. And at least buried in the castle by myself I know exactly what's going to happen. If I love nothing, then nothing can be taken from me. And if I blame myself for my wife's death, then it's so much easier to justify that. To call it recompense instead of cowardice. But I was hiding. From the world. And then from you. From my feelings for you. It isn't that I don't think I can love—it's that I was enraged because my heart hadn't learned. Because I can love, deeper and more profoundly than I ever could because I know how much it costs. I love you in ways I cannot describe, in ways that I wasn't capable of loving before I lost my wife. And all of that seems unfair, it seems terrifying and it seems like something I would rather run from than run to, but I can't exist inside of myself knowing that you're out there and I am there in the darkness. While my light is here…" He dragged his thumbs across her cheekbones. "I can't stay away from you, even if I should. I know that I should. For your safety, for your sake. But I want you too much to do that." He shook his head. "It could be argued that I perhaps don't love you enough, because that would mean letting you go, but I can't do that."

"Why do people do that?" she said, thinking back to what he had said about her earlier, about respect. "Why do they think if they love someone they need to let them go? Maybe, the truth is that if you really love someone, you need to fight through the hard parts, through the fear."

She leaned into him, resting her head on his shoulder. "Maybe you have to love someone enough to accept the fact that it sometimes means pain. That it might mean loss, that it might mean a struggle. That it might mean changing what you're doing and who you are. Sometimes those aren't bad things. Because I know for certain that before I loved you I wasn't whole."

"Belle…"

"I needed to change to have you," she continued as though he hadn't spoken. "And I don't think you're whole without me. So maybe we can dispense with this nonsense that superior love somehow means perfect happiness. I think it should mean passion. I think it should mean struggle, sacrifice, beauty and pain. I think it should mean that I have to open myself up and risk myself for you, and you have to be willing to be heard again for me. You keep telling me that you're darkness. And that I'm your light, but you never once thought that you might be mine?"

"How could that be?" he asked, his voice broken. "It makes no sense."

"I lived a passionless existence. I dated a man for eight months that I didn't even want. I probably would have married him, Adam, secure and happy in the fact that he didn't make me hurt. That he didn't make me ache or want. That I didn't have to risk anything to have him. But you showed me that I could have more—you made me want more. And then you gave it to me. You haven't taken anything from me. You have given me so much more than I could have ever hoped for. The only darkness I've experienced has been those moments without you."

He pulled her into his arms then, kissing her, over and over, deep, fierce and drugging kisses that left her in no doubt of his passion for her.

"You were never my captive," he said, sliding his thumb across her lower lip. "I was only ever yours. From that very first moment I saw you."

"Maybe you're the one with Stockholm syndrome."

He laughed. "Or maybe we just love each other."

She smiled, feeling like light was flooding her soul. "Yes," she said, "I think you're right."

When she had seen him that first day, that day he had told her she would be his prisoner, she had thought him a monster. But it had turned out Prince Adam Katsaros was the man she had always needed.

"I want you to be my wife," he said. "I don't think I have ever said that before. At least not in quite that way. I want you to marry me, be my princess, sleep with me always, give me children. I want it more than I want my next breath."

"I want that too," she said.

"You are my future," he said, drawing his knuckles across her cheek. "You are my heart."

She lifted her hands, tracing the deep lines of his scars that spoke of his pain, that spoke of his strength. Those scars that made him the man she loved.

"And you are mine."

And they lived happily ever after...

* * * * *

If you enjoyed
THE PRINCE'S CAPTIVE VIRGIN
watch out for the second part of Maisey Yates's
BRIDES OF INNOCENCE *trilogy*

THE PRINCE'S STOLEN VIRGIN
Available August 2017!

In the meantime, why not explore another
trilogy by Maisey Yates?

HEIRS BEFORE VOWS
THE SPANIARD'S PREGNANT BRIDE
THE PRINCE'S PREGNANT MISTRESS
THE ITALIAN'S PREGNANT VIRGIN
Available now!

**"You can ask me anything, Princess,"
Rodolfo heard himself say, in a lazy,
smoky sort of tone he'd never used in
her presence before.**

But this was the princess he was going to marry—
not one of the enterprising women who flung
themselves at him everywhere he went, looking
for a taste of Europe's favorite Daredevil Prince.

There was no denying it. Suddenly, out of
nowhere, he wanted his future wife.

Desperately.

As if she could tell—as if she'd somehow become
the sort of woman who could read a man's desire
and use it against him when he'd have sworn she
was anything but—Valentina deepened her smile.

She tilted her head to one side. "It's about your
shocking double standards," she said sweetly. "If
you can cat your way through all of Europe, why
can't I?"

Something black and wild and wholly unfamiliar
surged in him then, making Rodolfo's hands curl
into fists and his entire body go tense, taut.

Then he really shocked the hell out of himself.

"Because," he all but snarled—and there was no
pretending that wasn't exactly what he was doing,
no matter how unlikely, "like it or not, Princess,
you are mine."

*Introducing a new, sinfully scandalous duet
from Caitlin Crews…*

Scandalous Royal Brides

Married for passion, made for scandal!

When personal assistant Natalie and Princess Valentina meet they can't believe their eyes…they're the very image of one another. They're so similar it's impossible that they're anything but identical twins.

Dissatisfied with their lives, they impulsively agree to swap places—for six weeks only…

But will they want to return to their old lives when the alpha heroes closest to them are intent on making these scandalous women their brides?

Read Natalie and Prince Rodolfo's story in

The Prince's Nine-Month Scandal
Available now

And discover Princess Valentina
and Achilles Casilieris's story in

The Billionaire's Secret Princess
Available July 2017

THE PRINCE'S
NINE-MONTH
SCANDAL

BY
CAITLIN CREWS

All rights reserved including the right of reproduction in whole
or in part in any form. This edition is published by arrangement with
Harlequin Books S.A.

This is a work of fiction. Names, characters, places, locations and
incidents are purely fictional and bear no relationship to any real
life individuals, living or dead, or to any actual places, business
establishments, locations, events or incidents. Any resemblance is
entirely coincidental.

This book is sold subject to the condition that it shall not, by way of
trade or otherwise, be lent, resold, hired out or otherwise circulated
without the prior consent of the publisher in any form of binding or
cover other than that in which it is published and without a similar
condition including this condition being imposed on the subsequent
purchaser.

® and TM are trademarks owned and used by the trademark owner
and/or its licensee. Trademarks marked with ® are registered with the
United Kingdom Patent Office and/or the Office for Harmonisation in
the Internal Market and in other countries.

First Published in Great Britain 2017
By Mills & Boon, an imprint of HarperCollins*Publishers*
1 London Bridge Street, London, SE1 9GF

© 2017 Caitlin Crews

ISBN: 978-0-263-92524-1

Our policy is to use papers that are natural, renewable and recyclable
products and made from wood grown in sustainable forests. The logging
and manufacturing processes conform to the legal environmental
regulations of the country of origin.

Printed and bound in Spain
by CPI, Barcelona

USA TODAY bestselling and RITA® Award–nominated author **Caitlin Crews** loves writing romance. She teaches her favourite romance novels in creative writing classes at places like the UCLA Extension's prestigious Writers' Program, where she finally gets to utilise the MA and PhD in English Literature she received from the University of York in England. She currently lives in California, with her very own hero and too many pets. Visit her at caitlincrews.com.

Visit the Author Profile page
at millsandboon.co.uk for more titles.

CHAPTER ONE

NATALIE MONETTE HAD never done a rash thing in her entire twenty-seven years, something she'd always viewed as a great personal strength. After a childhood spent flitting about with her free-spirited, impetuous mother, never belonging anywhere and without a shred of anything resembling permanence including an address, Natalie had made her entire adulthood—especially her career—a monument to all things *dependable* and *predictable*.

But she'd finally had enough.

Her employer—never an easy man at the best of times—wasn't likely to accept her notice after five long years with anything like grace. Natalie shook her head at the very notion of grace and her cranky billionaire boss. He preferred a bull-in-china-shop approach to most things, especially his executive assistant. And this latest time, as he'd dressed her down for an imagined mistake in front of an entire corporate office in London, a little voice inside her had whispered: *enough*.

Enough already. Or she thought she might die. Internally, anyway.

She had to quit her job. She had to figure out what her life was like when not at the beck and call of a tyrant—because there had to be better things out there. There

had to be. She had to do *something* before she just…
disappeared.

And she was thinking that a rash move—like quitting here and now and who cared if her boss threw a
tantrum?—might just do the trick.

Natalie was washing her hands in the marbled sink
in the fancy women's bathroom that was a part of the
moneyed elegance evident everywhere in the high-class
lounge area at her boss's preferred private airfield outside
London. She was trying to slow her panicked breathing
and get herself back under control. She prided herself
on being unflappable under normal circumstances, but
nothing about the messy things swirling around inside
of her today felt *normal.* She hardly paid any attention
when one of the heavy stall doors behind her opened
and a woman stepped up to the sink beside hers. She had
the vague impression of the sort of marked glamour that
was usually on display in these places she only visited
thanks to her job, but then went back to wondering how
on earth she was going to walk out of this bathroom and
announce that she was done with her job.

She couldn't imagine how her boss would react. Or
she could, that was the trouble. But Natalie knew she had
to do it. *She had to do it.* Now, while there was still this
feverish thing inside her that kept pushing at her. Because if she waited, she knew she wouldn't. She'd settle
back in and it would be another five years in an instant,
and then what would she do?

"I beg your pardon, but you seem to look a great deal
like someone I know."

The woman's voice was cultured. Elegant. And it
made Natalie feel…funny. As if she'd heard it before
when she knew that was impossible. Of course she
hadn't. She never knew anyone in these ultra high-class

places her job took her. Then she looked up and the world seemed to tilt off its axis. She was shocked she didn't crumple to the ground where she stood.

Because the woman standing beside her, staring back at her through the mirror, had her face. *The exact same face.* Her coppery hair was styled differently and she wasn't wearing Natalie's dark-rimmed glasses over her own green eyes, but there was no denying that every other aspect was *exactly the same*. The fine nose. The faintly pointed chin. The same raised eyebrows, the same high forehead.

The other woman was taller, Natalie realized in a rush of something more complicated than simple relief. But then she looked down to see that her impossible, improbable twin was wearing the sort of sky-high stilettos only women who didn't have to walk very often or very far enjoyed, easily making her a few inches taller than Natalie in the far more serviceable wedges she wore that allowed her to keep up with her irascible employer's long, impatient stride.

"Oh." The other woman breathed the syllable out, like a sigh, though her eyes gleamed. "I thought there was an amusing resemblance that we should discuss, but this…"

Natalie had the bizarre experience of watching her own mouth move on another woman's face. Then drop open slightly. It was unnerving. It was like the mirror coming alive right in front of her. It was *impossible*.

It was a great deal more than an "amusing resemblance."

"What is this?" she asked, her voice as shaky as she felt. "How…?"

"I have no idea," the other woman said quietly. "But it's fascinating, isn't it?" She turned to look at Natalie directly, letting her gaze move up and down her body as if measuring her. Cataloging her. Natalie could hardly blame her. If she wasn't so frozen, she'd do the same. "I'm Valentina."

"Natalie."

Why was her throat so dry? But she knew why. They said everyone on earth had a double, but that was usually a discussion about mannerisms and a vague resemblance. Not *this*. Because Natalie knew beyond the shadow of any possible doubt that there was no way this person standing in front of her, with the same eyes and the same mouth and even the same freckle centered on her left cheekbone wasn't related to her. No possible way. And that was a Pandora's box full of problems, wasn't it? Starting with her own childhood and the mother who had always rather sternly claimed she didn't know who Natalie's father was. She tried to shake all that off—but then Valentina's name penetrated her brain.

She remembered where she was. And the other party that had been expected at the same airfield today. She'd openly scoffed at the notification, because there wasn't much on this earth she found more useless than royalty. Her mother had gotten that ball rolling while Natalie was young. While other girls had dressed up like princesses and dreamed about Prince Charming, Natalie had been taught that both were lies.

There's no such thing as happily-ever-after, her mother had told her. *There's only telling a silly story about painful things to make yourself feel better. No daughter of mine is going to imagine herself anything but a realist, Natalie.*

And so Natalie hadn't. Ever.

Here in this bathroom, face-to-face with an impossibility, Natalie blinked. "Wait. You're that princess."

"I am indeed, for my sins." Valentina's mouth curved in a serene sort of half smile that Natalie would have said she, personally, could never pull off. Except if someone with an absolutely identical face could do it, that meant she could, too, didn't it? That realization was…unnerving. "But I suspect you might be, too."

Natalie couldn't process that. Her eyes were telling her a truth, but her mind couldn't accept it. She played devil's advocate instead. "We can't possibly be related. I'm a glorified secretary who never really had a home. You're a royal princess. Presumably your lineage—and the family home, for that matter, which I'm pretty sure is a giant castle because all princesses have a few of those by virtue of the title alone—dates back to the Roman Conquest."

"Give or take a few centuries." Valentina inclined her head, another supremely elegant and vaguely noble gesture that Natalie would have said could only look silly on her. Yet it didn't look anything like silly on Valentina. "Depending which branch of the family you mean, of course."

"I was under the impression that people with lineages that could lead to thrones and crown jewels tended to keep better track of their members."

"You'd think, wouldn't you?" The princess shifted back on her soaring heels and regarded Natalie more closely. "Conspiracy theorists claim my mother was killed and the death hushed up. Senior palace officials assured me that no, she merely left to preserve her mental health, and is rumored to be in residence in a hospital devoted to such things somewhere. All I know is that I haven't seen her since shortly after I was born. According to my father, she preferred anonymity to the joys of motherhood."

Natalie wanted to run out of this bathroom, lose herself in her work and her boss's demands the way she usually did, and pretend this mad situation had never happened. This encounter felt rash enough for her as it was. No need to blow her life up on top of it. So she had no idea why instead, she opened up her mouth and shared her deepest, secret shame with this woman.

"I've never met my father," she told this total stranger who looked like an upscale mirror image of herself. There was no reason she should feel as if she could trust a random woman she met in a bathroom, no matter whose face she wore. It was absurd to feel as if she'd known this other person all her life when of course she hadn't. And yet she kept talking. "My mother's always told me she has no idea who he was. That Prince Charming was a fantasy sold to impressionable young girls to make them silly, and the reality was that men are simply men and untrustworthy to the core. And she bounces from one affair to the next pretty quickly, so I came to terms with the fact it was possible she really, truly didn't know."

Valentina laughed. It was a low, smoky sound, and Natalie recognized it, because it was hers. A shock of recognition went through her. Though she didn't feel like laughing. At all.

"My father is many things," the princess said, laughter and something more serious beneath it. "Including His Royal Majesty, King Geoffrey of Murin. What he is not now, nor has ever been, I imagine, is forgettable."

Natalie shook her head. "You underestimate my mother's commitment to amnesia. She's made it a life choice instead of a malady. On some level I admire it."

Once again, she had no idea why she was telling this stranger things she hardly dared admit to herself.

"My mother was the noblewoman Frederica de Burgh,

from a very old Murinese family." Valentina watched Natalie closely as she spoke. "Promised to my father at birth, raised by nuns and kept deliberately sheltered, and then widely held to be unequal to the task of becoming queen. Mentally. But that's the story they would tell, isn't it, to explain why she disappeared? What's your mother's name?"

Her hands felt numb, so Natalie shifted her bag from her shoulder to the marble countertop beside her. "She calls herself Erica."

For a moment neither one of them spoke. Neither one of them mentioned that *Erica* sounded very much like a shortened form of *Frederica,* but then, there was no need. Natalie was aware of too many things. The far-off sounds of planes outside the building. The television in the lounge on the other side of the door, cued to a twenty-four-hour news channel. She was vaguely surprised her boss hadn't already texted her fifteen furious times, wondering where she'd gone off to when it was possible he might have need of her.

"I saw everyone's favorite billionaire, Achilles Casilieris, out there in the lounge," Valentina said after a moment, as if reading Natalie's mind. "He looks even more fearsome in person than advertised. You can almost *see* all that brash command and dizzying wealth ooze from his pores, can't you?"

"He's my boss." Natalie ran her tongue over her teeth, that reckless thing inside of her lurching to life all over again. "If he was really oozing anything, anywhere, it would be my job to provide first aid until actual medical personnel could come handle it. At which point he would bite my head off for wasting his precious time by not curing him instantly."

She had worked for Achilles Casilieris—and by extension the shockingly hardy, internationally envied and recession-proof Casilieris Company—for five very long years. That was the first marginally negative thing she'd said about her job, ever. Out loud, anyway. And she felt instantly disloyal, despite the fact she'd been psyching herself up to quit only moments ago. Much as she had when she'd opened her mouth about her mother.

How could a stranger who happened to look like her make Natalie question who *she* was?

But the princess was frowning at the slim leather clutch she'd tossed on the bathroom counter. Natalie heard the buzzing sound that indicated a call as Valentina flipped open the outer flap and slid her smartphone out, then rolled her eyes and shoved it back in.

"My fiancé," she said, meeting Natalie's gaze again, her own more guarded. Or maybe it was something else that made the green in her eyes darker. The phone buzzed a few more times, then stopped. "Or his chief of staff, to be more precise."

"Congratulations," Natalie said, though the expression on Valentina's face did not look as if she was precisely awash in joyous anticipation.

"Thank you, I'm very lucky." Valentina's mouth curved, though there was nothing like a smile in her eyes and her tone was arid. "Everyone says so. Prince Rodolfo is objectively attractive. Not all princes can make that claim, but the tabloids have exulted over his abs since he was a teenager. Just as they have salivated over his impressive dating history, which has involved a selection of models and actresses from at least four continents and did not cease in any noticeable way upon our engagement last fall."

"Your Prince Charming sounds…charming," Natalie murmured. It only confirmed her long-held suspicions about such men.

Valentina raised one shoulder, then dropped it. "His theory is that he remains free until our marriage, and then will be free once again following the necessary birth of his heir. More discreetly, I can only hope. Meanwhile, I am beside myself with joy that I must take my place at his side in two short months. Of course."

Natalie didn't know why she laughed at that, but she did. More out of commiseration than anything else, as if they really were the same person. And how strange that she almost felt as if they were. "It's going to be a terrific couple of months all around, then. Mr. Casilieris is in rare form. He's putting together a particularly dramatic deal and it's not going his way and he...isn't used to that. So that's me working twenty-two-hour days instead of my usual twenty for the foreseeable future, which is even more fun when he's cranky and snarling."

"It can't possibly be worse than having to smile politely while your future husband lectures you about the absurd expectation of fidelity in what is essentially an arranged marriage for hours on end. The absurdity is that *he* might be expected to curb his impulses for a year or so, in case you wondered. The expectations for *me* apparently involve quietly and chastely finding fulfillment in philanthropic works, like his sainted absentee mother who everyone knows manufactured a supposed health crisis so she could live out her days in peaceful seclusion. It's easy to be philanthropically fulfilled while living in isolation in Bavaria."

Natalie smiled. "Try biting your tongue while your famously short-tempered boss rages at you for no reason, for the hundredth time in an hour, because he pays you to stand there and take it without wilting or crying or selling whinging stories about him to the press."

Valentina's smile was a perfect match. "Or the hours

and hours of grim palace-vetted pre-wedding press interviews in the company of a pack of advisors who will censor everything I say and inevitably make me sound like a bit of animated treacle, as out of touch with reality as the average overly sweet dessert."

"Speaking of treats, I also have to deal with the board of directors Mr. Casilieris treats like irritating schoolchildren, his packs of furious ex-lovers each with her own vendetta, all his terrified employees who need to be coached through meetings with him and treated for PTSD after, and every last member of his staff in every one of his households, who like me to be the one to ask him the questions they know will set him off on one of his scorch-the-earth rages."

They'd moved a little bit closer then, leaning toward each other like friends. *Or sisters,* a little voice whispered. It should have concerned Natalie like everything else about this. And like everything else, it did and it didn't. Either way, she didn't step back. She didn't insist upon her personal space. She was almost tempted to imagine her body knew something about this mirror image version of her that her brain was still desperately trying to question.

Natalie thought of the way Mr. Casilieris had bitten her head off earlier, and her realization that if she didn't escape him now she never would. And how this stranger with her face seemed, oddly enough, to understand.

"I was thinking of quitting, to be honest," she whispered. Making it real. "Today."

"I can't quit, I'm afraid," the impossibly glamorous princess said then, her green eyes alight with something a little more frank than plain mischief. "But I have a better idea. Let's switch places. For a month, say. Six weeks at the most. Just for a little break."

"That's crazy," Natalie said.

"Insane," Valentina agreed. "But you might find royal protocol exciting! And I've always wanted to do the things everyone else in the world does. Like go to a real job."

"People can't *switch places*." Natalie was frowning. "And certainly not with a princess."

"You could think about whether or not you really want to quit," Valentina pointed out. "It would be a lovely holiday for you. Where will Achilles Casilieris be in six weeks' time?"

"He's never gone from London for too long," Natalie heard herself say, as if she was considering it.

Valentina smiled. "Then in six weeks we'll meet in London. We'll text in the meantime with all the necessary details about our lives, and on the appointed day we'll just meet up and switch back and no one will ever be the wiser. Doesn't that sound like *fun*?" Her gaze met Natalie's with something like compassion. "And I hope you won't mind my saying this, but you do look as if you could use a little fun."

"It would never work." Natalie realized after she spoke that she still hadn't said no. "No one will ever believe I'm you."

Valentina waved a hand between them. "How would anyone know the difference? I can barely tell myself."

"People will take one look at me and know I'm not you," Natalie insisted, as if that was the key issue here. "You look like a *princess*."

If Valentina noticed the derisive spin she put on that last word out of habit, she appeared to ignore it.

"You too can look like a princess. This princess, anyway. You already do."

"There's a lifetime to back it up. You're elegant. Poised.

You've had years of training, presumably. How to be a diplomat. How to be polite in every possible situation. Which fork to use at dinner, for God's sake."

"Achilles Casilieris is one of the wealthiest men alive. He dines with as many kings as I do. I suspect that as his personal assistant, Natalie, you have, too. And have likely learned how to navigate the cutlery."

"No one will believe it," Natalie whispered, but there was no heat in it.

Because maybe she was the one who couldn't believe it. And maybe, if she was entirely honest, there was a part of her that wanted this. The princess life and everything that went with it. The kind of ease she'd never known—and a castle besides. And only for a little while. Six short weeks. Scarcely more than a daydream.

Surely even Natalie deserved a daydream. Just this once.

Valentina's smile widened as if she could scent capitulation in the air. She tugged off the enormous, eye-gouging ring on her left hand and placed it down on the counter between them. It made an audible *clink* against the marble surface.

"Try it on. I dare you. It's an heirloom from Prince Rodolfo's extensive treasury of such items, dating back to the dawn of time, more or less." She inclined her head in that regal way of hers. "If it doesn't fit we'll never speak of switching places again."

And Natalie felt possessed by a force she didn't understand. She knew better. Of course she did. This was a ridiculous game and it could only make this bizarre situation worse, and she was certainly no Cinderella. She knew that much for sure.

But she slipped the ring onto her finger anyway, and it fit perfectly, gleaming on her finger like every dream she'd ever had as a little girl. Not that she could live a magical life, filled with talismans that shone the way this ring did, because that was the sort of *impracticality* her mother had abhorred. But that she could have a home the way everyone else did. That she could *belong* to a man, to a country, to the sweep of a long history, the way this ring hugged her finger. As if it was meant to be.

The ring had nothing to do with her. She knew that. But it felt like a promise, even so.

And it all seemed to snowball from there. They each kicked off their shoes and stood barefoot on the surprisingly plush carpet. Then Valentina shimmied out of her sleek, deceptively simple sheath dress with the unselfconsciousness of a woman used to being dressed by attendants. She lifted her brows with all the imperiousness of her station, and Natalie found herself retreating into the stall with the dress—since she was not, in fact, used to being tended to by packs of fawning courtiers and therefore all but naked with an audience. She climbed out of her own clothes, handing her pencil skirt, blouse and wrap sweater out to Valentina through the crack she left open in the door. Then she tugged the princess's dress on, expecting it to snag or pull against her obviously peasant body.

But like the ring, the dress fit as if it had been tailored to her body. As if it was hers.

She walked out slowly, blinking when she saw…herself waiting for her. The very same view she'd seen in the mirror this morning when she'd dressed in the room Mr. Casilieris kept for her in the basement of his London town house because her own small flat was too far away to be to-ing and fro-ing at odd hours, according to him, and it was easier to acquiesce than fight. Not that it had kept him from firing away at her. But she shoved that aside because Valentina was laughing at the sight of Natalie in obvious astonishment, as if she was having the same literal out-of-body experience.

Natalie walked back to the counter and climbed into the princess's absurd shoes, very carefully. Her knees protested beneath her as she tried to stand tall in them and she had to reach out to grip the marble counter.

"Put your weight on your heels," Valentina advised. She was already wearing Natalie's wedges, because apparently even their feet were the same, and of course she had no trouble standing in them as if she'd picked them out herself. "Everyone always wants to lean forward and tiptoe in heels like that, and nothing looks worse. Lean back and you own the shoe, not the other way around." She eyed Natalie. "Will your glasses give me a headache, do you suppose?"

Natalie pulled them from her face and handed them over. "They're clear glass. I was getting a little too much attention from some of the men Mr. Casilieris works with, and it annoyed him. I didn't want to lose my job, so I started wearing my hair up and these glasses. It worked like a charm."

"I refuse to believe men are so idiotic."

Natalie grinned as Valentina took the glasses and slid them onto her nose. "The men we're talking about weren't exactly paying me attention because they found me enthralling. It was a diversionary tactic during negotiations and yes, you'd be surprised how many men fail to see a woman who looks smart."

She tugged her hair tie from her ponytail and shook out her hair, then handed the elastic to Valentina. The princess swept her hair back and into the same ponytail Natalie had been sporting only seconds before.

And it was like magic.

Ordinary Natalie Monette, renowned for her fierce work ethic, attention to detail and her total lack of anything resembling a personal life—which was how she'd become the executive assistant to one of the world's most ferocious and feared billionaires straight out of college and now had absolutely no life to call her own—became Her Royal Highness, Princess Valentina of Murin in an instant. And vice versa. Just like that.

"This is crazy," Natalie whispered.

The real Princess Valentina only smiled, looking every inch the smooth, super competent right hand of a man as feared as he was respected. Looking the way Natalie had always *hoped* she looked, if she was honest. Serenely capable. Did this mean…she always had?

More than that, they looked like twins. They had to be twins. There was no possibility that they could be anything but.

Natalie didn't want to think about the number of lies her mother had to have told her if that was true. She didn't want to think about all the implications. She couldn't.

"We have to switch places now," Valentina said softly, though there was a catch in her voice. It was the catch that made Natalie focus on her rather than the mystery that was her mother. "I've always wanted to be…someone else. Someone normal. Just for a little while."

Their gazes caught at that, both the exact same shade of green, just as their hair was that unusual shade of copper many tried to replicate in the salon, yet couldn't. The only difference was that Valentina's was highlighted with streaks of blond that Natalia suspected came from long, lazy days on the decks of yachts or taking in the sunshine from the comfort of her very own island kingdom.

If you're really twins—if you're sisters—it's your is-

land, too, a little voice inside whispered. But Natalie couldn't handle that. Not here. Not now. Not while she was all dressed up in princess clothes.

"Is that what princesses dream of?" Natalie asked. She wanted to smile, but the moment felt too precarious. Ripe and swollen with emotions she couldn't have named, though she understood them as they moved through her. "Because I think most other little girls imagine they're you."

Not her, of course. Never her.

Something shone a little too brightly in Valentina's gaze then, and it made Natalie's chest ache.

But she would never know what her mirror image might have said next, because her name was called in a familiar growl from directly outside the door to the women's room. Natalie didn't think. She was dressed as someone else and she couldn't let anyone see that—so she threw herself back into the stall where she'd changed her clothes as the door was slapped open.

"Exactly what are you doing in here?" growled a voice that Natalie knew better than her own. She'd worked for Achilles Casilieris for five years. She knew him much, much better than she knew herself. She knew, for example, that the particular tone he was using right now meant his usual grouchy mood was being rapidly taken over by his typical impatience. He'd likely had to actually take a moment and look for her, rather than her magically being at his side before he finished his thought. He hated that. And he wasn't shy at all about expressing his feelings. "Can we leave for New York now, do you think, or do you need to fix your makeup for another hour?"

Natalie stood straighter out of habit, only to realize that her boss's typical scowl wasn't directed at her. She was hidden behind the cracked open door of the bathroom stall. Her boss was aiming that famous glare straight at Valentina, and he didn't appear to notice that she wasn't Natalie. That if she was Natalie, that would mean she'd lightened her hair in the past fifteen minutes. But she could tell that all her boss saw was his assistant. Nothing more, nothing less.

"I apologize," Valentina murmured.

"I don't need you to be sorry, I need you on the plane," Achilles retorted, then turned back around to head out.

Natalie's head spun. She had worked for this man, night and day, for *half a decade*. He was Achilles Casilieris, renowned for his keen insight and killer instincts in all things, and Natalie had absolutely no doubt that he had no idea that he hadn't been speaking to her.

Maybe that was why, when Valentina reached over and took Natalie's handbag instead of her own, Natalie didn't push back out of the stall to stop her. She said nothing. She stood where she was. She did absolutely nothing to keep the switch from happening.

"I'll call you," Valentina mouthed into the mirror as she hurried to the door, and the last Natalie saw of Her Royal Highness Valentina of Murin was the suppressed excitement in her bright green eyes as she followed Achilles Casilieris out the door.

Natalie stepped out of the stall again in the sudden silence. She looked at herself in the mirror, smoothed her hair down with palms that shook only the slightest little bit, blinked at the wild sparkle of the absurd ring on her finger as she did it.

And just like that, became a fairy princess—and stepped right into a daydream.

CHAPTER TWO

CROWN PRINCE RODOLFO of the ancient and deeply, deliberately reserved principality of Tissely, tucked away in the Pyrenees between France and Spain and gifted with wealth, peace and dramatic natural borders that had kept things that way for centuries untold, was bored.

This was not his preferred state of existence, though it was not exactly surprising here on the palace grounds of Murin Castle, where he was expected to entertain the royal bride his father had finally succeeded in forcing upon him.

Not that "entertainment" was ever really on offer with the undeniably pretty, yet almost aggressively placid and unexciting Princess Valentina. His future wife. The future mother of his children. His future queen, even. Assuming he didn't lapse into a coma before their upcoming nuptials, that was.

Rodolfo sighed and stretched out his long legs, aware he was far too big to be sitting so casually on a relic of a settee in this stuffily proper reception room that had been set aside for his use on one of his set monthly visits with his fiancée. He still felt a twinge in one thigh from the ill-advised diving trip he'd taken some months back with a group of his friends and rather too many sharks. Rodolfo rubbed at the scarred spot absently, grateful that while his father had inevitably caught wind of the feminine talent who'd graced the private yacht off the coast of Belize, the fact an overenthusiastic shark had grazed the Crown Prince of Tissely en route to a friend's recently caught fish had escaped both the King's spies' and the rabid tabloids' breathless reports.

It was these little moments of unexpected grace, he often thought with varying degrees of irony, that made his otherwise royally pointless life worth living.

"You embarrass yourself more with each passing year," his father had told him, stiff with fury, when Rodolfo had succumbed to the usual demands for a command appearance upon his return to Europe at the end of last summer, the salacious pictures of his "Belize Booze Cruise" still fresh in every tabloid reader's mind. And more to the point, in his father's.

"You possess the power to render me unembarrassing forevermore," Rodolfo had replied easily enough. He'd almost convinced himself his father no longer got beneath his skin. Almost. "Give me something to do, Father. You have an entire kingdom at your disposal. Surely you can find a single task for your only son."

But that was the crux of the matter they never spoke of directly, of course. Rodolfo was not the son his father had wanted as heir. He was not the son his father would have chosen to succeed him, not the son his father had planned for. He was his father's only *remaining* son, and not his father's choice.

He was not Felipe. He could never be Felipe. It was a toss-up as to which one of them hated him more for that.

"There is no place in my kingdom for a sybaritic fool whose life is little more than an extended advertisement for one of those appalling survival programs, complete with the sensationalism of the nearest gutter press," his father had boomed from across his vast, appropriately majestic office in the palace, because it was so much easier to attack Rodolfo than address what simmered beneath it all. Not that Rodolfo helped matters with his increasingly dangerous antics, he was aware. "You stain the principality with every astonishingly bad decision you make."

"It was a boat ride, sir." Rodolfo had kept his voice even because he knew it irritated his father to get no reaction to his litanies and insults. "Not precisely a scandal likely to topple the whole of the kingdom's government, as I think you are aware."

"What I am aware of, as ever, is how precious little you know about governing anything," his father had seethed, in all his state and consequence.

"You could change that with a wave of your hand," Rodolfo had reminded him, as gently as possible. Which was perhaps not all that gently. "Yet you refuse."

And around and around they went.

Rodolfo's father, the taciturn and disapproving sovereign of Tissely, Ferdinand IV, held all the duties of the monarchy in his tight fists and showed no signs of easing his grip anytime soon. Despite the promise he'd made his only remaining son and heir that he'd give him a more than merely ceremonial place in the principality's government following Rodolfo's graduate work at the London School of Economics. That had been ten years back, his father had only grown more bitter and possessive of his throne, and Rodolfo had…adapted.

Life in the principality was sedate, as befitted a nation that had avoided all the wars of the last few centuries by simple dint of being too far removed to take part in them in any real way. Rodolfo's life, by contrast, was…stimulating. Provocative by design. He liked his sport extreme and his sex excessive, and he didn't much care if the slavering hounds of the European press corps printed every moment of each, which they'd been more than happy to do for the past decade. If his father wished him to be more circumspect, to preserve and protect the life of the hereditary heir to Tissely's throne the way he should—the way he'd raced about trying to wrap Felipe in cotton wool, restricting him from everything only to lose him to something as ignoble and silly as an unremarkable cut in his finger and what they'd thought was the flu—he needed only to offer Rodolfo something else with which to fill his time. Such as, perhaps, something to *do* besides continue to exist, thus preserving the bloodline by dint of not dying.

In fairness, of course, Rodolfo had committed himself to pushing the boundaries of his continued existence as much as possible, with his group of similarly devil-may-care friends, to the dismay of most of their families.

"Congratulations," Ferdinand had clipped out one late September morning last fall in yet another part of his vast offices in the Tisselian palace complex. "You will be married next summer."

"I beg your pardon?"

In truth, Rodolfo had not been paying much attention to the usual lecture until that moment. He was no fan of being summoned from whatever corner of the world he happened to be inhabiting and having to race back to present himself before Ferdinand, because his lord and father preferred not to communicate with his only heir by any other means but face-to-face. But of course, Ferdinand had not solicited his opinion. Ferdinand never did.

When he'd focused on his father, sitting there behind the acres and acres of his desk, the old man had actually looked…smug.

That did not bode well.

"You've asked me for a role in the kingdom and here it is. The Crown Prince of Tissely has been unofficially betrothed to the Murin princess since her birth. It is high time you did your duty and ensured the line. This should not come as any great surprise. You are not exactly getting any younger, Rodolfo, as your increasingly more desperate public displays amply illustrate."

Rodolfo had let that deliberate slap roll off his back, because there was no point reacting. It was what his father wanted.

"I met the Murin princess exactly once when I was ten and she was in diapers." Felipe had been fourteen and a man of the world, to Rodolfo's recollection, and the then Crown Prince of Tissely had seemed about as unenthused about his destiny as Rodolfo felt now. "That seems a rather tenuous connection upon which to base a marriage, given I've never seen her since."

"Princess Valentina is renowned the world over for her commitment to her many responsibilities and her role as her father's emissary," his father had replied coolly. "I doubt your paths would have crossed in all these years, as she is not known to frequent the dens of iniquity you prefer."

"Yet you believe this paragon will wish to marry me."

"I am certain she will wish no such thing, but the princess is a dutiful creature who knows what she owes to her country. You claim that you are as well, and that your dearest wish is to serve the crown. Now is your chance to prove it."

And that was how Rodolfo had found himself both hoist by his own petard and more worrying, tied to his very proper, very dutiful, very, very boring bride-to-be with no hope of escape. Ever.

"Princess Valentina, Your Highness," the butler intoned from the doorway, and Rodolfo dutifully climbed to his feet, because his life might have been slipping out of his control by the second, but hell, he still had the manners that had been beaten into him since he was small.

The truth was, he'd imagined that he would do things differently than his father when he'd realized he would have to take Felipe's place as the heir to his kingdom. He'd been certain he would not marry a woman he hardly knew, foisted upon him by duty and immaculate bloodlines, with whom he could hardly carry on a single meaningful conversation. His own mother—no more enamored of King Ferdinand than Rodolfo was—had long since repaired to her preferred residence, her ancestral home in the manicured wilds of Bavaria, and had steadfastly maintained an enduring if vague health crisis that necessitated she remain in seclusion for the past twenty years.

Rodolfo had been so sure, as an angry young man still reeling from his brother's death, that he would do things better when he had his chance.

And instead he was standing attendance on a strange woman who, in the months of their engagement, had appeared to be made entirely of impenetrable glass. She was about that approachable.

But this time, when Valentina walked into the reception room the way she'd done many times before, so they could engage in a perfectly tedious hour of perfectly polite conversation on perfectly pointless topics as if it was the stifling sixteenth century, all to allow the waiting press corps to gush about their visits later as they caught Rodolfo leaving, everything…changed.

Rodolfo couldn't have said how. Much less why.

But he *felt* her entrance. He *felt it* when she paused in the doorway and looked around as if she'd never laid eyes on him or the paneled ceiling or any part of the run-of-the-mill room before. His body tightened. He felt a rush of heat pool in his—

Impossible.

What the hell was happening to him?

Rodolfo felt his gaze narrow as he studied his fiancée. She looked the way she always did, and yet she didn't. She wore one of her efficiently sophisticated and chicly demure ensembles, a deceptively simple sheath dress that showed nothing and yet obliquely drew attention to the sheer feminine perfection of her form. A form he'd seen many times before, always clothed beautifully, and yet had never found himself waxing rhapsodic about before. Yet today he couldn't look away. There was something about the way she stood, as if she was unsteady on those cheeky heels she wore, though that seemed unlikely. Her hair flowed around her shoulders and looked somehow wilder than it usually did, as if the copper of it was redder. Or perhaps brighter.

Or maybe he needed to get his head examined. Maybe he really had gotten a concussion when he'd gone on an impromptu skydiving trip last week, tumbling a little too much on his way down into the remotest peaks of the Swiss Alps.

The princess moistened her lips and then met his gaze, and Rodolfo felt it like her sultry little mouth all over the hardest part of him.

What the hell?

"Hello," she said, and even her voice was…different, somehow. He couldn't put his finger on it. "It's lovely to see you."

"Lovely to see me?" he echoed, astonished. And

something far more earthy, if he was entirely honest with himself. "Are you certain? I was under the impression you would prefer a rousing spot of dental surgery to another one of these meetings. I feel certain you almost admitted as much at our last one."

He didn't know what had come over him. He'd managed to maintain his civility throughout all these months despite his creeping boredom—what had changed today? He braced himself, expecting the perfect princess to collapse into an offended heap on the polished floor, which he'd have a hell of a time explaining to her father, the humorless King Geoffrey of Murin.

But Valentina only smiled and a gleam he'd never seen before kindled in her eyes, which he supposed must always have been that remarkable shade of green. How had he never noticed them before?

"Well, it really depends on the kind of dental surgery, don't you think?" she asked.

Rodolfo couldn't have been more surprised if the quietly officious creature had tossed off her clothes and started dancing on the table—well, there was no need to exaggerate. He'd have summoned the palace doctors if the princess had done anything of the kind. After appreciating the show for a moment or two, of course, because he was a man, not a statue. But the fact she appeared to be teasing him was astounding, nonetheless.

"A root canal, at the very least," he offered.

"With or without anesthesia?"

"If it was with anesthesia you'd sleep right through it," Rodolfo pointed out. "Hardly any suffering at all."

"Everyone knows there's no point doing one's duty unless one can brag forever about the amount of suffering required to survive the task," the princess said, moving farther into the room. She stopped and rested her hand on the high, brocaded back of a chair that had likely cradled the posteriors of kings dating back to the ninth century, and all Rodolfo could think was that he wanted her to keep going. To keep walking toward him. To put herself within reach so he could—

Calm down, he ordered himself. *Now.* So sternly he sounded like his father in his own head.

"You are describing martyrdom," he pointed out.

Valentina shot him a smile. "Is there a difference?"

Rodolfo stood still because he didn't quite know what he might do if he moved. He watched this woman he'd written off months ago as if he'd never seen her before. There was something in the way she walked this afternoon that tugged at him. There was a new roll to her hips, perhaps. Something he'd almost call a swagger, assuming a princess of her spotless background and perfect genes was capable of anything so basic and enticing. Still, he couldn't look away as she rounded the settee he'd abandoned and settled herself in its center with a certain delicacy that was at odds with the way she'd moved through the old, spectacularly royal room. Almost as if she was more uncertain than she looked...but that made as little sense as the rest.

"I was reading about you on the plane back from London today," she told him, surprising him all over again.

"And here I thought we were maintaining the polite fiction that you did not sully your royal eyes with the squalid tabloids."

"Ordinarily I would not, of course," she replied, and then her mouth curved. Rodolfo was captivated. And somewhat horrified at that fact. But still captivated, all the same. "It is beneath me, obviously."

He sketched a bow that would have made his grandfather proud. "Obviously."

"I am a princess, not a desperate shopgirl who wants nothing more than to escape her dreary life, and must imagine herself into fantastical stories and half-truths presented as gospel."

"Quite so."

"But I must ask you a question." And on that she smiled again, that same serene curve of her lips that had about put him to sleep before. That was not the effect it had on him today. By a long shot.

"You can ask me anything, princess," Rodolfo heard himself say.

In a lazy, smoky sort of tone he'd never used in her presence before. Because this was the princess he was going to marry, not one of the enterprising women who flung themselves at him everywhere he went, looking for a taste of Europe's favorite daredevil prince.

There was no denying it. Suddenly, out of nowhere, he wanted his future wife.

Desperately.

As if she could tell—as if she'd somehow become the sort of woman who could read a man's desire and use it against him, when he'd have sworn she was anything but—Valentina's smile deepened.

She tilted her head to one side. "It's about your shocking double standard," she said sweetly. "If you can cat your way through all of Europe, why can't I?"

Something black and wild and wholly unfamiliar surged in him then, making Rodolfo's hands curl into fists and his entire body go tense, taut.

Then he really shocked the hell out of himself.

"Because you can't," he all but snarled, and there was no pretending that wasn't exactly what he was doing. *Snarling.* No matter how unlikely. "Like it or not, princess, you are mine."

CHAPTER THREE

Prince Rodolfo was not what Natalie was expecting.

No picture—and there were thousands, at a conservative estimate, every week he continued to draw breath—could adequately capture the *size* of Europe's favorite royal adrenaline junkie. That was the first thing that struck her. Sure, she'd seen the detailed telephoto shots of his much-hallowed abs as he emerged from various sparkling Mediterranean waters that had dominated whole summers of international swooning. And there was that famous morning he'd spent on a Barcelona balcony one spring, stretching and taking in the sunlight in boxer briefs and nothing else, but somehow all of those revealing pictures had managed to obscure the sheer *size* of the man. He was well over six feet, with hard, strong shoulders that could block out a day or two. And more than that, there was a leashed, humming sort of *power* in the man that photographs of him concealed entirely.

Or, Natalie thought, *maybe he's the one who does the concealing.*

But she couldn't think about what this man might be hiding beneath the surface. Not when the surface itself was so mesmerizing. She still felt as dazed as she'd been when she'd walked in this room and seen him waiting for her, dwarfing the furniture with all that contained physicality as he stood before the grand old fireplace. He looked like an athlete masquerading as a prince, with thick dark hair that was not quite tamed and the sort of dark chocolate eyes that a woman could lose herself in for a lifetime or three. His lean and rangy hard male beauty was packed into black trousers and a soft-looking button-down shirt that strained to handle his biceps and his gloriously sculpted chest. His hands were large and aristocratic at once, his voice was an authoritative rumble that seemed to murmur deep within her and then sink into a bright flame between her legs, his gaze was shockingly direct—and Natalie was not at all prepared. For any of it. For *him*.

She'd expected this real-life Prince Charming to be as repellent as he'd always been in the stories her mother had told her as a child about men just like him. Dull and vapid. Obsessed with something obscure, like hound breeding. Vain and huffy and bland, all the way through. Not...*this*.

Valentina had said that her fiancé was attractive in an offhanded, uncomplimentary way. She'd failed to mention that he was, in fact, upsettingly—almost incomprehensibly—stunning. The millions of fawning, admiring pictures of Crown Prince Rodolfo did not do him any justice, it turned out, and the truth of him took all the air from the room. From Natalie's lungs, for that matter. Her stomach felt scraped hollow as it plummeted to her feet, and then stayed there. But after a moment in the doorway where she'd seen nothing but him and the world had seemed to smudge a little bit around its luxe, literally palatial edges, Natalie had rallied.

It was hard enough trying to walk in the ridiculous shoes she was wearing—with her weight back on her heels, as ordered—and not goggle in slack-jawed astonishment at the palace all around her. *The actual, real live palace.* Valentina had pointed out that Natalie had likely visited remarkable places before, thanks to her job, and that was certainly true. But it was one thing to be treated as a guest in a place like Murin Castle. Or more precisely, as the employee of a guest, however valued by the guest in question. It was something else entirely to be treated as if it was all…hers.

The staff had curtsied and bowed when Natalie had stepped onto the royal jet. The guards had stood at attention. A person who was clearly her personal aide had catered to her during the quick flight, quickly filling her in on the princess's schedule and plans and then leaving her to her own devices. Natalie had spent years doing the exact same thing, so she'd learned a few things about Valentina in the way her efficient staff operated around her look-alike. That she was well liked by those who worked for her, which made Natalie feel oddly warm inside, as if that was some kind of reflection on her instead of the princess. That Valentina was not overly fussy or precious, given the way the staff served her food and acted while they did it. And that she was addicted to romance novels, if the stacks of books with bright-colored covers laid out for her perusal was any indication.

Then, soon enough, the plane had landed on the tiny little jewel of an island nestled in the Mediterranean Sea. Natalie's impressions were scattered as they flew in. Hills stretched high toward the sun, then sloped into the sea, covered in olive groves, tidy red roofs and the soaring arches of bell towers and churches. Blue water gleamed everywhere she looked, and white sand beaches nestled up tight to colorful fishing villages and picturesque marinas. There were cheerful sails in the graceful bay and a great, iconic castle set high on a hill. A perfect postcard of an island.

A dream. Except Natalie was wide-awake, and this was really, truly happening.

"Prince Rodolfo awaits your pleasure, Your Highness," a man she assumed was some kind of high-level butler had informed her when she'd been escorted into the palace itself, with guards saluting her arrival. She'd been too busy trying to look as if the splendor pressing in on her from all sides was so terribly common that she hardly noticed it to do more than nod, in some approximation of the princess's elegant inclination of her head. Then she'd had to follow the same butler through the palace, trying to walk with ease and confidence in shoes she was certain were not meant to be walked in at all, much less down endless marble halls.

She'd expected Prince Rodolfo to be seedier in person than in his photos. Softer of jaw, meaner of eye. And up himself in every possible way. She had not expected to find herself so stunned at the sight of him that she'd had to reach out and hold on to the furniture to keep her knees from giving out beneath her, for the love of all that was holy.

And then he'd spoken, and Natalie had understood—with a certain, sinking feeling that only made that breathlessness worse—that she was in more than a little hot water. It had never crossed her mind that *she* might find this prince—or any prince—attractive. It had never even occurred to her that she might be affected in any way by a man who carried that sort of title or courted the sort of attention Prince Rodolfo did. Natalie had never liked *flashy*. It was always a deliberate distraction, never anything real. Working for one of the most powerful men in the world had made her more than a little jaded when it came to other male displays of supposed strength. She knew what real might look like, how it was maintained and more, how it was wielded. A petty little princeling who liked to fling himself out of airplanes could only be deeply unappealing in person, she'd imagined.

She'd never imagined...*this.*

It was possible her mouth had run away with her, as some kind of defense mechanism.

And then, far more surprising, Prince Rodolfo wasn't the royal dullard she'd been expecting—all party and no substance. The sculpted mouth of his...*did things* to her as he revealed himself to be something a bit more intriguing than the airhead she'd expected. Especially when that look in his dark eyes took a turn toward the feral.

Stop, she ordered herself sternly. *This is another woman's fiancé, no matter what she might think of him.*

Natalie had to order herself to pay attention to what was happening as the Prince's surprisingly possessive words rang through the large room that teemed with antiques and the sort of dour portraits that usually turned out to have been painted by ancient masters, were always worth unconscionable amounts of money and made everyone in them look shriveled and dour. Or more precisely, she had to focus on their conversation, and not the madness that was going on inside her body.

You are mine didn't sound like the kind of thing the man Valentina had described would say. Ever. It didn't sound at all like the man the tabloids drooled over, or all those ex-lovers moaned about in exclusive interviews, mostly to complain about how quickly each and every one of them was replaced with the next.

In fact, unless she was mistaken, His Royal Highness, Prince Rodolfo, he of so many paramours in so many places that there were many internet graphs and user forums dedicated to tracking them all, looked as surprised by that outburst as she was.

"That hardly seems fair, does it?" she asked mildly, hoping he couldn't tell how thrown she was by him. Hoping it would go away if she ignored it. "I don't see why I have to confine myself to only you when you don't feel compelled to limit yourself. In any way at all, according to my research."

"Is there someone you wish to add to your stable, princess?" Rodolfo asked, in a smooth sort of way that was at complete odds with that hard, near-gold gleam in his dark eyes that set off every alarm in her body. Whether she ignored it or not. "Name the lucky gentleman."

"A lady never shares such things," she demurred. Then smiled the way she always had at the officious secretaries of her boss's rivals, all of whom underestimated her. Once. "Unlike you, Your Highness."

"I cannot help it if the press follows me everywhere I go." She sensed more than heard the growl in his voice. He was still standing where he'd been when she arrived, arranged before the immense fireplace like some kind of royal offering, but if he'd thought it made him look idle and at his ease he'd miscalculated. All she could see when she looked at him was how *big* he was. Big and hard and beautiful from head to toe and, God help her, she couldn't seem to control her reaction to him. "Just as I cannot keep them from writing any fabrication they desire. They prefer a certain narrative, of course. It sells."

"How tragic. I had no idea you were a misunderstood monk."

"I am a man, princess." He didn't quite bare his teeth. There was no reason at all Natalie should feel the cut of them against her skin. "Were you in some doubt?"

Natalie reminded herself that she, personally, had no stake in this. No matter how many stories her mother had told her about men like him and the careless way they lived their lives. No matter that Prince Rodolfo proved that her mother was right every time he swam with sharks or leaped from planes or trekked for a month in remotest Patagonia with no access to the outside world or thought to his country should he never return. And no matter the way her heart was kicking at her and her breath seemed to tangle in her throat. This wasn't about *her* at all.

I'm going to sort out your fiancé as a little wedding gift to you, she'd texted Valentina when she'd recovered from her shell shock and had emerged from the fateful bathroom in London to watch Achilles Casilieris's plane launch itself into the air without her. The beauty of the other princess having taken her bag when she'd left— with Natalie's phone inside it—was that Natalie knew her own number and could reach the woman who was inhabiting her life. You're welcome.

Good luck with that, Valentina had responded. He's unsortable. Deliberately, I imagine.

As far as Natalie was concerned, that was permission to come on in, guns blazing. She had nothing to lose by saying the things Valentina wouldn't. And there was absolutely no reason she should feel that hot, intent look he was giving her low and tight in her belly. No reason at all.

She made a show of looking around the vast room the scrupulously correct butler who had ushered her here had called a *parlor* in ringing tones. She'd had to work hard not to seem cowed, by the butler or the scale of the private wing he'd led her through, all dizzying chandeliers and astoundingly beautiful rooms clogged with priceless antiques and jaw-dropping art.

"I don't see any press here," she said, instead of debating his masculinity. For God's sake.

"Obviously not." Was it her imagination or did Rodolfo sound a little less…civilized? "We are on palace grounds. Your father would have them whipped."

"If you wanted to avoid the press, you could," Natalie pointed out. With all the authority of a person who had spent five years keeping Achilles Casilieris out of the press's meaty claws. "You don't."

Was it possible this mighty, beautiful prince looked… ill at ease? If only for a moment?

"I never promised you that I would declaw myself, Valentina," he said, and it took Natalie a moment to remember why he was calling her Valentina. Because that's who he thought she was, of course. Princess Valentina, who had to marry him in two months. Not mouthy, distressingly common Natalie, who was unlikely to marry anyone since she spent her entire life embroiled in and catering to the needs of a man who likely wouldn't be able to pick her out of a lineup. "I told you I would consider it after the wedding. For a time."

Natalie shrugged, and told herself there was no call for her to feel slapped down by his response. He wasn't going to marry *her*. She certainly didn't need to feel wounded by the way he planned to run his relationship. Critical, certainly. But not *wounded*.

"As will I," she said mildly.

Rodolfo studied her for a long moment, and Natalie forced herself to hold that seething dark glare while he did it. She even smiled and settled back against the delicate little couch, as if she was utterly relaxed. When she was nothing even remotely like it.

"No," he said after a long, long time, his voice dark

and lazy and something else she felt more than heard. "I think not."

Natalie held back the little shiver that threatened her then, because she knew, somehow, that he would see it and leap to the worst possible conclusion.

"You mistake me," she said coolly. "I wasn't asking your permission. I was stating a fact."

"I would suggest that you think very carefully about acting on this little scheme of yours, princess," Rodolfo said in that same dark, stirring tone. "You will not care for my response, I am certain."

Natalie crossed her legs and forced herself to relax even more against the back of her little couch. Well. To look it, anyway. As if she had never been more at her ease, despite the drumming of her pulse.

She waved a hand the way Valentina had done in London, so nonchalantly. "Respond however you wish. You have my blessing."

He laughed, then. The sound was rougher than Natalie would have imagined a royal prince's laugh ought to have been, and silkier than she wanted to admit as it wrapped itself around her. And all of that was a far second to the way amusement danced over his sculpted, elegant face, making him look not only big and surprisingly powerful, but very nearly approachable. Magnetic, even.

Something a whole lot more than magnetic. It lodged itself inside of her, then glowed.

Good lord, Natalie thought in another sort of daze as she gazed back at him. *This is the most dangerous man I've ever met.*

"I take it this is an academic discussion," Rodolfo said when he was finished laughing like that and using up all the light in the world, so cavalierly. "I had no idea you felt so strongly about what I did or didn't do, much less with whom. I had no idea you cared what I did at all. In fact, princess, I wasn't certain you heard a single word I've uttered in your presence in all these months."

He moved from the grand fireplace then, and watching him in motion was not exactly an improvement. Or it was a significant improvement, depending on how she looked at it. He was sleek for such a big man, and moved far too smoothly toward the slightly more substantial chair at a diagonal to where Natalie sat. He tossed himself into the stunningly wrought antique with a carelessness that should have snapped it into kindling, but didn't.

It occurred to her that he was far more aware of himself and his power than he appeared. That he was something of an iceberg, showing only the slightest bit of himself and containing multitudes beneath the surface. She didn't want to believe it. She wanted him to be a vapid, repellant playboy who she could slap into place during her time as a make-believe princess. But there was that assessing gleam in his dark gaze that told her that whatever else this prince was, he wasn't the least bit vapid.

And was rather too genuinely *charming* for her peace of mind, come to that.

He settled in his chair and stretched out his long, muscled legs so that they *almost* brushed hers, then smiled.

Natalie kept her own legs where they were, because shifting away from him would show a weakness she refused to let him see. She refused, as if her life depended on that refusal, and she didn't much care for the hysterical notion that it really, truly did.

"I don't care at all what you do or don't do," she assured him. "But it certainly appears that you can't say the same, for some reason."

"I am not the one who started making proclamations about my sexual intentions. I think you'll find that was you. Here. Today." That curve of his mouth deepened. "Entirely unprovoked."

"My mistake. Because a man who has grown up manipulating the press in no way sends a distinct message when he spends the bulk of his very public engagement 'escorting' other women to various events."

His gaze grew warmer, and that sculpted mouth curved. "I am a popular man."

"What I am suggesting to you is that you are not the only popular person in this arrangement. I'm baffled at your Neanderthal-like response to a simple statement of fact, when you have otherwise been at such pains to present yourself as the very image of modernity in royal affairs."

"We are sitting in an ancient castle on an island with a history that rivals Athens itself, discussing our upcoming marriage, which is the cold-blooded intermingling of two revered family lines for wealth and power, exactly as it might have been were we conducting this conversation in the Parthenon." His dark brows rose. "What part of this did you find particularly modern?"

"The two of us, I thought, before I walked in this room." She smiled brightly and let her foot dangle a bit too close to his leg. As if she didn't care at all that he was encroaching into her personal space. As if the idea of even so innocuous a touch did nothing at all to her central nervous system. As if he were not the sort of man she'd hated all her life, on principle. *And as if he were not promised to another,* she snapped at herself in disgust, but still, she didn't retreat the way she should have. In case she was wondering what kind of person she was.

"Now I suspect the Social Media Prince is significantly more caveman-like than he wants his millions of adoring followers to realize."

"I am the very soul of a Renaissance man, I assure you. I am merely aware of what the public will and will not support and I hate to break it you, princess, but the tabloids are not as forgiving of royal indiscretions as you appear to be."

"You surprise me again, Your Highness. I felt certain that a man in your position could not possibly care what the tabloid hacks did or did not forgive, given how much material you give them to work with. Daily."

"The two of us can sit in this room and bask in our progressive values, I am sure," Rodolfo murmured, and the look in his dark eyes did not strike Natalie as particularly progressive. "But public sentiment, I think you will find, is distressingly traditional. People may enjoy any number of their own extramarital affairs. It doesn't make them tolerant when a supposed fairy-tale princess strays from her charmed life. If anything, it makes the stones they cast heavier and more pointed."

"So, to unpack that, you personally wish to carry on as if we are single and free, but are prevented from following your heart's desire because you suddenly fear public perception?" She eyed him balefully and made no attempt to hide it. "That's a bit hard to believe, coming from the man who told me not twenty minutes ago that he refused to be *declawed*."

"You are not this naive, princess." And the look he gave her then seemed to prickle along her skin, lighting fires Natalie was terribly afraid would never go out. "You know perfectly well that I can do as I like with only minimal repercussions. It is you who cannot. You have built an entire life on your spotless character. What would happen were you to be revealed as nothing more or less than a creature as human as the rest of us?"

CHAPTER FOUR

RODOLFO HAD LONG ceased recognizing himself. And yet he kept talking.

"It will be difficult to maintain the fiction that you are a saint if your lovers are paraded through the tabloids of Europe every week," he pointed out, as if he didn't care one way or the other.

Somehow, he had the sense that the confounding woman who sat close enough to tempt him near to madness knew better. He could see it in the way her green eyes gleamed as she watched him. She was lounging in the settee as if it was a makeshift throne and she was already queen. And now she waved a languid hand, calling attention to her fine bones and the elegant fingers Rodolfo wanted all over his body. Rather desperately.

"It is you who prefer to ignore discretion," she said lightly enough. "I assume you get something out of the spotlight you shine so determinedly into your bedroom. I must congratulate you, as it is not every man who would be able to consistently perform with such an audience, so many years past his prime."

"I beg your pardon. Did you just question my… performance?"

"No need to rile yourself, Your Highness. The entire world has seen more than enough of your prowess.

I'm sure you are marvelously endowed with the—ah—necessary tools."

It took Rodolfo a stunned moment to register that the sensation moving in him then was nothing short of sheer astonishment. Somewhere between temper and laughter and yet neither at once.

"Let me make sure I am following this extraordinary line of thought," he began, trying to keep himself under control somehow—something that he could not recall ever being much of an issue before. Not with Princess Valentina, certainly. Not with any other woman he'd ever met.

"Whether or not it is extraordinary is between you and your revolving selection of aspiring hyphenates, I would think." When he could only stare blankly at her, she carried on almost merrily. "Model slash actress slash waitress slash air hostess, whatever the case may be. You exchange one for another so quickly, it's hard to keep track."

"I feel as if I've toppled off the side of the planet into an alternate reality," Rodolfo said then, after a moment spent attempting to digest what she'd said. What she'd actually dared say directly to his face. "Wherein Princess Valentina of Murin is sitting in my presence issuing veiled insults about my sexual performance and, indeed, my manhood itself."

"In this reality, we do not use the word *manhood* when we mean penis," Princess Valentina said with the same serene smile she'd always worn, back when he'd imagined she was boring. He couldn't understand how he'd misread her so completely. "It's a bit missish, isn't it?"

"What I cannot figure out is what you hope to gain from poking at me, Valentina," he said softly. "I am not given to displays of temper, if that is what you hoped.

Perhaps you forgot that I subject myself to extreme stress often. For fun. It is very, very difficult to get under my skin."

She smiled with entirely too much satisfaction for his comfort. "Says the man who had a rather strong reaction to the idea that what he feels constitutes reasonable behavior for him might also be equally appropriate for his fiancée."

"I assume you already recognize that there is no stopping the train we're on," he continued in the same quiet way, because it was that or give in to the simmering thing that was rumbling around inside of him, making him feel more precarious than he had in a long, long time. "The only way to avoid this marriage is to willfully cause a crisis in two kingdoms, and to what end? To make a point about free will? That is a lovely sentiment, I am sure, but it is not for you or me. We are not free. We belong to our countries and the people we serve. I would expect a woman whose very name is synonymous with her duty to understand that."

"That is a curious statement indeed from the only heir to an ancient throne who spends the bulk of his leisure time courting his own death." She let that land, that curve to her lips but nothing like a smile in her direct green stare. And she wasn't done. "Very much as if he was under the impression he did, in fact, owe nothing to his country at all."

Rodolfo's jaw felt like granite. "I can only assume that you are a jealous little thing, desperate to hide what you really want behind all these halfhearted feints and childish games."

The princess laughed. It was a smoky sound that felt entirely too much like a caress. "Why am I not surprised that so conceited a man would achieve that conclusion so quickly? Alas, I am hiding nothing, Your Highness."

He felt his lips curl in something much too fierce to be polite. "If you want to know whether or not I am marvelously endowed, princess, you need only ask for a demonstration."

She rolled her eyes, and perhaps that was what did it. Rodolfo was not used to being dismissed by beautiful women. Quite the contrary, they trailed around after him, begging for the scraps of his attention. He'd become adept at handling them before he'd left his teens. The ones who pretended to dislike him to get his attention, the ones who propositioned him straight out, the ones who acted as if they were shy, the ones so overcome and starstruck they stammered or wept or could only stare in silence. He'd seen it all.

But he had no way to process what was happening here with this woman he'd dismissed as uninteresting and uninterested within moments of their meeting as adults last fall. He had no idea what to do with a woman who set him on fire from across a room, and then treated him like a somewhat sad and boring joke.

He could handle just about anything, he realized, save indifference.

Rodolfo simply reached over and picked the princess up from the settee, hauling her through the air and setting her across his lap.

It was not a smart move. At best it was a test of that indifference she was flinging around the palace so casually, but it still wasn't smart.

But Rodolfo found he didn't give a damn.

The princess's porcelain cheeks flushed red and hot. She was a soft, slight weight against him, but his entire body exulted in the feel of her. Her scent was something so prosaic it hit him as almost shockingly exotic—soap. That was all. Her hands came up to brace against his chest, her copper hair was a silky shower over his arm and she was breathing hard and fast, making her exactly as much of a liar as he'd imagined she was.

She was many things, his hidden gem of a princess bride, but she was not *indifferent* to him. It felt like a victory.

"Do you think I cannot read women?" he asked her, his face temptingly, deliciously close to hers.

Her gaze was defiant. "There has long been debate about whether or not you can read anything else."

"I know you want me, princess. I can see it. I can feel it. The pulse in your throat, the look in your eyes. The way you tremble against me."

"That is sheer amazement that you think you can manhandle me this way, nothing more."

He moved the arm that wasn't wrapped around her back, sliding his hand to the delectable bit of thigh that was bared beneath the hem of her dress and just held it there. Her skin was a revelation, warm and soft. And her perfect, aristocratic oval of a face was tipped back, his for the taking.

Maybe he was the Neanderthal she'd claimed he was, after all. For the first time in his life, he felt as if he was that and more. A beast in every possible way, inside and out.

"What would happen if I slid my hand up under your skirt?" he asked her, bending even closer, so his mouth was a mere breath from hers.

"I would summon the royal guard and have you cast into the dungeons, the more medieval the better."

He ignored that breathy, insubstantial threat, along with the oddity of the Princess of Murin talking of dungeons in a palace that had never had any in the whole of its storied history. He concentrated on her body instead.

"What would I find, princess? How wet are you? How much of a liar will your body prove you to be?"

"Unlike you," she whispered fiercely, "I don't feel the need to prove myself in a thousand different sexual arenas."

But she didn't pull away. He noted that she didn't even try.

"You don't need to concern yourself with any arena but this one," he said, gruff against her mouth and his palm still full of her soft flesh. "And you need not prove yourself to anyone but me."

Rodolfo had kissed her once before. It had been a bloodless, mechanical photo op on the steps of Murin Castle. They had held hands and beamed insincerely at the crowds, and then he had pressed a chaste, polite sort of closemouthed kiss against her mouth to seal the deal. No muss, no fuss. It hadn't been unpleasant in any way. But there hadn't been anything to it. No fire. No raw, aching need. Rodolfo had experienced more intense handshakes.

That was not the way he kissed her today. Because everything was different, somehow. Himself included.

He didn't bother with any polite, bloodless kiss. Rodolfo took her mouth as if he owned it. As if there was nothing *arranged* about the two of them and never had been. As if he'd spent the night inside her, making her his in every possible way, and couldn't contain himself another moment.

Her taste flooded his senses, making him glad on some distant level that he'd had the accidental foresight to remain seated, because otherwise he thought she might have knocked him off his feet. He opened his mouth over hers, angling his jaw to revel in the slick, hot fit.

She was a marvel. And she was his, whether she liked it or not. No matter what inflammatory thing she said to rile him up or insult him into an international incident that would shame them both, or whatever the hell she was doing. How had he thought otherwise for even a moment?

Rodolfo lost his mind.

And his lovely bride-to-be did not push him off or slap his face. She didn't lie there in icy indifference. Oh, no.

She surged against him, wrapping her arms around his neck to pull him closer, and she kissed him back. Again and again and again.

For a moment there was nothing but that fire that roared between them. Wild. Insane. Unchecked and unmanageable.

And then in the next moment, she was shoving away from him. She twisted to pull herself from his grasp and then clambered off his lap, and he let her. Of course he bloody let her, and no matter the state of him as she went. That it was a new state—one he'd never experienced before, having about as much experience with frustrated desire as he did with governing the country he would one day rule—was something he kept to himself. Mostly because he hardly knew what to make of it.

The princess looked distressed as she threw herself across the room and away from him. She was trembling as she caught herself against the carved edge of the stone fireplace, and then she took a deep, long breath. To settle herself, perhaps, if she felt even a fraction of the things he did. Or perhaps she merely needed to steady herself in those shoes.

"Valentina," he began, but her name seemed to hit

her like a slap. She stiffened, then held up a hand as if to silence him. Yet another new experience.

And he could still taste her in his mouth. His body was still clamoring for her touch. He wanted her, desperately, so he let her quiet him like an errant schoolboy instead of the heir to an ancient throne.

"That must never happen again," she said with soft, intense sincerity, her gaze fixed on the fireplace, where an exultant flower arrangement took the place of the fires that had crackled there in the colder months.

"Come now, princess." He didn't sound like himself. Gruff. Low. "I think you know full well it must. We will make heirs, you and I. It is the primary purpose of our union."

She stood taller, then turned to face him, and he was struck by what looked like *torment* on her face. As if this was hard for her, whatever the hell was happening here, which made no sense. This had always been her destiny. If not with Rodolfo, then with some other Crown-sanctioned suitor. The woman he'd thought he'd known all these months had always seemed, if not precisely thrilled by the prospect, resigned to it. He imagined the change in her would have been fascinating if he wasn't half-blind from *wanting* her so badly.

"No," she said, and he was struck again by how different her voice sounded. But how could that be? He shook that off and concentrated instead on what she'd said.

"You must be aware that there can be no negotiation on this point." He tamped down on the terrible need making his body over into a stranger's, and concentrated instead on reality.

She frowned at him. "What if we can't produce heirs? It's more common than you think."

"And covered at some length in the contracts we

signed," he agreed, trying to rein in his impatience. "But we must try, Valentina. It is part of our agreement." He shook his head when she started to speak. "If you plan to tell me that this is medieval, you are correct. It is. Literally. The same provisions have covered every such marriage between people like us since the dawn of time. You cannot have imagined that a royal wedding at our rank would allow for anything else, can you?"

Something he would have called fierce inhabited her face for a moment, and then was gone.

"You misunderstand me." She ran her hands down the front of her dress as if it needed smoothing, but all Rodolfo could think of was the feel of her in his arms and the soft skin of her thigh against his palm. "I have every intention of doing my duty, Your Highness. But I will only be as faithful to you as you are to me."

He shook his head. "I am not a man who backs down from a challenge, princess. You must know this."

"It's not a challenge." Her gaze was dark when it met his. "It's a fact. As long as you ignore your commitments, I'll do the same. What have I got to lose? I'll always know that our children are mine. Let's hope you can say the same."

And on that note—while he remained frozen in his chair, stunned that she would dare threaten him openly with such a thing—Rodolfo's suddenly fascinating princess pulled herself upright and then swept out of the room.

He let her go.

It was clear to him after today that not only did he need to get to know his fiancée a whole lot better than he had so far, he needed to up his game overall where she was concerned. And when it came to games, Rodolfo had the advantage, he knew.

Because he'd never, ever lost a single game he'd ever played.

His princess was not going to be the first.

It was difficult to make a dramatic exit when Natalie had no idea where she was going.

She was on her third wrong turn—and on the verge of frustrated tears—when she hailed a confused-looking maid who, after a stilted conversation in which Natalie tried not to sound as if she was lost in what should have been her home, led her off into a completely different part of the palace and into what were clearly Valentina's own private rooms. Though "rooms" was an understated way to put it. The series of vast, exquisitely furnished chambers were more like a lavish, sprawling penthouse contained in the palace and sporting among its many rooms a formal dining area, a fully equipped media center and a vast bedroom suite complete with a wide balcony that looked off toward the sea and a series of individual rooms that together formed the princess's wardrobe. The shoe room alone was larger than the flat Natalie kept on the outskirts of London, yet barely used, thanks to her job.

Staff bustled about in the outer areas of the large suite, presumably adhering to the princess's usual schedule, but the bedroom was blessedly empty. It was there that Natalie found a surprisingly comfortable chaise, curled herself up on it with a sigh of something not quite relief and finally gave herself leave to contemplate the sort of person she'd discovered she was today.

It left a bitter taste in her mouth.

She'd always harbored a secret fantasy that should she ever stumble over a Prince Charming type—and not be forced into studied courtesy because she represented her employer—she'd shred him to pieces. Because even if the man in question wasn't the one who'd taught her mother to be so bitter, it was a fair bet that he'd ruined someone else's life. That was what Prince Charmings *did*. Even in the fairy tale, the man had left a trail of mutilated feet and broken families behind him everywhere he went. Natalie had been certain she could slap an overconfident ass like that down without even trying very hard.

And instead, she'd kissed him.

Oh, she tried to pretend otherwise. She tried to muster up a little outrage at the way Rodolfo had put his hands on her and hauled her onto his lap—but what did any of that matter? He hadn't held her there against her will. She could have stood up at any time.

She hadn't. Quite the contrary.

And when his mouth had touched hers, she'd *imploded*.

Not only had Natalie kissed the kind of man she'd always hated on principle, but she'd kissed one promised to another woman. If that wasn't enough, she'd threatened to marry him and then present him with children that weren't his. As punishment? Just to be cruel? She had no idea. She only knew that her mouth had opened and out the threat had come.

The worst part was, she'd seen that stunned, furious look on the Prince's face when she'd issued that threat. Natalie had no doubt that he believed that she would do exactly that. Worse, that *Princess Valentina* was the sort of person who, apparently, thought nothing of that kind of behavior.

"Great," she muttered out loud, to the soft chaise beneath her and the soothing landscapes on the walls. "You've made everything worse."

It was one thing to try to make things better for Valentina, who Natalie imagined was having no fun at all contending with the uncertain temper of Mr. Casilieris. Natalie was used to fixing things. That was what she did with her life—she sorted things out to be easier, smoother, better for others. But Rodolfo hadn't been as easily managed as she'd expected him to be, and the truth was, she'd never quite recovered from that first, shocking sight of him.

There was a possibility, Natalie acknowledged as she remained curled up on a posh chaise in a princess's bedroom like the sort of soft creature she'd never been, that she still hadn't recovered. *And that you never will,* chimed in a voice from deep inside her, but she dismissed it as unnecessarily dire.

Her clutch—Valentina's clutch—had been delivered here while she'd been off falling for Prince Charming like a ninny, sitting on an engaged man's lap as if she had no spine or will of her own, and making horrible threats about potential royal heirs in line to a throne. Was that treason in a kingdom like Murin? In Tissely? She didn't even know.

"And maybe you should find out before you cause a war," she snapped at herself.

What she did know was that she didn't recognize herself, all dressed up in another woman's castle as if that life could ever fit her. And she didn't like it.

Natalie pushed up off the chaise and went to sweep up the clutch from where it had been left on the padded bench that claimed the real estate at the foot of the great four-poster bed. She'd examined the contents on the plane, fascinated. Princesses apparently carried very little, unlike personal assistants, who could live out of their shoulder bags for weeks in a pinch. There was no money or identification, likely because neither was necessary when you had access to an entire treasury filled with currency stamped with your own face. Valentina carried only her mobile, a tube of extremely high-end lip gloss and a small compact mirror.

Natalie sat on the bench with Valentina's mobile in her hand and looked around the quietly elegant bedroom, though she hardly saw it. The adrenaline of the initial switch had given way to sheer anxiety once she'd arrived in Murin. She'd expected to be called out at any moment and forced to explain how and why she was impersonating the princess. But no one had blinked, not even Prince Rodolfo.

Maybe she shouldn't be surprised that now that she was finally alone, she felt a little lost. Maybe that was the price anyone could expect to pay when swapping identities with a complete stranger. Especially one who happened to be a royal princess to boot.

It was times like this that Natalie wished she had the sort of relationship with her mother that other people seemed to have with theirs. She'd like nothing more than to call Erica up and ask for some advice, or maybe just so she could feel soothed, somehow, by the fact of her mother's existence. But that had never been the way her mother operated. Erica had liked Natalie best when she was a prop. The pretty little girl she could trot out when it suited her, to tug on a heartstring or to prove that she was maternal when, of course, she wasn't. Not really. Not beyond the telling of the odd fairy tale with a grim ending, which Natalie had learned pretty early on was less for her than for her mother.

No wonder Natalie had lost herself in school. It didn't matter where they moved. It didn't matter what was going on in whatever place Erica was calling home that month. Natalie could always count on her studies. Whether she was behind the class or ahead of it when she showed up as the new kid, who cared? School always gave her a project of one sort or another. She'd viewed getting into college—on a full academic scholarship, of course, because Erica had laughed when Natalie had asked if there would be any parental contributions to her education and then launched into another long story about the evils of rich, selfish men—as her escape. College had been four years of an actual place to call home, at last. Plus classes. Basically nirvana, as far as Natalie had been concerned.

But that kind of overachieving behavior, while perfect for her eventual career as the type A assistant to the most picky and overbearing man alive, had not exactly helped Natalie make any friends. She'd always been the new kid in whatever school she'd ended up in. Then, while she wasn't the new kid at college, she was so used to her usual routine of studying constantly that she hadn't known how to stop it. She and her freshman-year roommate had gotten along well enough and they'd even had lunch a few times over the next few years, all very pleasant, but it hadn't ever bloomed into the sort of friendships Natalie knew other women had. She'd had a boyfriend her junior year, which had been more exciting in theory than in fact. And then she'd started working for Mr. Casilieris after graduation and there hadn't been time for anything but him, ever again.

All of this had been perfectly fine with her yesterday. She'd been proud of her achievements and the fact no one had helped her in equal measure. Well. She'd wanted to quit her job, but surely that was a reasonable response to five years of Achilles Casilieris. And today, sitting on the cushioned bench at the foot of a princess's bed with a medieval castle looming all around her like an accusation, it was clear to Natalie that really, she could have used someone to call.

Anyone except the person she knew she had to call, that was.

But Natalie hadn't dealt with a terrifying man like Achilles Casilieris for years by being a coward, no matter how tempting it was to become one now. She blew out a breath, then dialed her own mobile number. She knew that the flight she should have been on right now, en route to New York City, hadn't landed yet. She even knew that all the calls she'd set up would likely have ended—but she wasn't surprised when Valentina didn't answer. Mr. Casilieris was likely tearing strips out of the princess's hide, because no matter how she'd handled the situation, it wouldn't have been to his satisfaction. She was a bit surprised that Valentina hadn't confessed all and that the Casilieris plane wasn't landing in Murin right now to discharge her—and so Achilles Casilieris could fire Natalie in person for deceiving him.

Really, it hadn't been nice of Natalie to let Valentina take her place. She'd known what the other woman was walking into. God help the poor princess if she failed to provide Mr. Casilieris with what he wanted three seconds before he knew he wanted it. When she'd started, Achilles Casilieris had been famous for cycling through assistants in a matter of hours, sometimes, depending on the foulness of his mood. Everyone was an idiot, as he was all too happy to make clear, especially the people he paid to assist him. Everyone fell short of his impossibly high standards. If he thought Natalie had lost her ability to do her job the way he liked it done, he'd fire her without a second thought. She'd never been in any doubt about that.

Which meant that really, she should have been a little more concerned about the job Valentina was almost certainly botching up right this very minute, somewhere high above the Atlantic Ocean.

But she found she couldn't work up the usual worry over that eventuality. If he fired her, he fired her. It saved her having to quit, didn't it? And when she tried to stress out about losing the position she'd worked so hard to keep all these years, all she could think of instead was the fact he hadn't known Valentina wasn't her in that bathroom. That despite spending more time with Natalie than with his last ten mistresses combined, he'd failed to recognize her. And meanwhile, Rodolfo had looked at *her*. As if he wanted to climb inside of her. As if he could never, ever get enough. And that mouth of his was sculpted and wicked, knowing and hot…

She heard her own voice asking for a message and a phone number on the other end of the line, but she didn't leave a voice mail at the beep. What would she say? Where would she start? Would she jump right into the kissing and claims that she'd sleep her way around Europe in payback for any extramarital adventures Prince Rodolfo might have? She could hardly believe she'd done either of those things, much less think of how best to tell someone else that she had. Particularly when the someone else was the woman who was expected to marry the man in question.

The fact was, she had no idea what Valentina expected from her arranged marriage. A dry tone in a bathroom to a stranger when discussing her fiancé wasn't exactly a peek into the woman's thoughts on what happily-ever-after looked like for her. Maybe she'd been fine with the expected cheating, like half of Europe seemed to be. Maybe she hadn't cared either way. Natalie had no way to tell.

But it didn't matter what Valentina's position on any of this was. It didn't make Natalie any happier with herself that she was hoping, somewhere in there, that Valentina might give her blessing. Or her forgiveness, anyway. And it wasn't as if she could blame the Prince, either. Prince Rodolfo thought she *was* Valentina. His behavior was completely acceptable. He'd had every reason to believe he was with his betrothed.

Natalie was the one who'd let another woman's fiancé kiss her. So thoroughly her breasts still ached and her lips felt vulnerable and she felt a fist of pure need clench tight between her legs at the memory. Natalie was the one who'd kissed him back.

There was no prettying that up. *That* was who she was.

Natalie put the phone aside, then jumped when it beeped at her. She snatched it back up, hoping it was Valentina so she could at least unburden her conscience— another indication that she was not really the good person she'd always imagined herself to be, she was well aware—but it was a reminder from the princess's calendar, telling her she had a dinner with the king in a few hours.

She wanted to curl back up on that chaise and cry for a while. Perhaps a week or so. She wanted to look around for the computer she was sure the princess must have secreted away somewhere and see if she could track her actual life as it occurred across the planet. She wanted to rewind to London and her decision to do this insane thing in the first place and then think better of pulling such a stunt.

But she swallowed hard as she looked down at that reminder on the mobile screen. *The king.*

All those things she didn't want to think about flooded her then.

If Erica had shortened her name… If all that moving around had been less *wanderer's soul a*nd more *on the run*… If there was really, truly only one reasonable explanation as to how a royal princess and a glorified secretary could pass for each other and it had nothing to do with that tired old saying that *everyone had a twin somewhere*…

If all of those things were true, then the King of Murin—with whom she was about to have a meal— wasn't simply the monarch of this tiny little island kingdom, well-known for his vast personal wealth, many rumors of secret affairs with the world's most glamorous women and the glittering, celebrity-studded life he lived as the head of a tiny, wealthy country renowned for its yacht-friendly harbors and friendly taxes.

He was also very likely her father.

And that was the lure, it turned out, that Natalie couldn't resist.

CHAPTER FIVE

A LITTLE OVER a week later, Natalie thought she might actually be getting the hang of this princess thing. Or settling into her role well enough that she no longer had to mystify the palace staff with odd requests that they lead her to places she should have been able to find on her own.

She'd survived that first dinner with the king, who might or might not have been her father. The truth was, she couldn't tell. If she'd been expecting a mystical, magical sort of reunion, complete with swelling emotions and dazed recognition on both sides, she'd been bitterly disappointed. She'd been led to what was clearly her seat at one end of a long, polished table in what looked like an excruciatingly formal dining room to her but was more likely the king's private, casual eating area given that it was located in his private wing of the palace. She'd stood there for a moment, not knowing what she was supposed to do next. Sit? Wait? Prepare to curtsy?

The doors had been tossed open and a man had strode in with great pomp and circumstance. Even if she hadn't recognized him from the pictures she'd studied online and the portraits littering the castle, Natalie would have known who he was. King Geoffrey of Murin didn't exude the sort of leashed, simmering power Rodolfo did, she couldn't help thinking. He wasn't as magnificently built, for one thing. He was a tall, elegantly slender man who would have looked a bit like an accountant if the suit he wore hadn't so obviously been a bespoke masterpiece and if he hadn't moved with a sort of bone-deep imperiousness that shouted out his identity with each step. It was as if he expected marble floors to form themselves beneath his foot in anticipation that he might place it there. And they did.

"Hello," she'd said when he approached the head of the table, with perhaps a little too much *meaning* in those two syllables. She'd swallowed. Hard.

And the king had paused. Natalie had tensed, her stomach twisting in on itself. *This is it,* she'd thought. *This is the moment you'll not only be exposed as not being Valentina, but recognized as his long-lost daughter—*

"Are you well?" That was it. That was all he'd asked, with a vaguely quizzical look aimed her way.

"Ah, yes." She cleared her throat, though it didn't need clearing. It was her head that had felt dizzy. "Quite well. Thank you. And you?"

"I hope this is not an example of the sort of witty repartee you practice upon Prince Rodolfo," was what Geoffrey had said. He'd nodded at her, which Natalie had taken as her cue to sit, and then he'd settled himself in his own chair. Only then did he lift a royal eyebrow and summon the hovering servants to attend them.

"Not at all," Natalie had managed to reply. And then some demon had taken her over, and she didn't stop there. "A future king looks for many things in a prospective bride, I imagine, from her bloodlines to whether or not she is reasonably photogenic in all the necessary pictures. But certainly not wit. That sort of thing is better saved for the peasants, who require more entertainment to make it through their dreary lives."

"Very droll, I am sure." The king's eyes were the same as hers. The same shape, the same unusual green. And showed the same banked temper she'd felt in her own too many times to count. A kind of panicked flush had rolled over her, making her want to get up and run from the room even as her legs felt too numb to hold her upright. "I trust you know better than to make such an undignified display of inappropriate humor in front of the prince? He may be deep in a regrettable phase with all those stunts he pulls, but I assure you, at the end of the day he is no different from any other man in his position. Whatever issues he may have with his father now, he will sooner or later ascend the throne of Tissely. And when he does, he will not want a comedienne at his side, Valentina. He will require a queen."

Natalie was used to Achilles Casilieris's version of slap downs. They were quicker. Louder. He blazed into a fury and then he was done. This was entirely different. This was less a slap down and more a deliberate *pressing down,* putting Natalie firmly and ruthlessly in her place.

She'd found she didn't much care for the experience. Or the place Valentina was apparently expected to occupy.

"But you have no queen," she'd blurted out. Then instantly regretted it when Geoffrey had gazed at her in amazement over his first course. "Sir."

"I do not appreciate this sort of acting out at my table, Valentina," he'd told her, with a certain quiet yet ringing tone. "You know what is expected of you. You were promised to the Tisselians when I still believed I might have more children, or you would take the throne of

Murin yourself. But we are Murinese and we do not back out of our promises. If you are finding your engagement problematic, I suggest you either find a way to solve it to your satisfaction or come to a place of peace with its realities. Those are your only choices."

"Was that your choice?" she'd asked.

Maybe her voice had sounded different then. Maybe she'd slipped and let a little emotion in. Natalie hadn't known. What she'd been entirely too clear on was that this man should have recognized her. At the very least, he should have known she wasn't the daughter he was used to seeing at his table. And surely the king knew that he'd had twins. He should have had some kind of inkling that it was *possible* he'd run into his other daughter someday.

And yet if King Geoffrey of Murin noticed that his daughter was any different than usual, he kept it to himself. In the same way that if he was racked nightly by guilt because he'd clearly misplaced a twin daughter some twenty-seven years ago, it did not mar his royal visage in any way.

"We must all make choices," he'd said coolly. "And when we are of the Royal House of Murin, each and every one of those choices must benefit the kingdom. You know this full well and always have. I suggest you resign yourself to your fate, and more gracefully."

And it was the only answer he'd given.

He'd shifted the conversation then, taking charge in what Natalie assumed was his usual way. And he'd talked about nothing much, in more than one language, which would have made Natalie terrified that she'd give herself away, but he hadn't seemed to want much in the way of answers. In Italian, French, or English.

Clearly, the princess's role was to sit quietly and listen as the king expounded on whatever topic he liked. And not to ask questions. No wonder she'd wanted a break.

I have a confession to make, Natalie had texted Valentina later that first night. She'd been back in the princess's absurdly comfortable and elegant bedroom, completely unable to sleep as her conscience was keeping her wide awake.

Confession is good for the soul, I'm reliably informed, Valentina had replied after a moment or two. Natalie had tried to imagine where she might be. In the small room in Mr. Casilieris's vast New York penthouse she thought of as hers? Trying to catch up on work in the office suite on the lower floor? I've never had the pleasure of a life that required a confession. But you can tell me anything.

Natalie had to order herself to stop thinking about her real life, and to start paying attention to Valentina's life, which she was messing up left and right.

Rodolfo kissed me. There. Three quick words, then the send button, and she was no longer keeping a terrible secret to herself.

That time, the pause had seemed to take years.

That sounds a bit more like a confession Rodolfo ought to be making. Though I suppose he wouldn't know one was necessary, would he?

In the spirit of total honesty, Natalie had typed resolutely, because there was nothing to be gained by lying at that point and besides, she clearly couldn't live with herself if she didn't share all of this with Valentina no matter the consequences, I kissed him back.

She'd been sitting up against the headboard then, staring at the phone in her hand with her knees pulled up beneath her chin. She'd expected anger, at the very least. A denunciation or two. And she'd had no idea what that would even look like, coming from a royal princess—would guards burst through the bedroom doors and haul her away? Would Valentina declare her an imposter and have her carried off in chains? Anything seemed possible. Likely, even, given how grievously Natalie had slipped up.

If she'd been a nail-biter, Natalie would have gnawed hers right off. Instead, she tried to make herself breathe.

Someone should, I suppose, Valentina had texted back, after another pause that seemed to last forever and then some. *I've certainly never touched him.*

Natalie had blinked at that. And had then hated herself, because the thing that wound around inside of her was not shame. It was far warmer and far more dangerous.

I never will again, she'd vowed. And she'd wanted to mean it with every fiber of her being. *I swear.*

You can do as you like with Rodolfo, Valentina had replied, and Natalie could almost hear the other woman's airy tone through the typed words. *You have my blessing. Really. A hundred Eastern European models can't be wrong!*

But it wasn't Valentina's blessing that she'd wanted, Natalie realized. Because that was a little too close to outright permission and she'd hardly been able to control herself as it was. What she wanted was outrage. Fury and consequences. Something—*anything*—to keep her from acting like a right tart.

And instead it was a little more than a week later and Rodolfo was outplaying her at the game she was very much afraid she'd put into motion that first day in her new role as the princess. By accident—or at least, without thinking about the consequences—but that hardly mattered now.

Worse, he was doing it masterfully, by not involving her at all. Why risk what might come out of her mouth when he could do an end run around her and go straight to King Geoffrey instead? On some level, Natalie admired the brilliance of the move. It made Rodolfo look like less of a libertine in the king's eyes and far more of the sort of political ally for Murin he would one day become as the King of Tissely.

She needed to stop underestimating her prince. Before she got into the kind of trouble a text couldn't solve.

"Prince Rodolfo thinks the two of you ought to build more of an accessible public profile ahead of the wedding," the king said as they'd sat at their third dinner of the week, as was apparently protocol.

It had taken Natalie a moment to realize Geoffrey was actually waiting for her response. She'd swallowed the bite of tender Murinese lamb she'd put in her mouth and smiled automatically, playing back what he'd said—because she'd gotten in the terrible habit of nodding along without really listening. She preferred to study the King's features and ask herself why, if he was her father, she didn't *feel* it. And he didn't either, clearly. Surely she should *know him* on a deep, cellular level. Or something. Wasn't blood supposed to reveal itself like that? And if it didn't, surely that meant that she and Valentina only happened to resemble each other by chance.

In every detail. Down to resembling Geoffrey, too. So much so that the King himself couldn't tell the difference when they switched.

Natalie knew on a level she didn't care to explore that it was unlikely to be chance. That it couldn't be chance.

"A public profile?" she echoed, because she had to say something, and she had an inkling that flatly refusing to do anything Rodolfo suggested simply because it had come from him wouldn't exactly fly as far as the king was concerned.

"I rather like the idea." King Geoffrey's attention had returned to his own plate. "It is a sad fact that in these modern times, a public figure is judged as much on the image he presents to the world as his contributions to it. More, perhaps."

He didn't order her to do as Rodolfo asked. But then, he didn't have to issue direct orders. And that was how Natalie found herself flying off to Rome to attend a star-studded charity gala the very next day, because Rodolfo had decided it was an excellent opportunity to "boost their profile" in the eyes of the international press corps.

If she ignored the reason she was taking the trip and the man who'd engineered it, Natalie had to admit that it was lovely to have her every need attended to, for a change. All she had to do was wake up the following morning. Everything else was sorted out by a fleet of others. Her wardrobe attendant asked if she had any particular requests and, when Natalie said she didn't, nodded decisively and returned with tidily packed luggage in less than an hour. Which footmen then whisked away. Natalie was swept off to the same private jet as before, where she was fed a lovely lunch of a complicated, savory salad and served sparkling water infused with cucumber. Things she didn't know she craved, deeply, until they were presented to her.

"Your chocolate, Your Highness," the air steward said with a smile after clearing away the salad dishes, presenting her with two rich, dark squares on a gold-embossed plate. "From the finest chocolatiers in all of the kingdom."

"I do like my chocolate," Natalie murmured.

More than that, she liked the princess's style, she thought as she let each rich, almost sweet square dissolve on her tongue, as if it had been crafted precisely to appeal to her.

Which, if she and Valentina were identical twins after all, she supposed it had.

And the pampering continued. The hotel she was delivered to in Rome, located at the top of the Spanish Steps to command the finest view possible over the ancient, vibrant city, had been arranged for and carefully screened by someone else. All she had to do was walk inside and smile as the staff all but kowtowed before her. Once in her sprawling penthouse suite, Natalie was required to do nothing but relax as her attendants bustled around, unpacking her things in one of the lavishly appointed rooms while they got to work on getting the princess ready for the gala in another. A job that required the undivided attention of a team of five stylists, apparently, when Natalie was used to tossing something on in the five minutes between crises and making the best of it.

Her fingernails were painted, her hair washed and cut and styled just so, and even her makeup was deftly applied. When they were done, Natalie was dressed like a fairy-tale princess all ready for her ball.

And her prince, something inside her murmured.

She shoved that away. Hard. There'd been no room for fairy tales in her life, only hard work and dedication. Her mother had told her stories that always ended badly, and Natalie had given up wishing for happier conclusions to such tales a long, long time ago. Even if she and Valentina really were sisters, it hardly mattered now. She was a grown woman. There was no being swept off in a pumpkin and spending the rest of her life surrounded by dancing mice. That ship had sailed.

She had no time for fairy tales. Not even if she happened to be living one.

Natalie concentrated on the fact that she looked like someone else tonight. Someone she recognized, yet didn't. Someone far more sophisticated than she'd ever been, and she'd thought her constant exposure to billionaires like Mr. Casilieris had given her a bit of polish.

You look like someone beautiful, she thought in a kind of wonder as she studied herself in the big, round mirror that graced the wall in her room. *Objectively beautiful.*

Her hair was swept up into a chignon and secured with pins that gleamed with quietly elegant jewels. Her dress was a dove-gray color that seemed to make her skin glow, cascading from a strapless bodice to a wide, gorgeous skirt that moved of its own accord when she walked and made her look very nearly celestial. Her shoes were high sandals festooned with straps, there was a clasp of impossible sapphires and diamonds at her throat that matched the ring she wore on her hand and her eyes looked fathomless.

Natalie looked like a princess. Not just Princess Valentina, but the sort of magical, fantasy princess she'd have told anyone who asked she'd never, ever imagined when she was a child, because she'd been taught better than that.

Never ever. Not once.

She nodded and smiled her thanks at her waiting attendants, but Natalie didn't dare speak. She was afraid that if she did, that faint catch in her throat would tip over into something far more embarrassing, and then worse, she'd have to explain it. And Natalie had no idea how to explain the emotions that buffeted her then.

Because the truth was, she didn't know how to be beautiful. She knew how to stick to the shadows and more, how to excel in them. She knew how to disappear in plain sight and use that to her—and her employer's—advantage. Natalie had no idea how to be the center of attention. How to be *seen*. In fact, she'd actively avoided it. Princess Valentina turned heads wherever she went, and Natalie had no idea how she was going to handle it. If she *could* handle it.

But it was more than her shocking appearance, so princessy and pretty. This was the first time in all her life that she hadn't had to be responsible for a thing. Not one thing. Not even her own sugar consumption, apparently. This was the first time in recent memory that she hadn't had to fix things for someone else or exhaust herself while making sure that others could relax and enjoy themselves.

No one had ever taken care of Natalie Monette. Not once. She'd had to become Princess Valentina for that to happen. And while she hadn't exactly expected that impersonating royalty would feel like a delightful vacation from her life, she hadn't anticipated that it would feel a bit more like an earthquake, shaking her apart from within.

It isn't real, a hard voice deep inside of her snapped, sounding a great deal like her chilly mother. *It's temporary and deeply stupid, as you should have known before you tried on that ring.*

Natalie knew that, of course. She flexed her hand at her side and watched the ring Prince Rodolfo had given another woman spill light here and there. None of this was real. Because none of this was hers. It was a short, confusing break from real life, that was all, and there was no use getting all soppy about it. There was only surviving it without blowing up the real princess's life while she was mucking around in it.

But all the bracing lectures in the world couldn't keep that glowing thing inside her chest from expanding as she gazed at the princess in the mirror, until it felt as if it was a part of every breath she took. Until she couldn't tell where the light of it ended and that shaking thing began. And she didn't need little voices inside of her to tell her how dangerous that was. She could feel it deep in her bones, knitting them into new shapes she was very much afraid she would have to break into pieces when she left.

Because whatever else this was, it was temporary. She needed to remember that above all.

"Your Highness." It was the most senior of the aides who traveled with the princess, something Natalie had known at a glance because she recognized the older woman's particular blend of sharp focus and efficient movement. "His Royal Highness Prince Rodolfo has arrived to escort you to the gala."

"Thank you," Natalie murmured, as serenely and princessy as possible.

And this was the trouble with dressing up like a beautiful princess who could be whisked off to a ball at a moment's notice. Natalie started to imagine that was exactly who she was. It was so hard to keep her head, and then she walked into the large, comfortably elegant living room of her hotel suite to find Prince Rodolfo waiting for her, decked out in evening clothes, and everything troubling became that much harder.

He stood at the great glass doors that slid open to one

of the terraces that offered up stunning views of Rome at all times, but particularly now, as the sun inched toward the horizon and the city was bathed in a dancing, liquid gold.

More to the point, so was Rodolfo.

Natalie hadn't seen him since that unfortunate kissing incident. Not in person, anyway. And once again she was struck by the vast, unconquerable distance between pictures of the man on a computer screen and the reality before her. He stood tall and strong with his hands thrust into the pockets of trousers that had clearly been lovingly crafted to his precise, athletic measurements. His attention was on the red-and-gold sunset happening there before him, fanciful and lovely, taking over the Roman sky as if it was trying to court his favor.

He wasn't even looking at her. And still he somehow stole all the air from the room.

Natalie felt herself flush as she stood in the doorway, a long, deep roll of heat that scared her, it was so intense. Her pulse was a wild fluttering, everywhere. Her temples. Her throat. Her chest.

And deep between her legs, like an invitation she had no right to offer. Not this man. Not ever this man. If he was Prince Charming after all, and she was skeptical on that point, it didn't matter. He certainly wasn't hers.

She must have made some noise through that dry, clutching thing in her throat, because he turned to face her. And that wasn't any better. In her head, she'd downgraded the situation. She'd chalked it up to excusable nerves and understandable adrenaline over switching places with Valentina. That was the only explanation that had made any sense to her. She'd been so sure that when she saw Rodolfo again, all that power and compulsion that had sparked the air around him would be gone.

He would just be another wealthy man for her to handle. Just another problem for her to solve.

But she'd been kidding herself.

If anything, tonight he was even worse, all dressed up in an Italian sunset.

Because you know, something inside her whispered. *You know, now.*

How he tasted. The feel of those lean, hard arms around her. The sensation of that marvelous mouth against hers. She had to fight back the shudder that she feared might bring her to her knees right there on the absurdly lush rug, but she had the sneaking suspicion he knew anyway. There was something about the curve of his mouth as he inclined his head.

"Princess," he murmured.

And God help her, but she felt that everywhere. *Everywhere.* As if he'd used his mouth directly against her heated skin.

"I hear you wish to build our public profile, whatever that is," she said, rather more severely than necessary. She made herself move forward, deeper into the room, when what she wanted to do was turn and run. She seated herself in an armchair because it meant he couldn't sit on either side of her, and his fascinating mouth twitched as if he knew exactly why she'd done it. "King Geoffrey—" She couldn't bring herself to say *my father,* not even if Valentina would have and not even if it was true "—was impressed. That is obviously the only reason I am here."

"Obviously." He threw himself onto the couch opposite her with the same reckless disregard for the lifespan of the average piece of furniture that he'd displayed back in Murin. She told herself that was reflective of his character. "Happily, it makes no difference to me if you are here of your own volition or not, so long as you are here."

"What a lovely sentiment. Every bride dreams of such poetry, I am certain. I am certainly aflutter."

"There is no need for sarcasm." But he sounded amused. "All that is required is that we appear in front of the paparazzi and look as if this wedding is our idea because we are a couple in love like any other, not simply a corporate merger with crowns."

Natalie eyed him, wishing the Roman sunset was not taking quite so long, nor quite so many liberties with Rodolfo's already impossible good looks. He was bathed in gold and russet now, and it made him glow, as if he was the sort of dream maidens might have had in this city thousands of years ago in feverish anticipation of their fierce gods descending from on high.

She tried to cast that fanciful nonsense out of her head, but it was impossible. Especially when he was making no particular effort to hide the hungry look in his dark gaze as he trained it on her. She could feel it shiver through her, lighting her on fire. Making it as hard to sit still as it was to breathe.

"I don't think anyone is going to believe that we were swept away by passion," she managed to say. She folded her hands in her lap the way she'd seen Valentina do in the videos she'd watched of the princess these past few nights, so worried was she that someone would be able to see right through her because she forgot to do some or other princessy thing. Though she thought she gripped her own fingers a bit more tightly than the princess had. "Seeing as how our engagement has been markedly free of any hint of it until now."

"But that's the beauty of it." Rodolfo shrugged. "The story could be that we were promised to each other and were prepared to do our duty, only to trip over the fact we were made for each other all along. Or it could be that it was never arranged at all and that we met, kept everything secret, and are now close enough to our wedding that we can let the world see what our hearts have always known."

"You sound like a tabloid."

"Thank you."

Natalie glared at him. "There is no possible way that could be construed as a compliment."

"I've starred in so many tabloid scandals I could write the headlines myself. And that is what we will do, starting tonight. We will rewrite whatever story is out there and make it into a grand romance. The Playboy Prince and His Perfect Princess, etcetera." That half smile of his deepened. "You get the idea, I'm sure."

"Why would we want to do something so silly? You are going to be a king, not a Hollywood star. Surely a restrained, distant competence is more the package you should be presenting to the world." Natalie aimed her coolest smile at him. "Though I grant you, that might well be another difficult reach."

The sun finally dripped below the city as she spoke, leaving strands of soft pink and deep gold in its wake. But it also made it a lot easier to see Prince Rodolfo's dark, measuring expression. And much too easy to feel the way it clattered through her, making her feel...jittery.

It occurred to her that the way he lounged there, so carelessly, was an optical illusion. Because there wasn't a single thing about him that wasn't hard and taut, as if he not only kept all his brooding power on a tight leash—but could explode into action at any moment. That notion was not exactly soothing.

Neither was his smile. "We will spend the rest of the

night in public, princess. Fawned over by the masses. So perhaps you will do me the favor of telling me here, in private, exactly what it is that has made you imagine I deserve a steady stream of insult. One after the next, without end, since I last saw you."

Natalie felt chastened by that, and hated herself for it in the next instant. Because her own feelings didn't matter here. She shouldn't even have feelings where this man was concerned. Valentina might have given her blessing to whatever happened between her betrothed and Natalie, but that was neither here nor there. Natalie knew better than to let a man like this beguile her. She'd been taught to see through this sort of thing at her mother's knee. It appalled her that his brand of patented princely charm was actually *working*.

"Are you not deserving?" she asked quietly. She made herself meet his dark gaze, though something inside her quailed at it. And possibly died a little bit, too. But she didn't look away. "Are you sure?"

"Am I a vicious man?" Rodolfo's voice was no louder than hers, but there was an intensity to it that made that lick of shame inside of her shimmer, then expand. It made the air in the room seem thin. It made Natalie's heart hit at her ribs, hard enough to bruise. "A brute? A monster in some fashion?"

"Only you can answer that question, I think."

"I am unaware of any instance in which I have deliberately hurt another person, but perhaps you, princess, know something I do not about my own life."

It turned out the Prince was as effective with a slap down as her boss. Natalie sat a bit straighter, but she didn't back down. "Everyone knows a little too much about your life, Your Highness. Entirely too much, one might argue."

"Tabloid fantasies are not life. They are a game. You should know that better than anyone, as we sit here discussing a new story we plan to sell ourselves."

"How would I know this, exactly?" She felt her head tilt to one side in a manner she thought was more her than Valentina. She corrected it. "I do not appear in the tabloids. Not with any frequency, and only on the society pages. Never the front-page stories." Natalie knew. She'd checked.

"You are a paragon, indeed." Rodolfo's voice was low and dark and not remotely complimentary. "But a rather judgmental one, I fear."

Natalie clasped her hands tighter together. "That word has always bothered me. There is nothing wrong with rendering judgment. It's even lauded in some circles. How did *judgmental* become an insult?"

"When rendering judgment became a blood sport," Rodolfo replied, with a soft menace that drew blood on its own.

But Natalie couldn't stop to catalog the wounds it left behind, all over her body, or she was afraid she'd simply…collapse.

"It is neither bloody nor sporting to commit yourself to a woman in the eyes of the world and then continue to date others, Your Highness," she said crisply. "It is simply unsavory. Perhaps childish. And certainly dishonorable. I think you'll find that there are very few women on the planet who will judge that behavior favorably."

Rodolfo inclined his head, though she had the sense his jaw was tighter than it had been. "Fair enough. I will say in my defense that you never seemed to care one way or the other what I did, much less with whom, before last week. We talked about it at length and you said nothing. Not one word."

Valentina had said he talked at her, defending himself—hadn't she? Natalie couldn't remember. But she also wasn't here to poke holes in Valentina's story. It didn't matter if it was true. It mattered that she'd felt it, and Natalie could do something to help fix it. Or try, anyway.

"You're right, of course," she said softly, keeping her gaze trained to his. "It's my fault for not foreseeing that your word was not your bond and your vows were meaningless. My deepest apologies. I'll be certain to keep all of that in mind on our wedding day."

He didn't appear to move, and yet suddenly Natalie couldn't, as surely as if he'd reached out and wrapped her in his tight grip. His dark gaze seemed to pin her to her chair, intent and hard.

"I've tasted you," he reminded her, as if she could forget that for an instant. As if she hadn't dreamed about exactly that, night after night, waking up with his taste on her tongue and a deep, restless ache between her legs. "I know you want me, yet you fight me. Is it necessary to you that I become the villain? Does that make it easier?"

Natalie couldn't breathe. Her heart felt as if it might rip its way out of her chest all on its own, and she still couldn't tear her gaze away from his. There was that hunger, yes, but also a kind of *certainty* that made her feel…liquid.

"Because it is not necessary to insult me to get my attention, princess," Rodolfo continued in the same intense way. "You have it. And you need not question my fidelity. I will touch no other but you, if that is what you require. Does this satisfy you? Can we step away from the bloodlust, do you think?"

What that almost offhanded promise did was make

Natalie feel as if she was nothing but a puppet and he was pulling all her strings, all without laying a single finger upon her. And what sent an arrow of shame and delight spiraling through her was that she couldn't tell if she was properly horrified by that notion, or…not.

"Don't be ridiculous," was the best she could manage.

"You only confirm my suspicions," he told her then, and she knew she wasn't imagining the satisfaction that laced his dark tone. "It is not who I might or might not have dated over the past few months that so disturbs you. I do not doubt that is a factor, but it is not the whole picture. Will you tell me what is? Or will I be forced to guess?"

And she knew, somehow, that his guesses would involve his hands on her once more and God help her, she didn't know what might happen if he touched her again. She didn't know what she might do. Or not do.

Who she might betray, or how badly.

She stood then, moving to put the chair between them, aware of the way her magnificent gown swayed and danced as if it had a mind of its own. And of the way Rodolfo watched her do it, that hard-lit amusement in his dark eyes, as if she were acting precisely as he'd expected she would.

As if he was a rather oversize cat toying with his next meal and was in absolutely no doubt as to how this would all end.

Though she didn't really care to imagine him treating her like his dinner. Or, more precisely, she refused to allow herself to imagine it, no matter how her pulse rocketed through her veins.

"My life is about order," she said, and she realized as she spoke that she wasn't playing her prescribed role. That the words were pouring out of a part of her she hadn't even known was there inside of her. "I have duties, responsibilities, and I handle them all. I *like* to handle them. I like knowing that I'm equal to any task that's put in front of me, and then proving it. Especially when no one thinks I can."

"And you are duly celebrated for your sense of duty throughout the great houses of Europe." Rodolfo inclined his head. "I salute you."

"I can't tell if you're mocking me or not, but I don't require celebration," she threw back at him. "It's not about that. It's about the accomplishment. It's about putting an order to things no matter how messy they get."

"Valentina…"

Natalie was glad he said that name. It reminded her who she was—and who she wasn't. It allowed her to focus through all the clamor and spin inside of her.

"But your life is chaos," she said, low and fierce. "As far as I can tell, it always has been. I think you must like it that way, as you have been careening from one death wish to another since your brother—"

"Careful."

He looked different then, furious and something like thrown, but she only lifted her chin and told herself to ignore it. Because the pain of an international playboy had nothing to do with her. Prince Charming was the villain in all the stories her mother had told her, never the hero. And the brother he'd lost when he was fifteen was a means to psychoanalyze this man, not humanize him. She told herself that again and again. And then she forged on.

"He died, Rodolfo. You lived." He hissed in a breath as if she'd struck him, but Natalie didn't stop. "And yet your entire adult life appears to be a calculated attempt to change that. You and I have absolutely nothing in common."

Rodolfo stood. The glittering emotion she'd seen grip him a moment ago was in his dark gaze, ferocious and focused, but he was otherwise wiped clean. She would have been impressed if she'd been able to breathe.

"My brother's death was an unfortunate tragedy." But he sounded something like hollow. As if he was reciting a speech he'd learned by rote a long time ago. His gaze remained irate and focused on her. "I never intended to fill his shoes and, in fact, make no attempt to do so. I like extreme sports, that is all. It isn't a death wish. I am neither suicidal nor reckless."

He might as well have been issuing his own press release.

"If you die while leaping out of helicopters to get to the freshest ski slope in the world, the way you famously do week after week in winter, you will not only break your neck and likely die, you will leave your country in chaos," Natalie said quietly. His gaze intensified, but she didn't look away. "It all comes back to chaos, Your Highness. And that's not me."

She expected him to rage at her. To argue. She expected that dark thing in him to take him over, and she braced herself for it. If she was honest, she was waiting for him to reach out and his put his hands on her again the way he had the last time. She was waiting for his kiss as surely as if he'd cast a spell and that was her only hope of breaking it—

It was astonishing, really, how much of a fool she was when it counted.

But Rodolfo's hard, beguiling mouth only curved as if there wasn't a world of seething darkness in his eyes, and somehow that sent heat spiraling all the way through her.

"Maybe it should be, princess," he said softly, so softly, as if he was seducing her where he stood. As if he was the spell and there was no breaking it, not when he was looking at her like that, as if no one else existed in all the world. "Maybe a little chaos is exactly what you need."

CHAPTER SIX

THE CHARITY GALA took place in a refurbished ancient villa, blazing with light and understated wealth and dripping with all manner of international celebrities like another layer of decoration. Icons from the epic films of Bollywood mingled with lauded stars of the stages of the West End and rubbed shoulders with a wide selection of Europe's magnificently blooded aristocrats, all doing what they did best. They graced the red carpet as if they found nothing more delightful, smiling into cameras and posing for photographs while giving lip service to the serious charity cause du jour.

Rodolfo escorted his mouthy, surprising princess down the gauntlet of the baying paparazzi, smiling broadly as the press went mad at the sight of them, just as he'd suspected they would.

"I told you," he murmured, leaning down to put his mouth near her ear. As much to sell the story of their great romance as to take pleasure in the way she shivered, then stiffened as if she was trying to hide it from him. Who could have imagined that his distant betrothed was so exquisitely sensitive? He couldn't wait to find out where else she was this tender. This sweet. "They want nothing more than to imagine us wildly and madly in love."

"A pity my imagination is not quite so vivid," she replied testily, though she did it through a smile that perhaps only he could tell was not entirely serene.

But the grin on Rodolfo's face as they made their way slowly through the wall of flashing cameras and shouting reporters wasn't feigned in the least.

"You didn't mention which charity this gala benefits," the princess said crisply as they followed the well-heeled crowd inside the villa, past dramatic tapestries billowing in the slight breeze and a grand pageant of colored lights in the many fountains along the way.

"Something critically important, I am sure," he replied, and his grin only deepened when she slid a reproving look at him. "Surely they are all important, princess. In the long run, does it matter which one this is?"

"Not to you, clearly," she murmured, nodding regally at yet another photographer. "I am sure your carelessness—excuse me, I mean thoughtfulness—is much appreciated by all the charities around who benefit from your random approach."

Rodolfo resolved to take her out in public every night, to every charity event he could find in Europe, whether he'd heard of its cause or not. Not only because she was stunning and he liked looking at her, though that helped. The blazing lights caught the red in her hair and made it shimmer. The gray dress she wore hugged her figure before falling in soft waves to the floor. She was a vision, and better than all of that, out here in the glare of too many spotlights she could not keep chairs between them to ward him off. He liked the heat of her arm through his. He liked her body beside his, lithe and slender as if she'd been crafted to fit him. He liked the faint scent of her, a touch of something French and something sweet besides, and below it, the simplicity of that soap she used.

There wasn't much he didn't like about this woman, if he was honest, not even her intriguing puritan streak. Or her habit of poking at him the way no one else had ever dared, not even his disapproving father, who preferred to express his endless disappointment with far less sharpness and mockery. No one else ever threw Felipe in his face and if they'd ever tried to do such a remarkably stupid thing, it certainly wouldn't have been to psychoanalyze him. Much less find him wanting.

He took care of that all on his own, no doubt. And the fact that his own father found his second son so much more lacking than his first was common knowledge and obvious to all. No need to underscore it.

Rodolfo supposed it was telling that as little as he cared to have that conversation, he hadn't minded that Valentina had tried. Or he didn't mind too much. He didn't know where his deferential, disappearing princess had gone, the one who had hidden in plain sight when there'd been no one in the room but the two of them, but he liked this one much better.

The hardest part of his body agreed. Enthusiastically. And it didn't much care that they were out in public.

But there was another gauntlet to run inside the villa. One Rodolfo should perhaps have anticipated.

"I take it that you did not make proclamations about your sudden onset of fidelity to your many admirers," Valentina said dryly after they were stopped for the fifth time in as many steps by yet another woman who barely glanced at the princess and then all but melted all over Rodolfo. Right there in front of her.

For the first time in his entire adult life, Rodolfo found he was faintly embarrassed by his own prowess with the fairer sex.

"It is not the sort of thing one typically announces,"

he pointed out, while attempting to cling to his dignity, despite the number of slinky women circling him with that same avid look in their eyes. "It has the whiff of desperation about it, does it not?

"Of course, generally speaking, becoming engaged *is* the announcement." What was wrong with him, that he found her tartness so appealing? Especially when not a bit of it showed on her lovely, serene face? How had he spent all these months failing to notice how appealing she was? He'd puzzled it over for days and still couldn't understand it. "I can see the confusion in your case, given your exploits these last months."

"Yet here I am," he pointed out, slanting a look down at her, amused despite himself. "At your side. Exuding fidelity."

"That is not precisely what you exude," she said under her breath, because naturally she couldn't let any opportunity pass to dig at him, and then they were swept into the receiving line.

It felt like a great many hours later when they finally made it into the actual gala itself. A band played on a raised dais while glittering people outshone the blazing chandeliers above them. Europe's finest and fanciest stood in these rooms, and he'd estimate that almost all of them had their eyes fixed on the spectacle of Prince Rodolfo and Princess Valentina actually out and about together for once—without a single one of their royal relatives in sight as the obvious puppeteers of what had been hailed everywhere as an entirely cold-blooded marriage of royal convenience.

But their presence here had already done exactly what Rodolfo had hoped it would. He could see it in the faces of the people around them. He'd felt it on the red carpet outside, surrounded by paparazzi nearly incandescent with joy over the pictures they'd be able to sell of the two of them. He could already read the accompanying headlines.

Do the Daredevil Prince and the Dutiful Princess Actually Like *Each Other After All?*

He could feel the entire grand ballroom of the villa seem to swell with the force of all that speculation and avid interest.

And Rodolfo made a command decision. They could do another round of the social niceties that would cement the story he wanted to sell even further, assuming he wasn't deluged by more of the sort of women who were happy to ignore his fiancée as she stood beside him. Or he could do what he really wanted to do, which was get his hands on Valentina right here in public, where she would have no choice but to allow it.

This was what he was reduced to. On some level, he felt the requisite shame. Or some small shadow of it, if he was honest.

Because it still wasn't much of a contest.

"Let's dance, shall we?" he asked, but he was already moving toward the dance floor in the vast, sparkling ballroom that seemed to swirl around him as he spoke. His proper, perfect princess would have to yank her arm out of his grip with some force, creating a scene, if she wanted to stop him.

He was sure he could see steam come off her as she realized that for herself, then didn't do it. Mutinously, if that defiant angle of her pointed chin was any clue.

"I don't dance," she informed him coolly as he stopped and turned to face her. He dropped her arm but stood a little too close to her, so the swishing skirt of her long dress brushed against his legs. It made her have to tip her head back to meet his gaze. And he was well aware it created the look of an intimacy between them. It suggested all kinds of closeness, just as he wanted it to do.

As much to tantalize the crowd as to tempt her.

"Are you certain?" he asked idly.

"Of course I'm certain."

Other guests waltzed around them, pretending not to stare as they stood still in the center of the dance floor as if they were having an intense discussion. Possibly an argument. Inviting gossip and rumor with every moment they failed to move. But Rodolfo forgot about all the eyes trained on them in the next breath. He gazed down at his princess, watching as the strangest expression moved over her face. Had she been anyone else, he would have called it panic.

"Then I fear I must remind you that you have been dancing since almost before you could walk," he replied, trying to keep his voice mild and a little bit lazy, as if that could hide the intensity of his need to touch her. As if every moment he did not was killing him. He felt as if it was.

He reached over and took her hands in his, almost losing his cool when he felt that simple touch everywhere—from his fingers to his feet and deep in his aching sex—far more potent than whole weekends he could hardly recall with women he wouldn't remember if they walked up and introduced themselves right now. What the hell was she doing to him? But he ordered himself to pull it together.

"There is that iconic portrait of you dancing with your father at some or other royal affair. It was the darling of the fawning press for years. You are standing on his shoes while the King of Murin dances for the both of you." Rodolfo made himself smile, as if the odd intensity that gripped him was nothing but a passing thing. The work of a moment, here and then gone in the swirl of the stately dance all around them. "I believe you were six."

"Six," she repeated. He thought she said it oddly, but then she seemed to recollect herself. He saw her blink, then focus on him again. "You misunderstand me. I meant that I don't dance with *you*. By which I mean, I won't."

"It pains me to tell you that, sadly, you are wrong yet again." He smiled at her, then indulged himself—and infuriated her—by reaching out to tug on one of the artful pieces of hair that had been left free of the complicated chignon she wore tonight. He tucked it behind her ear, marveling that so small a touch should echo inside of him the way it did then, sensation chasing sensation, as if all these months of not quite seeing her in front of him had been an exercise in restraint instead of an oddity he couldn't explain to his satisfaction. And this was his reward. "You will dance with me at our wedding, in front of the entire world. And no doubt at a great many affairs of state thereafter. It is unavoidable, I am afraid."

She started to frown, then caught herself. He saw the way she fought it back, and he still couldn't understand why it delighted him on a deep, visceral level. His glass princess, turned flesh and blood and brought to life right there before him. He could see the way her lips trembled, very slightly, and he knew somehow that it was the same mad fire that blazed in him, brighter by the moment.

It made him want nothing more than to taste her here and now, the crowd and royal protocol be damned.

"You should know that I make it a policy to step on the feet of all the men I dance with, as homage to that iconic photograph." Her smile was razor sharp and her eyes had gone cool again, but he could still see that soft little tremor that made her mouth too soft. Too vulnerable.

He could still see the truth she clearly wanted to hide, and no matter that he couldn't name it. "Prepare yourself."

"All you need to do is follow my lead, princess," Rodolfo said then, low and perhaps a bit too dark, and he didn't entirely mean the words to take on an added resonance as he said them. But he smiled when she pulled in a sharp little breath, as if she was imagining all the places he could lead her, just as he was. In vivid detail. "It will be easy and natural. There will be no trodding upon feet. Simply surrender—" and his voice dipped a bit at that, getting rough in direct correlation to that dark, needy thing in her gaze "—and I will take care of you. I promise."

Rodolfo wasn't talking about dancing—or he wasn't only talking about a very public waltz—but that would do. He studied Princess Valentina as she stood there before him, taut and very nearly quivering with the same dark need that made him want to behave like a caveman instead of a prince. He wanted to throw her over his shoulder and carry her off into the night. He wanted to throw her down on the floor where they stood and get his mouth on every part of her, as if he could taste what it was that had changed in her, cracking her open to let the fascinating creature inside come out and making her irresistible seemingly overnight.

He settled for extending his hand, very formally and in full view of half of Europe, even throwing in a polite bow that, as someone more or less equal in rank to her, could only be construed as a magnanimous, even romantic gesture. Then he stood still in the center of the dance floor and waited for her to take it.

Her green eyes looked a little bit too wide and still far too dark with all the same simmering need and deep hunger he knew burned bright in him. She looked more beautiful than he'd ever seen her before, but then, he was closer than he'd ever been. He couldn't count those hot, desperate moments in the palace reception room where he'd tasted her with all the finesse of an untried adolescent, because he'd been too out of control—and out of his mind—to enjoy it.

This was different. This—tonight—he had every intention of savoring.

But he wasn't sure he would ever savor anything more than when she lifted that chin of hers, faintly pointed and filled with a defiance her vulnerable mouth contradicted, and placed her hand in his.

Rodolfo felt that everywhere, as potent as if she'd knelt down before him and declared him victor of this dark and delicious little war of theirs.

He pulled her a step closer with his right hand, then slid his left around to firmly clasp the back she'd left bared in the lovely dress she wore that poured over her slender figure like rain, and he heard her hiss in a breath. He could feel the heat of her like a furnace beneath his palm. He wanted to bend close and get his mouth on her more than he could remember wanting anything.

But he refrained. Somehow, he held himself in check, when he was a man who usually did the exact opposite. For fun.

"Put your hand on my shoulder," he told her, and he didn't sound urbane or witty or anything like lazy. Not anymore. "Have you truly forgotten how to perform a simple waltz, princess? I am delighted to discover how deeply I affect you."

He felt the hard breath she took, as if she was bracing herself. And he realized with a little shock that he had no idea what she would do. It was as likely that she'd yank herself out of his arms and storm away as it was that she'd melt into him. He had no idea—and he couldn't deny he felt that like a long, slow lick against the hardest part of him.

She was as unpredictable as one of his many adventures. He had the odd thought that he could spend a lifetime trying to unravel her mysteries, one after the next, and who knew if he'd ever manage it? It astonished him that he wanted to try. That for the first time since their engagement last fall, he wanted their wedding day to hurry up and arrive. And better than that, their wedding night. And all the nights thereafter, all those adventures lined up and waiting for him, packed into her lush form and those fathomless green eyes.

He could hardly wait.

And it felt as if ten years had passed when, with her wary gaze trained on him as if he couldn't be trusted not to harm her somehow, Valentina put her hand where it belonged.

"Thank you, princess." He curled his fingers around hers a little tighter than necessary for the sheer pleasure of it and smiled when the hand she'd finally placed on his shoulder dug into him, as if in reaction. "You made that into quite a little bit of theater. When stories emerge tomorrow about the great row we had in the middle of a dance floor, you will have no one to blame but yourself."

"I never do," she replied coolly, but that wariness receded from her green gaze. Her chin tipped up higher and Rodolfo counted it as a win. "It's called taking responsibility for myself, which is another way of acknowledging that I'm an adult. You should try it sometime."

"Impossible," he said, gripping her hand tighter in his and smiling for all those watching eyes. And because her defiance made him want to smile, which was far more dangerous. And exciting. "I am far too busy leaping out of planes in a vain attempt to cheat death. Or court death. Which is it again? I can't recall which accusation you leveled at me, much less when."

And before she could enlighten him, he started to move.

She was stiff in his arms, which he assumed was another form of protest. Rodolfo ignored it, sweeping her around the room and leading her through the steps she appeared to be pretending not to know, just as he'd promised he would.

"You cannot trip me up, princess," he told her when she relaxed just slightly in his hold and gave herself over to his lead. "I was raised to believe a man can only call himself a man when he knows how to dance well, shoot with unerring accuracy and argue his position without either raising his voice or reducing himself to wild, un-justified attacks on his opponent."

"Well," she said, and she sounded breathless, which he felt in every part of his body like an ache, "you obvi-ously took that last part to heart."

"I am also an excellent shot, thank you for asking."

"Funny, the tabloids failed to report that. Unless you're speaking in innuendo? In which case, I must apol-ogize, but I don't speak twelve-year-old boy."

He let out a laugh that had the heads nearest them turning, because no one was ever so giddy when on dis-play like this, especially not him. Rodolfo was infamous because he called attention to himself in other ways, but never like this. Never in situations like these, all stuffy protocol and too many spectators. Never with anything that might be confused for *joy*.

"You must be feeling better if you're this snappish, princess."

"I wasn't feeling bad. Unless you count the usual dismay anyone might feel at being bullied onto a dance floor in the company of a rather alarming man who dances very much like he flings himself off the sides of mountains."

"With a fierce and provocative elegance? The envy of all who witness it?"

"With astonishing recklessness and a total lack of regard for anyone around you. Much in the same vein as your entire life, Your Highness, if the reports are true." She lifted one shoulder, then let it drop in as sophisticated and dismissive a shrug as he'd ever seen. "Or even just a little bit true, for that matter."

"And if you imagine that was bullying, princess, you have led a very charmed life, indeed. Even for a member of a royal house dating back to, oh, the start of recorded history or thereabouts, surrounded by wealth and ease at every turn."

"What do you want, Rodolfo?" she asked then, and that near-playful note he was sure he'd heard in her voice was gone. Her expression was grave. As if she was yet another stranger, this one different than before. "I don't believe that this marriage is anything you would have chosen, if given the opportunity. I can't imagine why you're suddenly pretending otherwise and proclaiming your commitment to fidelity in random hotel suites. What I do understand is that we're both prepared to do our duty and have been from the start. And I support that, but there's nothing wrong with maintaining a civil, respectful distance while we go about it."

"I would have agreed with you in every respect," he said, and he should have been worried about that fervent intensity in his tone. He could feel the flames of it licking through him, changing him, making him something other than the man he'd thought he was all this time.

Something that should have set off alarms in every part of him, yet didn't. "But that was before you walked into your father's reception rooms and rather than blending into the furniture the way you usually did, opted to attack me instead."

"Of course." And Rodolfo had the strangest sensation that she was studying him as if he was a museum exhibit, not her fiancé. Hardly even a man—which should have chastened him. Instead, it made him harder. "I should have realized that to a man like you, with an outsize ego far more vast and unconquerable than any of the mountain peaks you've summited in your desperate quest for meaning, any questioning of any kind is perceived as an attack."

"You are missing the point, I think," Rodolfo said, making no attempt to hide either the laughter in his voice or the hunger in his gaze, not put off by her character assassinations at all. Quite the opposite. "Attack me all you like. It doesn't shame me in the least. Surely you must be aware that *shame* is not the primary response I have to you, princess. It is not even close."

She didn't ask him what he felt instead, but he saw a betraying, bright flush move over her face. And he knew she was perfectly aware of the things that moved in him, sensation and need, hunger and that edgy passion—and more, that she felt it, too.

Perhaps that was why, when they danced past a set of huge, floor-to-ceiling glass doors that led out to a wide terrace for the third time, he led her out into the night instead of deeper into the ballroom.

"Where are we going?" she asked.

Rodolfo thought it was meant to be a demand—a rebuke, even—but her cheeks were too red. Her eyes were too bright. And most telling, she made no attempt to tug her hand from his, much less lecture him any further about chaos and order and who was on which side of that divide.

"Nothing could be less chaotic than a walk on a terrace in full view of so many people," he pointed out, not bothering to look behind him at the party they'd left in full swing. He had no doubt they were all staring after him, the way they always did, and with more intensity than ever because he was with Valentina. "Unless you'd like it to be?"

"Certainly not. Some people admire the mountain from afar, Your Highness. They are perfectly happy doing so, and feel no need whatsoever to throw themselves off it or climb up it or attempt to ski down the back of it."

"Ah, but some people do not live, princess. They merely exist."

"Risking death is not living. It's nihilistic. And in your case, abominably selfish."

"Perhaps." He held her hand tighter in his. "But I would not underestimate the power of a little bout of selfishness, if I were you. Indulge yourself, princess. Just for an evening. What's the worst that could happen?"

"I shudder to think," she retorted, but there was no heat in it.

Rodolfo pretended not to hear the catch in her throat. But he smiled. He liberated two glasses of something exquisite from a passing servant with a tray, he pulled his fascinating princess closer to his side and then he led her deeper into the dark.

CHAPTER SEVEN

MAYBE IT WAS the music. Maybe it was the whirl of so many gleaming, glorious people.

Natalie had the suspicion that really, it was Rodolfo.

But no matter what it was, no matter why—she forgot.

That she wasn't really a princess, or if she was, she was the discarded kind. The lost and never-meant-to-be-found sort that had only been located by accident in a bathroom outside London.

She forgot that the dress wasn't hers, the ball inside the pretty old building wasn't a magical spectacle put on just for her and, most of all, that the man at her side—gripping her hand as he led her into temptation—wasn't ever going to be hers, no matter what.

He'd danced with her. It was as simple and as complicated as that.

Natalie had never thought of herself as beautiful before she'd seen herself in that mirror tonight, but it was more than that. She couldn't remember the last time anyone had treated her like a *woman*. Much less a desirable one. Not a pawn in whatever game the man in question might have been playing with her employer, which had only ever led to her wearing her hair in severe ponytails and then donning those clear glasses to keep the attention off her. Not an assistant. Not the person responsible for every little detail of every little thing and therefore the first one to be upbraided when something went wrong.

Rodolfo looked at her as if she was no more and no less than a beautiful woman. He didn't see a list of all the things she could *do* when he gazed at her. He saw only her. A princessed-out, formally made-up version of her, sure. And she couldn't really gloss over the fact he called her by the wrong name because he had every reason to believe she was someone else. Even so, she was the woman he couldn't seem to stop touching, who made his eyes light up with all that too-bright need and hunger.

And it was that, Natalie found, she couldn't resist.

She'd never done a spontaneous thing in her life before she'd switched places with Valentina in that bathroom. Left to her own devices, she thought it was likely she'd never have given her notice at all, no matter how worked up she'd been. And now it seemed she couldn't stop with the spontaneity. Yet somehow Rodolfo's grip on her hand, so strong and sure, made her not mind very much at all. She let this prince, who was far more charming than she wanted to admit to herself, tug her along with him, deeper into the shadows, until they were more in the dark than the light.

He turned to face her then, and he looked something like stern in the darkness. He set the two glasses of sparkling wine down on the nearby balustrade, then straightened again. Slowly. Deliberately, even. Natalie's heart thudded hard against her ribs, but it wasn't from fear. He pulled her hand that he'd been holding high against his chest and held it there, and Natalie couldn't have said why she felt as caught. As gripped tight. Only that she was—and more concerning, had no desire to try to escape it.

If anything, she leaned closer into him, into the shelter of his big body.

"Where did you come from?" he asked, his voice a mere scrape against the night. "What the hell are you doing to me?"

Natalie opened her mouth to answer him. But whatever that dark, driving force had been inside her, urging her to poke back at him and do her best to slap down the only real Prince Charming she'd ever met in the flesh, it was gone. Had she imagined herself some kind of avenging angel here? Flying into another woman's royal fairy tale of a life to do what needed doing, the way she did with everything else? Fighting her mother's battles all these years later and with a completely different man than the one Erica had never explicitly named?

It didn't matter, because that had been before he'd taken her in his arms and guided her around a dance floor, making her feel as if she could dance forever when she'd never danced a waltz before in her life. She had a vague idea of what it entailed, but only because she'd had to locate the best ballroom dancing instructor in London when Achilles Casilieris had abruptly decided he needed a little more polish one year. She'd watched enough of those classes—before Mr. Casilieris had reduced the poor man to tears—to understand the basic principle of a waltz.

But Rodolfo had made her feel as if they were flying.

He looked down at her now, out here in the seductive dark, and it made her tremble deep inside. It made her forget who she was and what she was doing. Her head cleared of everything save him. Rodolfo. The daredevil prince who made her feel as if she was the one catapulting herself out of airplanes every time his dark, hungry gaze caught hers. And held.

He took her bare shoulders in his hands, drawing her closer to him. Making her shiver, deep and long. On some distant level she thought she should push away from him. Remind them both of her boundaries, maybe. But she couldn't seem to remember what those were. Instead she tilted her head back while she drifted closer to his big, rangy body. And then she made everything worse by sliding her hands over the steel wall of his chest, carefully packaged in that gorgeous suit that made him look almost edible. To push him away, she told herself piously.

But she didn't push at him. She didn't even try.

His dark eyes gleamed with a gold she could feel low in her belly, like a fiery caress. "The way you look at me is dangerous, princess."

"I thought you courted danger," she heard herself whisper.

"I do," he murmured. "Believe me, I do."

And then he bent his head and kissed her.

This time, the first brush of his mouth against hers was light. Easy. Electricity sparked and sizzled, and then he did it again, and it wasn't enough. Natalie pressed herself toward him, trying to get more of him. Trying to crawl inside him and throw herself into the storm that roared through her. She went up on her toes to close the remaining distance between them, and her reward was the way he smiled, that dangerous curve of his mouth against hers.

It seemed to wash over her like heat then pool in a blaze of fire, high between her legs. Natalie couldn't keep herself from letting out a moan, needy and insistent.

And obvious. So terribly, blatantly obvious it might as well have been a scream in the dark. She felt Rodolfo turn to stone beneath her palms.

Then he angled his head, took the kiss deeper and wilder and everything went mad.

Rodolfo simply…took her over. He kissed her like he was already a great king and she but one more subject to his rule. His inimitable will. He kissed her as if there had never been any doubt that she was his, in every possible way. His mouth was demanding and hot, intense and carnal, and her whole body thrilled to it. Her hands were fists, gripping his jacket as if she couldn't bear to let go of him, and he only took the kiss deeper, wilder.

She arched against him as he plundered her mouth, taking and taking and taking even more as he bent her over his arm, as if he could never get enough—

Then he stopped, abruptly, muttering a curse against her lips. It seemed to pain him to release her, but he did it, stepping back and maneuvering so he stood between Natalie and what it took her far too long to realize was another group of guests making use of the wide terrace some distance away.

But she couldn't bring herself to care about them. She raised a hand to her lips, aware that her fingers trembled. And far more aware that he was watching her too closely as she did it.

"Why do you look at me as if it is two hundred years ago and I have just stolen your virtue?" he asked softly, his dark eyes searching hers. "Or led you to your ruin with a mere kiss?"

Natalie didn't know what look she wore on her face, but she felt…altered. There was no pretending otherwise. Rodolfo was looking at her the way any man might gaze at the woman he was marrying in less than two months, after kissing her very nearly senseless on the terrace of a romantic Roman villa.

But that was the trouble. No matter what fairy tale

she'd been spinning out in her head, Natalie wasn't that woman.

She was ruined, all right. All the way through.

"I'm not looking at you like that." Her voice hardly sounded like hers. She took a step away from him, coming up against the stone railing. She glanced down at the two glasses of sparkling wine that sat there and considered tossing them back, one after the next, because that might dull the sharp thing that felt a little too much like pain, poking inside of her. Only the fact that it might dull her a little *too* much kept her from it. Things were already bad enough. "I'm not looking at you like anything, I'm sure."

Rodolfo watched her, his eyes too dark to read. "You are looking at me as if you have never been kissed before. Much as that might pander to my ego, which I believe we've agreed is egregiously large already, we both know that isn't true." His mouth curved. "And tell the truth, Valentina. It was not so bad, was it?"

That name slammed into her like a sucker punch. Natalie could hardly breathe through it. She had to grit her teeth to keep from falling over where she stood. How did she keep forgetting?

Because you want to forget, a caustic voice inside her supplied at once.

"I'm not who you think I am," she blurted out then, and surely she wasn't the only one who could hear how ragged she sounded. How distraught.

But Rodolfo only laughed. "You are exactly who I think you are."

"I assure you, I am not. At all."

"It is an odd moment for a philosophical turn, princess," he drawled, and there was something harder about him then. Something more dangerous. Natalie could feel it dance over her skin. "Are any of us who others think we are? Take me, for example. I am certain that every single person at this gala tonight would line up to tell you exactly who I am, and they would be wrong. I am not the tabloid stories they craft about me, pimped out to the highest bidder. My wildest dream is not surviving an adventure or planning a new one, it's taking my rightful place in my father's kingdom. That's all." His admission, stark and raw, hung between them like smoke. She had the strangest notion that he hadn't meant to say anything like that. But in the next instant he looked fierce. Almost forbidding. "We are none of us the roles we play, I am sure."

"Are you claiming you have a secret inner life devoted to your sense of duty? That you are merely misunderstood?" she asked, incredulous.

"Do you take everything at face value, princess?" She told herself she was imagining that almost hurt look on his face. And it was gone when he angled his head toward her. "You cannot really believe you are the only one with an internal life."

"That's not what I meant."

But, of course, she couldn't tell him what she meant. She couldn't explain that she hadn't been feeling the least bit philosophical. Or that she wasn't actually Princess Valentina at all. She certainly couldn't tell this man that she was Natalie Monette—a completely different person.

Though it occurred to her for the first time that even if she came clean right here and now, the likelihood was that he wouldn't believe her. Because who could believe something so fantastical? Would she have believed it herself if it wasn't happening to her right now—if she wasn't standing in the middle of another woman's life?

And messing it up beyond recognition, that same interior voice sniped at her. *Believe that, if nothing else.*

"Do you plan to tell me what, then, you meant?" Rodolfo asked, dark and low and maybe with a hint of asperity. Maybe with more than just a hint. "Or would you prefer it if I guessed?"

The truth hit Natalie then, with enough force that she felt it shake all the way through her. There was only one reason that she wanted to tell him the truth, and it wasn't because she'd suddenly come over all honest and upstanding. She'd switched places with another person—lying about who she was came with the territory. It allowed her to sit there at those excruciatingly proper dinners and try to read into King Geoffrey's facial expressions and his every word without him knowing it, still trying to figure out if she really thought he was her father. And what it would mean to her if he was. Something that would never happen if she'd identified herself. If he'd been on the defensive when he met her.

She didn't want to tell Rodolfo the truth because she had a burning desire for him to know who she was. Or she did want that, of course, but it wasn't first and foremost.

It made her stomach twist to admit it, but it was true: what she wanted was him. This. She wanted what was happening between them to be real and then, when it was, she wanted to keep him.

He is another woman's fiancé, she threw at herself in some kind of despair.

Natalie thought she'd never hated herself more than she did at that moment, because she simply couldn't seem to govern herself accordingly.

"I need to leave," she told him, and she didn't care if she sounded rude. Harsh and abrupt. She needed to remove herself from him—from all that temptation he wore entirely too easily, like another bespoke suit—before she made this all worse. Much, much worse. In ways she could imagine all too vividly. "Now."

"Princess, please. Do not run off into the night. I will only have to chase you." He moved toward her and Natalie didn't have the will to step away. To ward him off. To do what she should. And she compounded it by doing absolutely nothing when he fit his hand to her cheek and held it there. His dark eyes gleamed. "Tell me."

He was so big it made her heart hurt. The dark Roman night did nothing to obscure how beautiful he was, and she could taste him now. A kind of rich, addicting honey on her tongue. She thought that alone might make her shatter into pieces. This breath, or the next. She thought it might be the end of her.

"I need to go," she whispered, aware that her hands were in useless, desperate fists at her sides.

She wanted to punch him, she told herself, but Natalie knew that was a lie. The sad truth here was she was looking for any excuse to put her hands on him again. And she knew exactly what kind of person that made her.

And even so, she found herself leaning into that palm at her cheek.

"I never wanted what our parents had," Rodolfo told her then, his voice low and commanding, somehow, against the mild night air. "A dance in front of the cameras and nothing but duty and gritted teeth in private. I promised myself that I would marry for the right reasons. But then it seemed that what I would get instead was a cold shoulder and a polite smile. I told myself it was more than some people in my position could claim. I thought I had made my peace with it."

Natalie found she couldn't speak. As if there was a hand around her throat, gripping her much too tight.

Rodolfo didn't move any closer, though it was as if he shut out the rest of the world. There was nothing but that near-smile on his face, that hint of light in his gaze. There was nothing but the two of them and the lie of who she was tonight, but the longer he looked at her like that, the harder it was to remember that he wasn't really hers. That he could never be hers. That none of the things he was saying to her were truly for her at all.

"Rodolfo…" she managed to say. Confession or capitulation, she couldn't tell.

"I like my name in your mouth, princess," he told her, sending heat dancing all over her, until it pooled low and hot in her belly. "And I like this. There is no reason at all we cannot take some pleasure in our solemn duty to our countries. Think of all the dreadfully tedious affairs we will enjoy a great deal more when there is this to brighten up the monotony."

His head lowered to hers again, and she wanted nothing more than to lose herself in him. In the pleasure he spoke of. In his devastating kiss, all over again.

But somehow, Natalie managed to recollect herself in the instant before his lips touched hers. She yanked herself out of his grip and stepped away from him, the night feeling cool around her now that she wasn't so close to the heat that seemed to come off him in waves.

"I'm sorry." She couldn't seem to help herself. But she kept her gaze trained on the ground, because looking at him was fraught with peril. Natalie was terribly afraid it would end only one way. "I shouldn't have…" She trailed off, helplessly. "I need to go back to my hotel."

"And do what?" he asked, and something in his voice made her stand straighter. Some kind of foreboding, perhaps. When she looked up at him, Rodolfo's gaze had gone dark again, his mouth stern and hard. "Switch personalities yet again?"

Valentina jerked as if he'd slapped her, and if he'd been a little more in control of himself, Rodolfo might have felt guilty about that.

Maybe he already did, if he was entirely honest, but he couldn't do anything about it. He couldn't reach out and put his hands on her the way he wanted to do. He couldn't do a goddamned thing when she refused to tell him what was going on.

The princess looked genuinely distraught at the thought of kissing him again. At the thought that this marriage they'd been ordered into for the good of their kingdoms could be anything but a necessary, dutiful undertaking to be suffered through for the rest of their lives.

Rodolfo didn't understand any of this. Didn't she realize that this crazy chemistry that had blazed to life out of nowhere was a blessing? The saving grace of what was otherwise nothing more than a royal chore dressed up as a photo opportunity?

Clearly she did not, because she was staring at him with something he couldn't quite read making her green eyes dark. Her lovely cheeks looked pale. She looked shaken—though that made no sense.

"What do you mean by that?" she demanded, though her voice sounded as thrown as the rest of her looked. "I have the one personality, that's all. This might come as a shock to you, I realize, but many women actually have *layers*. Many humans, in fact."

Rodolfo wanted to be soothing. He did. He prided himself on never giving in to his temper. On maintaining his cool under any and all extreme circumstances. There was no reason he couldn't calm this maddening woman, whether he understood what was going on here or not.

"Are you unwell?" he asked instead. And not particularly nicely.

"I am feeling more unwell by the moment," she threw back at him, stiff and cool. "As I told you, I need to leave."

He reached over and hooked a hand around her elbow when she made as if to turn, holding her there where she stood. Keeping her with him. And the caveman in him didn't care whether she liked it or not.

"Let go of me," she snapped at him. But she didn't pull her elbow from his grasp.

Rodolfo smiled. It was a lazy, edgy sort of smile, and he watched the color rush back into her face.

"No."

She stiffened, but she still didn't pull away. "What do you mean, *no*?"

"I mean that I have no intention of releasing you until you tell me why you blow so hot and cold, princess. And I do not much care if it takes all night. It is almost as if you are two women—"

Her green eyes flashed. "That or I find you largely unappealing."

"Until, of course, you do not find me unappealing in the least. Then you melt all over me."

Her cheeks pinkened further. "I find it as confusing as you do. Best not to encourage it, I think."

He savored the feel of her silky skin beneath his palm. "Ah, but you see, I am not confused in the least."

"If you do not let go of me, right now, I will scream," she told him.

He only smiled at her. "Go ahead. You have my blessing." He waited, and cocked an eyebrow when she only glared at him. "I thought you were about to scream down the villa, were you not? Or was that another metaphor?"

She took what looked like a shaky breath, but she didn't say anything. And she still didn't pull her elbow away. Rodolfo moved a little closer, so he could bend and get his face near hers.

"Tell me what game this is," he murmured, close to her ear. She jumped, and he expected her to pull free of him, but she didn't. She settled where she stood. He could feel her breathe. He could feel the way her pulse pounded through her. He could smell her excitement in the heated space between them, and he could feel the tension in her, too. "I am more than adept at games, I promise you. Just tell me what we're playing."

"This is no game." But her voice sounded a little broken. Just a little, but it was enough.

"When I met you, there was none of this fire," he reminded her, as impossible as that was to imagine now. "We sat through that extraordinarily painful meal—"

She tipped her head back so she could look him dead in the eye. "I loved every moment of it."

"You did not. You sat like a statue and smiled with the deepest insincerity. And then afterward, I thought you might have nodded off during my proposal."

"I was riveted." She waved the hand that wasn't trapped between them. "Your Royal Highness is all that is charming and so on. It was the high point of my life, etcetera, etcetera."

"You thanked me in your usual efficient manner, yes. But riveted?" He slid his hand down her forearm, abandoning his grip on her elbow so he could take her hand in his. Then he played with the great stone she wore on her finger that had once belonged to his grandmother and a host of Tisselian queens before her. He tugged it this way, then that. "You were anything but that, princess. You used to look through me when I spoke to you, as if I was a ghost. I could not tell if I was or you were. I imagined that I would beget my heirs on a phantom."

Something moved through her then, some electrical current that made that vulnerable mouth of hers tremble again, and she tugged her hand from his as if she'd suddenly been scalded. And yet Rodolfo felt as if he might have been, too.

"I'm not sure what the appropriate response is when a man one has agreed to marry actually sits there and explains his commitment to ongoing infidelity, as if his daily exploits in the papers were not enough of a clue. Perhaps you should count yourself lucky that all I did was look through you."

"Imagine my surprise that you noticed what I did, when you barely appeared to notice me."

"Is that what you need, Rodolfo?" she demanded, and this time, when she stepped back and completely away from him, he let her go. It seemed to startle her, and she pulled in a sharp breath as if to steady herself. "To be noticed? It may shock you to learn that the entire world already knows that, after having witnessed all your attention-seeking theatrics and escapades. That is not actually an announcement you need to make."

Rodolfo didn't exactly thrill to the way she said that, veering a bit too close to the sorts of things his father was known to hurl at him. But he admired the spirit in her while she said it. He ordered himself to concentrate on that.

"And now you are once again *this* Valentina," he replied, his voice low. "The one who dares say things to my face others would be afraid to whisper behind my back. Bold. Alluring. Who are you and what have you done with my dutiful ghost?"

She all but flinched at that and then she let out a breath that sounded a little too much like a sob. But before he could question that, she clearly swallowed it down. She lifted her chin and glared at him with nothing but sheer challenge in her eyes, and he thought he must have imagined the vulnerability in that sound she'd made. The utter loneliness.

"This Valentina will disappear soon enough, never fear," she assured him, a strange note in her voice. "We can practice that right now. I'm leaving."

But Rodolfo had no intention of letting her go. This time when she turned on her heel and walked away from him, he followed.

CHAPTER EIGHT

RODOLFO CAUGHT UP to her quickly with his long, easily athletic stride, and then refused to leave her side. He stayed too close and put his hand at the small of her back, guiding her through the splendid, sparkling crowd whether she wanted his aid or not. Natalie told herself she most emphatically did not, but just as she hadn't pulled away from him out on the terrace despite her threats that she might scream, she didn't yank herself out of his grasp now, either. She assured herself she was only thinking about what would be best for the real princess, that she was only avoiding the barest hint of scandal—but the truth was like a brand sunk deep in her belly.

She wanted him to touch her. She liked it when he did.

You are a terrible person, she told herself severely.

Natalie wanted to hate him for that, too. She told herself that of course she did, but that slick heat between her legs and the flush that she couldn't quite seem to cool let her know exactly how much of a liar she was. With every step and each shifting bit of pressure his hand exerted against her back.

He summoned their driver with a quick call, and then walked with her all the way back down the red carpet, smiling with his usual careless charm at all the paparazzi who shrieked out his name. Very much as if he enjoyed all those flashing lights and impertinent questions.

It was Natalie who wanted to curl up into a ball and hide somewhere. Natalie who wasn't used to this kind of attention—not directed at her, anyway. She'd fended off the press for Mr. Casilieris as part of her job, but she'd never been its focus before, and she discovered she really, truly didn't like it. It felt like salt on her skin. Stinging and gritty. But she didn't have the luxury of fading off into the background to catch her breath in the shadows, because she wasn't Natalie right now. She was Princess Valentina, who'd grown up with this sort of noisy spectacle everywhere she went. Who'd danced on her doting father's shoes when she was small and had cut her teeth on spotlights of all shapes and sizes and hell, for all she knew, enjoyed every moment of it the way Rodolfo seemed to.

She was Princess Valentina tonight, and a princess should have managed to smile more easily. Natalie tried her best, but by the time Rodolfo handed her into the gleaming black SUV that waited for them at the end of the press gauntlet, she thought her teeth might crack from the effort of holding her perhaps not so serene smile in place.

"I don't need your help," she told him, but it was too late. His hand was on her arm again as she clambered inside and then he was climbing in after her, forcing her to throw herself across the passenger seat or risk having him…all over her.

She hated that she had to remind herself—sternly— why that would be a bad idea.

"Would you prefer it if I had drop-kicked you into the vehicle?" he asked, still smiling as he settled himself beside her.

There was a gleam in his dark gaze that let her know he was fully aware of the way she was clinging to the far door as if it might save her. From him. As ever, he appeared not to notice the confines or restrictions of whatever he happened to be sitting on. In this case, he sprawled out in the backseat of the SUV, taking up more than his fair share of the available room and pretty much all of the oxygen. Daring her to actually come out and comment on it, Natalie was fairly sure, rather than simply twitching her skirts away from his legs in what she hoped was obvious outrage.

"I think you are well aware that neither I nor anyone else would prefer to be drop-kicked. And also that there exists yet another option, if one without any attendant theatrics. You could let me get in the car as I have managed to do all on my own for twenty-seven years and keep your hands to yourself while I did it."

He turned slightly in his seat and studied her for a moment, as the lights of Rome gleamed behind him, streaking by in the sweet, easy dark as they drove.

"Spoken like someone who has not spent the better part of her life being helped in and out of motorcades to the roars of a besotted crowd," Rodolfo said, his dark brows high as his dark eyes took her measure. "Except you have."

Natalie could have kicked herself for making such a silly mistake, and all because she'd hoped to score a few points in their endless little battle of words. She thought she really would have given herself a pinch, at the very least, if he hadn't been watching her so closely. She sniffed instead, to cover her reaction.

"You've gone over all literal, haven't you? Back on the terrace it was all metaphor and now you're parsing what I say for any hint of exaggeration? What's next?

Will you declare war on parts of speech? Set loose the Royal Tisselian Army on any grammar you dislike?"

"I am looking for hints, Valentina, but it is not figurative language that I find mysterious. It is a woman who has already changed before my eyes, more than once, into someone else."

Natalie turned her head so she could hold that stern, probing gaze of his. Steady and long. As if she really was Valentina and had nothing at all to hide.

"No one has changed before your eyes, Your Highness. I think you might have to face the fact that you are not very observant. Unless and until someone pricks at your vanity. I might as well have been a piece of furniture to you, until I mentioned I planned to let others sit on me." She let out a merry little laugh that was meant to be a slap, and hit its mark. She saw the flare of it in his gaze. "You certainly couldn't have *that*."

"Think for a moment, please." Rodolfo's voice was too dark to be truly impatient. Too rich to sound entirely frustrated. And still, Natalie braced herself. "What is the headline if I am found to be cavorting outside the bounds of holy matrimony?"

"A long, weary sigh of boredom from all sides, I'd imagine." She aimed a cool smile his way. "With a great many exclamation points."

"I am expected to fail. I have long since come to accept it is my one true legacy." Yet that dark undercurrent in his low voice and the way he lounged there, all that ruthless power simmering beneath his seeming unconcern, told Natalie that Rodolfo wasn't resigned to any such thing. "You, on the other hand? It wouldn't be *my* feelings of betrayal you would have to worry about, however unearned you might think they were. It would be the entire world that thought less of you, forever after. Is that really what you want? After you have gone to such lengths to create your spotless reputation?"

Natalie laughed again, but there was nothing funny. There was only a kind of heaviness pressing in upon her, making her feel as if she might break apart if she didn't get away from this man before something really terrible happened. Something she couldn't explain away as a latent Cinderella fantasy, lurking around inside of her without her knowledge or permission, that had put a ball and a prince together and then thrown her headfirst into an unfortunate kiss.

"What does it matter?" she asked him, aware that her voice was ragged, giving too much away—but she couldn't seem to stop herself. "There's no way out of this, so we might as well do as we like no matter what the headlines say or do not. It will make no difference. We will marry. You will have your heirs. Our kingdoms will be linked forever. Who cares about the details when that's the only part that truly matters in the long run?"

"An argument I might have made myself a month ago," Rodolfo murmured. "But we are not the people we were a month ago, princess. You must know that."

From a distance he would likely have looked relaxed. At his ease, with his legs thrust out and his collar loosened. But Natalie was closer, and she could see that glittering, dangerous thing in his gaze. She could feel it inside her, like a lethal touch of his too-talented hands, stoking fires she should have put out a long time ago.

"What I know," she managed to say over her rocketing pulse and that quickening, clenching in her core, "is that it is not I who am apparently unwell."

But Rodolfo only smiled.

Which didn't help at all.

The rest of the drive across the city was filled with

a brooding sort of silence that in many ways was worse than anything he might have said. Because the silence grew inside of her, and Natalie filled it with…images. Unhelpful images, one after the next. What might have happened if they hadn't been interrupted on that terrace, for example. Or if they'd walked a little farther into the shadows, maybe even rounding the corner so no one could see them. Would Rodolfo's hands have found their way beneath her dress again? Would they have traveled higher than her thigh—toward the place that burned the hottest for him even now?

"Thank you for the escort but I can see myself—" Natalie began when they arrived at her hotel, but Rodolfo only stared back at her in a sort of arrogant amazement that reminded her that he would one day rule an entire kingdom, no matter what the tabloids said about him now.

She restrained the little shiver that snaked down her spine, because it had nothing to do with apprehension, and let him usher her out of the car and into the hushed hotel lobby, done in sumptuous reds and deep golds and bursting with dramatic flowers arranged in stately vases. Well. It wasn't so much that she *let* him as that there was no way to stop him without causing a scene in front of all the guests in the lobby who were pretending not to gawk at them as they arrived—especially because really, yet again, Natalie didn't much *want* to stop him. Until she'd met Rodolfo, she'd never known that she was weak straight through to her core. Now she couldn't seem to remember that everywhere but here, she was known for being tough. Strong. Unflappable.

That Natalie seemed like a distant memory.

Rodolfo nodded at her security detail as he escorted her to the private, keyed elevator that led only to the penthouse suite, and then followed her into it. The door swished shut almost silently, and then it was only the two of them in a small and shiny enclosed space. Natalie braced herself, standing there just slightly behind him, with a view of his broad, high, solidly muscled back and beyond that, the gold-trimmed elevator car. She could feel the heat of him, and all that leashed danger, coming off him like flames. He surrounded her without even looking at her. He seemed to loop around her and pull tight, crushing her in his powerful grip, without so much as laying a finger upon her. She couldn't hear herself think over the thunder of her heart, the clatter of her pulse—

But nothing happened. They were delivered directly into the grand living room of the hotel's penthouse. Rodolfo stepped off and moved into the room, shrugging out of his jacket as he went. Natalie followed after him because she had no choice—or so she assured herself. It was that or go back downstairs to the hotel lobby, where she would have to explain herself to her security, the hotel staff, the other guests still sitting around with mobile phones at the ready to record her life at will.

The elevator doors slid shut behind her, and that was it. The choice was made. And it left her notably all alone in her suite's living room with the Prince she very desperately wanted to find the antithesis of charming.

There was no Roman sunset to distract her now. There was only Rodolfo, far too beautiful and much too dangerous for anyone's good. She watched the way he moved through the living room with a kind of liquid athleticism. The light from the soft lamps scattered here and there made the sprawling space feel close. Intimate.

And it made him look like some kind of god all over

again. Not limned in red or gold, but draped in shadows and need.

Her throat was dry. Her lungs ached as if she'd been off running for untold miles. Her fingers trembled, and she realized she was as jittery as if she'd pulled one of her all-nighters before a big meeting and had rivers of coffee running through her veins in place of blood. It made her stomach clench tight to think that it wasn't caffeine that was messing with her tonight. It was this man before her who she should never have touched, much less kissed.

What was she going to do now?

The sad truth was, Natalie couldn't trust herself to make the right decision, or she wouldn't still be standing where she was, would she? She would have gone straight on back to her bedchamber and locked the door. She would have summoned her staff, who she knew had to be nearby, just waiting for the opportunity to serve her and usher Rodolfo out. She would have done *something* other than what she did.

Which was wait. Breathlessly. As if she really was a princess caught up in some or other enchantment. As if she could no more move a muscle than she could wave a magic wand and turn herself back into Natalie.

Rodolfo shrugged out of his jacket and tossed it over the back of one of the fussy chairs, and then he took his time turning to face her again. When he did, his dark eyes burned into her, the focused, searing hunger in them enough to send her back a step. In a wild panic or a kind of dizzy desire, she couldn't have said.

Both, something whispered inside of her. And not with any trace of fear. Not with anything the least bit like fear.

"Rodolfo," she managed to say then, in as measured

a tone as she could manage, because she thought she should have been far more afraid of all those things she could feel in the air between them than she was. Either way, this was all too much. It was all temptation and need, and she could hardly think through the chaos inside of her. "This has all gotten much too fraught and strange. Why don't I have some coffee made? We can sit and talk."

"I am afraid, *princesita*, that it is much too late for talk."

He moved then. His long stride ate up the floor and he was before her in an instant. Or perhaps it was that she didn't want to move out of his reach. She couldn't seem to make herself run. She couldn't seem to do anything at all. All she did was stand right where she was and watch him come for her, that simmering light in his dark eyes and that stern set to his mouth that made everything inside her quiver.

Maybe there was no use pretending this wasn't what she'd wanted all along. Since the very first moment she'd crossed the threshold of that reception room at the palace and discovered he was so much more than his pictures. She'd wanted to eviscerate him and instead she'd ended up on his lap with his tongue in her mouth. Had that really been by chance?

Something dark and guilty kicked inside of her at that, and she opened her mouth to protest—to do *something,* to say *anything* that might stop this—but he was upon her. And he didn't stop. Her breath left her in a rush, because he kept coming. She backed up when she thought he might collide into her, but there was nowhere to go. The doors to the elevator were at her back, closed up tight, and Rodolfo was there. *Right there.* He crowded into her. He laid a palm against the smooth metal on either side of her head and then he leaned in, trapping her between the doors of the elevator and his big, hard body.

And there was nothing but him, then. He was so much bigger than her that he became the whole world. She could see nothing past the wall of his chest. There was no sky but his sculpted, beautiful face. And if there was a sun in the heated little sliver of space that was all he'd left between their bodies, Natalie had no doubt it would be as hot as that look in his eyes.

"I think," she began, because she had to try.

"That is the trouble. You think too much."

And then he simply bent his head and took her mouth with his.

Just like that, Natalie was lost. The delirious taste of him exploded through her, chasing fire with more fire until all she did was burn. His kiss was masterful. Slick and hot and greedy. He left absolutely no doubt as to who was in control as he took her over and sampled her, again and again, as if he'd done it a thousand times before tonight alone. As if he planned to keep doing it forever, starting now. Here.

There was no rush. No desperation or hurry. Just that endless, erotic tasting as if he could go on and on and on.

And Natalie forgot, all over again, who she was and what she was meant to be doing here.

Because she could feel him everywhere. In her fingers, her toes. In the tips of her ears and like a breeze of sensation pouring down her spine. She pushed up on her feet, high on her toes, trying to get as close to him as she could. His arms stayed braced against the elevator doors like immovable barriers, leaving her to angle herself closer. She did it without thought, grabbing hold of his soft shirt in both fists and letting the fire that burned through her blaze out of control.

Sensation stormed through her, making and remaking her as it swept along. Telling her stark truths about herself she didn't want to know. She felt flushed and wild from her lips to the tight, hard tips of her breasts, all the way to that ravenous heat between her legs.

She would have climbed him if she could. She couldn't seem to get close enough.

And then Rodolfo slowed down. His kiss turned lazy. Deep, drugging—but he made no attempt to move any closer. He kept his hands on the wall.

After several agonies of this same stalling tactic, Natalie tore her lips from his, jittery and desperate.

"Please…" she whispered.

His mouth chased hers, tipped up in the corners as he sampled her, easy and slow. Teasing her, she understood then. As if this was some kind of game, and one he could play all night long. As if she was the only one being burned to a crisp where she stood. Over and over again.

"Please, what?" he asked against her mouth, an undercurrent of laughter making her hot and furious and decidedly needy all at once. "I think you can do better than that."

"Please…" she tried again, and then lost her train of thought when his mouth found the line of her jaw.

Natalie shivered as he dropped lower, trailing fire down the side of her neck and somehow finding his way to every sensitive spot she hadn't known she had. And then he used his tongue and his teeth to taunt her with each and every one of them.

"You will have to beg," he murmured against her flushed, overwarm skin, and she could feel the rumble of his voice deep inside of her, low in her belly where all that heat seemed to bloom into a desperate softness that made her knees feel weak. "So that later, there can be no confusion, much as you may wish there to be. Beg me, *princesita*."

Natalie told herself that she would do no such thing. Of course not. Her mother had raised a strong, tough, independent woman who did not *beg,* and especially not from a man like this. Prince Charming at his most dangerous.

But she was writhing against him. She was unsteady and wild and out of her mind, and all she wanted was his hands on her. All she wanted was *more.* And she didn't care what that made her. How could she? She hardly knew who the hell she was.

"Please, Rodolfo," she whispered, because it was the only way she could get her voice to work, that betraying little rasp. "Please, touch me."

His teeth grazed her bare shoulder, sending a wild heat dancing and spinning through her, until it shuddered into the scalding heat at her core and made everything worse.

Or better.

"I am already touching you."

"With your hands." And her voice was little more than a moan then, which ought to have embarrassed her. But she was far beyond that. "Please."

She thought he laughed then, and she felt that, too, like another caress. It wound through her, stoking the flames and making her burn brighter, hotter. So hot she worried she might simply…explode.

And then Rodolfo dropped his arms from the wall, leaning closer to her as he did. He took her jaw in his hand and guided her mouth to his. The kiss changed, deepened, losing any semblance of laziness or control. Natalie welcomed the crush of his chest against her, the contrast between all his heat and the cool metal at her back. She wound her arms around his neck and held on to all that corded strength as he claimed her mouth over and over, as if he was as starved for her as she was for him.

She hardly dared admit how very much she wanted that to be true.

With his other hand, he reached down and began pulling up the long skirt of her dress. He took his time, plundering her mouth as he drew the hem higher and higher. She felt the faintest draft against her calf. Her knee. Then her thigh, and then his hand was on her flesh again, the way it had been that day in the palace.

Except this time, he didn't leave it one place.

He continued to kiss her, again and again, as he smoothed his way up her thigh, urging her legs apart. And Natalie felt torn in two. Ripped straight down the center by the intensity of the hunger that poured through her, then. A tumult of need and hunger and the wild flame within her that Rodolfo kept burning at a fever pitch.

When his seeking fingers reached the edge of the satiny panties she wore, he lifted his head just slightly, taking his mouth away from her. It felt like a blow. Like a loss almost too extreme to survive.

It hurts to breathe, Natalie thought dimly, still lost in the mad commotion happening everywhere in her body. Still wanting him—needing him—almost more than she could bear.

"I will make it stop," Rodolfo said, and she realized with a start that she'd spoken out loud. His mouth crooked slightly in one corner. "Eventually."

And then he dipped his fingers beneath the elastic of her panties and found the heat of her.

Natalie gasped as he stroked his way through her

folds, bold and sure, directly into her softness. His other hand was at her neck, his thumb moving against her skin there the way his clever fingers played with her sex below. He traced his way around the center of her need, watching her face as she clutched at his broad wrist— but only to maintain that connection with him, not to stop him. Never that. Not now.

And then, without warning, he twisted his wrist and drove two fingers into her, that hard curve of his mouth deepening when she moaned.

"Like that, princess," he murmured approvingly. "Sing for me just like that."

And Natalie lost track of what he was doing, and how. He dropped his head to her neck again, teasing his way down to toy with the top of her bodice. He dragged his free hand over her nipples, poking hard against the fabric of the dress, and it was like lightning storming straight down the center of her body to where she was already little more than a flame. And he was stoking that fire with every thrust of his long, blunt fingers deep into her, as if he knew. As if he knew everything. Her pounding heart, that slick, impossible pleasure crashing over her, and that delicious tightening that was making her breath come too fast and too loud.

She lost herself in the slide, the heat. His wicked, talented hands and what they were doing to her. Her hips lifted of their own accord, meeting each stroke, and then the storm took her over. She let her head fall back against the elevator doors. She let herself go, delivering herself completely into his hands, as if there was nothing but this slick, insistent rhythm. As if there was nothing but the sensation he was building in her, higher and higher.

As if there was nothing left in all the world but him.

And then Rodolfo did something new, twisting his wrist and thrusting in a little bit deeper, and everything seemed to shudder to a dangerous halt. Then he did it again, and threw her straight over the edge into bliss.

Sheer, exultant bliss.

Natalie tumbled there, lost to herself and consumed by all that wondrous fire, for what seemed like a very long time.

When the world stopped spinning he was shifting her, lifting her up and into his arms. She had the vague thought that she should protest as he held her high against his chest so her head fell to his wide shoulder when she couldn't hold it up, but his gaze was dark and hungry—still so very hungry—and she couldn't seem to find her tongue to speak.

Rodolfo carried her to the long couch that stretched out before the great wall of windows with all of Rome winking and sparkling there on the other side, like some kind of dream. He laid her down carefully, as if she were infinitely precious to him, and it caught at her. It made the leftover fire still roaring inside of her bleed into…something else. Something that ached more than it should.

And that was the trouble, wasn't it?

Natalie wanted this to be real. She wanted all of this to be real. She wanted to stay Valentina forever, so it wouldn't matter what she did here because *she* would live the consequences of it. She could marry Rodolfo herself. She could—

You could lose yourself in him, a voice that sounded too much like her mother's, harsh and cold, snapped at her. It felt like a face full of cold water. *And then you could be one more thing he throws away when he gets bored. This is a man who has toys, not relationships.*

How can you be so foolish as to imagine otherwise—no matter how good he is with his hands?

"I should have done this a long time ago," he was saying, in a contemplative sort of way that suggested he was talking to himself more than her. But his gaze was so hot, so hungry. It made her shiver, deep inside, kindling the same fire she would have sworn was already burned out. "I think it would have made for a far better proposal of marriage, don't you?"

"Rodolfo…" she began, but he was coming down over her on the couch. He held himself up on his arms and gazed down at her as he settled himself between her legs, fitting his body to hers in a way that made them both breathe a little bit harder. Audibly. And there was no pretending that wasn't real. It made her foolish. "You may imagine you know who I am, but you don't. You really don't."

"Quiet, *princesita*," he said in a low sort of growl that made everything inside her, still reeling from what he'd done with his hands alone, bloom into a new, even more demanding sort of heat. He shifted so he could take her face between his hands, and that was better. Worse. Almost too intense. "I am going to taste you again. Then I will tell you who are, though I already know. You should know it, too." He let his chest press against her, and dipped his chin so his mouth was less than a gasp away. Less than a breath. *"Mine."*

And then he set his mouth to hers and the flames devoured her.

Again.

This time, Natalie didn't need to be told to beg for him. There was no space between them, only heat and the intense pressure of the hardest part of him, flush against her scalding heat. There was no finesse, no strategy, no teasing. Only need.

And that hunger that rolled between them like so much summer thunder.

She didn't know who undressed whom and she didn't—couldn't—care. She only knew that his mouth was a torment and a gift, both at the same time. His hands were like fire. He pulled down her bodice and feasted on the nipples he'd played with before, until Natalie was nothing but a writhing mess beneath him. Begging. Pleading. Somehow his shirt was open, and she was finally able to touch all those hard muscles she'd only imagined until now. And he was so much better than the pictures she'd seen. Hot and extraordinarily male and perfect and *here,* right here, stretched out on top of her. It was her turn to use her mouth on him, tasting the heat and salt of him until his breath was as heavy as hers, and everything was part of the same shattering, impossible magic.

At some point she wondered if it was possible to survive this much pleasure. If anyone could live through it. If she would recognize herself when this was done—but that was swept away when he took her mouth again.

She loved his weight, crushing her down into the cushions. She loved it even more when he pulled her skirts out of the way and found her panties again. This time, he didn't bother sneaking beneath them. This time he simply tugged, hard and sure, until they tore away in his hand.

And somehow that was so erotic it seemed to light her up inside. She could hardly breathe.

Rodolfo reached down and tore at his trousers, and when he shifted back into place Natalie felt him, broad and hard, nudging against her entrance. His gaze traveled over her body from the place they were joined to the skirt of the dress rucked up and twisted around her hips. Then higher, to where her breasts were plumped up above the dress's bodice, her nipples still tight and swollen from his mouth. Only then did his gaze touch her face.

Suddenly, the world was nothing but that shuddering beat of her heart, so hard she thought he must surely feel it, and that stark, serious expression he wore. He dropped down to an elbow, bringing himself closer to her.

This was happening. This was real.

He was the kind of prince she'd never dared admit she dreamed about, so big and so beautiful it hurt to be this close to him. It hurt in a way dreams never did. It ached, low and deep, and everywhere else.

"Are you ready, princess?" he asked, and his voice was another caress, rough and wild.

Natalie wanted to say something arch. Witty. Something to cut through the intensity and make her feel in control again. Anything at all that might help make this less than it was. Anything that might contain or minimize all those howling, impossible things that flooded through her then.

But she couldn't seem to open her mouth. She couldn't seem to find a single word that might help her.

Her body knew what to do without her guidance or input. As if she'd been made for this, for him. She lifted her hips and pushed herself against him, impaling herself on his hardness, one slow and shuddering inch. Then another. He muttered something in what she thought was the Spanish he sometimes used, but Natalie was caught in his dark gaze, still fast on her face.

"What are you doing to me?" he murmured. He'd asked it before.

Like then, he didn't wait for an answer. He didn't give her any warning. He wrapped an arm around her hips, then hauled them high against him. And in the next instant, slammed himself in deep.

"Oh, my God," Natalie whispered as he filled her, and everything in her shuddered again and again, nudging her so close to the edge once more that she caught her breath in anticipation.

"'Your Highness' will do," Rodolfo told her, a thread of amusement beneath the stark need in his voice.

And then he began to move.

It was a slick, devastating magic. Rodolfo built the flames in her into a wildfire, then fanned the blaze ever higher. He dropped his mouth to hers, then shifted to pull a nipple into the heat of his mouth.

Natalie wrapped herself around him, and gave herself over to each glorious thrust. She dug her fingers into his back, she let her head fall back and then she let herself go. As if the woman she'd been when she'd walked into this room, or into this life, no longer existed.

There was only Rodolfo. There was only this.

Perfect, she thought, again and again, so it became a chant inside her head. *This is perfect.*

She might even have chanted it aloud.

He dropped down closer, wrapping his arms around her as his rhythm went wilder and more erratic. He tucked his face in her neck and kept his mouth there as he pounded into her, over and over, until he hurled her straight back off that cliff.

And he followed her only moments later, releasing himself into her with a roar that echoed through the room and deep inside of Natalie, too, tearing her apart in a completely different way as reality slammed back into her, harsh and cruel.

Because she'd never felt closer to a man in all her life, and Rodolfo had called out to her as if he felt the same. She was as certain as she'd ever been of anything that he felt exactly the same as she did.

But, of course, he thought she was someone else.

And he'd used the wrong name.

CHAPTER NINE

RODOLFO HAD BARELY shifted his weight from Valentina before she was rolling out from beneath him, pulling the voluminous skirt of her dress with her as she climbed to her feet. He found he couldn't help but smile. She was so unsteady on her feet that she had to reach out and grab hold of the nearby chair to keep from sagging to the ground.

He was male enough to find that markedly satisfying.

"You are even beautiful turned away from me," he told her without meaning to speak. It was not, generally, his practice to traffic in flattery. Mostly because it was never required. But it was the simple truth as far as Valentina was concerned. Not empty flattery at all.

She shivered slightly, as if in reaction to his words, but that was all. She didn't glance back at him. She was pulling her dress back into place, shaking back her hair that had long since tumbled from its once sleek chignon. And all Rodolfo wanted to do was pull her back down to him. He wanted to indulge himself and take a whole lot more time with her. He wanted to strip her completely and make sure he learned every last inch of her sweet body by heart.

He was more than a little delighted at the prospect of a long life together to do exactly that.

Rodolfo zipped himself up and rolled to a sitting position, aware that he felt lighter than he had in a long time. Years.

Since Felipe died.

Because the truth was, he'd never wanted his brother's responsibilities. He'd wanted his brother. Funny, irreverent, remarkably warm Felipe had been Rodolfo's favorite person for the whole of his life, and then he'd died. So suddenly. So needlessly. He'd locked himself in his rooms to sleep through what he'd assumed was a flu, and he'd been gone within the week. There was a part of Rodolfo that would never accept that. That never had. That would grieve his older brother forever.

But Rodolfo was the Crown Prince of Tissely now no matter how he grieved his brother, and that meant he should have had all of the attendant responsibilities whether he liked it or not. His father had felt otherwise. And every year the king failed to let Rodolfo take Felipe's place in his court and his government was like a slap in the face all over again, of course. It was a very public, very deliberate rebuke.

More than that, it confirmed what Rodolfo had always known to be true. He could not fill Felipe's shoes. He could not come anywhere close and that would never change. There was no hope.

Until now, he'd assumed that was simply how it would be. His father would die at some point, having allowed Rodolfo no chance at all to figure out his role as king. Rodolfo would have to do it on the fly, which was a terrific way to plunge a country straight into chaos. It was one of the reasons he'd dedicated himself to the sort of sports that required a man figure out how to remain calm no matter what was coming at him. Sharks. The earth, many thousands of feet below, at great speed. Assorted impossible mountain peaks that had killed many men before him. He figured it was all good practice for the little gift his father planned to leave him, since he suspected the old man was doing his level best to ensure that all his dire predictions about the kind of king Rodolfo would be would come true within days of his own death.

This engagement was a test, nothing more. Rodolfo had no doubt that his father expected him to fail, somehow, at an arranged marriage that literally required nothing of him save that he show up. And perhaps he'd played into that, by continuing to see other women and doing nothing to keep that discreet.

But everything was different now. Valentina was his. And their marriage would be the kind of real union Rodolfo had always craved. Without even meaning to, Rodolfo had beaten his father at the old man's own cynical little game.

And it was more than that. Rodolfo had to believe that if he could make the very dutiful princess his the way he had tonight, if he could take a bloodless royal arrangement and make it a wildfire of a marriage, he could do anything. Even convince his dour father to see him as more than just an unwelcome replacement for his beloved lost son.

For the first time in a long, long while, Rodolfo felt very nearly *hopeful*.

"Princess," he began, reaching out to wrap a hand around her hip and tug her toward him, because she was still showing him her back and he wanted her lovely face, "you must—"

"Stop calling me that!" she burst out, sounding raw. And something like wild.

She twisted out of his grasp. And he was so surprised by her outburst that he let her go.

Valentina didn't stop moving until she'd cleared the vast glass table set before the couch, and then she stood there on the other side, her chest heaving as if she'd run an uphill mile to get there.

His princess did not look anything like *hopeful*. If anything, she looked… Wounded. Destroyed. Rodolfo couldn't make any sense out of it. Her green eyes were dark and that sweet, soft mouth of hers trembled as if the hurt inside her was on the verge of pouring out even as she stood there before him.

"I can't believe I let this happen…" she whispered, and her eyes looked full. Almost blank with an anguish Rodolfo couldn't begin to understand.

Rodolfo wanted to stand, to go to her, to offer her what comfort he could—but something stopped him. How many times would she do this back and forth in one way or another? How many ways would she find to pull the rug out from under him—and as he thought that, it was not lost on Rodolfo that unlike every other woman he'd ever known, he cared a little too deeply about what this one was about. All this melodrama and for what? There was no stopping their wedding or the long, public, political marriage that would follow. It was like a train bearing down on them and it always had been.

From the moment Felipe had died and Rodolfo had been sat down and told that in addition to losing his best friend he now had a different life to live than the one he'd imagined he would, there had been no deviating from the path set before them. Princess Valentina had already been his—entirely his—before he'd laid a single finger on her. What had happened here only confirmed what had always been true, not that there had been any doubt. Not for him, anyway.

The only surprise was how much he wanted her.

Again, now, despite the fact he'd only just had her. She made him…thirsty in a way he'd never experienced before in his life.

But it wouldn't have mattered if she'd stayed the same pale, distant ghost he'd met at their engagement celebration. The end result—their marriage and all the politics involved—would have been the same.

He didn't like to see her upset. He didn't like it at all. It made his jaw clench tight and every muscle in his body go much too taut. But Rodolfo remained where he was.

"If you mean what happened right here—" and he nodded at the pillow beside him as if could play back the last hour in vivid color "—then I feel I must tell you that it was always going to happen. It was only a question of when. Before the wedding or after it. Or did you imagine heirs to royal kingdoms were delivered by stork?"

But it was as if she couldn't hear him. "Why didn't you let me leave the gala alone?"

He shrugged, settling back against the pillows as if he was entirely at his ease, though he was not. Not at all. "I assume that was a rhetorical question, as that was never going to happen. You can blame the unfortunate optics if you must. But there was no possibility that my fiancée was ever going to sneak out of a very public event on her own, leaving me behind. How does that suit our narrative?"

"I don't care about your narrative."

"*Our* narrative, Valentina, and you should. You will. It is a weapon against us or a tool we employ. The choice is ours."

She was frowning now, and it was aimed at him, yet Rodolfo had the distinct impression she was talking to herself. "You should never, ever have come up here tonight."

He considered her for a moment. "This was not a mistake, *princesita*. This was a beginning."

She lifted her hands to her face and Rodolfo saw that they were shaking. Again, he wanted to go to her and again, he didn't. It was something about the stiff way she was standing there, or what had looked like genuine torment on her face before she'd covered it from his view. It gripped him, somehow, and kept him right where he was.

As if, he realized in the next moment, he was waiting for the other shoe to drop. The way he had been ever since he'd discovered at too young an age that anything and anyone could be taken from him with no notice whatsoever.

But that was ridiculous. There was no "other shoe" here. This was an arranged marriage set up by their fathers when Valentina was a baby. One crown prince of Tissely and one princess of Murin, and the kingdoms would remain forever united. Two small countries who, together, could become a force to be reckoned with in these confusing modern times. The contracts had been signed for months. They were locked into this wedding no matter what, with no possibility of escape.

Rodolfo knew. He'd read every line of every document that had required his signature. And still, he didn't much like that thing that moved him, dark and grim, as he watched her. It felt far too much like foreboding.

His perfect princess, who had just given herself to him with such sweet, encompassing heat that he could still feel the burn of it all over him and through him as if he might feel it always, dropped her hands from her face. Her gaze caught his and held. Her eyes were still too dark, and filled with what looked like misery.

Sheer, unmistakable misery. It made his chest feel tight.

"I should never have let any of this happen," she said, and her voice was different. Matter-of-fact, if hollow. She swallowed, still keeping her eyes trained on his. "This is my fault. I accept that."

"Wonderful," Rodolfo murmured, aware his voice sounded much too edgy. "I do so enjoy being blameless. It is such a novelty."

She clenched her hands together in front of her, twisting her fingers together into a tangle. There was something about the gesture that bothered him, though he couldn't have said what. Perhaps it was merely that it seemed the very antithesis of the sort of thing a woman trained since birth to be effortlessly graceful would do. No matter the provocation.

"I am not Princess Valentina."

He watched her say that. Or rather, he saw her lips move and he heard the words that came out of her mouth, but they made no sense.

Her mouth, soft and scared, pressed into a line. "My name is Natalie."

"Natalie," he repeated, tonelessly.

"I ran into the princess in, ah—" She cleared her throat. "In London. We were surprised, as you might imagine, to see…" She waved her hand in that way of hers, as if what she was saying was reasonable. Or even possible. Instead of out-and-out gibberish. "And it seemed like a bit of a lark, I suppose. I got to pretend to be a princess for a bit. What could be more fun? No one was ever meant to know, of course."

"I beg your pardon." He still couldn't move. He thought perhaps he'd gone entirely numb, but he knew, somehow, that the paralytic lack of feeling was better than what lurked on the other side. Much better. "But where, precisely, is the real princess in this ludicrous scenario?"

"Geographically, do you mean? She's back in London. Or possibly Spain, depending."

"All tucked up in whatever your life is, presumably." He nodded as if that idiocy made sense. "What did you say your name was, again?"

She looked ill at ease. As well she should. "Natalie."

"And if your profession is not that of the well-known daughter of a widely renowned and ancient royal family, despite your rather remarkable likeness to Princess Valentina, dare I ask what is it that you do? Does it involve a stage, perhaps, the better to hone these acting skills?"

"I'm a personal assistant. To a very important businessman."

"A jumped-up secretary for a man in trade. Of course." He was getting less numb by the second, and that was no good for anyone—though Rodolfo found he didn't particularly care. He hadn't lost his temper in a long while, but these were extenuating circumstances, surely. She should have been grateful he wasn't breaking things. He shook his head, and even let out a laugh, though nothing was funny. "I must hand it to you. Stage or no stage, this has been quite an act."

She blinked. "Somehow, that doesn't sound like a compliment."

"It was really quite ingenious. All you had to do was walk in the room that day and actually treat me like another living, breathing human instead of a cardboard cutout. After all those months. You must have been thrilled that I fell into your trap so easily."

The words felt sour in his own mouth. But Valentina only gazed back at him with confusion written all over her, as if she didn't understand what he was talking about. He was amazed that he'd fallen for her performance. Why hadn't it occurred to him that her public persona, so saintly and retiring, was as much a constriction as his daredevil reputation? As easily turned off as on. And yet it had never crossed his mind that she was anything but the woman she'd always seemed to be, hailed in all the papers as a paragon of royal virtue. A breath of fresh air, they called her. The perfect princess in every respect.

He should have known that all of it was a lie. A carefully crafted, meticulously built lie.

"The trap?" She was shaking her head, looking lost and something like forlorn, and Rodolfo hated that even when he knew she was trying to play him, he still wanted to comfort her. Get his hands on her and hold her close. It made his temper lick at him, dark and dangerous. "What trap?"

"All of this so you could come back around tonight and drop this absurd story on me. Did you really think I would credit such an outlandish tale? You *happen* to resemble one of the wealthiest and most famous women in the world, yet no one remarked on this at any point during your other life. Until, by chance, you stumbled upon each other. How convenient. And that day in the palace, when you came back from London—am I meant to believe that you had never met me before?"

She pressed her lips together as if aware that they trembled. "I hadn't."

"What complete and utter rubbish." He stood then, smoothing his shirt down as he rose to make sure he kept his damned twitchy hands to himself, but there wasn't much he could do about the fury in his voice. "I am not entirely certain which part offends me more. That you would go to the trouble to concoct such a childish, ridiculous story in the first place, or that you imagined for one second that I would believe it."

"You said yourself that I was switching personalities. That I was two women. This is why. I think—I mean, the only possible explanation is that Valentina and I are twins." There was an odd emphasis on that last word, as if she'd never said it out loud before. She squared her shoulders. "Twin sisters."

Rodolfo fought to keep himself under control, despite the ugly things that crawled through him then, each worse than the last. The truth was, he should have known better than to be hopeful. About anything. He should have known better than to allow himself to think that anything in his life might work out. He could jump out of a thousand planes and land safely. There had never been so much as a hiccup on any of his adventures, unless he counted the odd shark bite or scar. But when it came to his actual life as a prince of Tissely? The things he was bound by blood and his birthright to do whether he wanted to or not? It was nothing but disaster, every time.

He should have known this would be, too.

"Twin sisters," he echoed when he trusted himself to speak in both English and a marginally reasonable tone. "But I think you must mean *secret* twin sisters, to give it the proper soap opera flourish. And how do you imagine such a thing could happen? Do you suppose the king happily looked the other way while Queen Frederica swanned off with a stolen baby?"

"No one talks about where she went. Much less who she went with."

"You are talking about matters of state, not idle gossip." His hands were in fists, and he forced them to open, then shoved them in his pockets. "The queen's mental state was precarious. Everyone knows this. She would hardly have been allowed to retreat so completely from public life with a perfectly healthy child who also happened to be one of the king's direct heirs."

Valentina frowned. "Precarious? What do you mean?"

"Do not play these games with me," he gritted out, aware that his heart was kicking at him. Temper or that same, frustrated hunger, he couldn't tell. "You know as well as I do that she was not assassinated, no matter how many breathless accounts are published in the dark and dingy corners of the internet by every conspiracy theorist who can type. That means, for your story to make any kind of sense, a king with no other heirs in line for his throne would have to release one of the two he did have into the care of a woman who was incapable of fulfilling a single one of her duties as his queen. Or at the very least, somehow fail to hunt the world over for the child once this same woman stole her."

"I didn't really think about that part," she said tightly. "I was more focused on the fact I was in a palace and the man with the crown was acting as if he was my father. Which it turns out, he probably is."

"Enough." He belted it out at her, with enough force that her head jerked back a little. "The only thing this astonishing conversation is doing is making me question your sanity. You must know that." He let out a small laugh at that, though it scraped at him. "Perhaps that is your endgame. A mental breakdown or two, like mother, like daughter. If you cannot get out of the marriage before the wedding, best to start working on how to exit it afterward, I suppose."

Her face was pale. "That's not what this is. I'm trying to be honest with you."

He moved toward her then, feeling his lips thin as he watched her fight to stand her ground when she so clearly wanted to put more furniture between them—if not whole rooms.

"Have I earned this, Valentina?" he demanded, all that numbness inside him burning away with the force of his rage. His sense of betrayal—which he didn't care to examine too closely. It was enough that she'd led him to hope, then kicked it out of his reach. It was more than enough. "That you should go to these lengths to be free of me?"

He stopped when he was directly in front of her, and he hated the fact that even now, all he wanted to do was pull her into his arms and kiss her until the only thing between them was that heat. Her eyes were glassy and she looked pale with distress, and he fell for it. Even knowing what she was willing to do and say, his first instinct was to believe her. What did that say about his judgment?

Maybe his father had been right about him all along.

That rang in him like a terrible bell.

"Here is the sad truth, princess," he told her, standing above her so she was forced to tilt her head back to keep her eyes on him. And his body didn't know that everything had changed, of course. It was far more straightforward. It wanted her, no matter what stories she told. "There is no escape. There is no sneaking away into some fantasy life where you will live out your days without the weight of a country or two squarely on your shoulders. There is no switching places with a convenient twin and hiding from who you are. And I am terribly afraid that part of what you must suffer is our marriage. You are stuck with me. Forever."

"Rodolfo." And her voice was scratchy, as if she had too many sobs in her throat. As if she was fighting to hold them back. "I know it all sounds insane, but you have to listen to me—"

"No," he said with quiet ferocity. "I do not."

"Rodolfo—"

And now even his name in her mouth felt like an insult. Another damned lie. He couldn't bear it.

He silenced her the only way he knew how. He reached out and hooked a hand around her neck, dragging her to him. And then he claimed her mouth with his.

Rodolfo poured all of the dark things swirling around inside of him into the way he angled his jaw to make everything bright hot and slick. Into the way he took her. Tasted her. As if she was the woman he'd imagined she was, so proper and bright. As if he could still taste that fantasy version of her now despite the games she was trying to play. He gave her his grief over Felipe, his father's endless shame and fury that the wrong son had died—all of it. If she'd taken away his hope, he could give her the rest of it. He kissed her again and again, as much a penance for him as any kind of punishment for her.

And when he was done, because it was that or he would take her again right there on the hotel floor and he wasn't certain either one of them would survive that, he set her away from him.

It should have mattered to him that she was breathing too hard. That her green eyes were wide and there were tears marking her cheeks. It should have meant something.

Somewhere, down below the tumult of that black fury that roared in him, inconsolable and much too wounded, it did. But he ignored it.

"I only wanted you to know who I am," she whispered.

And that was it, then. That was too much. He took her shoulders in his hands and dragged her before him, up on her toes and directly in his face.

"I am Rodolfo of Tissely," he growled at her. "The accidental, throwaway prince. I was called *the spare* when I was born, always expected to live in my brother's shadow and never, ever expected to take Felipe's place. Then the spare became the heir—but only in name. Because I have always been the bad seed. I have always been unworthy."

"That's not true."

He ignored her, his fingers gripping her and keeping her there before him. "Nothing I touch has ever lasted. No one I love has ever loved me back, or if they did, it was only as long as there were two sons instead of the one. Or they disappeared into the wilds of Bavaria, pretending to be ill. Or they died of bloody sepsis in the middle of a castle filled with royal doctors and every possible medication under the sun."

She whispered his name as if she loved him, and that hurt him worse than all the rest. Because more than all the rest, he wanted that to be true—and he knew exactly how much of a fool that made him.

"What is one more princess who must clearly hate the very idea of me, the same as all the rest?" And what did it matter that he'd imagined that she might be the saving of him, of the crown he'd never wanted and the future he wasn't prepared for? "None of this matters. You should have saved your energy. This will all end as it was planned. The only difference is that now, I know exactly how deceitful you are. I know the depths of the games you will play. And I promise you this, princess. You will not fool me again."

"You don't understand," she said, more tears falling from her darkened green eyes as she spoke and wetting her pale cheeks. "I wanted this to be real, Rodolfo. I lost myself in that."

He told himself to let go of her. To take his hand off her shoulders and step away. But he didn't do it. If anything, he held her tighter. Closer.

As if he'd wanted it to be real, too. As if some part of him still did.

"You have to believe me," she whispered. "I never meant it to go that far."

"It was only sex," he told her, his voice a thing of granite. He remembered what she'd called herself as she'd spun out her fantastical little tale. "But no need to worry, *Natalie*." She flinched, and he was bastard enough to like that. Because he wanted her to hurt, too—and no matter that he hated himself for that thought. Hating himself didn't change a thing. It never had. "I will be certain to make you scream while we make the requisite heirs. I am nothing if not dependable in that area, if nowhere else. Feel free to ask around for references."

He let her go then, not particularly happy with how hard it was to do, and headed for the elevator. He needed to clear his head. He needed to wash all of this away. He needed to find a very dark hole and fall into it for a while, until the self-loathing receded enough that he could function again. Assuming it ever would.

"It doesn't have to be this way," she said from behind him.

But Rodolfo turned to face her only when he'd stepped into the elevator. She stood where he'd left her, her hands tangled in front of her again and something broken in her gaze.

Eventually, she would have as little power over him as she'd had when they'd met. Eventually, he would not want to go to her when she looked at him like that, as if she was small and wounded and only he could heal her.

Eventually. All he had to do was survive long enough to get there, like anything else.

"It can only be this way," he told her then, and he hardly recognized his own voice. He sounded like a broken man—but of course, that wasn't entirely true. He had never been whole to begin with. "The sooner you resign yourself to it, the better. I am very much afraid this is who we are."

Natalie didn't move for a long, long time after Rodolfo left. If she could have turned into a pillar of stone, she would have. It would have felt better, she was sure.

The elevator doors shut and she heard the car move, taking Rodolfo away, but she still stood right where he'd left her as if her feet were nailed to the floor. Her cheeks were wet and her dress caught at her since she'd pulled it back into place in such a panicked hurry, and her fingers ached from where she'd threaded them together and held them still. Her breathing had gone funny because her throat was so tight.

And for a long while, it seemed that the only thing she could do about any of those things was stay completely still. As if the slightest movement would make it all worse—though it was hard to imagine how.

Eventually, her fingers began to cramp, and she unclasped them, then shook them out. After that it was easier to move the rest of her. She walked on stiff, protesting legs down the long penthouse hallway into her bedroom, where she stood for a moment in the shambles of her evening, blind to the luxury all around her. But that could only last so long. She went to kick off her shoes and realized she'd lost them somewhere, but she didn't want to go back out to the living room and look. She was sure Rodolfo's contempt was still clinging to every gleaming surface out there and she couldn't bring herself to face it.

She padded across the grandly appointed space to the adjoining bathroom suite and stepped in to find the bath itself was filled and waiting for her, steam rising off the top of the huge, curved, freestanding tub like an invitation. That simple kindness made her eyes fill all over again. She wiped the blurriness away, but it didn't help, and the tears were flowing freely again by the time she got herself out of her dress and threw it over a chair in the bedroom. She didn't cry. She almost never cried. But tonight she couldn't seem to stop.

Natalie returned to the bathroom to pull all the pins out of her hair. She piled the mess of it on her head and knotted it into place, ignoring all the places she felt stiff or sore. Then she walked across the marble floor and climbed into the tub at last, sinking into the warm, soothing embrace of the bath's hot water and the salts that some kind member of the staff had thought to add.

She closed her eyes and let herself drift—but then there was no more hiding from the events of the night. The dance. That kiss out on the terrace of the villa. And then what had happened right here in this hotel. His mouth against her skin. His wickedly clever hands. The bold, deep surge of his possession and how she'd fallen to pieces so easily. The smile on Rodolfo's face when he'd turned her around to face him afterward, and how quickly it had toppled from view. And that shuttered, haunted look she'd put in his eyes later, that had been there when he'd left.

As if that was all that remained of what had swelled and shimmered between them tonight. As if that was all it had ever been.

Whatever else came of these stolen days here in Valentina's life, whatever happened, Natalie knew she would never forgive herself for that. For believing in a fairy tale when she knew better and hurting Rodolfo—to say nothing of herself—in the process.

She sat in the tub until her skin was shriveled and the water had cooled. She played the night all the way through, again and again, one vivid image after the next. And when she sat up and pulled the plug to let the water swirl down the drain, she felt clean, yes. But her body didn't feel like hers. She could still feel Rodolfo's touch all over, as if he'd branded her with his passion as surely as he'd condemned her with his disbelief.

Too bad, she told herself, sounding brisk and hard like her mother would have. *This is what you get for doing what you knew full well you shouldn't have.*

Natalie climbed out of the tub then and wrapped herself in towels so light and airy they could have been clouds, but she hardly noticed. She stood in the still-fogged-up bathroom and brushed out her hair, letting the copper strands fall all around her like a curtain and then braiding the heavy mess of it to one side, so she could toss it over one shoulder and forget it.

When she walked back into the bedroom, her dress was gone from the chair where she'd thrown it and in its place was the sort of silky thing Valentina apparently liked to sleep in. Natalie had always preferred a simple T-shirt, but over the past couple of weeks she'd grown to like the sensuous feel of the fine silk against her bare skin.

Tonight, however, it felt like a rebuke.

Her body didn't want silk, it wanted Rodolfo.

She would have given anything she had to go back in time and keep herself from making that confession. To accept that of course he would call her by the wrong name and find a way to make her peace with it. Her mind spun out into one searing fantasy after another about how the night would have gone if only she'd kept her mouth shut.

But that was the trouble, wasn't it? She'd waited too long to tell him the truth, if she was going to. And she never should have allowed him to touch her while he thought she was Valentina. Not back in the palace. Certainly not tonight. She should have kept her distance from him entirely.

Because no matter what her traitorous heart insisted, even now, he wasn't hers. He could never be hers. The ring on her finger belonged to another woman and so did he. It didn't matter that Valentina had given her blessing, whatever that meant in the form of a breezy text. Natalie had never wanted to be the sort of woman who took another woman's man, no matter the circumstances. She'd spent her whole childhood watching her mother flit from one lover to the next, knowing full well that many of the men Erica juggled had been married already. Natalie always vowed that she was not going to be one of those women who pretended they didn't know when a man was already committed elsewhere. In this case, she'd known going in and she'd still ended up here.

How many more ways was she going to betray herself?

How many more lives was she going to ruin besides her own?

Natalie looked around the achingly gorgeous room, aware of every last detail that made it the perfect room for a princess, from the soaring canopy over her high, proud bed to the deep Persian rugs at her feet. The epic sweep of the drapery at each window and the stunning view of Rome on the other side of the glass. The artistry in every carved leg of each of the chairs placed *just so* at different points around the chamber. She looked down at her own body, still warm and pink from her bath and barely covered in a flowy, bright blue silk that cascaded lazily from two spaghetti straps at her shoulders. Her manicure and pedicure were perfect. Her skin was as soft as a baby's after access to Valentina's moisturizing routine with products crafted especially for her. Her hair had never looked so shiny or healthy, even braided over one shoulder. And she was wearing nothing but silk and a ring fit for a queen. Literally.

But she didn't belong here with these things that would never belong to her. She might fit into this borrowed life in the most physical sense, but none of it suited her. *None of it was hers.*

"I am Natalie Monette," she told herself fiercely, her own voice sounding loud and brash in the quiet of the room. Not cool and cultured, like a princess. "My fingernails are never painted red. My toes are usually a disaster. I live on pots of coffee and fistfuls of ibuprofen, not two squares of decadent chocolate a day and healthy little salads."

She moved over to the high bed, where Valentina's laptop and mobile phone waited for her on a polished bedside table, plugged in and charged up, because not even that was her responsibility here.

It was time to go home. It was time to wake up from this dream and take back what was hers—her career—before she lost that, too.

It was time to get back to the shadows, where she belonged.

She picked up the mobile and punched in her own number, telling herself this would all fade away fast when she was back in her own clothes and her own life. When she had too much to do for Mr. Casilieris to waste her time brooding over a prince she'd never see again. Soon this little stretch of time would be like every other fairy tale she'd ever been told as a girl, a faded old story she might recall every now and then, but no part of anything that really mattered to her.

And so what if her heart seemed to twist at that, making her whole chest ache?

It was still time—past time—to go back where she belonged.

"I am Natalie Monette," she whispered to herself as the phone on the other end rang and rang. "I am not a princess. I was never a princess and I never will be."

But it didn't matter what she told herself, because Valentina didn't answer.

Not that night.

And not for weeks.

CHAPTER TEN

RODOLFO WAS CONFLICTED.

He hadn't seen Valentina since that night in Rome. He'd had his staff contact her to announce that he thought they'd carried out their objectives beautifully and there would be no more need for their excursions into the world of the paparazzi. And that was before he'd seen their pictures in all the papers.

The one most prominently featured showed the two of them on the dance floor, in the middle of what looked like a very romantic waltz. Rodolfo was gazing down at her as if he had never seen a woman before in all his life. That was infuriating enough, given what had come afterward. It made his chest feel too tight. But it was the look on the princess's face that had rocked Rodolfo.

Because the picture showed her staring up at the man who held her in his arms in open adoration. As if she was falling in love right then and there as they danced. As if it had already happened.

And it had all been a lie. A game.

The first you've ever lost, a vicious voice inside of him whispered.

Today he stood in the grand foyer outside his father's offices in the palace in Tissely, but his attention was across Europe in Murin, where the maddening, still-more-fascinating-than-she-should-have-been woman who was meant to become his wife was going about her business as if she had not revealed herself to be decidedly unhinged.

She'd kept a low profile these last few weeks. As had Rodolfo.

But his fury hadn't abated one bit.

Secret twins. The very idea was absurd—even if she hadn't been the daughter of one of the most famous and closely watched men in the world. There was press crawling all over Murin Castle day and night and likely always had been, especially when the former queen had been pregnant with the heir to the country's throne.

"Ridiculous," he muttered under his breath.

But his trouble was, he didn't want to be bitter. He wanted to believe her, no matter how unreasonable she was. That was what had been driving him crazy these past weeks. He'd told himself he was going to throw himself right back into his old habits, but he hadn't. Instead he'd spent entirely too much time mired in his old, familiar self-pity and all it had done was make him miss her.

He had no earthly idea what to do about that.

The doors opened behind him and he was led in with the usual unnecessary ceremony to find his father standing behind his desk. Already frowning, which Rodolfo knew from experience didn't bode well for the bracing father/son chat they were about to have.

Ferdinand nodded at the chair before his desk and Rodolfo took it, for once not flinging himself down like a lanky adolescent. Not because doing so always irritated his father. But because he felt like a different man these days, scraped raw and hollow and made new in a variety of uncomfortable and largely unpleasant ways he could blame directly on his princess, and he didn't have it in him to needle his lord and king whenever possible.

His father's frown deepened as he beheld his son before him, because, of course, he always had it in him to poke at his son. It was an expression Rodolfo knew well. He had no idea why it was harder to keep his expression impassive today.

"I hope you have it in you to acquit yourself with something more like grace at your wedding," Ferdinand said darkly, as if Rodolfo had been rousted out of a den of iniquity only moments before and still reeked of excess. He'd tried. In the sense that he'd planned to go out and drown himself in all the things that had always entertained him before. But he'd never made it out. He couldn't call it fidelity to his lying, manipulative princess when the truth was, he'd lost interest in sin—could he? "The entire world will be watching."

"The entire world has been watching for some time," Rodolfo replied, keeping his tone easy. Even polite. Because there was no need to inform his father that he had no intention of marrying a woman who had tried to play him so thoroughly. How could he? But he told himself Ferdinand could find out when he didn't appear at the ceremony, like everyone else. "Has that not been the major point of contention all these years?"

His father ignored him. "It is one thing to wave at a press call. Your wedding to the Murin princess will be one of the most-watched ceremonies in modern Europe. Your behavior must, at last, be that of a prince of Tissely. Do you think you can manage this, Rodolfo?"

He glared at him as if he expected an answer. And something inside of Rodolfo simply...cracked.

It was so loud that first he thought it was the chair beneath him, but his father didn't react. And it took Rodolfo a moment to understand that it wasn't his chair. It was him.

He died, Rodolfo, his princess had said in Rome, before she'd revealed herself. *You lived.*

And he'd tried so hard to reverse that, hadn't he? He'd told himself all these years that the risks he took were what made him feel alive, but that had been a lie. What he'd been doing was punishing himself. Pushing himself because he hadn't cared what happened to him. Risking himself because he'd been without hope.

Until now.

"I am not merely *a* prince of Tissely," he said with a great calm that seemed to flood him then, the way it always did before he dropped from great heights with only a parachute or threw himself off the sides of bridges and ravines attached to only a bouncy rope. Except this time he knew the calm was not a precursor to adrenaline, but to the truth. At last. "I am the only prince of Tissely."

"I know very well who you are," his father huffed at him.

"Do you, sir? Because you have seemed to be laboring under some misconceptions as to my identity this last decade or two."

"I am your father and your king," his father thundered.

But Rodolfo was done being put into his place. He was done accepting that his place was somehow lower and shameful, for that matter.

All he'd done was live. Imperfectly and often foolishly, but he'd lived a life. He might have been lying to himself. He might have been hopeless. But he'd survived all of that.

The only thing he was guilty of was of not being Felipe.

"I am your son," Rodolfo replied, his voice like steel.

"I am your only remaining son and your only heir. It doesn't matter how desperately you cling to your throne. It doesn't matter how thoroughly you convince yourself that I am worthless and undeserving. Even if it were true, it wouldn't matter. Nothing you do will ever bring Felipe back."

His father looked stiff enough to break in half. And old, Rodolfo thought. How had he missed that his father had grown old? "How dare you!"

He was tired of this mausoleum his father had built around Felipe's memory. He was tired of the games they played, two bitter, broken men who had never recovered from the same long-ago loss and instead, still took it out on each other.

Rodolfo was done with the game. He didn't want to live like this any longer.

He wanted to feel the way he did when he was with Valentina. Maybe it had all been a lie, but he'd been *alive*. Not putting on a show. Not destined to disappoint simply by showing up.

And there was something he should have said a decade or two ago.

"I am all you have, old man." He stood then, taking his time and never shifting his gaze from his father's, so perhaps they could both take note of the fact that he towered over the old man. "Whether you like it or do not, I am still here. Only one of your sons died all those years ago. And only you can decide if you will waste the rest of your life acting as if you lost them both."

His father was not a demonstrative man. Ferdinand stood like a stone for so long that Rodolfo thought he might stand like that forever. So committed to the mausoleum he'd built that he became a part of it in fact.

But Rodolfo wanted no part of it. Not anymore. He

was done with lies. With games. With paying over and over for sins that were not his.

He inclined his head, then turned for the door. He was reaching for the knob to let himself out—to leave this place and get on with his life—when he heard a faint noise from behind him.

"It is only that I miss him," came his father's voice, low and strained. It was another man's sob.

Rodolfo didn't turn around. It would embarrass them both.

"I know, Papa," he said, using a name he hadn't thought, much less spoken aloud, since he was little more than a baby himself. But it was the only one that seemed appropriate. "I do, too."

The first week after that shattering trip to Rome, Natalie tried Valentina so many times she was slightly afraid it would have bordered on harassment—had she not been calling her own mobile number. And it didn't matter anyway, because the princess never answered, leaving Natalie to sit around parsing the differences between a ringing phone that was never picked up and a call that went straight to voice mail like an adolescent girl worrying over a boy's pallid attentions.

And in the meantime, she still had to live Valentina's life.

That meant endless rounds of charity engagements. It meant approximately nine million teas with the ladies of this or that charity and long, sad walks through hospitals filled with ill children. It was being expected to "say a few words" at the drop of a hat, and always in a way that would support the crown while offending no one. It meant dinners with King Geoffrey, night after night, that she gradually realized were his version of preparing Valentina for the role she would be expected to fill once she married and was the next Queen of Tissely. It also meant assisting in the planning of the impending royal wedding, which loomed larger with every day that passed.

Every call you don't answer is another questionable decision I'm making for YOUR wedding, she texted Valentina after a particularly long afternoon of menu selecting. *I hope you enjoy the taste of tongue and tripe. Both will feature prominently.*

But the princess didn't respond.

Which meant Natalie had no choice but to carry on playing Valentina. She supposed she could fly to London and see if she was there, but the constant stream of photographs screeching about her *fairy-tale love affair* in the papers made her think that turning up at Achilles Casilieris's property this close to Valentina's wedding would make everything worse. It would cause too much commotion.

It would make certain that when they finally did switch, Natalie wouldn't be able to seamlessly slip back into her old life.

Meanwhile, everything was as Rodolfo had predicted. The public loved them, and the papers dutifully recycled the same pictures from Rome again and again. Sometimes there were separate shots of them going about their business in their separate countries, and Natalie was more than a little embarrassed by the fact she pored over the pictures of Rodolfo like any obsessed tabloid reader. One day the papers were filled with stories about how daredevil, playboy Rodolfo encouraged Valentina to access her playful side, bringing something real and rare to her stitched-up, dutiful life. The next day the same papers were crowing about the way the proper princess had brought noted love cheat Rodolfo to heel, presumably with the sheer force of her *goodness*. It didn't matter what story the papers told; the people ate it up. They loved it.

Natalie, meanwhile, was miserable. And alone.

Everything was in ruins all around her—it was just too bad her body didn't know it.

Because it wanted him. So badly it kept her up at night. And made her hoard her vivid, searing memories of Rome and play them out again and again in her head. In her daydreams. And all night long, when she couldn't sleep and when she dreamed.

She was terribly afraid that it was all she would ever have of him.

The longer she didn't hear from Rodolfo or see him outside of the tabloids, the more Natalie was terrified that she'd destroyed Valentina's marriage. Her future. Her destiny. That come the wedding day, there would be no groom at the altar. Only a princess bride and the wreck Natalie had made of her life.

Because she was a twin that shouldn't exist. A twin that couldn't exist, if Rodolfo had been right in Rome.

Do you suppose the king happily looked the other way while Queen Frederica swanned off with a stolen baby? he'd asked, and God help her, but she could still see the contempt on his face. It still ricocheted inside of her, scarring wherever it touched.

And it was still a very good question.

One afternoon she locked herself in Valentina's bedroom, pulled out her mobile and punched in her mother's number from memory.

Natalie and her mother weren't close. They never had been, and while Natalie had periodically wondered what it might be like to have the mother/daughter bond so many people seemed to enjoy, she'd secretly believed she was better off without it. Still, she and Erica were civil. Cordial, even. They might not get together for holidays or go off on trips together or talk on the phone every Sunday, but every now and then, when they were in the same city and they were both free, they had dinner. Natalie wasn't sure if that would make pushing Erica for answers harder or easier.

"Mother," she said matter-of-factly after the perfunctory greetings—all with an undercurrent of some surprise because they'd only just seen each other a few months back in Barcelona and Natalie wasn't calling from her usual telephone number—were done. "I have to ask you a very serious question."

"Must you always be so intense, Natalie?" her mother asked with a sigh that only made her sound chillier, despite the fact she'd said she was in the Caribbean. "It's certainly not your most attractive trait."

"I want the truth," Natalie forged on, not letting her mother's complaint distract her. Since it was hardly anything new. "Not some vague story about the evils of some or other Prince Charming." Her mother didn't say anything to that, which was unusual. So unusual that it made a little trickle of unease trail down Natalie's back... but what did she have to fear? She already knew the answer. She'd just been pretending, all this time, that she didn't. "Is your real name Frederica de Burgh, Mother? And were you by chance ever married to King Geoffrey of Murin?"

She was sitting on the chaise in the princess's spacious bedroom with the laptop open in front of her, looking at pictures of a wan, very unsmiling woman, pale with copper hair and green eyes, who had once been the Queen of Murin. Relatively few pictures existed of the notorious queen, but it really only took one. The woman Natalie knew as Erica Monette was always tanned. She had dark black hair in a pixie cut, brown eyes and was almost never without her chilly smile. But how hard could it be, for a woman who didn't want to be found or connected to her old self, to cut and dye her hair, get some sun and pop in color contacts?

"Why would you ask such a thing?" her mother asked.

Which was neither an answer nor an immediate refutation of her theory, Natalie noted. Though she thought her mother sounded a little…winded.

She cleared her throat. "I am sitting in the royal palace in Murin right now."

"Well," Erica said after a moment bled out into several. She cleared her throat, and Natalie thought that was more telling than anything else, given that her mother didn't usually do emotions. "I suppose there's no use in telling you not to go turning over rocks like that. It can only lead to more trouble than it's worth."

"Explain this to me," Natalie whispered, because it was that or shout, and she wasn't sure she wanted to give in to that urge. She wasn't sure she'd stop. "Explain *my life* to me. How could you possibly have taken off and gone on to live a regular life with one of the King's children?"

"I told him you died," her mother said matter-of-factly. So matter-of-factly, it cut Natalie in half. She couldn't even gasp. She could only hold the phone to her ear and sit there, no longer the same person she'd been before this phone call. Her mother took that as a cue to keep going, once again sounding as unruffled as she always did. "My favorite maid took you and hid you until I could leave Murin. I told your father one of the twins was stillborn and he believed it. Why wouldn't he? And of course, we'd hid the fact that I was expecting twins from the press, because Geoffrey's mother was still alive then and she thought it was unseemly. It made sense to hide that there'd been a loss, too. Geoffrey never liked to show a weakness. Even if it was mine."

A thousand questions tracked through Natalie's head then. And with each one, a different emotion, each one buffeting her like its own separate hurricane. But she couldn't indulge in a storm. Not now. Not when she had a charity event to attend in a few short hours and a speech to give about its importance. Not when she had to play the princess and try her best to keep what was left of Valentina's life from imploding.

Instead, she asked the only question she could.

"Why?"

Erica sighed. And it occurred to Natalie that it wasn't just that she wasn't close to her mother, but that she had no idea who her mother was. And likely never would. "I wanted something that was mine. And you were, for a time, I suppose. But then you grew up."

Natalie rubbed a trembling hand over her face.

"Didn't it occur to you that I would find out?" she managed to ask.

"I didn't see how," Erica said after a moment. "You were such a bookish, serious child. So intense and studious. It wasn't as if you paid any attention to distant European celebrities. And of course, it never occurred to me that there was any possibility you'd run into any member of the Murinese royal family."

"And yet I did," Natalie pushed out through the constriction in her throat. "In a bathroom in London. You can imagine my surprise. Or perhaps you can't."

"Oh, Natalie." And she thought for a moment that her mother would apologize. That she would try, however inadequately, to make up for what she'd done. But this was Erica. "Always so intense."

There wasn't much to say after that. Or there was, of course—but Natalie was too stunned and Erica was too, well, *Erica* to get into it.

After the call was over, Natalie sat curled up in that chaise and stared off into space for a long time. She tried to put all the pieces together, but what she kept coming back to was that her mother was never going to change. She was never going to be the person Natalie wanted her to be, whether Natalie was a princess or a secretary. None of that mattered, because it was Erica who had trouble figuring out how to be a mother.

And in the meantime, Natalie really, truly was a princess, after all. Valentina's twin with every right to be in this castle. It was finally confirmed.

And Rodolfo still isn't yours, a small voice inside her whispered. *He never will be, even if he stops hating you tomorrow. Even if he shows up for his wedding, it won't be to marry you.*

She let out a long, hard breath. And then she sat up.

It took a swipe of her finger to bring up the string of texts Valentina still hadn't answered.

It turns out we really are sisters, she typed. Maybe you already suspected as much, but I was in denial. So I asked our mother directly. I'll tell you that story if and when I see you again.

She sent that and paused, lifting a hand to rub at the faint, stubborn headache that wouldn't go away no matter how much water she drank or how much sleep she got, which never felt at all like enough.

I don't know when that will be, because you've fallen off the face of the planet and believe me, I know how hard it is to locate Achilles Casilieris when he doesn't wish to be found. But if you don't show up soon, I'm going to marry your husband and I didn't sign up to pretend to be you for the rest of my life. I agreed to six weeks and it's nearly been that.

She waited for long moments, willing the other woman to text back. To give her some clue about…anything. To remind her that she wasn't alone in this madness despite how often and how deeply she felt she was.

If you're not careful, you'll be Natalie Monette forever. Nobody wants that.

But there was nothing.

So Natalie did the only thing she could do. She got to her feet, ignored her headache and that dragging exhaustion that had been tugging at her for over a week now, and went out to play Valentina.

Again.

CHAPTER ELEVEN

A FEW SHORT hours before the wedding, Rodolfo strode through the castle looking for his princess bride, because the things he wanted to say to her needed to be said in person.

He'd followed one servant and bribed another, and that was how he finally found his way to the princess's private rooms. He nodded briskly to the attendants who gaped at him when he entered, and then he strode deeper into her suite as if he knew where he was headed. He passed an empty media center and an office, a dining area and a cheerful salon, and then pushed his way through yet another door to find himself in her bedroom at last.

To find Valentina herself sitting on the end of the grand four-poster bed that dominated the space as if she'd been waiting for him.

She was not dressed in her wedding clothes. In fact, she was wearing the very antithesis of wedding clothes: a pair of very skinny jeans, ballet flats and a slouchy sort of T-shirt. There was an apricot-colored scarf wrapped around her neck several times, her hair was piled haphazardly on the top of her head and she'd anchored the great copper mess of it with a pair of oversize sunglasses. He stopped as the door shut behind him and could do nothing but stare at her.

This was the sort of outfit a woman wore to wander down to a café for a few hours. It was not, by any possible definition, an appropriate bridal ensemble for a woman who was due to make her way down the aisle of a cathedral to take part in a royal wedding.

"You appear to be somewhat underdressed for the wedding," he pointed out, aware he sounded more than a little gruff. Deadly, even. "Excuse me. I mean *our* wedding."

There was something deeply infuriating about the bland way she sat there and did nothing at all but stare back at him. As if she was deliberately slipping back into that old way she'd acted around him. As if he'd managed to push her too far away from him for her to ever come back and this was the only way she could think to show it.

But Rodolfo was finished feeling sorry for himself. He was finished living down to expectations, including his own. He was no ghost, in his life or anyone else's. After their conversation in Tissely, Ferdinand had appointed Rodolfo to his cabinet. He'd called it a wedding gift, but Rodolfo knew what it was: a new beginning. If he could manage it with his father after all these years and all the pain they'd doled out to each other, this had to be easier.

He'd convinced himself that it had to be.

"I am sorry, princess," he said, because that was where it needed to start, and it didn't seem to matter that he couldn't recall the last time he'd said those words. It was Valentina, so they flowed. Because he meant them with every part of himself. "You must know that above all else."

She straightened on the bed, though her gaze flicked away from his as she did. It seemed to take her a long time to look back at him.

"I beg your pardon?"

"I am sorry," he said again. There was too much in

his head, then. Felipe. His father. Even his mother, who had refused to interrupt her solitude for a wedding, and no matter that it was the only wedding a child of hers would ever have. She'd been immovable. He took another step toward Valentina, then stopped, opening up his hands at his sides. "I spent so long angrily not being my brother that I think I forgot how to be me. Until you. You challenged me. You stood up to me. You made me want to be a better man."

He heard what he assumed were her wedding attendants in the next room, but Valentina only regarded him, her green eyes almost supernaturally calm. So calm he wondered if perhaps she'd taken something to settle her nerves. But he forgot that when she smiled, serene and easy, and settled back on the bed.

"Go on," she murmured, with a regal little nod.

"In my head, you were perfect," he told her, drifting another step or so in her direction. "I thought that if I could win you, I could fix my life. I could make my father treat me with respect. I could clean up my reputation. I could make myself the Prince I always wanted to be, but couldn't, because I wasn't my brother and never could be." He shook his head. "And then at the first hint that you weren't exactly who I wanted you to be, I lost it. If you weren't perfect, then how could you save me?"

That was what it was, he understood. It had taken him too long to recognize it. Why else would he have been so furious with her? So deeply, personally wounded? He was an adult man who risked death for amusement. Who was he to judge the games other people played? Normally, he wouldn't. But then, he'd spent his whole life pretending to be normal. Pretending he wasn't looking for someone to save him. Fix him. Grant him peace.

No wonder he'd been destroyed by the idea that the

only person who'd ever seemed the least bit capable of doing that had been deliberately deceiving him.

"I don't need you to save me," he told her now. "I believe you already have. I want you to marry me."

Again, the sounds of her staff while again, she only watched him with no apparent reaction. He told himself he'd earned her distrust. He made himself keep going.

"I want to love you and enjoy you and taste you, everywhere. I do not want a grim march through our contractual responsibilities for the benefit of a fickle press. I want no *heir and spare,* I want to have babies. I want to find out what our life is like when neither one of us is pretending anything. We can do that, princess, can we not?"

She only gazed back at him, a faint smile flirting with the edge of her lips. Then she sat up, folding her hands very nicely, very neatly in her lap.

"I'm moved by all of this, of course," she said in a voice that made it sound as if she wasn't the least bit moved. It rubbed at him, making all the raw places inside him…ache. But he told himself to stand up straight and take it like a man. He'd earned it. Which wasn't to say he wouldn't fight for her, of course. No matter what she said. Even if she was who he had to fight. "But you think I'm a raving madwoman, do you not?"

And that was the crux of it. There was what he knew was possible, and there was Valentina. And if this was what Rodolfo had to do to have her, he was willing to do it. Because he didn't want their marriage to be like his parents'. The fake smiles and churning fury beneath it. The bitterness that had filled the spaces between them. The sharp silences and the barbed comments.

He didn't want any of that, so brittle and empty. He wanted to live.

After all this time being barely alive when he hadn't

felt he deserved to be, when everyone thought he should have died in Felipe's place and he'd agreed, Rodolfo wanted to *live*.

"I do not know how to trust anyone," he told her now, holding her gaze with his, "but I want to trust you. I want to be the man you see when you look at me. If that means you want me to believe that there are two of you, I will accept that." His voice was quiet, but he meant every word. "I will try."

Still, she didn't say anything, and he had to fight back the temper that kicked in him.

"Am I too late, Valentina? Is this—" He cut himself off and studied her clothes again. He stood before her in a morning coat and she was in jeans. "Are you planning to run out on this wedding? Now? The guests have already started arriving. You will have to pass them on your way out. Is that what you planned?"

"I was planning to run out on the wedding, yes," she replied, and smiled as she said it, which made no sense. Surely she could not be so *flippant* about something that would throw both of their kingdoms into disarray—and rip his heart out in the process. Surely he'd only imagined she'd said such a thing. But Valentina nodded across the room. "But the good news is that *she* looks like she's planning to stay."

And on some level he knew before he turned. But it still stole his breath.

His princess was standing in the door to what must have been her dressing room, clad in a long white dress. There was a veil pinned to a shining tiara on her head that flowed to the ground behind her. She was so lovely it made his throat tight, and *her* green eyes were dark with emotion and shone with tears. He looked back to check, to make sure he wasn't losing his own mind, but the spitting image of her was still sitting on the end of the bed, still dressed in the wrong clothes.

He'd known something was off about her the moment he'd walked in. *His* princess lit him up. She gazed at him and he wanted to fly off into the blue Mediterranean sky outside the windows. More, he believed he could.

She was looking at him that way now, and his heart soared.

He thought he could lose himself in those eyes of hers. "How long have you been standing there?"

"Since you walked in the door," she whispered.

"Natalie," he said, his voice rough, because she'd heard everything. Because he really had been talking to the right princess after all. "You told me you were Natalie."

She smiled at him, a tearful, gorgeous smile that changed the world around. "I am," she whispered. "But I would have been Valentina for you, if that was what you wanted. I tried."

Valentina was talking, but Rodolfo was no longer listening. He moved to *his princess* and took her hands in his, and there it was. Fire and need. That sense of homecoming. *Life.*

He didn't hesitate. He went down on his knees before her.

"Marry me, Natalie," he said. Or begged, really. Her hands trembled in his. "Marry me because you want to, not because our fathers decided a prince from Tissely should marry a princess from Murin almost thirty years ago. Marry me because, when you were not pretending to be Valentina and I was not being an ass, I suspect we were halfway to falling in love."

She pulled a hand from his and slid it down to stroke over his cheek, holding him. Blessing him. Making him whole.

"I suspect it's a lot more than halfway," she whispered. "When you said *mine,* you meant it." Natalie shook her head, and the cascading veil moved with her, making her look almost ethereal. But the hand at his jaw was all too real. "No one ever meant it, Rodolfo. My mother told me I grew up, you see. And everything else was a job I did, not anything real. Not anything true. Not you."

"I want to live," he told her with all the solemnity of the most sacred vow. "I want to live with you, Natalie."

"I love you," she whispered, and then she bent down or he surged up, and his mouth was on hers again. At last.

She tasted like love. Like freedom. Like falling end over end through an endless blue sky only with this woman, Rodolfo didn't care if there was a parachute. He didn't care if he touched ground. He wanted to carry on falling forever, just like this.

Only when there was the delicate sound of a throat being cleared did he remember that Valentina was still in the room.

He pulled back from Natalie, taking great satisfaction in her flushed cheeks and that hectic gleam in her green eyes. Later, he thought, he would lay her out on a wide, soft bed and learn every single inch of her delectable body. He would let her do the same when he was sated. He estimated that would take only a few years.

Outside, the church bells began to ring.

"I believe that is our cue," he said, holding fast to her hand.

Natalie's breath deserted her in a rush, and Rodolfo braced himself.

"I want to marry you," she said fiercely. "You have no idea how much. I wanted it from the moment I met you, whether I could admit it to myself or not." She shook her head. "But I can't. Not like this."

"Like what?" He lifted her fingers to his mouth. "What can be terrible enough to prevent us from marrying? I haven't felt alive in two decades, princess. Now that I do, I do not want to waste a single moment of the time I have left. Especially if I get to share that time with you."

"Rodolfo, listen to me." She took his hand between hers, frowning up at him. "Your whole life was plotted out for you since the moment you were born. Even when your brother was alive. My mother might have made some questionable choices, but because she did, I got something you didn't. I lived exactly how I wanted to live. I found out what made me happy and I did it. That's what you should do. *Truly live.* I would hate myself if I stood between you and the life you deserve."

"You love me," he reminded her, and he slid his hand around to hold the nape of her neck, smiling when she shivered. "You want to marry me. How can it be that even in this, you are defiant and impossible?"

"Oh, she's more than that," Valentina chimed in from the bed, and then smiled when they both turned to stare at her. A little too widely, Rodolfo thought. "She's pregnant."

His head whipped back to Natalie and he saw the truth in his princess's eyes, wide and green. He let go of her, letting his gaze move over what little of her body he could see in that flowing, beautiful dress, even though he knew it was ridiculous. He could count—and he knew exactly when he'd been with her on that couch in Rome. To the minute.

He'd longed for her every minute since.

But mostly, he felt a deep, supremely male and wildly possessive triumph course through him like a brand-new kind of fire.

"Bad luck, *princesita*," he murmured, and he didn't

try very hard to keep his feelings out of his voice. "That means you're stuck with me, after all."

"That's the point," she argued. "I don't want to be stuck. I don't want *you* to be stuck!"

He smiled at her, because if she'd thought she was his before, she had no idea what was coming. He'd waited his whole life to love another this much, and now she was more than that. Now she was a family. "But I do."

And then, to make absolutely sure there would be no talking her way out of this or plotting something new and even more insane than the secret twin sister who was watching all of this from her spot on the bed, he wrenched open the door behind him and called for King Geoffrey himself.

"Make him hurry," he told the flabbergasted attendants as they raced to do his bidding. "Tell him I'm seeing double."

In the end, it all happened so fast.

King Geoffrey strode in, already frowning, only to stop dead when he saw Natalie and Valentina sitting next to each other on the chaise. Waiting for him.

Natalie braced herself as Valentina stood and launched into an explanation. She rose to her feet, too, shooting a nervous look over at Rodolfo where he lounged against one of the bed's four posters, because she expected the king to rage. To wave it all away the way Erica had. To say or do something horrible—

But instead, the King of Murin made a small, choked sound.

And then he was upon them, pulling both Natalie and Valentina into a long, hard, endless hug.

"I thought you were dead," he whispered into Natalie's neck. "She told me you were dead."

And for a long while, there was nothing but the church bells outside and the three of them, not letting go.

"I forget myself," Geoffrey said at last, wiping at his face as he stepped back from their little knot. Natalie made as if to move away, but Valentina gripped her hand and held her fast. "There is a wedding."

"My wedding," Rodolfo agreed from the end of the bed.

The king took his time looking at the man who would be his son-in-law one way or another. Natalie caught her breath.

"You were promised this marriage the moment you became the Crown Prince, of course, as your brother was before you."

"Yes." Rodolfo inclined his head. "I am to marry a princess of Murin. But it does not specify which one."

Valentina blinked. "It doesn't?"

The king smiled. "Indeed it does not."

"But everyone expects Valentina," Natalie heard herself say. Everyone turned to stare at her and she felt her cheeks heat up. "They do. It's printed in the programs."

"The programs," Rodolfo repeated as if he couldn't believe she'd said that out loud, and his dark gaze glittered as it met hers, promising a very specific kind of retribution.

She couldn't wait.

"It is of no matter," King Geoffrey said, sounding every inch the monarch he was. He straightened his exquisite formal coat with a jerk. "This is the Sovereign Kingdom of Murin and last I checked, I am its king. If I wish to marry off a daughter only recently risen from the dead, then that is exactly what I shall do." He started for the door. "Come, Valentina. There is work to be done."

"What work?" Valentina frowned at his retreating

back. But Natalie noticed she followed after him anyway. Instantly and obediently, like the proper princess she was.

"If I have two daughters, only one of them can marry into the royal house of Tissely," King Geoffrey said. "Which means you must take a different role altogether. Murin will need a queen of its own, you know."

Valentina shot Natalie a harried sort of smile over her shoulder and then followed the King out, letting the door fall shut behind her.

Leaving Natalie alone with Rodolfo at last.

It was as if all the emotions and revelations of the day spun around in the center of the room, exploding into the sudden quiet. Or maybe that was Natalie's head— especially when Rodolfo pushed himself off the bedpost and started for her, his dark gaze intent.

And extraordinarily lethal.

A wise woman would have run, Natalie was certain. But her knees were in collusion with her galloping pulse. She sank down on the chaise and watched instead, her heart pounding, as Rodolfo stalked toward her.

"Valentina arrived in the middle of the night," she told him as he came toward her, all that easy masculine grace on display in the morning coat he wore entirely too well, every inch of him a prince. And something far more dangerous than merely charming. "I never had a sister growing up, but I think I quite like the idea."

"If she appears in the dead of night in my bedchamber, princess, it will not end well." Rodolfo's hard mouth curved. "It will involve the royal guard."

He stopped when he was at the chaise and squatted down before her, running his hands up her thighs to find and gently cup her belly through the wedding gown she wore. He didn't say a word, he just held his palm there, the warmth of him penetrating the layers she wore and sinking deep into her skin. Heating her up the way he always did.

"Would you have told me?" he asked, and though he wasn't looking at her as he said it, she didn't confuse it for an idle question.

"Of course," she whispered.

"Yet you told me to go off and be free, like some dreadfully self-indulgent Kerouac novel."

"There was a secret, nine-month limit on your freedom," Natalie said, and her voice wavered a bit when he raised his head. "I was trying to be noble."

His gaze was dark and direct and filled with light.

"Marry me," he said.

She whispered his name like a prayer. "There are considerations."

"Name them."

Rodolfo inclined his head in that way she found almost too royal to be believed, and yet deeply alluring. It was easy to imagine him sitting on an actual throne somewhere, a crown on his head and a scepter in his hand. A little shiver raced down her spine at the image.

"I didn't mean to get pregnant," she told him, very seriously. "I'm not trying to trap you."

"The hormones must be affecting your brain." He shook his head, too much gold in his gaze. "You are already trapped. This is an arranged marriage."

"I wasn't even sick. Everyone knows the first sign of pregnancy is getting sick, but I didn't. I had headaches. I was tired. It was Valentina who suggested I might be pregnant. So I counted up the days and she got a test somewhere, and…"

She blew out a breath.

"And," he agreed. He smiled. "Does that truly require consideration? Because to me it sounds like something of a bonus, to marry the father of your child. But I am alarmingly traditional in some ways, it turns out."

Natalie scoffed at the famous daredevil prince who had so openly made a mockery of the very institutions he came from, saying such things. "What are you traditional about?"

His dark eyes gleamed. "You."

Her heart stuttered at that, but she pushed on. "And we've only had sex the one time. It could be a fluke. Do you want to base your whole life on a fluke?"

His gaze was intent on hers, with that hint of gold threaded through it, and his hands were warm even through layers and layers of fabric.

"Yes," he said. "I do."

It felt like a kiss, like fire and need, but Natalie kept going.

"You barely know me. And the little while you have known me, you thought I was someone else. Then when I told you I wasn't who you thought I was, you were sure I was either trying to con you, or crazy."

"All true." His mouth curved. "We can have a nice, long marriage and spend the rest of our days sorting it out."

"Why are you in such a rush to get married?" she demanded, sounding cross even to her own ears, and he laughed.

It was that rich, marvelous sound. Far better than Valentina's gold-plated chocolate. Far sweeter, far more complex and infinitely more satisfying.

Rodolfo stood then, rising with an unconscious display of that athletic grace of his that never failed to make her head spin.

"We are dressed for it, after all," he said. "It seems a pity to waste that dress."

She gazed up at him, caught by how beautiful he was. How intense. And how focused on her. It was hard to think of a single reason she wouldn't love him wildly and fiercely until the day she died. Whether with him or not.

Better to be with him.

Better, for once in her life, to stay where she belonged. Where after all this time, she finally *belonged*.

"Natalie." And her name—her real name at last—was like a gift on his tongue. "The bells are ringing. The cathedral is full. Your father has given his blessing and your secret twin sister, against all odds, has returned and given us her approval, too, in her fashion. But more important than all of that, you are pregnant with my child. And I have no intention of letting either one of you out of my sight ever again."

She pulled in a breath, then let it out slowly, as if she'd already decided. As if she'd already stayed.

"I risked death," Rodolfo said then, something tender in his gaze. "For fun, princess. Imagine what I can do now I have decided to live."

"Anything at all," she replied, tears of joy in her voice. Her eyes. Maybe her heart, as well. "I think you're the only one who doesn't believe in you, Rodolfo."

"I may or may not," he said quietly. "That could change with the tides. But it only matters to me if you do."

And she didn't know what she might have done then, because he held out his hand. The way he had on that dance floor in Rome.

Daring her. Challenging her.

She was the least spontaneous person in all the world, but Rodolfo made it all feel as if it was inevitable. As if she had been put on this earth for no other purpose but to love him and be loved by him in turn.

Starting right this minute, if she let it.

"Come." His voice was low. His gaze was clear. "Marry me. Be my love. All the rest will sort itself out, *princesita*, while we make love and babies with equal vigor, and rule my country well. It always does." And his smile then was brighter than the Mediterranean sun. "I love you, Natalie. Come with me. I promise you, whatever else happens, you will never regret it."

"I will hold you to that," she said, her heart in her voice.

And then she slipped her hand into Rodolfo's and let him lead her out into the glorious dance of the rest of their lives.

* * * * *

If you enjoyed
THE PRINCE'S NINE-MONTH SCANDAL
why not explore these other Caitlin Crews stories?

CASTELLI'S VIRGIN WIDOW
EXPECTING A ROYAL SCANDAL
THE RETURN OF THE DI SIONE WIFE
THE GUARDIAN'S VIRGIN WARD
BRIDE BY ROYAL DECREE
Available now!

And watch out for the second part of Caitlin's
SCANDALOUS ROYAL BRIDES duet,
coming June 2017!

MILLS & BOON®

MODERN™

POWER, PASSION AND IRRESISTIBLE TEMPTATION

A sneak peek at next month's titles...

In stores from 15th June 2017:

- **The Pregnant Kavakos Bride** – Sharon Kendrick *a*
  The Secret Kept from the Greek – Susan Stephen
- **Sicilian's Baby of Shame** – Carol Marinelli *and*
  Salazar's One-Night Heir – Jennifer Hayward

In stores from 29th June 2017:

- **The Billionaire's Secret Princess** – Caitlin Crews *a*
  Claiming His Convenient Fiancée – Natalie Anders
- **A Ring to Secure His Crown** – Kim Lawrence *and*
  Wedding Night with Her Enemy – Melanie Milburn

Just can't wait?
Buy our books online before they hit the shops!
www.millsandboon.co.uk

Also available as eBooks.

0617/19

MILLS & BOON®

EXCLUSIVE EXTRACT

Ariston Kavakos makes impoverished Keeley Turner a
proposition: a month's employment on his island, at his
command. Soon her resistance to their sizzling chemistry
weakens! But when there's a consequence, Ariston makes
one thing clear: Keeley *will* become his bride…

Read on for a sneak preview of
THE PREGNANT KAVAKOS BRIDE

'You're offering to *buy* my baby? Are you out of your
mind?'

'I'm giving you the opportunity to make a fresh start.'

'Without my *baby*?'

'A baby will tie you down. I can give this child
everything it needs,' Ariston said, deliberately allowing his
gaze to drift around the dingy little room. 'You cannot.'

'Oh, but that's where you're wrong, Ariston,' Keeley
said, her hands clenching. 'You might have all the houses
and yachts and servants in the world, but you have a great
big hole where your heart should be—and therefore you're
incapable of giving this child the thing it needs more than
anything else!'

'Which is?'

'Love!'

Ariston felt his body stiffen. He loved his brother and
once he'd loved his mother, but he was aware of his limi-
tations. No, he didn't do the big showy emotion he suspected
she was talking about and why should he, when he knew
the brutal heartache it could cause? Yet something told him
that trying to defend his own position was pointless. She

would fight for this child, he realised. She would fight with all the strength she possessed, and that was going to complicate things. Did she imagine he was going to accept what she'd just told him and play no part in it? Politely dole out payments and have sporadic weekend meetings with his own flesh and blood? Or worse, no meetings at all. He met the green blaze of her eyes.

'So you won't give this baby up and neither will I,' he said softly. 'Which means that the only solution is for me to marry you.'

He saw the shock and horror on her face.

'But I don't want to marry you! It wouldn't work, Ariston—on so many levels. You must realise that. Me, as the wife of an autocratic control freak who doesn't even like me? I don't think so.'

'It wasn't a question,' he said silkily. 'It was a statement. It's not a case of *if* you will marry me, Keeley—just when.'

'You're mad,' she breathed.

He shook his head. 'Just determined to get what is rightfully mine. So why not consider what I've said, and sleep on it and I'll return tomorrow at noon for your answer—when you've calmed down. But I'm warning you now, Keeley—that if you are wilful enough to try to refuse me, or if you make some foolish attempt to run away and escape…' he paused and looked straight into her eyes '…I will find you and drag you through every court in the land to get what is rightfully mine.'

Don't miss
THE PREGNANT KAVAKOS BRIDE
by Sharon Kendrick

Available July 2017
www.millsandboon.co.uk

Copyright ©2017 Sharon Kendrick

Join Britain's BIGGEST Romance Book Club

2 in 1

MARINELLI

50% OFF your first parcel

- **EXCLUSIVE offers** every month

- **FREE delivery direct** to your door

- **NEVER MISS a title**

- **EARN Bonus Book** points

Call Customer Services
0844 844 1358*

or visit
llsandboon.co.uk/subscriptions

* This call will cost you 7 pence per minute plus your phone company's price per minute access charge.

MILLS & BOON®

Why shop at millsandboon.co.uk?

Each year, thousands of romance readers find their perfect read at millsandboon.co.uk. That's because we're passionate about bringing you the very best romantic fiction. Here are some of the advantages of shopping at www.millsandboon.co.uk:

* **Get new books first**—you'll be able to buy your favourite books one month before they hit the shops

* **Get exclusive discounts**—you'll also be able to buy our specially created monthly collections, with up to 50% off the RRP

* **Find your favourite authors**—latest news, interviews and new releases for all your favourite authors and series on our website, plus ideas for what to try next

* **Join in**—once you've bought your favourite books, don't forget to register with us to rate, review and join in the discussions

Visit **www.millsandboon.co.uk** for all this and more today!